The
Last
Everything

Book 1: The Impossible Future

Frank Kennedy

Dedicated to all those who like to keep life interesting.

Cover art by Fiona Jayde
fionajaydmedia.com

Exogenesis

Lake Vernon, Alabama
3 years ago

MARLENA SHERIDAN BROUGHT ONE SON and one monster to this version of Earth because the fool she married sought adventure.

"No-no," Tom argued. "They aren't cave dwellers; their homes have environmental controls. Communication tech is rudimental, but they show progress. True, they slaughter livestock, disregard their poor, and pollute their oceans. How is this different from most of the colonies?"

Her fate might have been worse. They could have been ordered to 19th-century Ukraine on another Earth disguised as Cossacks or sent to a fold in the jungles of Indonesia Prime. She visited there once – a day trip from the Ark Carrier Oasis – and returned with a virus. She vowed never to set foot on a colony world again.

Not that this Earth knew anything about colonies. She scoffed at their scientific limitations: A few trips to the moon, a shell of a space station, robot crawlers on Mars.

And seven billion planet-wrecking people in need of culling.

Tom often talked her down. "Remember what is at stake," he said. "Keep the boys in line until recovery day. Our sacrifice saves the future."

Marlena needed to hear those words every month, even as the calendars flipped, and their escape grew closer. Twelve years behind, a thousand unending days ahead.

She watched the young one – her monster – from a cushioned wicker chair on the lake house deck. The boy and his best friend were cannonballing off the end of the dock.

1

"Jamie seems happy today," Tom said from a matching chair. "He and Michael appear to be each other's tonic."

Marlena bemoaned her husband's dreadful judgment.

"They're criminals, Tom."

He nodded. "Yes, they do have fun together. They are fourteen years old, Marlena. Teenagers."

She dunked a slice of lemon in her sweet tea. "Teenagers. Criminals. One and the same on this world. Honestly, Tom. Look at them."

Jamie and Michael clung to the bottom of a ladder, their shoulders above the water. After a moment of inaudible back-and-forth, they burst into manic laughter. Jamie gazed back, catching Marlena's eyes.

"They're conspiring," she said. "The next prank, the next theft, the next joy ride. They think we're blind to it all. Smug, self-indulgent criminals. As I have told you many times: One word to the Coopers, and Michael will be gone. One less variable."

Tom adjusted his sun hat. "No, Marlena. This is where we draw the line. Michael may not be the best influence but imagine Jamie without him. He's had more bad days this year than ever. Confrontations at school, the bullies, the depression. Benjamin hasn't been able to get through to him and frankly, that worries me. Jamie admires his brother, but he only listens to his peers now. I never see him with anyone other than Michael. We need to keep him whole for three more years. Then none of this will matter."

Grace Huggins joined them on the deck carrying a tray of cream cheese and pimentos on crackers. She forced a curt smile.

"You two," she said. "Still having this debate, are you?"

"Every day," Marlena rolled her eyes. "I'm not sure playing the role of passive parents has served us well. If the Mentor program had done its job, Jamie might not be so fragile. He'd have purpose. He'd value each day."

"It is a quandary," Grace said, taking a seat. "And you are certain the Mentor is still silent?"

Marlena studied Jamie as he climbed onto the dock. A lean, strapping boy, surging past six feet tall in the past few months. A runner's body, his rarely-brushed blond hair falling below his shoulders.

"There was a moment at breakfast two years ago," she said. "He hadn't touched his food. He was staring at me. His eyes were glassy, as if in a trance. I expected him to reveal what Mentor told him. But the moment passed. He picked up his spoon and ate. The moment never repeated. But he suspected something was off about me."

Tom stirred uneasily and leaned forward. "We'll be more vigilant. I'll speak to Ignatius. He'll keep a closer watch. He's done a button-up job of shielding our little thieves from handcuffs so far. When the Mentor does decide to kick in, the rest will take care of itself. In the meantime, I think the boy could use a little love from his mother. Just a thought."

Marlena plucked an ice cube from her tea and flicked it at Tom.

"His mother is not here, Tom, and it wouldn't matter if she was." Marlena leaned toward Grace. "He expected me to love Jamie by now. I've seen what short-term love does to a person. The idiots on this Earth attach themselves to dogs and cats, few of which live past fifteen. They give their whole hearts to these animals. They grieve when the predictable arrives then buy replacements to repeat the cycle. I refuse to grieve that boy when he is gone."

She reset her icy glare upon her husband. "That was never the plan."

"Find your humanity, love," Tom said. "That boy may yet save us all."

"He's just as likely to kill us all if the design is breaking down."

Grace widened her eyes. "Voices," she warned, pointing toward the dock. The boys slipped into their sandals and started in. Each draped a towel over his shoulder but didn't bother drying. They dripped on everything reaching for the tray of appetizers without so much as hello.

Their pairing made no sense to Grace. Michael buried himself in movies and video games, while Jamie preferred a skateboard, a sketchpad, and running trails. Michael rotated between afro and dreadlocks, while Jamie streaked his hair with varied highlights.

"Ma," Jamie said between bites. "Coop and me are heading out. Gonna hike up to the store for snacks. Got a twenty I could borrow?"

She glared. "Borrow implies a loan."

"Don't worry, Mrs. S.," Michael said. "J and I got it covered. You want us to get you folks something? We'll keep the change."

Tom pulled a twenty from his shirt pocket. "Consider this your snacks for today and tomorrow. Yes? Spend wisely."

"Sweet, Dad." Jamie and Michael pumped fists.

"Ebony and ivory on the case," Michael said. "Catch you on the flipside."

Marlena groaned as the boys turned to leave. "Ebony and ivory? Is that your new catchphrase, Michael?"

He frowned. "Don't reckon. It's just ..." He pointed back and forth between himself and Jamie. "Ebony. Ivory. Stevie Wonder? Get it?"

"No. Is Stevie another friend I haven't met?"

The boys fell upon each other in stitches. "Let's just go, dude," Jamie insisted. "Wait, what?" Michael said as they shuffled off. "How does she not know Stevie Freaking Wonder? Dude. Seriously."

She punched Tom's arm. "I guarantee they will leave this house with a lighter and a couple of joints. The snacks will come after."

Tom shrugged. "If this is the worst they do, then at least Jamie will be happy for the next three years. He's earned it, even if he has no idea why." Tom shifted to Grace. "So? Walt and Sammie are running a bit late. Yes?"

"Sammie wanted more time on the range," she said of her daughter. "Which reminds me. Walt wanted you to see his latest acquisition. Since the boys are gone ... shall we?"

Marlena and Tom followed Grace inside to the master bedroom. She pulled open the double-closet doors and reached to the top shelf. She retrieved a long, wide case and set it on the bed. She placed a key in the lock and turned three rotations. Tom whistled and Marlena felt cold as they studied the two weapons.

"M16s," Tom said, grabbing one. "Walt's contact came through. How big is the Huggins arsenal now?"

"We're getting closer, although I doubt Walt will ever be satisfied. He'll have no relief until recovery is complete and we cross the fold alive."

Marlena had not fired a weapon in twenty years, but that didn't worry her. "Why so much firepower?" She asked. "You already have more than enough to kill the others. Does Walt sincerely doubt their loyalty?"

Grace smiled. "Walt trusts no one. Except for me and Sammie."

"But," Marlena said, "have you heard any of the others say a single word against this mission in twelve years? Even a hint of disloyalty?"

"Of course not, but none would dare make a premature move. They know how Walt will respond. No, Walt expects the trouble to come toward the end, perhaps not even until the final hours. Some might choose to go rogue and stay here; others might move against the Jewel before transformation. Walt believes the last hours will be treacherous."

The same thoughts plagued Marlena since the day she arrived. Fifteen years was too long an exile, on this or any other planet. Too much time to become satisfied, to forget about the traditions of home, to doubt the mission parameters, to justify killing friends.

Marlena doubted she would see her home world again.

PART ONE
FROM THE DARKNESS

Son,

In these, your final hours, we hope you will find the capacity to forgive us. Please understand that the force of history requires promises be kept and destinies be fulfilled. We were faced with a dilemma; we made the choice that was in the best interests of humanity. It is our sincerest hope you were able to find a life of reasonable happiness and fulfillment in the short time given to you.

With Fondest Regards,
Mother
Father

1

Albion, Alabama
1:58 a.m.

J AMIE SHERIDAN NEEDED a few more smash-and-grabs to refine his technique, with less emphasis on "smash." He made a mess of the back door to Ol' Jack's General Store because he stole the wrong key from the old man's master ring. He used the butt of his flashlight to crack enough glass for a gloved reach-in.

"You suck, Sheridan," he muttered as he brushed hair out of his face and followed the light.

He passed the bait and tackle display then the grain and feed, reaching the tiny office where Jamie expected to find the object of his first official robbery. He long ago decided the other thefts didn't count because he never kept what he stole.

This time, no give-backs.

Jamie pulled open the top drawer of Jack's file cabinet. He squeezed the hanging folders forward and focused his light on a brown metal lockbox. He set the box on a desk littered with the chaotic paperwork of a man who trafficked only in cash, check and handwritten receipts - and trust of a boy who swept floors and bagged groceries three times a week.

"He'll never get it," Jamie said. "None of them will."

Jamie took a deep breath. He knew where Jack kept the bolt cutters, but he played a hunch. The box opened without resistance. He should have known. *Ain't nobody robbed me in forty-two years,* Jack insisted at least once a week. *Who in hell's gonna bother now?*

Jamie wondered whether the old man was begging to be robbed - any excuse to quit the business he said was dragging him to the grave.

Jamie understood the sentiment too well. Albion was the town where dreams came to die. A dreary blip on the map, not enough traffic lights to count on one hand, and sufficient whispers of judgmental busybodies to drive a boy out of his skin. He knew what they thought every time they saw him riding a skateboard or jogging the quiet streets after sunset. They turned down their noses at his long, blond ponytail, gossiped about fights at school, and spread rumors about drugs and booze. Then they tied it together to what happened two years ago and lost all pity.

You're 17 now, they said. Get on with life. Learn a craft. Earn your diploma. Go down to Burton's for a proper haircut.

They wouldn't be surprised to learn he took up crime.

Jamie reeled when he shined his light on the contents of the box.

"Shit."

The money was there - upwards of a thousand dollars, enough to send him on his way and keep food in his belly until he found a new town and his next grab. However, he didn't predict the Glock lying atop the cash.

Jamie's heart raced, so he took a seat. He ran his gloved hands over the gun and wondered whether this was a gift from burglar heaven or a warning. The old man never spoke of a gun, keeping only a hard-to-find baseball bat tucked amid clutter under the front counter. Jamie hadn't fired a weapon in years - a .22, squirrel hunting with Ben six years ago. He studied the Glock, found the safety, and released the magazine. Full.

"I can't," he whispered. "This is beyond stupid."

He restored the magazine, set the pistol aside and gathered the cash, tucking it into a bank deposit bag lying underneath. He opened the desk drawer and found a pack of Jack's Marlboros and a lighter. The old man chain-smoked while laboring through paperwork.

Jamie lit a cigarette and took a long drag.

"What the hell is wrong with me?"

Go home. Go home. Every instinct told him to go back to that rat box called an apartment, find Ben passed out on the couch reeking of alcohol and the perfume of another woman.

Don't let Coop down. He needs me tomorrow. He can't finish the plan without me. He and Michael Cooper expected their prank to be a fitting end to their junior year. "Alternative cow residue" instead of frozen beef patties would bring them legendary status - and possible expulsion. Jamie almost backed off the last time they texted, just before 1 a.m. He typed the words, *I'm out,* but he never sent the message.

He didn't want to disappoint Coop, the only boy who didn't see him with suspicion or condescension. But if he went to school, he'd have to sit for Ms. Bidwell's English III exam. The thought of it - and her imperious sneer at his inevitable failure - frightened him more than expulsion.

He took a deep puff and thought of Samantha. Weird, shy, beautiful Sammie. He'd just begun to think she might be his first. And she loved him - never said the words, but he saw it in her eyes. He felt the love every time she tried to steer him back on course. What would she think of him now?

What would any of them think?

"You're a good man, J," Ben told him six hours ago before heading across the county line to drown himself at his usual dive. "They'll see that someday. They'll get past what happened. So will you."

You're wrong, Jamie thought. Just like with everything else.

"Gotta blow this town," he said. "Not one more day."

Jamie tucked the pistol inside the deposit bag and zipped it shut.

He took another puff, enough to give him the courage to head out. A packed bag awaited him at the apartment. He only needed Ben's car keys. He figured that step would be easy. From there ...

"This is not what Tom and Marlena wanted for you."

Jamie dropped the cigarette. The voice, husky and rigid, escaped from the darkness. Jamie knew it at once. He focused the flashlight, and Deputy Ignatius Horne - all 6-foot-8 and 270 pounds of him - filled the doorway, his badge shining in the narrow beam.

The deputy flipped on the office light but kept a hand by his holster. Jamie saw heartbreak crack the deputy's stern, militaristic features.

"This is not for you, J," Ignatius said. "You're a lousy thief and a bigger coward."

"You'd never understand, Iggy. Please. I'll be out of town before morning, and you'll never have to deal with me again. Please?"

Ignatius smiled. "Did you think old Jack didn't see how curious you were every time he put money in the box and stowed it away in here? He predicted you'd try this by the start of the week. He sure hoped he was wrong. The pistol was my idea. I really thought it might scare you off, given everything you've been through."

"I never would've used it ... not to hurt anyone. You know me."

"Used to. Let's go."

The deputy backed away, but Jamie did not follow. He unzipped the bag and reached for the Glock. He aimed the gun.

"I can't live here anymore. Let me screw up my life on my own."

The deputy unholstered his weapon. "Or I could put it to an end right here. A third Sheridan lying on the floor in a pool of blood. That what you want, J?" He advanced. "Maybe they were right after all."

"Who?"

10

Ignatius took a deep breath. "You'll know soon enough. Your timing is ironic, to say the least. I always gave you more credit than the others."

"What others?"

In a blink-and-miss-it maneuver, Ignatius used his free hand to disarm Jamie, who fell back into the chair.

"I wish there was enough time to cover it all," Ignatius said. "Perhaps you'd understand. No matter. Let me just say this: I was named after a great man whose courage and sacrifice changed the course of human history. You've never heard of him. He lived and died far away from here and a very long time ago. Since you lost your folks, I have tried to carry myself with the same honor and dedication to a selfless cause. What of James Sheridan? Will he be remembered as a worthless thief gunned down during a heist? Or will he become something more?"

Jamie tossed the deposit bag onto the desk.

"What now?"

"We have a long drive ahead of us."

"Huh? You're not arresting me? Are we meeting Ben?"

Ignatius studied his phone and frowned.

"First, I have a question. Think carefully. Right before you smashed the door, did you experience anything out of the ordinary? Headache? Dizziness? Nausea?"

The questions flummoxed Jamie but triggered a memory. "What? I was scared. Almost passed out. But I was scared. What's going on, Iggy?"

"Hmm. Guess that clinches it. Too bad. But maybe it's all for the best. Maybe if we had more time, I could explain."

The deputy cocked his weapon and ordered Jamie to move.

2

O UTSIDE THE BACK DOOR, Ignatius looked at the mess. "Suppose I'll have to warn Jack before he comes in. I really did not want things to end this way."

"What things? Iggy, what aren't you telling me?"

"Listen, Jamie. There are things in motion we can't stop. Things that have been coming for a very long time. If we had known for sure it was happening tonight, I don't think Ben would have ..."

"Where's Ben? What's happening?"

"I texted him right after I saw you enter Jack's. Hopefully, he's not too far gone yet."

Another memory dislodged. Shortly after supper hours earlier, after a row between he and Ben, Jamie saw his brother out on the street, talking to Ignatius, arguing, gesticulating. At the time, he assumed it was all part of the continuing struggle to keep Ben on this side of the county line and away from the gushing booze. Jamie dismissed the moment, except to reinforce the idea that he needed to put distance between himself and Albion.

"What's been going on between you and Ben?"

"None of that matters anymore, J. We need to move."

"I don't know what's happening, but I left my phone and a packed bag at the apartment. Can we stop by and ..."

"No. You were right about one thing, J. It's time for you to leave this town, albeit for a more honorable reason than as a thief. I ..."

Ignatius cut himself off the instant they reached Main Street, which usually rolled up by 7 p.m. He found his Albion County sheriff's sedan where he left it, two stores up from Jack's. But his eyes focused on the headlights approaching from a block away. He stepped back, hiding himself and Jamie behind the corner of Sylvia's Beauty Salon.

"What's wrong?" Jamie asked to no response.

Ignatius kept his eyes glued on the other car, which slowed as it neared the sheriff's vehicle. The car idled for a moment then slid in a full length behind the police sedan.

"They wouldn't," Ignatius said. He grabbed his phone, fired off a text then turned to Jamie. "Possible change of plans."

He handed Jamie the Glock. "I know you wouldn't hurt anyone if you didn't have to."

Even in the dim glow of the streetlight, Jamie saw fear cross the deputy's face.

"What's happening, Iggy? Speak to me."

"This has a trigger safety. Don't release it unless you have to. I might be wrong about them. Just stay here and let me doing the talking. Understand, J?"

"OK. Sure. I guess. I'll ..."

"Stay here. Don't show yourself. Not for a second."

Ignatius headed up the sidewalk. Jamie heard car doors open and the engine stall. The headlights cast distorted beams down Main Street. He moved as close to the street edge as possible and listened. At first, the voices stayed low. Back and forth, civil, disciplined. Soon, they raised.

"This was sorted," Ignatius told someone. "The vote was unanimous. We had fifteen years to debate. Go home. Wait it out."

"I beg to differ," a woman said. "We are guided by a moral imperative which supersedes your obstructionist attempts at ..."

13

Jamie lost track of the words when he recognized her voice.

"No way," he whispered. "Can't be."

"Last warning," Ignatius said. "We will see this through and then all of us go home. Just as we agreed."

"You are not in charge," another man insisted. "We abided your wishes for too long. We have to end that thing before it evolves. Like Agatha said, this is a moral choice. For the future. For everyone."

"And if I don't let you near him?"

"Do you think we have anything to lose?"

Jamie knew the third voice as well. He released the trigger safety and stepped out into the open. He had no idea what he was doing. He also didn't realize all three residents of Albion already drew on each other.

"Don't make me do this," Ignatius said as Jamie stepped into the partial headlight beams.

"There," the woman pointed.

A series of pops followed. Jamie froze as Ignatius groaned and fell to the sidewalk, two silhouettes approaching him. One of them stopped over the deputy and lowered a weapon. Flashes erupted from a long, slender suppressor. Ignatius lay silent and still.

Jamie's heart pounded as it might at the end of one of his evening jogs, yet he could not move his legs. He could not wrap his mind around this new nightmare, especially when he recognized the portly profile of Rand Paulus, a flour mill foreman who visited the house often after the Sheridan murders. Jamie tried to retreat, but the sidewalk betrayed him and he stumbled backward over uneven pavement.

Rand Paulus aimed his weapon as the other, now familiar shadow closed in alongside him.

"Sorry, son," Rand said. "Has to be done. Everyone's best interest."

In the instant before Rand pulled the trigger, Jamie regained his balance and fired the pistol without aiming. Bullets ricocheted off the beauty salon and the sheriff's vehicle.

"This ain't real," he jabbered. "It's a freaking dream. Shit. Oh, shit. Not real."

Undaunted, Iggy's attackers advanced in no particular hurry.

"Once he's down," the woman told Rand, "empty your clip in him. No sense taking chances with it."

Both open fired at once, and Jamie responded in kind. He felt a pair of stings and stumbled backward, then turned down the alley next to Jack's. He grabbed his flashlight, dropped in the confrontation, and took off full speed into the darkness. His lungs burned and his tears flowed.

Bullets pinged the ground about him.

He did not slow down, his newfound pain an unbearable yet clear signal he was still alive. As he dashed toward the shadows, he heard muffled pops, originating farther behind. A bullet grazed his left shoulder.

Jamie didn't know where he was running or why, fully expecting a bullet to rip through his back and end his pain at any second. He cursed Ben and cried out for his help. Jamie saw nothing ahead but empty streets, a lonely park and no one in this stifling little town to save him.

3

JAMIE SENSED THEY were all around, but he rarely saw them — fleeting shadows beneath distant streetlamps, a slow-moving car with the headlights off. The pain in his sides and belly grew sharper, his shirt soaked in sweat and blood. He didn't know where the bullets hit him, only that as long as he stayed on concrete, he left a trail of red splotches for them to follow.

He made quick work of the business district, which was no more than a few blocks of tiny shops, a barbershop with a pole that no longer lit, and a diner where he used to eat all the chicken and dumplings he wanted for free (a gift to an orphan). He hoped someone might be about, a rogue light in a window offering sanctuary.

Yet only the pale hue of streetlamps gave him direction — as it did his pursuers. He raced through the town park, around which Albion was built. He cut past Horton's Feed Store, dodged through an alley behind the Bowl-a-rama, sprinted across Coverdale Street, and ran into the woods bordering Alamander River.

He stood at the edge of a dense collection of low scrub, tall pines and fallen branches, none of which he saw well. Sweat fell as tears over his eyes, which he wiped clear. He heard the pressing echo of a runner less than a block away. He convinced himself to press on, even without hope of aid. Perhaps the shots he fired woke the town. Perhaps not. He heard their apathy: Fools with firecrackers. Go back to sleep. Nothing to see here.

"Nobody's coming," Jamie whispered. "I'm dead."

He didn't stop running until he stumbled into the river, which was no more than a turbulent stream and never reached the bottom of his shorts as he crossed, fighting a testy current that wanted to drag him downstream. The bottom was soft and sandy, and the water seemed a brief, cool refresher that lessened the sting of his wounds. He heard a dog bark in the distance then climbed from the river, ambling over a log, where he sat.

He set the gun on a rock then removed his shirt, fighting to contain a scream of agony, but he saw little in the dark. So many thoughts competed against the relentless pounding of his heart and the sudden, desperate thirst scorching his throat. He tried to control his breathing, something he did with ease when he jogged. He listened for pursuers but heard only the coursing of the river.

He used his flashlight to find the bullet wounds. He discovered a tiny hole about an inch from his side. Jamie felt little pain, more like a tingle, but the slow current of blood was undeniable. Then, right about where his appendix was removed years ago, Jamie found the second hole. He remembered some of Iggy's last words.

"A thief shot dead. That's how they're going to remember me."

With his last fumes came dizziness. He grabbed hold of the log for support, certain he lost far more blood than he realized. How long before he'd lose consciousness? Should he tear the shirt into strips, tie it together, perhaps wrap it around, put pressure on the wounds?

"No, this is stupid. Gotta find help. Gotta ..."

He was cold, his teeth chattering, and Jamie asked one word: Why?

He thought he heard a twig snap.

17

"I'm so sorry it has come to this," a soft feminine voice said. "Expected yet still somewhat surprising."

Jamie froze and ducked. The voice came from several feet behind him, the second time someone stunned him from the darkness. He fought the dizziness and remembered the familiar voice of the woman who finished off Iggy with a silencer-equipped gun. This was not the same woman, her voice somehow softer.

She emerged from the shadows wearing high heels, a smart business ensemble, the skirt cut beneath her knees. She was hefty in the midsection, her face full and eyes soft below distinctive wrinkles. Her jewelry glowed in the thick of night; a necklace of pearls complemented pearl earrings. Her red hair was coiffed, fresh from the salon. She smiled like a reassuring grandmother and bent down beside Jamie. She stretched a hand toward a bullet hole, but he jerked back, pressing hard against the log.

"Who .... Who are you? C-can you help me?"

"Oh, I wish I could, my sweet child. You cannot know how much."

"Look, lady. If you're one of *them*, then just go ahead and do me, because I can't take any more of this crap. But if you ain't, please help me. They shot me, see ..."

She studied the wounds, a gentle sheen bouncing off her, as if the director of this absurd play had cast a spotlight on her.

"I'm sure the creators never envisioned the end to be so sloppy," she said. "Then again, they didn't expect my program to take so long to boot."

"What? What the ..."

"Yes. Must have been the Caryllan pulse that shook me loose. Dear, dear. All these years. I should have had ample time to prepare you. Now I'll have to improvise. This will be a sizable challenge."

"Lady, what's wrong with you? You some kind of nut that goes wandering round in the woods in the middle of the night?"

18

She laughed. "Any other time, I might suggest you get immediate help for your wounds. However, Jamie, they have become manageable."

Jamie found strength in his legs and lifted himself.

"You … you know who I am? You *are* one of them."

"If you're referring to the assassins, no my child. Alas, I can offer you no means of escape. My assignment was to prepare you. To condition you for the end, for the event that always was and always will be."

"I'm outta here, lady. You're a whack-job."

"Please, Jamie. Hear me out. You are part of something that extends far beyond your imagination. Far beyond this universe, truth be told."

Jamie didn't try to process her words. "Screw you."

"Run if you must. But know this, my dear sweet child: Even if you can elude the assassins, in just a few hours from now the boy known as Jamie Sheridan will cease to exist. I am so very, very sorry."

All at once, nature intervened with a shrill symphony. Jamie heard crickets, perhaps millions in unison, a chorus escalating to fever pitch. They seemed to be everywhere and closing in fast, screaming in his ears, their echoes bouncing off the tree tops like thunder. Just as Jamie raised his hands to cover his ears, the sound morphed into crackling, as if the land and the trees were covered in tin foil, all of it being crumpled by unseen, godlike hands. He looked to the sky, certain the loss of blood was sending him into shock. He saw a clear blanket of stars, his eyes fully adjusted to the natural light. And as the crackling turned into a scream, a shadow reached out and smudged the stars from existence.

"The final stage has begun," the woman shouted. "I am sorry for your pain, my dear sweet Jamie. But you had a good life, for a while."

Jamie stumbled into the woods, anything to get away from the scream. The shadow fell over the trees, slinking beyond the low brush and twisting into a horrid shape that seemed to have legs. He ran, the adrenaline rampaging through his blood once more. As the scream faded, Jamie heard the pounding of the forest floor, many legs scurrying at once, almost upon him. He had no sense of his bearings, no care for how much blood he lost or what was directly behind him. He forgot about the bullet holes in his gut.

4

10 miles west of Albion, Alabama
2:30 a.m.

BEN SHERIDAN FOUND pleasure in the sensation of warm liquor filling his belly and leaching into his bloodstream. He parked on an old hunting road a hundred yards off the highway. He sat on the hood of his blue Dodge pickup and toasted the moon, even though the moon wasn't out.

"Wherever the hell you are," he said, raising his bottle.

Ben tossed back the whiskey like someone chugging water on the hottest day of the year. Some of the whiskey missed its target and trickled onto his perpetual week-old beard.

Ben always worked through this sordid business far from the eyes of a boy who once idolized him. He didn't want to explain why he needed the booze. Jamie wouldn't understand all the sacrifices and the desperate gambles. They argued enough without adding on the whole truth. So he found a liquid escape in the nearest wet county.

He knew he had no business leaving Jamie alone. There was simply too much at stake, as Ignatius reminded him every day. He

21

owed this much to Jamie: Be home, comfort him all the way to the end. Send him to his rest with peace and dignity. Even Tom and Marlena would have agreed.

"Bastards," he said, toasting his parents like he did every night.

Ben shivered. As quickly as the ghostly image of his parents snuck in through the back door, he kicked them out.

"Get a grip, Sheridan," he mumbled. "Iggy knows what he's doing."

He took out his phone, wondering why he received no texts.

"Damn it." Somewhere along the way, he muted the phone.

That's when he saw it.

Caryllan pulse confirmed. Walt triangulating. Rebirth beginning. I have him. You know where to find us. He will need you.

"Oh, hell. It's too soon."

Ben called Ignatius. No response. Sent a text. No response. He called Jamie. No response. Then he saw the second text.

traitors rp ab ??

He took another swig and tossed the bottle aside. He fumbled for his keys and felt nauseous, but not because of the liquor.

"What have I done?"

He opened the driver's door, braced himself against the side of the truck until the dizziness passed, and jumped in, dropping his keys between the seats. He cursed, wondering how to make the drive home. After taking a few deep breaths, Ben found his keys, flipped open the glove compartment, reached beneath the owner's manual and grabbed his .45 semi-automatic. He attached a suppressor and sat the gun on the passenger seat.

The truck jerked as he hit the gas. He struggled to keep the Dodge out of either ditch as he made several rough attempts at turning around. When he found his bearings, Ben did not know what was worse: The nausea or the panic. Neither compared to the sickening realization that even if he got to his brother in time, and even if his craziest theories were right, Ben couldn't save Jamie from the inevitable.

He balanced the wheel in one hand, his cell phone in the other. He called Jamie and Ignatius, but both phones went to voicemail.

He glanced at his watch. Ten minutes before three.

"Seven hours to go. Damn, J. We didn't have enough time."

Entering Albion from the northwest, he passed the K-12 school, two churches, and the field where Jamie used to run track. The instant he turned onto Main Street - three blocks from home - Ben felt a wave of foreboding.

The street was quiet, empty, yet Ben slowed the Dodge. He knew something was off. Then he saw it: An Albion County sheriff's car parked in the alley next to Ol' Jacks.

Drive, you stupid bastard. Drive. Ben stopped the car anyway, grabbed his flashlight and gun, and stumbled to the police sedan.

"The hell?"

This made no sense. Ignatius and Jamie should have been far from Albion by now. Unless ...

That's when he saw the dark red stain on the trunk, a handprint in blood. He dropped to one knee and vomited. After the final heave, and as he tried to regain his senses, Ben tried to lift the trunk. No luck. He raced around, opened the driver door, and pulled the trunk-release lever. He said a prayer before looking inside.

"Shit. No. No. Shit, no."

Ben drew close and saw at least three bullet holes in the chest.

"I'm sorry, my friend. Should have been here. You warned me."

In that instant, Ignatius gasped, his eyes wandering. Ben jumped.

"Betrayed," the deputy said between bloody coughs. "Walt right. Thought they try this."

"J. Where is he? Did they kill him?"

"Ran. Has gun. Heard when they came back. Still looking for him. Thought I was dead. Tossed me here. Buy time. Chancellors don't die easy."

23

"Who?"

"Rand. Agatha. More? Find him, Ben. Give him a chance."

"What?"

"Third option." Ignatius took rapid breaths. "Give him third way out. Deserves. We hurt him. All of us."

"I want to, but it won't work. And it won't stop the inevitable."

Ignatius used what strength he still had to grab Ben by the arm. "Remember your father. How he looked at you like a stranger when he threw you out. Ben, there's nothing to lose ..."

Ignatius held his stare as he died.

Ben fought off another wave of nausea and focused. He had little time, few resources, and only one man to trust. He summoned all the cold-hearted, rigid principles he learned from the parents he came to despise. The same parents who, fifteen years earlier, robbed him of the life of his dreams on the world of his birth.

5

J AMIE EMERGED ON the other side of the woods into a
soybean field. The world dropped into utter silence, and
he found his bearings. He saw the First Baptist Church to his
south next to Pine Grove Cemetery. He recognized Morry's
Lane, tracked it north, and saw a night light over the distant
outline of McNally's Gas n' Grab at the corner of Morry's and
Coverdale Street. He formed a plan.

If he got to the phone booth outside McNally's, he'd call 911;
they'd send help. Only when he thought about the police did he feel
the loss of Ignatius Horne. Iggy had been a true friend after Jamie's
parents died. It was Iggy who made the quick capture of his parents'
killer and offered daily support to both the Sheridan brothers during
the trial, which Jamie insisted on attending despite everyone's advice
to the contrary. Iggy motivated Jamie to return to running after a
long absence.

The field was muddy, and his feet sank, but Jamie pushed on like
an athlete, relying upon instinct and training. He flew as if running
cross country, handling the challenges of changing topography at a
steadied pace. The gun felt light in his right hand, the flashlight in his
left.

Jamie regained his senses as he reached the intersection and crouched in the ditch. To the east, Coverdale Street disappeared into the countryside, winding past fields and farmhouses on the way to the interstate. Jamie knew his pursuers would likely be coming from the west, where he saw the first of Albion's street lights, illuminating entry into the town. Just beyond, he saw a jumbled mess of cars and pickups at Autry's Body Shop, followed by a short bridge over Alamander River, and a towering wood frame at Albion Mills Flour Co.

Jamie took a deep breath and sprinted across Coverdale, avoided running beneath the nightlight at McNally's, and reached the phone booth. He punched the first key then slammed against the inside of the booth when he heard a familiar voice.

"The problem, my sweet child, is that I should have kicked in ten years ago. Your subconscious was still malleable. That was the whole purpose of my program, you see."

The woman in the smart business ensemble stood against the open door. Jamie froze.

"What? How did ..."

She sighed. "My challenge is to make your remaining hours one of reconciliation with your destiny. This will be difficult. After all, when you die, so will I. Fortunately, I am not burdened by petty emotion." She reached out her hand, but Jamie backed away. "The program refers to me as Mentor. But that seems shallow. So I have decided to borrow the name of the sweet lady who lived next door to your parents. Call me Lydia."

He closed his eyes, figuring this delusion would go away if he wished hard enough. When he opened his eyes, she was still there, twirling a finger around her pearl necklace.

"Look, I don't know who you are or what loony-tune factory they let you out of. But if you can't help, get the hell out of my face, lady."

Jamie dialed 911. He didn't know how to respond to the dispatcher when she asked the nature of the emergency.

"Please let me wake up," he whispered. "Please let me wake up."

"Excuse me? Young man, what is ...?"

"I ... uh ... I'm in trouble. You see, I wasn't doing anything, right? This guy ... Rand ... he shot me. He and my ..." He knew how crazy the rest would sound. "I don't know why. Please help."

"You're going to be all right. Calm down and tell me your location."

He never did. As the dispatcher tried to coax anything out of him, Jamie saw the first sign of salvation. He looked through his tears, west along Coverdale, past the body shop and the bridge. Jamie saw a blue truck that looked exactly like ...

"Ben?"

Jamie dropped the phone and ran through the intersection at a dead sprint and crossed the bridge. He didn't care what he was doing to his wounds of if his pursuers were close, because he would get to safety before they reached him. Maybe this once, Ben would save him.

He sprinted across the meager asphalt parking lot, leaped onto Albion Mills' front loading dock, and opened his mouth to call for help. Then, as he prepared to round the corner, he heard the low hum of another car engine. He grabbed hold of the corner of the building and yanked himself back at the same instant he felt a sting in his heart.

His pursuers' car, its headlights still off, wheeled past the blue Chevy that did not belong to Ben. Jamie recognized the profile of Rand at the wheel. Jamie fell on his stomach and prayed not to be seen. He was exposed on the dock and didn't dare move. He saw tall figures inside but not how many. The engine idled for almost a minute before it died.

Jamie spied around the corner and looked for anyone who might be lurking. Pavement ended at the back corner of the mill and became gravel. The property slipped away in a steady decline toward the tiny river. A pale blue nightlight cast long shadows beyond a pair of delivery trucks parked at the base of the property under a spreading oak. Three men emerged from around the back of the mill, their faces obscured but profiles clear as they walked beneath the

27

light. Each man carried a gun at his side. One of them pulled on a cigarette, surrounding himself in a smoky haze.

He heard laughter and muffled voices. Seconds later, Rand Paulus emerged from the car and reached out to the smoker. He received a fresh cigarette, which he lit. Jamie could not reconcile this man with the one who had been so generous to the Sheridans in the months after their parents were killed. He brought sacks of groceries to their pitiful apartment each week free of charge and told a thousand of the world's corniest jokes.

The passenger door of the dark vehicle slammed shut, and a new shadow emerged into the blue light. This one, however, walked toward the mill, her face visible. She was an imperious woman with short, graying hair, narrow cheekbones and a protruding jaw that gave her cadaverous features. Jamie sometimes joked she could play frontcourt for the Los Angeles Lakers - but then, most of those gathered around this woman ranked among the tallest and most imposing in the county. Before Jamie knew true fear, he dreaded taking this woman's English III exam.

He watched her fire two bullets point-blank into Ignatius.

"This ain't happening," he whispered. "No way. I am screwed."

Jamie did not hear the words of his intended killers, and he dared not risk moving closer. All the terror masked by adrenaline broke through. The reality that he was alone in the night, barely clothed, hearing imaginary monsters, listening to a crazy woman, and bleeding while people he knew hunted him in the shadows, overtook Jamie. The horror oozed through his blood and overwhelmed every thought.

He felt three years old, trapped deep underground in a coffin, buried alive. His teeth chattered.

Jamie took stock of his location and thought of the only person he might still count on. However, she was three blocks away, and Jamie wasn't sure he would survive long enough to reach her. He walked with as gentle a touch as possible until at last he cleared Albion Mills.

He ran north of Coverdale Street. He cut through backyards, swerved to avoid dogs on chains, and limped zigzag in a crouch when next to a street. *They're gonna take me down like an animal.*

He was surprised when he reached his destination at 614 Truman Street and ecstatic to see a light from the first-floor bedroom window. He made sure he saw no movement among the shadows. Then he took a chance, believing this moment was meant to be.

Jamie tapped on her window, and the curtain swung back.

In that moment, she was the most beautiful girl in the world, and Jamie prayed she could save him.

6

2:40 a.m.

A GATHA BIDWELL SLAMMED shut the passenger door of Rand Paulus' fifteen-year-old Toyota sedan, produced a tissue from her purse, and dabbed at her lipstick. She approached her four compatriots with a purposeful gait, her unblinking eyes staring through each of them like long knives. She lifted the tissue for all to see.

"The conclusion that must be reached," she began, "is that my lips have made a considerably greater impression upon this tissue than upon your collective psyches. Yes?" She offered a crooked smile. "You are intelligent men of considerable foresight and moral complexity; yet I felt the need to resort to a visual analogy to make my point.

"We had a simple plan, gentlemen, with carefully constructed objectives. However, here we stand, in the parking lot of a flour factory, without which the locals would be unable to prepare country ham biscuits. My pride swells, gentlemen."

The youngest of the four men snickered.

"Good one," he said, taking a puff from his cigarette.

Agatha snatched the cigarette from his mouth and tossed it. She raised a sharp index finger and tightened her jowls.

"Christian, I have repeatedly warned you about those despicable instruments of death," she said. "No more."

"Come on, Mom. I only got a few more hours. There won't be any cigs where we're going. Bad enough I won't be able to walk at graduation."

"And I will not see the wreckage wrought by my finals. We will survive. Do I now have your absolute attention?"

Christian Bidwell, wearing a black t-shirt bearing Albion County School's blue rams head logo, tucked his gun into his pants. He crossed his broad, muscular arms, and the all-sport star who doubled as Student Council President nodded to the others to listen to his mother.

She revealed a cell phone that was not her own.

"Young James left this behind at his flat," she said. "We have only this limited evidence because of a heavy-handed approach clearly fueled by a desire to favor savagery over rational diplomacy."

"In other words," Christian told Rand, "you blew it."

"Don't be vulgar," Agatha hissed.

"Just saving time, Mom."

Rand took a long drag on his cigarette and exhaled through his nose.

"I can speak for myself, thank you. Ignatius drew. I know we agreed to avoid extreme measures, but the way I saw it ..."

"You did not follow my explicitly detailed guidelines," Agatha interrupted. "Consequently, we found ourselves hiding the remains of a Chancellor with whom we might have reached detente."

"I beg to differ. The kid was right there. We had him. Might be dead as we speak. And your son is right. You could stand to trim a bit of fat from your imperial English."

Christian reached for his pack of cigarettes. "What I've been saying for years, Mom. Cut to the chase. Less is more." He grabbed a

31

cigarette and stuck it between his lips then turned to the others. "She's been called the Queen Bee around this town for so long, I think she likes it."

Agatha stepped back. She watched as her son lit another cigarette despite her express orders. Instead, Agatha massaged her left temple, the very place where every teenager-induced headache began.

"Enough," she announced. "Killing young James was never going to be that simplistic. However, I have studied the boy's phone. He was communicating with Michael Cooper, his friend, for the past several hours. The final text came shortly after 1 a.m. I believe a visit to Mr. Cooper's home would be strategically prudent. Christian, I believe you are acquainted with Mr. Cooper?"

Christian laughed after a puff. "Sure. Coop's an ass, but an easy mark. Face to face, he's a tool."

"Let us hope you are correct," Agatha told her son. "He needs to turn over James, and you will convince him."

"What about me?" Rand said.

"An opportunity to redeem yourself," Agatha smiled. "Benjamin has been repeatedly texting and calling James. He is on his way back to Albion from his usual late-night indulgences. I suspect by now his conscience and his inebriation have left him in a dire strait. Intercept him at his apartment, Rand. Interrogate him."

"If he fights back ..."

"Understand, I do not wish injury to come to any of our people. For all our considerable disagreements, we are Chancellors. We came here in united cause fifteen years ago. I want all of us to return home and be welcomed into the fold of those who value our choices. Three of us have already fallen." She paused for a moment of silence. "Diplomacy first, Rand. Remind him of the morality of our case. Yes?"

She told Rand to return on foot, and he obeyed. Agatha turned to the twin 6-foot-10 Cobb brothers, Jonathan and Dexter, who ran a small auto-body shop on the outskirts of town.

"Begin reconnaissance across the southern perimeter. Follow our coordinated grid approach and report to me every ten minutes. Unless James has fallen into Walter's hands, we must assume the boy is desperate and wounded. Monitor all police transmissions. We took care of the matter of those gunshots. I contacted Sheriff Everson, told him the Marlette boys had gone firecracker mad and that he might visit them in the morning. He seemed satisfied. That spineless man does not work after sunset. However, I suspect there will soon be concerns about a certain deputy's radio silence."

"What about Walter?" Jonathan said. "Shouldn't we deal with him?"

"I am. I rerouted Arthur Tynes and Arlene Winters from escape preparations in order to observe Walter's residence. They should arrive shortly. If James finds his way there, we will have sufficient response. But we know the dangers of a frontal assault against Walter and that family."

"If Walter hadn't been so damn stubborn," Dexter said, "all this would be over by now."

"True. But he has been our guiding light for most of this exile. He kept our morale in place during those first critical months. I prefer he have a final chance to come around to our vision." She turned to her son. "You, Christian, have a classmate to torture. Put out that odious cigarette and drive."

Christian took a long, final puff. "Go Rams!"

7

JAMIE CLIMBED THROUGH the window and tumbled forward onto pure white shag carpet. He tried to scramble to his feet, but the sensation of a deep, soft floor and an air-conditioned room with a friend he trusted kept Jamie on solid ground. He pushed himself to a mirrored door that hid a walk-in closet and got a look at the monster he'd become: Muddy, sweaty, blood-stained, with tangled hair sufficient to pass for a wolf boy.

Samantha Huggins rested on her knees beside him, her eyes scattered between Jamie and the mess he embedded in the carpet.

"Oh, Jamie. The blood. And a gun? What have you done?"

His heart slowed. He never saw her dressed like this, wearing only an oversized, dark blue t-shirt. She wasn't the little girl who used to beg that he play dolls with her. She filled out well beyond even the freshman who he once thought would be the solution to his virginity. She became tall and lanky, like him. More important, she was his savior.

"They killed him," he whispered. "They killed him, Sammie."

"What? Who?"

"Iggy Horne. They shot him."

"The deputy? He's ...?"

"Dead. I was there, Sammie. It was ... you won't believe me. Hell, I don't. It was Rand Paulus. Ms. Bidwell. They did it. Wanted to kill me too, but I ran. I shot at them, but I was scared. I am royally screwed."

Jamie rambled, recounting every detail from the moment Ignatius interrupted his burglary, to his adventures in the river, at the Gas n' Grab, with the smartly-dressed woman who followed him around being no help whatsoever, to the flour mill. He didn't look Sammie in the eyes. Rather, he shifted his eyes around her room, taking in the shelves of antique dolls, the canopy bed overloaded with pink ruffles and stuffed animals. He smelled cinnamon potpourri. This bedroom hadn't changed in the years since he was last allowed in: soft and comfortable, how a home should be.

"Hold on," she said. "You tried to rob Jack's?"

Jamie didn't realize he was sobbing until he looked through the veil of tears into Sammie's stunned, disbelieving eyes. He knew the look – she tilted her head ever so slightly, her right eye squinting. Sammie possessed a keen sense for Jamie's tall tales, of which he'd sprouted many. She caressed him as if calming a small child.

"Jamie, have you been sleepwalking again?"

A single mocking laugh broke through his anger. "You kidding? Look at me, Sammie. It's not like those other times." He held up the gun. "How you think I got hold of this?"

He took to sleepwalking through town since his parents died. Jamie confided to Sammie last summer at her father's lake house.

"Jamie, everything you've told me ... don't you see how it's crazy?"

Jamie seethed. "You think I took Ben's gun and shot myself then made up some loony story so I wouldn't come off like a total dumbass?"

35

"I wanna believe you, Jamie. I do. But ... the Queen Bee? Really? Ms. Bidwell?" She looked away for an instant. "And there's something else. You have blood stains, but I don't see where you're bleeding. Look."

Jamie swept his right hand over his side, across his belly, front to back, fully expecting his fingers to land in the holes. He found nothing odd, looked down and saw no wounds.

"No way." He twisted about and posed for the mirror, feeling himself all over in a desperate search for bullet holes. "They were there, Sammie. I crossed the river and I stopped to look. I was bleeding. See? Look at all this blood. See? See?"

He was talking to the mirror, staring through the glass at her reflection, watching her disbelief turn into something deeper – the frightened look of a girl locked in a room with a nutcase wearing a hockey mask. He rested his head against the mirror. Jamie never considered that he'd just gone through the mother of all sleepwalking adventures.

Sammie tried to touch him, but Jamie recoiled. "You don't have a shirt. Maybe you walked into some briars. Maybe the cuts are small and it's hard to see through all the stains. Doesn't that make sense?"

"I took off my shirt at the river. I told you. You think briars caused all this goddamn blood?"

"Fine, Jamie. Look, this gun scares me. Put it down on the dresser. I'll get a first aid kit and clean the blood. Maybe we'll find the injury."

Sammie disappeared into the bathroom. Jamie was speechless. After all he went through, he would've expected her to be as panicked as he, turning off the bedroom light and racing to find her dad in case bad men were outside. Jamie couldn't fathom how calm and rational she was. Was this the Sammie who threw a conniption fit when her dad suggested she find other friends because Jamie was "a poor influence?"

"Please, Sammie. Go wake up your dad. I know I'm not his favorite dude right now ..."

She emerged from the bathroom carrying a towel, a first aid kit and a pair of soaked wash cloths. "No, you're not. That new window cost him four hundred dollars. Here." She handed him the wash cloths, which were drenched in warm water and soap. "Let's clean you up."

"So when did you become Florence Nightingale?"

"I have many talents. My whole life doesn't revolve around you."

He wanted to ask, "Since when?" However, he bit his tongue. They stopped cleaning for a few awkward seconds but didn't make eye contact.

"Some good news," she said without looking up. "No bullet holes, or holes or scratches of any kind that I can see. I can't explain the blood."

The girl was steady as a rock. He wanted to believe her, to put all his hope into another sleepwalking fiasco. He looked around again, and his eyes widened. He glanced at his watch.

"Sammie, why are you up so late? It's almost three in the morning."

She shrugged. "Reading. Sometimes I lose myself in a book and there's no stopping me. Besides, I only have one exam tomorrow, and it's a cakewalk. What do I need to sleep for?"

He should have known. She'd always been a bookworm, except when Jamie visited and talked her into many ill-fated adventures, most of which included Coop. Afterward, she endured the inevitable, awkward lectures from disappointed parents then came back for more. She never hid her feelings. As Sammie finished cleaning him, Jamie grabbed her hand.

"Sammie, I need you to look at me." She did, offering no hint of a smile. "Tell me the truth. I know you will because of how you feel about me. OK? Do you really think I'm making all this up? You really believe I dreamed everything while I was sleepwalking? You think I stole the gun from Ben, don't you?"

"Come on, Jamie. You know me better than ..."

"No, Sammie. Just be honest with me."

She set aside the blood-stained cloths and stammered for words then leaned in to Jamie. She reached out as if to hug him, then pulled her arms back, settling for a kiss on his cheek.

"I care so much about you. Gosh, for as long as I can remember. But this story … it's beyond crazy. Think about it for a minute. This is Albion. Albion? 'The town time forgot?' So, you're saying Mr. Paulus from the flour mill and Ms. Bidwell, your English teacher, tried to gun you down on Main Street? And then there's this woman … what, Lydia? She's talking about how you're only going to live a few more hours, and she shows up out of thin air. How's that possible, Jamie?"

He fought back new tears. "I'm not crazy."

Jamie felt small. He always used to be in control when he was with Sammie because she adored him. Now, he felt her judging him, reevaluating all those years she wasted in hopes he'd make her his girlfriend. Was he so self-absorbed he couldn't see the girl she became? Somewhere along the way, her features softened. He never really noticed how blue her eyes were, or how much her long brown hair shined.

"I'm thirsty," he whispered.

"Dummy me. I should've thought of that right off. I'll get you a glass of water. Otherwise, you're good to go." She started to the bathroom. "Oh, and I think you best get some clothes on before Daddy hears us. I've got some t-shirts and jogging shorts in the top drawer." She pointed to the chest of drawers next to the window Jamie flung himself through.

Jamie threw on a white tank top and grey shorts with a flexible waist band. Sammie brought him a glass of water, which he drank in one long, continuous gulp. She took the glass and went for seconds.

"Oh, and here's a ponytail tie," she said. "You'll feel better when you get your hair out of your face."

"Guess you've thought of everything."

She shrugged. "I just want you to feel better. That's all."

Jamie sat on the edge of her bed and tied up his hair. She was the only person close to him who never asked when he'd be getting a haircut. He drank a second glass of water while Sammie watched, sitting beside him. Excess driveled off his chin.

"I needed this," he said. He handed the glass to Sammie, and they shared a cautious smile. "I do feel better," he whispered. "Thank you, Sammie. Thank you."

He didn't hesitate to kiss her on the cheek. When he leaned back, Jamie stared into her eyes and felt something else. He couldn't define it. The notion was vague and awkward, one he never sensed around her before, as if something were misplaced.

That's when someone pounded on her door.

"Samantha, what's going on in there? I heard voices. Samantha?"

Her father's arrival should've scared him. Walter Huggins banished Jamie from this room four years ago, when he decided no boy was going to carry hormones behind closed doors with his little girl.

Jamie wasn't frightened now because Walt would listen. Walt was older, knew the world was a cruel place, and would help.

"It's OK, Daddy. Hold on just a second." She grabbed Jamie by the hand. "We're gonna figure this out, Jamie. I promise. You're safe. You don't have to worry about those assassins breaking in here."

She smiled, looking every bit the angel who opened her window to him. And he was almost enamored. Almost. Jamie's smile disappeared as soon as Sammie started for the door. What did she say? *Assassins?* She called them *assassins?*

The pain sliced through his gut with a jagged blade. His heart broke into another jog, and Jamie understood what was wrong.

Jamie grabbed the bedpost as Sammie reached for the door handle. *She wouldn't say that. Why would she call them that?* She dismissed his story too easily. That's when he noticed the suitcase next to her bed. He also realized his gun had vanished.

39

8

3:05 a.m.

MICHAEL COOPER WAS alone in the house, and he had only himself to blame. His parents all but begged him to come with them to his cousin's wedding. They offered numerous incentives, but Michael was having nothing of it. Privately, his father painted the long weekend as an opportunity for debauchery, starting with a Thursday night bachelor party certain to go into the wee hours.

"Listen up, Pops," Michael explained. "I appreciate what you're trying to do. I reckon it's no different than shoving a whole chocolate cake in front of a six-year-old and saying, 'Dig in.' Here's the thing. I already got my hand in that cake, if you get my speed."

The "speed" was littered with half-truths. Yes, Michael enjoyed a fine cigar on occasion – when he found the opportunity to swipe them using Jamie as an accomplice. Moreover, a few beers had gone missing from select Albion refrigerators over the years.

"Tell you the God's honest truth, Pops, those Starkville Coopers ... hell, something ain't screwed on right with those folks. I can't cotton to them. And Starkville, Mississippi? She ain't exactly the jewel in the crown, if you get my speed."

His father sighed. "Why can't you speak like everyone else?"

Michael laughed. "It's all about style, Pops. A comedian's got to have a style all his own. Dig me?"

"You're a card, Mike, but one of these days that style of yours is gonna get you in a mess of trouble. Life isn't a series of one-liners and bizarre analogies."

Then his father acquiesced to Michael's wishes, and his parents left for Starkville by mid-afternoon, leaving behind a list of mandatory chores that leaned toward scrubbing, mopping and dusting. Michael moaned as he studied the list then turned his focus to the chaos he planned to introduce at Albion County School the next day.

He texted regularly with his fellow conspirators, who put the final touches on the special packages he'd deliver after midnight. Michael and four others, including Jamie, gathered ample cow manure, which they mixed with ground beef and molded into thin patties cut to the identical dimensions of the so-called hamburgers the state's vendors provided its schools. They wore surgical masks and latex gloves and slipped the patties between wax paper. They placed the patties into boxes stolen from the cafeteria dumpster and stored them in a deep freezer that Arnold Wilcox's father never used.

"They'll never make it to the serving line," Michael said. "That don't matter so long as they get thrown in the oven. The odor, the panic. I reckon there's gonna be something rotten, but not in Denmark."

Jamie was supposed to help him deliver the goods, but Michael's "No. 1 hombre" waffled all night. He saw Jamie fall into these funks ever since the murders. Michael tried to understand, and his tactics for perking up Jamie usually worked. Not this time. Jamie insisted he was ready to leave this hellhole. Michael tried to offer original wisecracks, but he couldn't break his best friend's depression. Jamie texted Michael to look at the bigger picture, to see life beyond Albion. If they hit the road together …

Michael responded with sarcasm, and Jamie texted nothing more after 1 a.m. Michael texted several follow-ups, but at some point, he laid his head on a pillow and envisioned alternative plans.

The next thing he knew, Michael woke up coughing. He flapped about like a freshly-landed trout until the object in his mouth was removed. When he realized he wasn't drowning or dreaming, Michael took stock of his surroundings, and specifically the familiar face who towered over him pointing a suppressor-equipped pistol between the boy's eyes.

"Here's how it's going to play," Christian Bidwell said. "I'm not planning on shooting your sorry ass right now, but if you don't go with the flow on this, no one is ever going to find your ashes. Got me, Coop?"

Michael searched his mind for outrageous possibilities. Perhaps he woke up to the wrong end of a prank. Maybe his Starkville cousins were trying to scare the hell out of him. Not likely, unless they were in the habit of recruiting the local star quarterback, power forward, pole-vaulter, and all-around Johnny All-America rolled into one.

"Bidwell. Dude. *Mi casa su casa.* So, what's with the heater?"

Christian snickered. "You're a funny guy, Coop. Think you are, anyhow." He dropped his smile. "I'm going to lay it down once: This is not a joke. You do what I say or I'm going to shove his gun down your throat and blow the back of your head off. Crystal?"

"Crystal, dude." Michael felt an urge to pee.

As he sat up, Michael saw another person standing in the doorway. As if on cue, the other visitor flicked the light switch. When Michael saw Agatha Bidwell, he wet the bed.

"Oh … you got to be …" He scrambled his thoughts, his brain still half-asleep. Although Michael never had to endure a Bidwell English class – he made a point of avoiding a semester of such well-known terror — he listened to ample tales of peers who wilted under her dominion.

"Look, I get what this is," Michael stammered. "You found out. OK. I get that. But aren't you … I mean, this is a little over the top, ain't it?"

"Explain yourself, Mr. Cooper," Agatha said as she approached the bed holding a pistol.

"The scheme. The prank. You found out, right? Look, I'll turn myself in first thing. We weren't going through with it anyway."

"Scheme?"

"The cafeteria? Hamburger sabotage?" He saw their confusion. "You got no idea."

Agatha rubbed her temple. "I have had fourteen of the most confounding years of my life to study teenaged children who possess a level of intellectual mediocrity that will astound and mystify historians for centuries to come. Yes? Trust me, Mr. Cooper. I have more than sufficient idea. What I don't have, however, is James Sheridan. I want to know where he is, and you will lead me to him." She turned to Christian. "Did I 'cut to the chase' sufficiently enough for you?"

"You're getting there, Mom. Keep working on it." He leveled the gun at Michael's lips. "Now open wide and start talking, dumbass."

9

SAMMIE TURNED THE lock, grabbed the handle and looked back at Jamie with a reassuring glint in her eyes. He was ten feet from the window and ready to run.

However, the tall, domineering frame of Walt Huggins bore down on him, ignoring Sammie and focusing his wrath exclusively on the teenager who had no business there. Walt grabbed him by the shoulder and jerked him. Although Jamie was 6-foot-3, he stared upward to meet this man's fiery eyes.

"Move an inch, boy, and I'll knock you ten ways to Sunday."

His deep voice came across like finely-honed granite. Walt filled out everywhere – the neck and shoulders of a linebacker, the biceps of a weightlifter half his age, the chest of a circus strongman. Only his receding hairline betrayed the notion of a superman. Walt leaned in, his breath a reminder of the onions he ate with a distant meal.

"You've got one chance to make this good, James. Explain why I'm standing here looking at your sorry mug in my daughter's bedroom at three in the morning."

Jamie stammered. The man who once compared Jamie to Dennis the Menace and predicted a stint in the state penal system, seemed more than the equal to Iggy's killers. His breaths shortened. He panicked.

Sammie came to his aid, grabbing her father by the arm.

"Daddy, please hear him out. He said he saw horrible things tonight. Incredible things."

Walt turned and winked. "Don't worry, Pumpkin. I'm not going to kill him." He asked Sammie to back off then inspected Jamie's clothes. "Are you wearing my daughter's things?"

Jamie and Sammie shared an awkward glance. She shrugged. "Yes, Daddy. He had blood all over him. Something happened. Please let go of Jamie and hear him out."

Walt did as she asked but told Sammie to get her mother. "I can handle this, Pumpkin."

Sammie gave Jamie the same reassuring smile he didn't trust the last time he saw it. She nodded and left the room. Her father saw the bloody clothes and backed away.

"Sit down, James. My daughter seems to think you have a story to share. I'm listening."

Jamie pieced his thoughts together. Before he began, he apologized.

"Mr. Huggins, first of all, I know you think I'm a major screw-up ... and OK, yeah, I ain't gonna deny it. But I didn't come here to take advantage of Sammie or ..."

"Give it a rest, James. I realize you didn't come here for Samantha, because you know very well that if you had, I'd string you up from the lowest branch on the tallest tree. Now get on with your story. I heard something about blood. Time is wasting."

He spared no details. Walt Huggins never interrupted, although Jamie saw him furrow an eyebrow at the mention of Iggy Horne's death. Walt checked his watch as Jamie reached the conclusion. Walt stepped away, his back turned to Jamie.

As Walt turned and said, "You're safe," Jamie heard the scratching again, the same as in the woods. It sounded muffled, as if outside the window. *Not now*, he thought. *Please not now.*

"I know what to do," Walt said, his voice intermingled with the growing chorus that steadily morphed into a symphony of crickets. "We'll figure this out together, James. James?"

He lost track of Walt's words as the shrill song returned. He put his hands to his ears, ignoring Walt's demands to pay attention. Jamie stepped toward the window. The crickets were everywhere, millions of them coating the glass, invisible to the naked eye but too close to be denied. The window cracked, the tiniest sliver piercing the pane like lightning in reverse.

He saw her out of the corner of his eyes. Lydia sat on an easy chair, her legs crossed. She nodded as she smiled, then her eyes darted back across the room, looking behind Jamie. Her smile disappeared.

He felt a thud against the base of his skull and dropped into a flash of white light.

10

3:15 a.m.

BEN SLOWED THE Dodge as he approached his apartment. He studied every visible detail, looking for any unusual shadows beneath the streetlights. Jamie left his second-floor window open – no surprise, since the heat must have been stifling. The AC had not worked for days.

Terror snatched him. Ben double-checked the clip in his pistol and took a deep breath. Adrenaline rushed forward. Ben hadn't felt such an overwhelming sense of fear in two years. The pistol shook in his hand, but he knew he had to go inside. He wouldn't find Jamie, and he assumed the traitors already tore it apart. But he remembered Iggy's final plea. Hope for the third option.

Inside, he found the front door open. He held his weapon with firm aim and focus. He glanced into Jamie's bedroom, which was a confusion of disorganized possessions that represented the life of a 17-year-old boy. Ben couldn't remember the last time he'd come into this room just to sit down and chat with Jamie, to be the man his parents would have expected.

In the bathroom, he took a handful of aspirin. Then he grabbed a pocket knife, dragged his frayed couch away from the living room wall and pried open a one-inch-square section of wood. He reached into the hole and felt a tiny envelope. Ben opened it and allowed a flash drive to fall in his hand. He wrapped his fingers around the compact metal device, which was the perfect size for a key ring but carried forty gigabytes of data, and breathed a deep sigh of relief.

Ben wanted to show this to Jamie for so long, but he never found the right time, knowing Jamie couldn't accept these contents until he was told the truth about everything else. Ben didn't know if he'd have enough time, but he had to find Jamie before anyone else and explain.

Ben was ready to leave when his phone rang.

He heard the granite tone of Walt Huggins. "He's safe, Sheridan. I have him."

Unseen weight fell from Ben's shoulders. "I've been calling. What took you so long?"

"Unexpected business. I'll need your help for that. As for James, we're en route to the safe house. Twenty minutes out. Are you drunk?"

"What ...? No, Huggins. I've had a bad night, that's all."

"We all have. Would have been less bad if you had stayed around to protect James."

"Please, I already feel enough like a schmuck. Did you know the others betrayed us?"

"I know about Ignatius. Rand and Agatha, too. I can guess who else is with them."

The aspirin was not working as quickly as Ben had hoped.

"Do we know who we can count on?"

"Other than the four of us," Walt said, "No one. Where are you?"

"The apartment. I ..."

"And you're still alive? Interesting. There are assassins about."

"I know. I saw their work."

Walt spoke after a long pause. "Here's what I need from you, Sheridan. Leave now. My wife and daughter are in a predicament.

They should be able to handle themselves; they're well trained. But I would prefer backup. Oh, and Sheridan, do hurry. We have much to do, and we want James to be comfortable in his final hours."

Ben cringed. "As always, Walt, you are a beacon of hope."

The instant Ben closed the phone, he felt the muzzle of a gun push into the back of his neck. In better, more sober times, he never would have allowed anyone to come so close without detection.

"You still believe his orthodoxy, even now, at the end?" Rand Paulus sounded amazed. "How could you have listened all these years and not realized who held the moral high ground? Drop the gun."

Ben did as told. "Rand. The debate ended. We took a vote. It was unanimous. I thought we were together on this."

Rand chuckled. "We could have voted thirteen to one against Walt, and he still would have overruled us."

"Is that why you killed Ignatius? Because you knew he never would have turned against Walt? I don't understand any of you. We had fifteen years to prepare, and now at the end you try to change the outcome."

Rand pressed the muzzle deeper. "A few random casualties at most. Nothing compared to the horror we'll see in less than seven hours if we don't stop the Jewel."

"You don't know that, Rand. You're trying to violate laws that have infinite consequences." Ben decided he was not going to continue this pointless debate. He took two steps forward and turned around. Rand's gun was aimed directly between his eyes.

"If you feel the need to shoot someone you've known all your life, go for it. I can't stop a bullet, and nobody will hear a thing. All I want is to be with Jamie at the end. I want to tell him how sorry I am, that he didn't deserve any of this. I don't expect him to forgive me, especially when he learns the whole truth. Still, I think he's entitled to as much. Don't you?"

Rand wavered. He lowered the gun slightly.

"I don't hate you for what you did," Ben said. "I just wish you had tried to talk. Ignatius was an understanding man. He would have listened."

In a flash, Ben ducked and jammed an elbow in Rand's gut, enough to cause his fellow Chancellor to drop the gun. Ben got to the weapon first, then spun about and aimed.

"Me? I don't listen anymore."

Ben pulled the trigger once. A hole opened in the center of Rand's forehead, and the flour mill foreman collapsed.

Ben grabbed both guns and made a quick exit for the Huggins house.

11

THE HUGGINS HOUSE was dark save for the flashlights that guided Sammie and her mother, Grace, to their duties. At one point, Sammie lost her composure. She had returned to her bedroom at the moment her father leveled Jamie with a carefully placed chop to the back of his neck. Her emotions got the better of her, and she screamed. With Jamie lying unconscious, her father whirled about, grabbed her by the shoulders and stared deep into her eyes.

"I had no choice, Pumpkin. I have to take control of this situation. I always did. You understand? Put your emotions aside. He can't be saved."

Walt towered over her like an iron giant, but Sammie felt comfort in his assuring arms. He knew what was best. He allowed Jamie to stay in her life despite everything.

"I know," she whispered. "I just wish we had more time."

"You'll have that chance with someone else. A stronger man. Someone guaranteed a future." He kissed her on the lips and ordered her to the garage to retrieve duct tape and cord. Sammie did as she was told, passing her mother in the doorway. She didn't expect her

51

father to add one last nugget. "Did you know he's a drunk like his brother?"

She heard those sorts of claims before. He would tell her about Jamie's supposed involvement in petty crime — some of which she knew to be true — but also suggested he was at times a marijuana user and/or seller who graduated to harder drugs as he entered high school. Walt never followed-up on his accusations, so she filed them away as the rants of an overzealous dad. She knew Jamie fought a daily battle with his lingering grief and his anger toward Ben.

Walt bound Jamie and carried him to the garage, where he plopped the boy in the trunk of his Buick. The family stood together as Walt explained the next step.

"Obviously, Agatha has swayed several of our colleagues to her cause. And apparently, the Caryllan pulse triggered earlier than I predicted. Nonethless, stick to the plan. Only difference: I want lights out as soon as I leave. Finish everything quickly as you can. No more than twenty minutes."

Sammie and her mother could have finished the list of evacuation duties quickly under normal circumstances. Once Grace shut off the power, each step required more care. They needed to box up all documents that might have indicated the Hugginses ever lived at 614 Truman Street. They moved swiftly through every drawer and cabinet. Sammie changed into jeans, t-shirt, blouse and her best athletic shoes then boxed up her schoolbooks and papers.

They divvied up ten incendiary devices. Earlier, she asked her father why they needed to take such an extreme step.

"Because endings like this always come in fire."

They followed Walt's design and planted the devices along the walls close to the baseboard. Grace took the second floor. Sammie stayed below, placing the first of her devices by the breakfast nook. She started toward the den when a shiver gripped her. She swung around, stepped gingerly to the back door, crouched down and peeked through the corner of the door's flowered lavender curtain. She ducked.

The trespasser wasn't more than ten feet from the door. Sammie stayed low, the flashlight pointed to the floor as she ran upstairs. She stumbled into her mother, who was leaving the master bedroom having planted the fourth of her devices.

"Mom. Out back. Trouble. He's got a gun and he's wearing night vision. Can't tell who because of the goggles."

Grace nodded. "OK. They must have been tracking Jamie. Saw your father leave. Suspected something. How many?"

"Just one that I saw, but I haven't looked out front."

"I'm sure there are others. Agatha wouldn't send just one to go up against us. She's not that bold." Grace handed a key to Sammie. "They probably don't know what they're facing. That's why they haven't entered. Open the cabinet. I'll scout for any other assassins. Give me the devices. I'll place them." She stroked her daughter's hair. "You've rehearsed this, dear. You'll do fine."

Sammie hugged her mother. "I won't let you down."

Sammie and Grace went in opposite directions. Sammie opened a small utility closet with the key and surveyed the family's arsenal. She loaded two shotguns with efficiency and strapped them over each shoulder. She opened two metal boxes and slid clips into four pistols, equipping each with thin, black suppressors. She made sure the safeties were turned on as she tucked two of the weapons behind her belt. She carried the other guns in her left hand, leading with the flashlight in her right. She raced downstairs and found her mother, who rushed to plant the final devices.

Grace grabbed two pistols and a shotgun.

"I saw another out front. Take position. You know where to go?"

"Yes, Mom. I'm ready."

"Good. It's time you had a chance to validate your field training. Remember, no hesitation. If you have one in your sights, pull the trigger. But take care with your aim: Ben may be on his way."

Sammie nodded, returned to the top of the stairs, and heard her mother on the cell phone.

"We'll do our best," Grace said. "Don't come back for us."

Sammie could not contain the rush of her heart. She turned off the safeties. She was ready for this. She remembered the broad smile on her father's face when she finished field training.

"You will be respected as a soldier of the Guard," he told her.

She wondered whether she would ever get a chance to see the Earth where her parents were born. Ultimately, she focused on her ability to survive the next five minutes.

12

J AMIE CAME TO, blind and sweating. He felt a cloth sack over his head and a plastic cord binding his legs and arms, chafing at his wrists and cutting off circulation. Nothing terrified Jamie more than the duct tape over his mouth. His lungs burned; he tried to breathe steadily through his nose.

His mind became a blank slate; he felt no pain, no anxiety, as if a resignation took hold. All hope vanished, and Jamie was left with a single, gnawing sensation, the one that stalked him for two years. He sensed Mom and Dad trapped in their bedroom, staring down the barrel of a hunting rifle, a single question on their lips as their killer pulled the trigger. *Why?*

Suddenly, he smelled perfume. The aroma was subtle, like a soft, scented pillow, not the splashed-on, belt-me-upside-the-head variety every girl in school wore to impress the guys. A hand pulled the sack off his face.

He gasped. "You."

Lydia the mentor patted her lips into a reassuring smile, like a grandmother doling out chocolate chip cookies and milk to a scared little boy. She caressed him on the cheek, her fingers warm and feather-soft. "There, there," she whispered before disappearing into the shadows. She returned seconds later with a chair and sat next to him. She was cast in a glow.

"I knew," Jamie stammered. "I knew you were with them. That's how they tracked me."

"Sweet child, I fear my answers are far more complicated than you're prepared to accept. First, please know that I am neither human nor a figment of your imagination. I am part of you, but I have only now begun to behave as my creators intended. I was designed to have a phantom presence in your life, starting five years into the redesign. I was to manipulate your subconscious, whisper to you as you slept, or appear in spectral form to comfort you while in pain. I was to be a second mother."

Jamie tried to sit up. He wanted to knock Lydia off her perch.

"Mother? Don't you dare. You didn't know my mother, and you sure as shit ..."

"Not on a personal basis. But I was able to observe."

"You are out of your freaking mind. Who brought me here? What is this place?"

Lydia crossed her legs in the opposite direction and sighed.

"Alas, dear child, I must apologize for my ramblings earlier. The program was excited to be unlocked, and I tried to say too much too fast. I can see why you thought I was unbalanced."

"You know something, lady. If I told folks about what's happened to me tonight, nobody on this rock would believe me. I don't think Sammie even believed. Why won't you just level with me?"

"Ah, yes. Samantha Huggins. Tricky, that one. As I was saying ..."

"Don't try making me think I've gone round to the nuthatch. You're just as real as the ones who killed Iggy. You're ..."

"Real? In what sense? That you see me, or that I eat and breathe?"

He laughed even though his throat hurt. "Lady, you can cut the head games. If you weren't real, you couldn't take the sack off my head and I sure as smack wouldn't smell your perfume. You see, I'm pretty good with that whole logic deal."

"I suppose you are. Dear child, do me a favor. Close your eyes."

"What?"

"Just for an instant. I won't hurt you. I can't."

Jamie had nothing to lose, so he played along.

"Good. Now open."

He stared into a wall of darkness and felt the sack over his head, as well as something else that didn't seem possible. Lydia asked the obvious questions before they passed his lips.

"Are you certain I removed the sack? Do you remember anyone pulling the tape off your mouth? Odd, isn't it? You've been talking to me quite freely."

The tape remained plastered over his mouth. He still breathed through his nose. Jamie felt a tinge of panic. *They're not going to crack me.* Faster than a wink, the sack disappeared, and Lydia glowed where she sat. Jamie flexed his jaw and felt no tape.

"Reality, my sweet child, is nothing more than perspective colored with bias. I am here, I am a part of you, and we need to face the challenges ahead. We have very little time."

Lydia knelt beside Jamie and ran her fingers along his face, down his neck and through his hair. She spoke to him barely above a whisper, as if wishing him good-night.

"Your mother gave you all her heart would allow, given her limitations. I suppose Marlena Sheridan could have been quite popular had she allowed others into her life." Jamie bristled. "How often did friends come over? Other than the Hugginses – and perhaps the real Lydia – how many people did you see associating with your mother?

"I remember when you were twelve. You had the first inkling that something was wrong with her. You saw it in her eyes, Jamie. Remember? It started one morning at breakfast. You finished your cereal and looked across the table. You couldn't help but stare. She had a newspaper in front of her and cup of coffee in one hand, but she seemed to be somewhere else. She gazed upward and caught your stare. You saw a coldness that frightened you. She was your mother and yet ..."

Jamie trembled. *How can she know this? I never told anyone.*

"... she wasn't." Lydia sighed. "I wish I could have been there to soften the blow. I don't know what wisdom I might have provided, but you would not have been alone with your fears."

Jamie stared into Lydia's crystal blue eyes and saw a twinkle.

"Who are you?" He asked.

"Someone who is now prepared to tell you the truth. I will apologize in advance; what I'm about to say will hurt you. But it can't be helped."

Jamie decided to play along once he realized Lydia had to be part of an elaborate mind game. He would've preferred a bullet between the eyes to this cruelty, but he'd been given no choice, no escape.

Lydia stretched her arms to her sides then paced around Jamie. "All the threads of life are interlaced. It is the heartbeat of creation itself. You'd have learned that someday, had you been given the chance. You've shown curiosity for the world beyond Albion. Thus, you may be open to accepting life's more extreme possibilities."

"Oh, yeah? You mean like the possibility that a guy who used to give me and Ben free cans of tuna might try to gun me down? Then a lady who's not real but looks like she's fetched and ready for church says, 'Yo, Jamie. Nice meeting you in the woods at two in the morning. Oh, and by the way, you're gonna die real soon.' Those possibilities?"

Lydia stopped in her tracks, her back to Jamie. "Actually, now that you mention it, yes." She swiveled about, clasped her hands together and nodded in glee. "You have borne witness to these improbable turns. Now I must ask you to consider that these events represent the tiniest threads in a tapestry more enormous and complex than a narrow mind could ever accept. Jamie, you believe in the idea of multiple universes. I know this because you and Michael Cooper have discussed it often. He's particularly fond of the what-if nature of this concept. Your choice in film and television reinforces the curiosity."

Jamie rolled his eyes. "Oh, c'mon. Really? I mean, really? You gonna tell me that's what this is all about?"

"After a fashion. The notion of multiverses is well-grounded scientific theory, even on this relatively juvenile Earth. Let us suppose humans have figured out how to travel between these rifts in the fabric of creation. Don't you consider the possibilities astounding?"

Jamie tried laughing, but his dry throat gagged, sending him into a coughing frenzy. "Lady, you're making up this crap as you go."

Lydia crossed her arms and wouldn't allow eye contact. "I have an obligation to explain why you are here and why your fate has been sealed." Her face turned red. "I have no other mission. We were born together. We will die together." She flew from her seat, her eyes bulging as she practically fell on top of Jamie and grabbed his neck. "You will allow me to finish my mission, and you will not mock me. I have a name, and I prefer to be addressed with respect."

Her eyebrows flared. A hair on the back of his neck alerted him to the dreadful possibility that this woman believed she was being honest. Lydia let go of his neck without ever having squeezed.

"Fine," he said. "I'll shut up. Just say your peace. Then get the hell out of my mind."

13

3:30 a.m.

MICHAEL COOPER FELT a tooth chip and a pool of blood rise in his mouth after the third time Christian Bidwell pistol-whipped him. The latest blow sent Michael reeling to the floor beside his bed. After chewing off a string of random curses beneath his breath, Michael spit out blood.

"Dude, this is not happening," Michael started. "Even if I knew where Jamie was, I'm not going to spill to a douche like you."

Christian offered the cocky smirk that Michael often saw when Mr. Everything sauntered down the halls of the high school with his entourage.

"*Douche*," Christian mocked. "Clever guy. Look, Coop, don't know if you're a fan of irony, but we're swimming in it, my friend. You see, if you'd given up Sheridan right out of the gate, I wouldn't have reason to knock you around. I'd be out of your life. Turns out, though, you're just a clueless son of a bitch. That means the guy with the gun has nowhere to go and needs to work out his frustration. Follow?"

"I get your speed," Michael said. "But messing me up don't change a damn thing. Bad enough you and the Queen Bee won't even tell me why you're after Jamie."

Christian stepped back and dropped the gun to his side. He lost all pretense of a smirk.

"Huh. Skipped that detail, didn't we?" He shrugged. "Simple, really. When I find him, I'm going to kill him. Do the world a favor."

Michael considered the absurdity of the past fifteen minutes of interrogation and torture then responded to Christian with a howl of laughter. He fell against his bed as the lunacy of this scene – staring into the face of a pistol wielded by the most popular 18-year-old in Albion County – left him certain he was lost inside the most painfully stark nightmare of his life. If only he could figure out when the script called for him to wake up ...

"No, seriously," Christian continued. "I will literally be doing this world a favor. Don't feel like I should have to, but Mom says it's for the best, so who am I to fight the Queen?"

Michael's laughter died as he looked closer and saw what appeared to be sincerity in Christian's olive eyes. Christian had always been the sort of guy Michael envied and despised at the same time: He could do no wrong in the class, on the field, or in the arms of girls, and he could punch a ticket to any future he chose. That he was a vacuous, self-absorbed Adonis who offered nothing of true value to society apparently escaped his adoring legion of hangers-on. And now, on top of everything else, Christian was taking his talents into the fields of torture and murder.

"Yessir," Michael said, "you're gonna kill a kid who never looked cross-eyed at you, but oh, you're gonna save the world in the process. Yessir, you got the whole package." Michael scared up his best impression of the high-pitched blondes who practically bowed before their young god and said, "I love you so much, Christian Bidwell. You're totally lit."

Christian again shrugged before he mumbled, "Screw this," and tightened his aim, setting the muzzle square between Michael's eyes. "Too many comedians, Coop. Nobody's going to miss one less."

In the instant that followed, Michael felt the first taste of his mortality. He saw the coldness in Christian's eyes, and the finger pull back on the trigger.

He was going to die. He was actually going to die.

"No," Agatha Bidwell shouted as she re-entered. "Not this way."

Christian pulled back. "He's worthless, Mom. Knows nothing, but he sure has a mouth that needs to be shut down for good."

"I think not. Our objective today is to save innocent life when practical. We have already lost too many friends and colleagues." She dropped a hand on her son's shoulder and waited for him to lower the gun. "We need to reevaluate our stratagem. I've just spoken with Arthur. We have a problem and we need to leave here now."

"And Cooper? He's seen us. All he has to do is ..."

"Come with us. Based on what has happened, he may yet have appreciable value."

"Appreciable value," Michael mumbled. "Stock's going up, huh?"

The next time Michael tried a sarcastic retort – while sitting in the back seat of Agatha's car – he received a crossing blow from the butt of Christian's gun. He cupped his nose and felt blood.

Michael did not pay attention to where Agatha was driving them or that she slowed down at the entrance to Truman Street. He did, however, see the sun come out much earlier than it should have. Flames raged from a house halfway down the street, and the yellow glow lit up the neighborhood. Small explosions erupted from inside the two-story structure. Neighbors emerged from their homes, some running and others gawking.

"I should have anticipated this," Agatha said as she pulled off the road. "Walter always had a special love for fire."

"Holy shit on a stick," Michael said, recognizing at last where they were. "Walt Huggins? You trying to say he's ..."

"There," Agatha pointed without paying Michael any mind. Seconds later, the front passenger door opened, and a man stumbled into the seat gripping his left arm, his shirt sleeve coated in blood.

He coughed. "They were waiting for us. Drive."

Michael leaned forward when he recognized the voice. When he caught enough of the profile, Michael forgot all about his broken nose.

"No way. You? I mean, look, I can buy into the Ice Queen and Prince Charming over here, but you? Coach?"

Arthur Tynes, who coached track at Albion and trained both Jamie and Michael since they were 12, glanced back at Michael. He offered only a brief nod and turned away.

"Sorry, sport," Arthur said. "I didn't figure you to get caught in the crossfire. Then again," he faced Agatha, who had sped the car away, "nobody expected an outcome like this."

"I don't think Sheriff Everson will be inclined to stay in bed any longer. Our timetable just accelerated."

"This is whacked," Michael said.

"You don't know the half of it, sport."

Agatha ordered Michael silent then turned to Arthur. "Status?"

"They got Arlene. I saw her down. The Huggins girl – she's good."

"The others?"

"We couldn't touch them, but I'm not sure we would have under any circumstance. Walt knew we would make this play. That house was rigged. Benjamin drove in right as they needed backup. They're gone – who knows where? – and they've got the Jewel. You were right about taking him on."

No one spoke as they entered the heart of town. Agatha stopped at the only light on main street, even though she had green. The car idled.

"Benjamin, you said? Rand was supposed to intercept him, and he has not responded to my texts." Agatha maintained control. "Arthur, are you saying Walter knew about our strategy? Predicted our moves?"

"What I'm suggesting, Agatha, is that Walt allowed us to think we had the advantage. He sat there during the vote and knew we were lying to his face. He knew we would turn against his family. He always put together the pieces with an intuition like no one I've ever seen."

"Sure," Christian chimed in. "And maybe he just guessed right."

"Maybe, sport. Truth is, we got lucky his calculations about the pulse were off by three days. Be glad your mother predicted correctly. If time were on his side, he probably would have eliminated us all before rebirth. We've been too timid, Agatha."

"And your suggestion?" She asked.

"We drop the pursuit altogether, allow events to play out, and make our way to the fold, just as Walt always insisted. Or ..."

"Yes?"

"We drop any pretext of caution. We not concern ourselves with who gets hurt or why. We use all our resources and attack Walt in a way he didn't foresee. He thinks we are conscientious objectors. He believes there are lines we will not cross. If we prove him wrong, we end that thing before it's born. Whatever else happens here won't matter after we're gone."

Christian turned to Michael and cocked his gun.

"Now that's what I'm talking about, Arthur. Time to start crossing the line. How about it, Coop?"

Michael had no comeback, no quip. His well of snarky humor went into hiding and left Michael with an emptiness in his belly. He contemplated the very real possibility that he would be dead by sunrise.

14

L YDIA SAT ON the floor next to Jamie and stroked his hair. "The Earth of my creators, of your parents, of your birthplace, and of several others in Albion," she began, "exists across a divide between universes. It is an Earth of vast technological wonder thousands of years ahead, but also fraught with unrest and violent division. It is that very unrest that ultimately led to your unfortunate fate."

Jamie was numb. He knew he should have been breaking into laughter, but Jamie couldn't get past the nagging sensation that the woman was sincere.

"The ruling class known as the Chancellory first led humans to the stars thousands of years ago and maintained control of the population as it expanded to thirty-nine colony worlds. Their wealth was infinite, their political and military power unchallenged throughout what became known as the Collectorate.

"But some of these Chancellors remained unsatisfied. They sought answers to questions about infinity that few others bothered to ask. Their search led them to uncover secrets that have since changed the fate of the Chancellory and led them to radical choices designed to preserve the future of their caste.

"Among their discoveries were interdimensional folds - small incisions between universes. Scattered through the galaxy, few in number, but mapped and known only to the most powerful."

Jamie coughed as he played along. "Chancellors. Right. Interdimensional whatevers. Sure."

Lydia wagged her finger in disapproval. "You will listen, Jamie. You have nowhere else to go." She sighed but continued.

"An incident of enormous impact occurred thirty-five years ago, according to Collectorate Standard Years. I shall not relate those precise details, as they are not relevant to your end. But you will find this of great interest: The man who changed the fate of the Chancellory went by the name Ignatius Horne."

Jamie perked up. He remembered Iggy's declaration of the pride he took in carrying that name.

"Yes," Lydia said. "The same. Ignatius Horne brought about a genetic cataclysm that is leading to the slow, painful collapse not only of the Chancellory's power but also the ability of Chancellors to reproduce. Unless they alter this path, Chancellors as a subset of the human race will die out in a few generations."

Jamie sniffed. "OK, so you're trying to make this believable by giving Iggy a role. Whatever. You still haven't said what this has to do with me. Ain't that the point?"

Lydia smiled. "Indeed it is. The most important discovery – the one that helped bring down the Chancellory and may yet restore it - was the retrieval of an ancient energy source, created by another race a million years ago. A sentient composition capable of remaking worlds, powering empires, and creating new life.

"They are called the Jewels of Eternity. They were harvested by the same researchers who found the folds between universes. Later, others acquired pieces of this energy and researched ways to slow the fall of the Chancellory. They redesigned humans at the genetic level using Jewel energy. These new hybrids were hidden away until reaching maturity and rebirth. The Chancellors hope they will herald a new future."

Hairs stood up on Jamie's neck, and his eyes widened. Although he consciously refused to believe any of this gobbledygook, Jamie's heart was beginning to tug at him, as if to suggest he needed to stop fighting, that the truth was closing in.

"So let's say this is a cool story," he said. "Again, what's my deal?"

"Your deal, dearest Jamie, is that you are a prototype. Ten were brought to term. Born as normal humans but with a key difference - each acts as a natural incubator for the Jewel within, to determine the viability of the new species. When the incubation concludes, the original personality is exterminated and the newly designed species emerges in totality. Consume every cell, rewrite the genome. An infancy unaware of any past life and acting only for the interests of the Chancellory. A new being of staggering power, fully capable of remaking mankind on a planetary scale."

Jamie tried to resist. "No, no, no. You're whacked. Did you really think I'd believe any of this crap?"

"Tonight?" Lydia shook her head. "I was skeptical. Now, if the Mentor had worked as programmed, you would have been resigned to this concept years ago. Again, I do apologize for the design flaw."

"OK. You're *so* creative, Lydia, that I have already figured out the end to this story. Before long, the Jewel is going to rewrite me slam out of the picture. I'll be dead, but something else that looks like me will be walking around instead. Right?"

"In simplest terms, yes. Humans always like to oversimplify. The final stage of the incubation began at 1:56 a.m., which was precisely 90 seconds before you broke into the general store. That dizziness you experienced - remember?"

His stomach twisted. The details were so precise. He wanted to resist, but he felt the barriers falling. She had an answer for everything.

If I'm supposed to become this incredible new … thing … then why are people trying to kill me?"

"Tricky, that. I cannot speak to their precise motivation, as I have only had your point of view through which to observe. My suspicion is that some of these observers have changed their opinion about this mission and no longer believe your rebirth should be made viable."

"Observers?"

"Yes. The team that escaped through the interdimensional fold with you. Engineers, guardians, some of their children. You see, in the years after the Chancellory began to collapse, factions of Chancellors turned against each other - the unrest and division I mentioned earlier. There was an insurgency called The United Green. Word of the Jewel program reached the leaders of the Green, who called for its destruction. They considered the program an abomination to humanity. They wanted more rational biological methods to be employed to preserve Chancellors.

"Rather than allow the prototypes to be destroyed, observer teams were dispatched to various folds, where they disappeared. They planned to live there until incubation concluded. Fifteen Standard Years. Their allies on the other side would send a Caryllan pulse through each of the folds, timed for simultaneous incision. The pulse serves two purposes: One, to triangulate the exact position of the fold's entry rift; two, to launch the concluding stage of incubation. The Jewels are made of Caryllan energy, thus acting as receivers for the pulse. Triangulation would not be possible were you already dead. Your observers would be stranded here, perhaps forever. Hence, why the attempt on your life did not occur until *after* the pulse arrived."

Jamie fought his bindings. "Don't you even dare say it."

Lydia laid on her side, her lips only inches from Jamie and her perfume enveloping him in a cloud that was equal parts toxic and soothing. Jamie's breaths and the pace of his heartbeat quickened. He vowed to fight her, to fight them all as long he could. They might kill him, but they weren't going to make him believe any of this madness.

"When you are reborn, you will pass through the fold and you will join with the other hybrids. Then you will clear a path for the birth of the new species. At least, that was the plan fifteen years ago. Like you, I will not be around to see its conclusion."

Jamie closed his eyes. "You are fragging with my head. I almost started to believe this shit. I'm supposed to be a ..."

"Berserker. Named after the fierce warriors of Norse legend. A Berserker could be programmed to a level of destruction befitting the fury of its handler. If necessary, it might eliminate whole cities, whole regions. In theory, whole worlds." Even this thought caused Lydia to pause. "You can understand why some might not wish you to survive the rebirth."

Lydia again kissed Jamie on the cheek.

"The Chancellors brought to this world the greatest secret in a universe of secrets. Big enough to die for. Big enough to kill for. Today is your endgame. This was ordained decades ago and far away. In a few hours, your destiny will be complete, as will mine. You will cease to exist, but you will reshape a galaxy."

Jamie shut down. He didn't notice moments later when a door opened and footsteps descended wooden stairs. The sack came off his head for real, the cellar where he lay bathed in fluorescent light. Jamie reflexively turned away, the light blinding him at first. He remained numb even as Walt Huggins sat him up, removed the gag and handed him a bottle of water. Walt didn't stick around long enough to be thanked.

Jamie searched his mind for anything to place him in the real world, not the fantasy he was force-fed. His wrists bound together, he did his best to gulp, not caring how much dribbled down his chest. He finished the bottle on his second try, dropped it aside and took stock of where he was.

The basement was empty except for a workbench, a pegboard decorated in hand tools, and a padlocked door. Jamie tested the binding cords but didn't need long to realize these knots were tied by an expert. He closed his eyes and wished all this away.

"You're smart to give up," Lydia said, sending a jolt through Jamie.

Jamie's heart sank the instant he saw her, any shred of hope that she was a product of his imagination now gone.

"Nice of Walt to bring you water, considering what he put you through. I wasn't sure about him until tonight. He is a hardened believer."

Jamie flashed back to that final moment in Sammie's bedroom. The crickets returned, the window was cracking, Lydia sat in the corner, then ...

"You and Walt are in this together. You and all the others."

Lydia sighed. "I cannot say who is with whom anymore. These assassins ... Rand Paulus, Agatha Bidwell ... I knew they were observers, but fifteen years on this limited world must have worn heavily upon them. Walt will kill them if he has the chance. He will keep you hidden here so you can die and be reborn before the others reach you. They used to be such allies." Jamie stared into space, his jaw hanging. "Walt is a defender of Chancellory genetic regeneration. As is Grace Huggins. And their daughter."

Jamie picked through the scrambled mush that was his brain.

"Sammie," he whispered, almost believing what he was hearing.

"Yes, Jamie. They despise this town, much as you do. They will celebrate their return through the fold. Twenty miles north of Albion. They have triangulated it by now. The folds are not stationary, you see. No doubt sent an observer to verify. Packed their bags, so to speak."

"Where are we now?" He asked.

"The lake house. You've been here before. Three years ago."

Lydia was right. He was here with all the Hugginses, his parents, and Michael. It was a great weekend. Cookouts, swimming, hiking, some pot on the side.

Jamie closed his eyes, his anger seething to the boiling point.

He screamed. "Huggins! Walt Huggins! I wanna talk to you."

Jamie created a stir for five minutes, until he heard footsteps above. A second later, the fluorescent light flickered and the basement went dark. Jamie continued to shout, adding a series of profanities that might have peeled wallpaper. Lydia didn't interfere.

He stretched his voice for almost half an hour, certain that sooner or later Sammie's muscle-bound father would storm downstairs with a fist specially prepared for Jamie's face. When the door opened at last and the light returned, Jamie didn't believe what he saw.

15

J AMIE'S TORTURE DIDN'T end when he saw a familiar face appear on the stairs leading into the cellar. Instead, his confusion deepened and his temper burned. Ben stopped at the bottom step and stared, his bloodshot eyes glistening as puddles of water formed. Ben lowered his head for an instant, muttered words Jamie couldn't understand, and started slowly toward the boy, who was bound as if he were a dangerous criminal.

Jamie didn't try to decode what piece of the puzzle his brother fit into. Ben presented him with so many identities over the years: the big brother who pushed him high on the swings, the alcoholic who now stood over him reeking of booze. Jamie felt cold and empty and waited for Ben to make the first move.

Ben knelt then pulled apart the Velcro band wrapping Jamie's wristwatch on the left arm and compared that watch to his own. He played with the buttons on Jamie's watch and returned it to his little brother.

"Nine fifty-six," Ben said. "Don't forget. Everything leads there, J. Nine fifty-six."

Ben removed a switchblade from his pants pocket and sliced through Jamie's cords. Jamie dropped his freed arms into his lap and watched the knife do its magic on his leg bindings. When those cords fell away, Jamie wasn't sure what he was supposed to do.

Jamie felt this paralysis before. He sat on the couch in the Coopers' den when Sheriff Bill Everson arrived in the middle of the night two years ago. The sheriff spread a cloud of heavy musk as he sat next to Jamie and explained what happened to Tom and Marlena Sheridan. Jamie remembered the words because they slithered out matter-of-fact beneath the sheriff's abundant gray mustache, carrying not the first hint of concern.

"Young man, it's my sad duty to inform you that your momma and daddy have met with a tragic end. It appears a man broke into your home with intent to rob. That individual fired shots at both your momma and daddy. They did not survive. I want to offer you my condolences and promise you the Albion County Sheriff's Office will find the individual who did this. He'll never harm another momma or daddy."

Sheriff Everson rambled on, but Jamie heard none of it and had no memory of the rest of that night, only that he woke up around noon in mid-scream. For a few seconds, he believed it was all a nightmare. Then his brother appeared, face ashen and eyes drooping. Jamie knew. They fell into each other's arms without saying a word.

Jamie turned his unbearable grief into seething anger, at first blaming himself for not being at home. Maybe he could have done something to save them. He assigned blame everywhere. He stirred his anger in a cauldron deep inside until he couldn't breathe. He saw no way back from the abyss.

The next day, he awoke to the voices of adults in the Coopers' kitchen. They were all there – Michael's parents, Sammie's parents, Ben. They talked about how to break the news that the killer, a thug just released from prison, was caught overnight and claimed his innocence – even though the sheriff insisted the case was open-and-shut. They said they never saw Jamie so withdrawn. He allowed his rage to consume his every thought. Later, he said he didn't remember grabbing the baseball bat from Michael's closet. He ran a mile into town, never slowing down, not even as he burst into the sheriff's office. He raced past the dispatcher, the deputies' desks, and down a short hall to the only occupied cell.

Jamie spewed forth words rarely heard from a 15-year-old, banged the bat against the cell and vowed to kill the balding, goateed prisoner who was about Ben's age. He spat as he shouted at the prisoner. Only when one deputy grabbed him around the chest and another swiped the bat did Jamie's temperament dissolve from screaming lunatic to rabid, trapped animal. His curses became grunts, and his tears returned in steady streams.

Jamie didn't realize what he did until he heard the whispers at his parents' funeral. He saw the frowns that mingled sympathy with fear. Many of the kids who expressed their condolences in the first few days distanced themselves. Rumors flew of Jamie having fought mental disorders for years and once threatening his parents with a pistol. The stories grew into myths that never died in a town such as Albion. That's when Jamie began jogging through the town at night, allowing the bubbling stress of life in Albion to become more endurable.

He forgot all about his vow as he stood barefoot in the basement of Walt Huggins' lake house at 4:30 a.m., glaring at Ben. Jamie had grown like a string bean in the past two years, and he almost faced his brother at eye level. Jamie didn't realize he balled his fists until, suddenly, he reared back with his right arm and leaped forward while delivering a cross that smacked Ben in the left eye. His brother staggered.

Jamie took to the offensive, marshalling the tempest built the past few hours. Both fists found their targets, and his legs showed no signs of having been bound; they danced and kicked with abandon. Ben didn't try to fight back; he blocked his brother's blows with open-faced hands. He grunted then pleaded with Jamie to stop.

"This is all your fault," Jamie told him between blows. "I knew you were the reason they've been trying to kill me. Dude, you're a waste."

"Jamie, c'mon. Get hold of yourself."

"Screw you. You done nothing for me since Mom and Dad got ..."

"Yes. I've done wrong by you ... but listen to me, will you?"

"Go to hell."

"I will, J. Guaranteed. But you gotta listen. You gotta calm down and hear me out. There's little time, and we have work to do. You hear me?"

Jamie flailed at random, and his fists missed as the bountiful energy dwindled. Ben, with one eye blackened and blood pouring from a busted lip, let loose with a lightning-fast left kick, cutting Jamie's legs out from under him. Jamie landed on his back with a thud and a groan. Ben backed away, tended to his bloody lip and gathered his breath.

"I deserved that," Ben said. "Long time coming. Dammit, Jamie. You got no idea how sorry I am. You gotta let me try to explain. I don't know if there's enough time to tell you the whole sordid business."

Jamie grabbed a sore spot in the nap of his back. "Dude, I ain't in the mood for some crazy-ass story. I heard enough of that already. You tell me one thing, Ben. You just tell me nobody's coming after me anymore. Can you promise me that?"

Ben's eyes widened. "What have you heard?"

Jamie narrowed his eyes into suspicious slits. "Nothing I believe. Some whacked-out lady ... shows up out of nowhere. She's just ..."

"Jamie, did this woman ... did she call herself Mentor?"

Death passed through Jamie with icy fingers. He fought back the terror and gritted his teeth.

"How could you know?"

Ben wiped his forehead and sighed. "Oh, damn, J. We figured something was wrong with the program, but why did it wait until

75

tonight to unlock? Did she tell you about the Jewel?" Ben didn't wait for a response. "The fold? The observers?"

Jamie felt a tremor in his heartbeat. All he could do was nod.

"Chancellors?" Ben asked. Again, Jamie nodded. "Everything at once. Makes no sense. Why would the Mentor ...?" Ben paused. "The Caryllan Wave pulse. Must be it. Did it ... you called it a woman ... did she mention the pulse and what's happening to you now?"

Jamie crinkled his face. "You tell me this is all some kind of giant put-on." He wouldn't allow reality to set in, but he felt the walls pressing against him from all sides.

"Please, Ben."

Ben turned his back on Jamie and placed his hands on his hips. "It wasn't supposed to happen this way. But here we are. Jamie, as much as you hate the idea, you're going to have to follow my instructions."

Jamie released a mocking laugh. "Why should I start now?"

Ben started up the stairs. Without turning around, he said, "Get your head together. We have things to do before you die."

16

4:15 a.m.

THE MORE FAMILIAR faces he saw, the less Michael could fathom the depth of this late-night pursuit of his best friend. Michael saw a cross-section of Albion join forces and come loaded for bear. These people gathered in a field south of town, arriving in three cars: A teacher, a fellow student, a track coach, two mechanics, a writer, and a married couple who operated a bed-and-breakfast. He recognized every face, if not the names, right away. Everyone sported a weapon – most carried pistols, but at least two (the Cobb brothers) packed AK-47s.

As he looked at these white faces, illuminated by headlights, Michael drew upon the stories of his grandfather, who lived through the depths of the Jim Crow era and the battle for civil rights. He came to an inescapable conclusion.

"This must have been what it was like for a black boy to get drug to a Klan meeting," he mumbled even as he felt the butt of a rifle in his back. Christian had upgraded his personal arsenal when they arrived at the field. The student council president kept guard over Michael as the older observers consolidated.

"Klan?" Christian said. "You comparing us to that sorry bunch of backcountry yahoos? Got news for you, Coop. Us Chancellors understand the true nature of the human race. We know how to segregate undesirables, and race is not how we do it."

"Chancellors? That's what you people call yourselves? So you got a club name. Good for you, Chrissy. Good for you."

Christian leaned in. "Tell me something, Coop. What you figure it would feel like to have your balls ripped out and fed to a dog?"

"I reckon it'd hurt like a mother, but at least the dog would think he's eating steak and walk off satisfied. A damn sight better than the garden peas he'd get from you."

Michael couldn't believe he still had the gumption. The past half-hour proved to be sobering, as Michael endured what he thought was little more than a death march. He sat in the rear of Agatha's car under guard as the English teacher and the track coach searched Jamie and Ben's apartment, confiscated the brothers' laptop, and offered praise for the courage of the late Rand Paulus despite the flour mill foreman's failure to kill either of the Sheridans.

He listened as Agatha contacted all the others whom he now knew as Chancellors and coordinated their rendezvous in the field. He discerned that the Huggins family and Ben escaped town with Jamie in tow, and their destination – the "safe house" - was a mystery. The Chancellors gathered to decipher where Jamie might be hidden.

"Walter was always guarded," Agatha told Arthur Tynes as they drove south. "He never spoke of the safe house. He believed security might be compromised were all of us made aware."

"Compromised by whom?" Arthur asked. "The United Green?"

"Naturally." They shared a laugh. "He never explained how they might possibly exploit our defenses, assuming they even managed to traverse the fold. When we came through the fold, Green operatives were years away from such inroads. My miscalculation was that his true paranoia was focused not upon the Green but upon us."

Michael thought to ask who in hell these 'Green' were, but he wasn't sure he wanted to know. No one answered any of his questions; he still had no idea why Jamie was so important or why they kept talking about "the rebirth." Now, as he stood in the field with people who might as well have been from another planet, Michael assumed only minutes remained before someone put a bullet in his head and threw him in a ditch.

The Chancellors did not need long to turn their complete attention in his direction. Agatha ordered Michael to his knees; Christian pushed his fellow student to the ground.

"We have something to show you," Agatha said. "I fully expect you to explain what you see. And I should caution you, Mr. Cooper, against any further sarcasm or feeble attempts at a brand of humor most intelligent humans would find insufferable. Yes?"

The laptop screen filled with the image of three teenagers posing arm-in-arm. In the center, Michael flashed a clownish grin exposing brilliant white teeth. To Michael's right, a blond, fair-skinned boy perhaps an inch taller tried to force a smile, but his teeth remained hidden. To Michael's left, a girl who had not yet escaped braces mustered an also-limited smile.

Arthur read the caption. "'Me, Coop, Sammie. Lake house. August. Great weekend.'"

Michael saw part of a rugged home in the background fashioned with dark wood planks and a platform extending over water. Beyond the house, the trees were taller and thicker than the pines that dominated the landscape around Albion.

"Look, I got no idea why you're doing this. I mean, I don't remember that too well."

Agatha dropped to his eye level and tightened her jowls. "I intended for you to survive this experience, Mr. Cooper. I have now reconsidered."

Michael paused, his eyes drifting away. "Oh. Yeah. That. I only been there once. How the hell am I gonna remember something like that when you got me by the balls in the middle of a cotton pickin' cornfield?"

"So, you know this place? Might the Huggins family be there?"

"I reckon. Sure. I seem to recall they own it."

"Own? That's not ..." Agatha caught herself. "Are you sure?"

"Yeah. That's what Sammie told me. Come to think on it, she tried to take it back, or at least wanted to make sure I didn't tell anybody else."

Agatha faced the others. "We had a strict agreement to report all property ownership. Walter never disclosed this information." She smiled. "I have an idea of the location. Walter often talked about how he loved Lake Vernon, how he sometimes rented a cabin when he took Samantha to field training." She switched back to Michael. "What is the exact address?"

He coughed. "It was one time. I dunno. It's down some road right off Highway 39. Lake Vernon, like you said."

Agatha turned to Arthur. "Manipulate the image. Search for any geographic detail that might narrow the possibilities. Is this the only image?"

"Uncertain. He stored hundreds of photos. I'm also scouring Ben's files, but they're proving difficult. Impressive encryption. Tom and Marlena taught him well."

Agatha sighed. "Now, Mr. Cooper. I'm faced with a quandary. I can assume we'll soon have an address and directions to this residence. In that case, I would be merciful and kill you now. Or I can give you the chance to jog your memory and guide us to our new destination. In which case, your life is extended. Which option best serves your needs?"

Michael didn't hesitate. "All else being equal, I like to breathe."

"Of course you do." Agatha ordered him into the car with Christian.

As he did so, Michael heard Agatha speak to her colleagues.

"Now we know where. We must do this in a way dear Walter will not see coming. The currents of the future can only be altered with extraordinary force. Arthur has opened my eyes to that very concept. When we arrive, no holding back. When we're done and the Jewel is destroyed, perhaps even Walter will understand why we had to finish our mission in this extraordinary manner. We have the moral imperative, my friends, but we need to hurry. We have very limited time."

Minutes later, as the cars sped south on Highway 39 in search of a house on a lake, Michael struggled with a new sensation. Not only was he going to die, but he handed a death sentence to the best friend he ever knew.

17

4:40 a.m.

W HEN JAMIE RACED from the cellar upstairs toward the kitchen of the lake house, he planned to give everyone a piece of his mind. They were lunatics, all of them. He'd laugh at them. Spit in their faces. Yet just before he stepped into the kitchen, reality smacked him upside the head like a two-by-four with well-positioned nails. He heard Walt.

"We need to extract answers from Arlene before she leaves us. Grace and Samantha are tending to her wounds. Once she's conscious, we need to learn what the others are planning."

"Good luck," Ben said. "I don't think she's in a confessing mood. She made her choice. Either way, she has no future, and she knows it."

Jamie felt a jolt as he heard Sammie.

"Daddy, it's not good. Mom's trying to slow the bleeding, but she's not optimistic."

"I know, Pumpkin. All we need is to stabilize her for a short spell. Long enough to talk. Wash those rags quickly."

Jamie steeled himself and entered the kitchen. Ben turned away, and Jamie saw shame in his brother's features. Jamie still wasn't ready to accept the truth until he saw Sammie standing behind the sink, a bloody rag in her hand, the sweet innocence gone from her blue eyes, and a pistol behind her belt.

Ben grabbed him, pulled open the sliding door, and forced Jamie through. He stumbled onto the deck overlooking Lake Vernon. He paid no mind to the sweet mixture of gentle lake breeze and fragrance of cedar. Instead, he tried to level another fist at Ben. This time, Ben blocked him.

"Get a grip," Ben said in a hushed tone. "I know this is too much to take, but you've got to hear me out." Ben closed the sliding door. Inside, Walt wrapped an arm around Sammie, and they disappeared from the kitchen. "There's more you have to know, but not in front of them. Trust is in very short supply."

"I'm supposed to stand here and believe a dude who's wearing booze like a Sunday suit?"

"No. You believe me because you know it in your heart. Nobody could make this up if they tried."

Jamie supported himself against the railing. The world wasn't spinning so much as punching him like an invisible boxer.

"You knew all along," he told Ben. "You knew these whackos were coming for me, so you took off to get yourself plastered."

"No. We did not expect it to happen tonight. If it did, I expected Ignatius to bring you here without any problems."

Jamie laughed. "Great plan, bro. Worked to perfection. Why's this happening to me, you bastard?"

"I'm sorry, J. I won't bother with a history lesson; I think the Mentor has already explained how we got to this point. The bottom line is ... I love you. I've done everything I could to keep this from happening."

Jamie backed away for fear of unleashing his temper again.

"I ain't seen love from you since Mom and Dad died. My life has been hell every day for two years, and all you've done is soak up the booze and sleep around with them damned whores. Only good thing you did was put me up in that sorry apartment without AC. I was leaving, Ben. On my way out of this shithole tonight. Broke into Ol' Jack's. Did you know that? Had the cash and a gun. I was ready. Then Iggy ..." He held firm to the railing. "Why, Ben? Why do the others want me dead?" He pointed inside. "What about the Hugginses? Sammie was ... who are these people?"

"Calm down. I think you already know the answer. We're all Chancellors. We came here as an extra layer of protection for you. That's why our families were always close, why ..."

Jamie raced through the incomprehensible slew of back story Lydia provided in the cellar, and he reached a quick conclusion.

"Dude. Give me a break. We weren't close. Walt and Grace wouldn't say two words to me if they could avoid it. They put up with me because of Sammie. And you can't stand them. I almost never saw them over at our house, even when Mom and Dad were alive." He heard water lapping against the deck; he used to love that sound – it would carry him to sleep. "Look, let's say I believe this story. Maybe everything about the other universe and these whacked Chancellors and this – thing – inside me ... maybe it's all true." He trembled and held fast to the railing. "Just answer one question. Please, Ben. How do I get out of this?"

Water clustered in Ben's eyes; his shoulders sagged. "You don't, J. No matter what happens, you'll die at 9:56. Sooner if we can't protect you from the others. I've got a theory for a third option. It's hope, but it's a long shot and won't stop the inevitable. All the Mentor told you is gospel. I only wish it hadn't waited until tonight. You would've been ready."

Jamie laughed even as tears streamed down his cheeks. "Ready? What? To die? When I'm 17? Who's ready for that? 9:56? Why then? Tell me everything."

84

Ben threw up his hands. "If this will give you some comfort, I'll answer your questions best I can. But it's a reality we've all had to live with for fifteen years. I guarantee, knowledge won't change the outcome."

"Because I got what ... something like five hours to live?"

Ben nodded as he looked at his watch. "And nine minutes."

Jamie faced the lake. He felt much older, but none the wiser. He listened with little patience as Ben verified what Lydia told him about the Jewel's incubation, how it received Caryllan Wave energy, and was resequencing his DNA. At the end of eight hours, he would die, replaced by a new personality primed as a Berserker.

"We'll be able to return the hybrid to our people on the other side of the fold." Ben touched Jamie on the shoulder. "What they do next, I have no idea. There was talk of an army of prototypes, but it's been years. Plans might have changed. The Chancellors behind the program might have lost power to The United Green. Jamie, do you really want me to keep going?"

"Why the hell not?" His voice faded. He shrugged. "I mean, if I only got five hours until I become a nuke - if this is all I got, then better now than later. Right? Hell, Ben, maybe I'm just one of them pricks that's gotta know every little detail. Or maybe, dammit, you owe me."

Ben wanted a drink. "That's what our parents said about a month after we arrived. 'You owe him,' they said. 'Be the best brother you can.'" He paused, staring out across the dark lake. A few distant house lights speckled the shoreline. "Yeah, so I owe you. You want to know about the fold and how we got to this point? You really want to know?"

"Yeah, bro. I really do."

Ben sighed. "These folds do not appear at fixed points in space. Like Earth, every solar system, every galaxy, they are constantly moving. If the rotation of this Earth and the other were identical, the fold rift would be easy to find. But the rotations and revolutions vary

85

by seconds, and that's enough - especially over a period of years. Without Chancellory tech, without Caryllan energy, the rifts are almost impossible to track. It's like walking through a hall of mirrors and never finding your way out. Dammit, Jamie, you have no idea what we sacrificed to reach this day."

Jamie's head began to hurt. "Here we go. Now the pity party. I'm the one's gonna die, but this whole mission hurt you, too. Whatever, bro. So, let me guess: Your mission didn't go as planned, huh?"

Ben's eyes drifted toward the stars. "I was 8. You got no idea what it was like; I gave up so much." He coughed. "Mom and Dad said we were going on a great adventure. They said studying a primitive culture would enlighten me.

"The observers brought a small transmitter that allowed us to maintain the lock on the fold rift. We used it long enough to upgrade local tech in order to detect a Caryllan pulse. First, we used pagers. Recently, we turned our phones into receivers.

"I lost the most important fifteen years of my life, J. Everything a Chancellor might become is determined by the age of 14. If I went back now, I wouldn't know how to fit in."

Jamie tried to push everything he was hearing into the far, hidden depths of his consciousness.

"I don't give a shit about how you've you lost fifteen years on account of me. The one time I'm actually the center of attention, and you still try to turn it all back on yourself. Unreal."

Ben reached out to Jamie, who recoiled. "I know, J. Trust me, I know. But you have to understand: They took me from my home. The Earth I left behind … you wouldn't recognize it. Think if you lived in the Dark Ages and suddenly you were thrust into the 21st century. Your mind couldn't conceive it. So how about the 54th century? The difference is beyond comprehension. It was stunning, it was exciting, it was dangerous. But it was my home."

"Home?" Jamie couldn't look Ben in the eyes. "Is there where I break out the violin?"

"Please. Let's focus on the time we have left together. You are going to start to feel changes the closer you get to the rebirth. Have you been seeing or hearing anything unusual? Experiencing distortions in reality?"

The sounds of a million crickets and shattering of glass remained fresh in his memory, but he couldn't bring himself to talk about it.

"Unusual? You mean like my neighbors trying to waste me? Lydia told me that Rand and Queen Bee are trying to kill me because they decided the rebirth is a bad idea for everyone. What about you and the Hugginses?"

"We believe the same as Mom and Dad. You deserved to have a full life, and we tried to give you as much of one as we could. But we can't stop the program."

Jamie let go of the railing and started for the sliding door.

"Full life? Dude, my whole life's been a lie. Mom and Dad were the worst. You know how much I loved them? You know how much I missed them? Now they ain't worth my tears. None of you people."

Jamie grabbed the sliding door and yanked it open. Ben raced after and grabbed him by the shoulder, but Jamie swiped him away.

"J, there's a third option. It may give you a chance at that full life."

"What? You already said that ain't gonna happen."

"No, I can't prevent you from dying. But there may be another way, if you'll just ..."

Jamie sped through the kitchen. He listened for voices and took a hard left into the front hallway past the den toward the bedrooms. He saw Sammie standing in a doorway staring inside. When Sammie saw him, she started toward him, her arms extended.

"Jamie, stop. You can't ..."

He brushed her aside and swept through the doorway.

"You people think I'm just gonna do what you want and die in a few hours, but ..."

Jamie's rage subsided as Walt and Grace parted to reveal a familiar woman on the bed, her chest covered in blood, her eyes drooping and her face awash in sweat. "What are you people doing?"

He recognized Arlene Winters, a waitress at the Denny's a few miles outside of town, right near the interstate. His parents used to take him there for breakfast. He couldn't get enough of the pancakes, and Arlene always made sure to provide him with an extra stack.

Walt dropped his bloody rag, firmed his left hand, and smacked Jamie across the cheek. The sickly wallop almost knocked Jamie off his feet, but he remained standing long enough for Walt to grab him by his ponytail with one hand, beneath his armpit with the other, and proceed to fling the boy across the room, slamming face-first into the wall beneath a clock that read 4:56. Jamie crumpled to the floor. Sammie yelled in protest, and Ben rushed in dismayed.

"Sheridan, contain your brother, or he'll spend his remaining hours in the cellar. Understood? We have important work to do."

18

J AMIE SHOOK OFF his dizziness, gathered himself to his feet, and prepared to go after the biggest target in the room. He reached for a side-table lamp, its base replicating a Grecian urn. He would have tested it against Walt's head had Ben not come between Jamie and additional pain.

"You won't solve anything this way," Ben mumbled as he dragged Jamie away from the bed, where Arlene Winters offered a slight but steady moan. "Come on. We can't stay here."

Walt cocked his pistol. "Son, you have the slightest idea what a bullet can do to a man's kneecap? How about both?"

"Daddy," Sammie said. "You wouldn't ..."

"Pumpkin, this is not your concern. I won't kill you, James. The program will take care of that. But a man can lose both his kneecaps and survive long enough for my needs."

Grace, who was patting Arlene's forehead with a clean rag, intervened. "That's more than enough, sweetheart. We can't afford to bicker. Our mission has already been compromised."

Sammie stepped forward. "Let me talk to Jamie alone." She didn't make eye contact with her would-be boyfriend. "Jamie needs a friend." Her voice cracked. "He knows he can trust me."

Jamie's instant, bellowing laugh bounced off the walls. Sammie's cheeks turned red, but she didn't back away. "There are things we

89

need to talk about while there's still time. Daddy, I won't let anything happen."

Jamie caught their knowing glance as she placed a hand near the gun behind her belt. Jamie couldn't imagine how he'd been fooled into believing she was so sweet, awkward, and shy.

"Yeah," Jamie mocked. "Reckon I won't jump her, even if this is my last chance to get laid."

Walt grumbled as he turned to his daughter. "All right, Pumpkin. Take him to your room but leave the door open. Keep him at a distance."

Neither spoke nor made eye contact once in her bedroom, and the door stayed open. Sammie sat on the corner of her bed, her cheeks a dark cherry. She slumped her shoulders and rubbed her hands back and forth against her thighs, a nervous tick reminiscent of the girl Jamie once knew.

"I'm sure you hate me," she said. "It's understandable."

Jamie wanted to rail against Sammie, yet something happened when he twisted about in fury and saw her long strands of hair falling over her shoulders, cloaking her face. Jamie's heart sank.

"Hate?" He said. "I been so mad the last two years, I didn't know how to get through the day unless I was freaking pissed. I don't hate you. I feel like a chump."

Sammie's gaze glistened as water pooled in her eyes.

"Jamie, I never really thought it would come to this."

"No? Tell me something. All them weekends you and your folks went to Texas and Louisiana, were they training you for this?"

"In a way."

"What does that mean?"

"We knew there might be enemies."

"Huh. Looks like ol' Daddy guessed right."

"No, Jamie. No, he didn't. This is the worst possible ending. We thought we might have to face enemies coming through the fold. We never expected to be fighting each other." Sammie paused. "I won't lie to you, not now. I'm fully trained on a variety of weapons. Pistols, shotguns, rifles, automatics, rocket-propelled grenades. But so are we all, including the people who are after you."

"Sure. Why not? So … Queen Bee is a regular Rambo?"

Sammie broke a smile. "If she wanted to be. Fact is, we're all Chancellors … you've been told about us?" Jamie nodded. "Most Chancellors go through military service. If I were living in the Collectorate, I'd be a soldier in the Unification Guard."

Jamie snapped his fingers. "Reality check, colonel. We're living in the sticks of Alabama, and we're in high school. We don't get to go around playing GI Joe till we're 18."

"Mom and Daddy wanted me to be prepared for when we return."

"Oh, yeah. That fold. After I get all Berserker on you. Right?"

"My parents said when we returned, a lot would be expected of me. They said I would be considered weak if I went through the fold lacking the necessary maturity. They only wanted the best for me."

Jamie's head was spinning. "You know, I think most folks that do right by their kids give them nice clothes or send them to really good schools. Maybe even buy them an Xbox. But they ain't hauling them off down to the freaking bayou to train them to be soldiers."

He walked to the window and peered through the curtains. The urge to run bounded through this blood. Those thoughts barely had time to gestate before he heard the bedroom door close. He swung about. Sammie leaned against the door, as if listening to make sure her mother hadn't caught on to what she'd done.

"They told me the truth when I was old enough to understand," she said. "It was so hard, Jamie. I wanted to tell you a thousand times. I thought maybe if there was one person in the whole world who might believe in me …" She dropped her head back against the door and sighed. "But I had to be careful. Don't you see? Even if I joked about who I really was and you didn't pay it any mind, Daddy would go ballistic. He wouldn't let me anywhere near you. And you

91

were the only friend I had." Her lips quivered, but Jamie's heart felt cold and impassive.

"OK. So ... you were what? A spy for big ol' Daddy?"

"No, Jamie. Never. I just wanted a friend. You don't know how hard it is to pretend to be the kind of person you're not. I was born five months after my parents came through the fold. I've lived my entire life in the wrong universe. I just wanted a friend. I wanted you, Jamie."

"There's a newsflash. So, why didn't you just fess up a couple hours ago when I was in your bedroom? You knew all about what was going on."

"Not true. I knew the resequencing began, but everyone had voted to protect you to the end. I think Daddy suspected he would be betrayed, but he had no proof. When you showed up at my window, I'd been sitting on my bed wondering if I'd ever get a chance to tell you how I really felt. I didn't know what to feel or say. Jamie, I ..."

He raised one hand as a stop sign, and Sammie relented.

"I was running for my life. Then I figured, 'Sammie can help. She's always been there for me.' I saw you in that window, and you looked like an angel." Jamie felt something cracking inside. "Sometimes, I have dreams about you. I used to think they were silly. But then I'd wake up feeling good. You know? Warm. I got these ideas that maybe you and me ..."

He couldn't look Sammie in the eyes as she started toward him.

"I love you," she said. "I suppose you already knew that. But you have no idea how much. Everything I've ever fantasized about had to do with you." Her tears flowed freely as she stepped within arm's reach. "You don't know how many times I prayed the Chancellors were wrong, that your program would never be triggered, and the fold would never open again."

He wanted revenge, but the tears rolling down her cheeks seemed genuine, as if she morphed back into the sweet, fragile girl he knew. Then he imagined tender Sammie running through the backwoods and swamps of Louisiana in camouflage dress and Army-style boots, toting an AK-47.

She touched his hand, a gentle caress. Jamie didn't try to push her away. Rather, he stepped closer.

"I reckon you're gonna tell me you want to kiss me."

A smile broke her tears. "It's our last chance."

He sniffled. "What the hell? Ain't like I got many options." He lowered his head. Their noses almost touched. "For what it's worth," he whispered, "you might've been my first, if things had worked out."

Jamie rested his left hand against her cheek, and Sammie smiled as she tilted her face into the warm comfort of his fingers. Jamie moistened his lips, felt her short breaths, and watched her eyes close the instant before they would've kissed. His right hand did the rest.

He completed the move in a second, swiping the pistol and pushing off. The gun felt like another enemy, especially as he dropped a finger over the trigger. He took two steps back, raised the weapon, aimed between her eyes, and was surprised to discover his right hand was not shaking.

"That was pretty dumb, colonel," he said. "I thought you were a trained soldier. Oh, well. I might not be as good with one of these as you, but I ain't gonna miss from this close. Time to get the car keys."

"Jamie, this won't work. What are you going to do? Lead me out that door? You think I'll just be able to go up to Mom or Dad and ask for the car keys? They'll never let you leave."

"So we'll go out the window." His eyes widened into energetic balls. "The hiking trails. Take them into the deep forest. They'll never find me."

"Sure they will. Daddy knows every inch of those trails. Please don't do this. We need to spend the time we have left ..."

"Running. That's how we're gonna spend it. I'm betting there's a flashlight in the bed stand, right?" She nodded. "Good. Get it."

Sammie did as he asked and tested it to make sure the batteries were strong. Jamie had a nagging sensation she could have disarmed him if she wanted to. She turned to the window without looking Jamie in the eyes.

"This is going to happen, no matter how much you fight it."

Jamie joined her by the window. "I still got time. If that program, or whatever you people call it, was so reliable, how come the Mentor didn't kick in until tonight? You got no way of knowing if this thing is even working. Tech fails all the time."

She rolled her eyes. "Of course it's working, Jamie. I saw what happened to you in my bedroom right before Daddy put you down. You were hearing things. Probably seeing things, too."

He heard her patronizing tone, as if she were one of those smug school guidance counselors whose phony concern always left him in a worse mood leaving the office than entering. He stepped forward and planted the gun in her chest directly above her heart.

"You crawl out that window, or swear to God, I'll kill you."

Her eyes glistening with water, Sammie pulled back the window latch, pushed up the frame and removed the screen, dropping it outside. As she began to climb through, flashlight in hand, Sammie ducked her head and faced Jamie.

"No matter what happens, I love you."

Jamie felt a wave of sarcasm. "I'll bet you say that to all your best friends when they're gonna die in the morning."

As he climbed through, a cell phone rang at full volume in another room, and he heard Grace Huggins shout. He stepped outside onto the ground strewn with pine needles. As he stood beside Sammie and told her to lead the way to the trail heading west along the shoreline, Jamie knew he was now living for the moment. He had no use for the past and less understanding of the future. No plan at all, just a desperate desire to run.

He cocked the hammer. "Move."

19

4:50 a.m.

MICHAEL COOPER DARED not move. To his left, Dexter Cobb maintained a stoic pose, his gun stuck in Michael's side. To his right, Christian Bidwell focused on the rifle he tucked securely, as if ready to fire at an instant's notice. Neither said a word since leaving the cornfield outside Albion. Agatha Bidwell and Arthur Tynes reviewed the findings on Jamie's laptop and debated options with their cohorts by phone.

These four white people were not the cracker supremacists his Grandfather Earl – still something of a paranoiac – once spoke about. Earl talked of how black men would disappear in the middle of the night, spirited away in cars full of white men with guns, never to be seen again or perhaps to be found hanging from a tree. No, Michael thought, these people represented something more ominous. The determination in their voices and the focus in their eyes was unrelenting.

When Michael was 8, Grandfather Earl gave him a slingshot for his birthday, telling Michael to use it exclusively for "cracker hunting." Earl then took Michael aside and explained three hundred years of

American racial history in less than three minutes, concluding his series of epithets with a simple message.

"Smack them crackers in the ass."

When Michael saw a white boy his age swimming naked in the Alamander River, he armed the slingshot with a quarter-sized rock, aimed and released. The rock skipped the water twice and plunked, enough to get the boy's attention. The boy stood in chest-high water and studied Michael for a few seconds.

"Oh. Hey. C'mon in and have a swim. Water ain't too cold today."

Michael decided the boy completely missed the point, so he searched for another rock.

"Don't move," he told the boy. "I'm gonna smack you. Hold on."

"Why you wanna do that?"

"Cause you're a cracker."

The boy tilted his head. "Cracker? You mean like a Saltine?"

Michael took aim. "You a dumb cracker, ain't you?"

"I seen you at school. Who's your teacher?"

Michael pulled back the slingshot. "Miss Huber."

"Oh, yeah? I heard she's mean." The boy started toward shore. "Want a sandwich? I got some bread and some Skippy."

The rock fell from the slingshot. "Peanut butter? Jelly, too?"

"Sure. You wanna see something cool?"

The boy was a few feet from the edge, but Michael turned away. "Reckon, but get your britches on first. That's a damn sight, right there."

The boy laughed and made his way to a small encampment which included clothes, a grocery bag containing lunch, and a thermos; sitting atop a flat boulder was a pad of graph paper and a box of colored pencils. Michael followed, after the boy slipped on a pair of shorts.

The boy handed Michael the peanut butter, two slices of bread and a plastic knife. "I'm not hungry yet. Gonna draw. C'mon over, take a look."

96

As Michael made his sandwich, he studied the boy's drawings, all of which were confined to panels. Most were fully colored, while a few toward the bottom were pencil sketches. Although the panels didn't have words, the boy had drawn bubbles for the dialogue.

"Cool, huh? Still trying to get my characters right. I just need to keep practicing. They gotta be different from everybody else. I'm Jamie Sheridan. Come down to the river much? I like it down here. Gotta name?"

"Michael Cooper."

"Good to meet you, Coop."

Jamie flipped the pages until he came to the first empty grids.

"You wanna try, Coop? It's fun once you get the hang of it."

Michael saw generosity in Jamie's deep brown eyes, partly hidden between the waterfalls of his dripping, snowy hair. How could Michael not trust a kid offering peanut butter?

Coop, he thought. *Kinda cool, I reckon.*

They met by the river often. They developed chemistry and a shorthand language only they understood.

Michael found his No. 1 hombre.

Now, as he stared into the face of imminent death, a desperate Michael looked for anything to get him and Jamie out of this nightmare, yet he saw no exit. Once the cars entered Lake Vernon National Park, the phone calls increased. He heard words such as "maximum force," "air power," and "precision assault." They talked in staccato tones until the car stopped, its destination reached.

"Bring him," Agatha told Dexter Cobb as they opened the doors.

The national park's ranger station was a long, narrow, one-floor structure glowing pale green beneath a single nightlight, its frame trimmed with logs. Dexter kept one hand to Michael's neck while the other steadied the gun in the boy's side.

Agatha ordered Jonathan Cobb to search the property for a park-service helicopter. As he disappeared into the shadows, the others approached the front door, weapons extended. Arthur Tynes wasn't surprised to find it locked. He stepped back, dropped his weapon to his side, and kicked at the door with enough force to throw it open. He entered, gun shoulder-high, Agatha and Christian following. From outside, Michael he heard a shuffle, whispers, and saw a light emerge from a back room. Arthur ordered someone to his knees, asked whether anyone else was present then gave the all-clear. The instant Michael and his captor entered, the front office lit up. Arthur stood behind the counter, aiming his gun at someone on the floor.

"Complete schematics to the national park," Arthur demanded. "Specific directions to an address. Access to your helicopter. Ask no questions." Dexter brought Michael to the counter. "Otherwise, this young gentleman will lie on your floor in a pool of his own blood." Arthur turned to Michael. "Sorry, sport."

The ranger nodded. He wore only a white t-shirt and boxers, his feet bare. The ranger came to his feet and followed Arthur's instructions. Christian flipped on the computer, examined the other available tech, and studied the wall map behind the counter.

No one spoke for several minutes, but Michael recognized their smiles: They were making progress. Only when Jonathan burst into the office did the quiet tension change.

"Out back," Jonathan said. "She's exactly what we need."

Moments later, Arthur and Agatha reviewed the property owners database. Suddenly, Agatha lit up.

"There," she said. "Walter Pynn." When Christian offered a quizzical look, she added, "His birth name. Not as clever as I would expect from dear Walter."

When apprised of the address, Jonathan added a note of excitement.

"The helicopter has GPS. We'll be right on top of the target."

Agatha instructed Jonathan to fly the bird. As Christian grabbed the maps, Agatha stopped her son.

"I believe your opportunity has come, Christian. Perhaps you should join Mr. Cobb in the air assault." Christian's eyes lit up. His mother turned to the ranger. "You, sir, did an exceptional job. For the moment, Mr. Cooper here will not have to die. But you, unfortunately, have too many answers."

Agatha leveled her gun at the ranger and fired point-blank. As the ranger dropped behind the counter with a thud, Michael jerked.

"Shit." His heart raced; the truth could not have been more evident – they weren't going to leave any witnesses behind.

Agatha stood over the body in silence for a moment. She looked first to Christian, an empty pall in her eyes.

"You understand, Son?" She asked. "While our cause is morally just, we must temporarily abandon whatever foibles we might have regarding the sanctity of life." She stretched her attention to Arthur and the Cobb brothers. "The slightest hesitation, and we lose to Walter. Yes?"

They nodded with enthusiasm and hustled outside.

The Cobbs opened their car's trunk and distributed heavy-duty weapons Michael recognized from news reports about the wars overseas. These were M16s, the U.S. Army's assault weapons of choice. Agatha gave quick instructions, all of which concerned the need for perfect timing. Michael found himself in a fog as Dexter forced him into the backseat. Agatha took the wheel as Jonathan and Christian bolted into the darkness toward the helicopter. Michael knew his death sentence would be complete if they found Jamie and the Hugginses in the lake house. The digital clock on the dashboard said 5:05.

Michael looked to his right. He had a free path to the door. It was his only chance, but his courage wasn't focused. Before he realized what happened, the car returned to Highway 39. Michael felt his life slipping.

Arthur held the wheel, and Agatha communicated with the helicopter crew; they were confident the assault would succeed. Shortly after the car turned off Highway 39 and headed toward the lake, Agatha gave new orders to her son.

"We're less than three minutes from the target. The next time I contact you, commence your attack run. Understood?"

Michael looked through the window to his right. Dense forest opened up to unveil a swath of ebony glass – Lake Vernon. He guessed the road was fifty yards above the lake. He recognized the bluffs along the northern face. The car moved at a swift pace, but the speed was limited by the road's wild curves.

Agatha turned around and faced him.

"Mr. Cooper, I fill the need to clarify what you witnessed at the ranger station." Michael did not take his eyes off the bluffs as she continued. "We are not murderers by trade or by choice. Our mission, however confounding you may find it, has always been to serve the greater interests of humanity. I have neither the time nor the inclination to explain this contradiction, except to assure you that for everyone who will be sacrificed today, millions of lives – some of them yet to exist – will be saved." She sighed. "I wish you could have experienced my English class. Naturally, you would have failed, but I believe your undisciplined humor might have been appreciated on occasion."

He knew what was coming next. Michael chose life.

He flung himself through the passenger door without being shot. However, he knew he was in trouble as soon as he hit the edge of the pavement, kneecap first, and rolled over. He scrambled to his feet, hoping this was nothing more than a stinger. His right leg wobbled, and he collapsed in agony. He knew better than to ponder the wound, so he balanced himself on his left leg and shuffled forward on one working foot.

Brakes squealed, and his heart sank. If he scrambled another ten, twelve feet, he'd roll down the bluff, pray that something less than deadly would catch his fall, and the lunatics with assault rifles wouldn't waste time tracking him.

He wasn't halfway when the car stopped bathed him in high beams. He expected his ex-track coach to hit the gas and run him over. Rather, he heard patient footsteps pressing the pavement and crunching the gravel just behind him.

Michael pushed himself toward the edge. He wasn't going to be a roadside kill like so many possums.

He heard ear-splitting thunder, and the first bullet entered just below his left shoulder blade. The initial sensation of a pinprick turned into fire in his chest as a lung deflated. Michael thought he saw the images of his mom and dad caught in the high beams and twisted a second time as another bullet sliced through him, entering centimeters from his spine just beneath his neck.

The momentum of the bullet propelled him forward. He lost all sense of control and, like a rag doll, keeled into the darkness below.

He rolled downward, his body thumping against exposed roots, his head whacking the base of a tree, and his mouth swallowing chunks of soil. He fell end over end into a clump of myrtle, dangled in the bush for a few seconds until the thin branches gave way, and landed gently in mud.

Michael wanted to cry out, but he had no strength, not even enough for tears. Opening his eyes was all he could bear. The world was silent, peaceful. Michael knew he was going to die alone.

He refused to go to his creator asking why this happened. A tiny voice buried deep in his memory whispered, "When the Lord is ready to call you home, open your arms and fly." He recognized his Grandmother Celeste, who always said she had no fear of passing.

Michael figured he would see her first.

Right before he closed his eyes, Michael found joy in his agony. He discovered that everything he ever heard was correct: The passage to the other side did indeed begin with a bright light.

20

FIFTEEN MINUTES AFTER Jamie disappeared into Samantha's bedroom, the torture continued elsewhere in the lake house. Ben held Arlene Winters still as Walt threaded a spliced electrical cord down the woman's sinus cavity. She convulsed, over and over, but seemed not to care.

Ben felt ashamed. Was this how all Chancellors behaved? Was this what he was too young to see before crossing the fold?

Pieces of crap, he told himself. *We're nothing special at all.*

"Size and disposition of Agatha's allies," Walt demanded of his prisoner. "Do they know our location? What is their next move?"

Arlene wet her blood-caked lips and smiled to show teeth.

"Time," she whispered, her hoarse voice breaking the single word into two syllables. "Your ... time ... is coming. You ruined us."

Walt balled a fist as he turned to Ben. "I've never understood their argument. Chancellors must evolve. This is for all of us."

Ben lost patience for this business. The clock was ticking on his chance to show his little brother the flash drive that was Ben's last meaningful gift, perhaps a way to defy the impossible.

"Walt, I have a proposal," Ben said. "Since we've obviously been compromised, why don't we just pack up and head into the woods?

We won't have to hold out but five hours. These people might be determined, but they don't know the terrain."

Walt smirked. "Of course we'll leave. Soon."

A cell phone sprang to life in the kitchen, its melodic ring at full volume echoing through the house. Ben and Walt froze as Grace shouted. She must have lunged for the phone, as it didn't ring twice. Walt started for the door, but he didn't make it all the way.

Grace was already talking into it as she entered the doorway.

"... no, no, no. Sheriff, I'm sure Alberta must have been mistaken. Hold on, Sheriff." She looked up, her eyes darting in panic, her free hand palm-up to maintain silence. She held the phone tight against her chest.

"Sheriff Everson. He's at the house. Calling to make sure we're safe. Apparently, Alberta Weatherington said she saw us leaving right before the explosions. She thinks someone kidnapped us and set fire to the place."

Walt seemed unconcerned.

"I'll take it from here." He grabbed the phone, shoved it to his chest, and faced Ben. "Work her over." He pointed to Arlene. "I want answers before her heart gives out."

Ben nodded but did nothing at first, listening to Walt as he stepped into the hallway and conned Sheriff Everson, his dramatic technique perfectly emulating a distraught family man whose house went up in flames. He turned to thanking God they weren't inside and insisted they were at a hunting camp thirty miles outside Baton Rouge, Louisiana.

Ben heard no more, as Grace shut the bedroom door. The distractions piled up, and time wasted away. He knew what would come next: Walt would conclude they had drawn too much attention, and for everyone's safety they should take enough supplies to carry them through the day in the deep woods. He would insist Jamie be bound and gagged for the journey and left that way until the re-sequencing concluded at 9:56. Ben searched for an alternative plan and felt the keys to the blue Dodge in his pants pocket next to the flash drive. Behind his back, tucked inside his belt, the gun that once belonged to Rand Paulus now called out.

"He knows."

Arlene's haggard voice shook Ben from his trance. The bloodied woman no longer seemed disoriented, as her eyes focused like lasers upon Ben. Her smile was satisfied.

"He knows everything," she said.

Ben felt a lump in his throat. "Who? Walt?"

"I know about you and Ignatius ..." She coughed blood. "What you did two years ago. Walt must know, too. He let it happen."

Ben felt a chill. He wanted to believe she was desperate, throwing out whatever wild accusations might give her a final chance at life. He even understood. He used to enjoy visiting Denny's and chatting with Arlene during slow hours. She carried herself with such vigor despite having been a Chancellor exobiologist of great repute. She settled for menial work because Walt always insisted none of them could use their intellect to draw attention to themselves.

"He knows," she said. "He's been preparing. Kill me."

Ben recoiled. "No. Already too much blood. Not again."

"Doesn't matter," she said. "I have no future."

Ben knew she was right, at so many levels, including the ones he had blinded himself to for the past two years. He saw similar pain in her eyes, and he did not want her to suffer anymore. She did not deserve this.

Ben released any moral restraints and shot Arlene twice through the heart. Arlene stared into eternity, a thin dribble of blood coursing from her left nostril.

Ben trembled, the gun's smoking suppressor hovering inches above the dead Chancellor's chest. A cold emptiness swept over him as he studied the second defenseless person he killed tonight and the fourth since he was dragged across the fold. Ben felt no remorse, only a deep, unbending regret that he became precisely the man he once vowed never to be. A string of profanities snapped him out of his trance. He felt Walt's hot breath.

"Have you completely lost your mind, Sheridan?"

Ben found courage. "No. If she knew anything concrete, she was never going to tell us. She said I chose the wrong side, that Jamie would be dead before the rebirth. They'd shoot him and burn his body. I snapped."

Walt loosened his fists. "As much as I despise to admit it, you're right, Sheridan. We were wasting time and resources. We have to make preparations for our next move."

"The, um, sheriff. Is everything taken care of with him?"

"Everson is a moron. I told him I'd drive back at first light. That would give us more than enough time for the mission objectives to be completed and allow us to start back toward the fold. The problem is not limited to our burned-out shell of a house."

Ben nodded. "The neighbors. They claim they saw us."

"The neighbors were half-asleep. Dim-witted buffoons. Of no concern now." He turned to Grace, who was standing in the doorway. "We need to prepare the lake house for departure."

Grace paused on her way out. "Complete preparation?"

"Yes. All of it." Grace hurried off. "After I explained how we were in Louisiana — in fact, the very camp where Grace and I have been field-training Samantha for years — he sprung additional news on me. It appears one of his deputies was found shot several times along with another man ... in your apartment, of course."

Ben felt light-headed, as if he were watching Ignatius die in his arms all over again.

Walt continued. "This provides a considerable complication. Everson might be a moron, but even he would see there must be a connection between our fire and his deputy's demise. I don't think there's been this much excitement in Albion since ... oh, since your parents were murdered. Once they verify that we have not been in

Louisiana … suffice to say, the farther we are from Albion, the better. It's time."

"Fine, Walt. I concede your point. But promise me one thing. I'll have a chance to spend time alone with my brother before the end."

Walt dropped a sympathetic hand on Ben's shoulder.

"Sheridan, I once had a cousin. He was as close as a brother, so he did not understand when I could not tell him the truth about our mission. On the final night, the two of us barely spoke. If you feel this strange need to bond with James, I won't stand in your way. However, he will be properly secured to the end."

A fierce banging on another door drew their attention. They raced into the hallway and saw Grace pounding her fist against Sammie's bedroom door.

"Samantha? Samantha? Open up now. Samantha?"

Walt wasted no time and launched a powerful kick that threw the door open. Ben saw the open window. Walt grunted but otherwise contained his temper, scanning the room with the quiet professionalism of a detective at a crime scene. He sauntered past Grace uttering the word "incompetent" over and over.

Standing in the doorway, Walt put a finger in Ben's chest.

"James has lost his bonding privileges. We'll search lakeside."

Ben raced through the kitchen, opened the sliding door and tore out onto the deck. He searched east and west, assisted only by the spotlights on the deck. He called out to Jamie and waited in the dark stillness for a response he knew wasn't coming. He didn't have a chance to ponder how Jamie pulled this off.

He heard an unexpected hum in the distance, breaking the silence of the night. He couldn't determine the sound's origin, as it bounced across the lake and through the forest. His stomach tightened.

Walt screamed. "Sheridan, get in here."

As Ben entered the kitchen, Grace raced up from the cellar, and Walt took out his keys.

"No time to search. They're coming," Walt said, glancing at his watch. He turned his attention to a long, narrow cabinet just inside the kitchen from the foyer.

"Who?" Ben asked. "Agatha Bidwell?"

"Who else?" Walt forged a smile as he turned a key into a lock and opened the cabinet.

"I thought the cabin was secure."

Walt hesitated but offered no answer. He reached into a deep cabinet stocked with assault weapons in vertical braces with magazines neatly arranged in cubbies below.

Walt grabbed a pair of AK-47s, which he tossed to Ben and Grace, followed by an extra magazine for each. He grabbed an M16, two pistols and extra clips.

"Lights," he told Grace, who retreated toward the cellar. "Sheridan, come with me."

"What about Jamie and Sammie?"

"Not an issue."

Stunned by Walt's nonchalance, Ben opened his mouth to say, "What do you mean?" Yet in that instant, the distant hum became a vicious roar. The next few seconds happened on instinct.

Ben realized which side of the house the helicopter was on, so he rushed through the kitchen toward Walt and the position that might have given them some defense. He loaded the magazine into the AK, a weapon he used once before.

The lights inside blinked out a second before the house became bathed in a blinding glare, as if time flashed forward to midday. Ben and Walt didn't speak, but Ben knew they were too late. Escape wasn't an option.

The bullets came like a meteor shower as bursts of machine-gun fire competed against the helicopter's roar. At first, the glass of the sliding door and windows tinkled as bullets cut through them without a care, followed by the chaotic symphony of clangs, slams, bangs and thuds of impact deeper inside the house. Within seconds, however, the glass shattered, spraying in every possible direction. Shielded for the moment in the foyer, Ben glanced to his left, saw Walt's eyes racing in a panic, no doubt plotting their escape plan. Then he realized what was missing. He looked over his shoulder into the kitchen, which was being shredded.

Grace Huggins glowed in the helicopter's searchlight, her twisted body sprawled across the floor, her bullet wounds visible, hundreds of tiny shards of glass shining as they intermingled with the blood.

"We have to move out," Walt yelled over the insane cacophony. "On my mark, through the front door. Follow my lead. Understand, Sheridan?"

As Ben slipped through the open door, bullets ricocheted through the foyer. The men raced out onto the wooden deck, their cars a few yards away. The searchlight's glare cast the house in a bizarre glow. The barrage of bullets from the other side seemed muffled. That's when Ben heard the crackle of single rifle shots. The first bullet ricocheted off the landing a few feet ahead, splintering the wood. Ben brought up his weapon, but he was too late. The first shots intensified. Ben tripped down the short flight of steps, never letting go of his rifle.

He lost track of Walt for a second, but that was long enough to feel the piercing of a bullet as it entered just above his right collar bone. A hand reached out and tugged at him, but Ben had no sense of where he was anymore.

21

J AMIE NEVER LOOKED back. He and Sammie were almost a half-mile from the lake house, following the trail westward less than ten feet from the shoreline.

Jamie kept the pistol aimed at the back of Sammie's head. They passed through tiny whiskers of fog creeping along the shore like misshapen ghosts hunting for bodies. The path was muddy at times and overgrown in brief stretches, but otherwise as Jamie remembered from his last visit. It continued for two miles if they remained close to the water, or they could take a sudden turn where it branched off not far ahead. It would turn sharply up the bluff, a tricky incline in which the soil often gave way, and exposed roots acted like rungs on a ladder. The trail then intersected the lake road and continued on the northern side, winding in convoluted swoops through the deep, unspoiled forests.

Jamie followed the flashlight's beam, making sure they didn't miss the intersection.

He resisted Sammie's nonstop efforts to end this nonsense.

"We don't have to do it this way," she said. "You're scared, for good reason. You just found out you're dying."

"If I'm dying, it's because of people like your parents and mine. Besides, if I go nuke, you and your folks get to take a trip back

109

home. I'll bet you'll be heroes. Then you can go off and play soldier girl. I mean, that's what your folks been training you for, right?"

"Is it so bad to want to be who you were always meant to be?"

Jamie laughed. "I figured I was made to be a cartoonist. But that's just too damn bad for me, now ain't it?"

Jamie wanted to lay it on thick, to be as sarcastic and angry about his fate as he thought Sammie could take, but he didn't have the chance. The echo of squealing tires distracted him.

"What's that?" Sammie asked.

The echo came from well ahead of them and above the bluffs. He swore the sound came from a car approaching from the west. Jamie perked his ears. This time he heard the sounds of brush being battered as something tumbled down the bluff, perhaps thirty yards ahead. The car burned rubber once more, this time heading east toward the lake house and beyond. Jamie caught a glimpse of the headlights.

"Rednecks. Probably throwing their empties down the bluff. Or a used refrigerator. Just rednecks."

"No, Jamie. I really think we should turn back."

He insisted she keep moving. The air off Lake Vernon was moist and cool. He almost forgot how perfect the summer nights out here could be. The gentle lake breezes gave way to an idyllic stillness as peaceful and cleansing as the stars above were brighter and closer.

Sammie stopped without warning. Jamie stumbled into her, the gun pressing into her back.

"Jamie, wait. I don't think the people in that car were throwing out beer bottles. Look."

She focused the flashlight on an object, and Jamie recognized the back of a human head on its side in a mud pack. Jamie thought the young black man's profile was familiar. He grabbed the flashlight, shined it on the face and fell to his knees.

"Oh, God. Oh, God. It's Coop." He dropped the gun to his side, handed the flashlight to Sammie and told her to come in close. "Please, Coop. Don't do this to me. Please."

He wrapped one hand gently under the side of Michael's face, which was caked in mud. His best friend's eyes were closed, but blood stained the side of his forehead, just above the ear.

"C'mon, Coop. Wake up, dude. How did you ...?"

"What's he doing out here, Jamie? How could he ...?"

"Shut up." He placed two fingers on Michael's neck and tried to calm his own panicked breathing. "A pulse. I can feel a pulse. He's still alive. I don't understand. How did this happen?"

Jamie and Sammie shared a knowing glance. Before Sammie said anything, Jamie cut her off. "No way. They couldn't know anything about Coop. He wasn't even at my place."

"There's no other explanation. This can't be a coincidence."

Jamie ignored her, wrapping an arm around Michael and trying to lift him from the mud. Only then did the flashlight display the blood intermingled with the packed wet soil and painted across Michael's back. The bullet holes were brown and obvious. Jamie lost control of his emotions. Tears flowed as a river while he hugged Michael, trying to keep his friend up and alive, desperation overcoming him.

"Oh, God. I left my phone at home. They must've found out who I was texting. It's your fault, Sammie," he snarled. "All of you. He didn't have anything to do with all this crazy shit. Look what you people did."

Sammie became drenched in tears as well, and she tried to reach out to Jamie, but his desperate growl forced her back.

"It's not our fault, Jamie. Please. Understand. I don't know how Coop got involved, but it means ..." Sammie froze, her tears dissolving as her eyes widened. "Agatha and the others. The car. It must have been them. They're tracking us. Mom. Dad. They've got to be warned."

She started to stand up, but Jamie grabbed her by the wrist, driving his nails into her skin.

"No way. You're not going back. You're going to help me, Sammie. There's a house. We gotta get Coop some help. He'll die soon."

"No, Jamie. It's too late."

"You owe me." Jamie held Michael up with one arm and reached behind himself with the other. When he felt the gun, he brought it across his body and aimed. "We're taking him to get help. That's all there is to it."

"But my parents. Your brother."

"To hell with them. My best friend ain't gonna die out here in the mud. Hold that light and help me lift him. Do it, Sammie."

Jamie wrapped an arm through Michael's left armpit and around his best friend's back, which was wet with blood. He wiped his tear-blotted eyes with his free arm and watched as Sammie supported Michael's right side. On a count of three, they lifted.

At the instant Jamie thought he could do this, that maybe he could pull off a miracle and get Michael to safety, the buzzing in his head returned. It was faint at first, like a swarm of bees a mile away but closing fast. Not as vicious as the million crickets, but equally exasperating.

"It's happening again. The sounds. Like in your bedroom."

Sammie stopped and looked away, her ears perked.

"No, Jamie. It's not you. I can hear it too. It's something coming. Something like …"

The buzz became a hum, and the hum developed a steady, rhythmic beat that included rapid mechanical clicks. That's when a helicopter appeared as if launched from the forest. It curled until forming a course parallel to the shoreline, heading directly toward them from the west, red signals flashing and a search light poised in a narrow beam straight ahead. The rhythmic beat became a roar as the chopper flew over them.

Michael became much heavier; Jamie realized Sammie let go.

"It's them," she shouted as the roar lessened. "They're coming to kill us all."

"Grab Coop's shoulder. There's nothing you can do."

"I can't leave them, Jamie. They're my parents. Your brother."

"They can fend for themselves. I'm going to save Coop, and you're going to help."

She twisted her panicked expression between Jamie, the gun, and the eastern shoreline.

"Help me, Sammie. Now."

"I'm sorry," she said. Her voice cracked when she added, "Forgive me. I always loved you."

She grabbed the pistol from his hand and dropped the flashlight in a move so fast he didn't have a chance to blink. She ran toward the lake house. Jamie lost his hold on Michael, and they crumpled to the ground together. Jamie shouted after Sammie, but he didn't expect her to respond. He held tight to the last person in the world he could trust.

22

J AMIE MANAGED TO reach his feet and shoulder Michael onward while keeping a wobbly flashlight focused on the trail. He sobbed because he didn't see how help would come soon enough to save his best friend.

"I can't let you do this, dude," he mumbled, his voice choked. "If I'd just let them kill me when they had the chance, you'd be OK. Please, Coop. Don't do this."

Jamie's lungs resisted his every step. The weight seemed overwhelming, as if Jamie never exercised a day in his life. Michael weighed ten pounds less, so Jamie didn't understand at first why his runner's body no longer had the stamina to move faster. Then he remembered what everyone told him about the program running through his DNA. If it was reshaping him, perhaps it was tearing down his organs.

A minute after Sammie turned and ran, Jamie heard gunfire from behind. The bursts of machine-gun blasts splintered across the still waters of the lake like hundreds of small explosions, each muffled and somehow drawn out as if delivered in slow motion. At times the gunfire snapped the air like thunder from a distant storm.

Jamie didn't turn around. He thought of Ben but couldn't bear to consider what might be happening to those left behind. The chaos droned for a seeming eternity, as if whole armies were battling to the death. He cared only about Michael, so he trudged onward.

He panted. "They're killing each other. It's what they deserve."

The lake bent to the north, and as the trail wound around, Jamie grabbed a flicker of hope. He saw a pale night light, perhaps no more than a hundred yards ahead, atop a pole at the foot of a dock. Trees blocked his view up the slope, but Jamie knew he was approaching the Hugginses' closest neighbor. He remembered the house from his summer hikes.

"They'll call 911, Coop. We'll get help." Jamie didn't believe his own words. "We've gotten out of a mess before, Coop. We'll do it again. Dude. Just hang with me."

Jamie pressed onward, trying to block out the insanity behind him and focusing instead on the last great escape he and Michael made together.

"Remember that night, Coop?" He whispered. "Autry's body shop?"

Jamie focused on the terrifying thrill of an adventure they experienced two days after Michael's fourteenth birthday. In the middle of the night, they ducked as they raced between cars – some of them heaps of junk – behind the decades-old body shop on Coverdale Street.

"There it is." Michael pointed to a 1979 brown Impala. "Just came in yesterday." Michael kept track of the inventory as he walked past each day to and from school. The boys' decision to become car thieves was easy, after countless plays of a video game called *Grand Theft Auto* and any movie with "fast" and "furious" in the title. On this first escapade, Jamie brought along a coat hanger. He claimed the driver's seat.

Jamie removed the casing under the dashboard and spent five minutes trying to rearrange the wires. The engine kicked in on his fifth try. He placed his hands on the wheel, registered a deep sigh, and froze.

"So, uh, tell me something, dude. How do you drive a car?"

Michael busted out laughing. He couldn't control himself and banged his head against the passenger window.

After Michael's shorthand course – finger-pointing while referring to gears and pedals as "this here" or "that there" – Jamie shifted out of park, pressed his foot on the gas and rammed into the back-right corner of a 1985 Chevy pickup. Five minutes later, the Impala found its way to Highway 39.

After a half mile, Michael switched the headlights on.

Their first twenty miles, most of which they spent on unpaved back roads, were easy. They switched roles several times, experienced the joy of driving on the wrong side of the road, and concluded they would become outstanding car thieves. They ignored speed limit signs when they returned to Highway 39 - until they passed an Alabama state trooper. They knew they were in trouble the instant the trooper hit the brakes and swung about.

Michael made a simple plea. "Dude, this ain't the way to start our career. Hit it."

Jamie forced the car to give all it could. That was enough to top 90. Fear and exaltation fueled Jamie as he gripped the wheel with frozen hands.

Michael told Jamie they had to lose this trooper before reaching town, so he hatched a plan. With bulging eyes, Michael told Jamie to get ready to tap the brakes, surge around the bend coming up and be ready to make a hard left into Haley Watson's cornfield.

Jamie's exhilaration blocked out the blurry shapes whipping by on either side of the road. He rounded the bend, waited for Coop's instructions, and turned the wheel hard. The Impala launched for a second, swerved as it slammed to the ground, and weaved across Haley Watson's front yard. The boys screamed and whooped as Jamie regained control, spun out the car and hit the gas. He found Watson's road to the back fields.

Jamie felt like any slew of good ol' boys he'd seen on television escaping from a dumb Southern sheriff. Not bad for a 14-year-old, he thought. Not bad at all.

He took a hard right into the pea fields, swerved again and drove the Impala into a shallow ditch and left it there, idling. They took off on foot. Only when they left the farms behind and found themselves in Michael's neighborhood less than two blocks from his house did they stop to gather their breath. They knocked fists and smiled.

"They're gonna lock us up one day," Jamie whispered.

"Gotta catch us first," Michael said. They couldn't stop laughing.

Jamie treasured that night. They were partners in everything since the day they met on the Alamander River, and Jamie refused to allow that partnership to die. He trudged onward lakeside, even as the gunfire stopped, not thinking of the possible carnage.

His lungs burned. He heard footsteps. Suddenly, Michael became much lighter, and Jamie's knees stopped wobbling. He shined the flashlight across his friend's chest.

Trails of tears fell from Sammie as she reinforced Michael.

"You were right," she said, her lips trembling. "There's nothing I could do."

She held the pistol in her right hand, pointed to the ground. Jamie wanted to lash out, but her tears reminded him of someone he grew up with, someone fragile and loyal, sensitive and shy. She was his angel at the window three hours ago, and now she stood where he needed her.

"Jamie, I'm ..."

"Don't say a word. Just help me."

They powered through the final distance. The neighbor's house sat on a slope fifty yards above them. They saw no evidence of life from inside, only another pale nightlight beside the driveway, which was empty. They laid Michael down and searched their surroundings for options. The dockside light illuminated an outboard.

"Stay here," Sammie said. "I'll see if anyone's home."

117

The deadened look in her eyes told Jamie what he already assumed – they weren't going to find help here. As Sammie disappeared around the side of the house, Jamie scanned the lake shore as far as he could see. The nearest lights were a quarter mile off. He turned the flashlight on Michael and placed his fingers over his friend's neck. He knew he'd find no pulse.

Instead, he felt a beat. Michael's chest rose and fell. He was alive, but this couldn't last forever. That's when Jamie realized what he had to do. Just before Sammie returned, yelling that no one was home, Jamie gathered up Michael and moved him toward the dock.

"What are you doing?" Sammie said as she helped. "There's nowhere else to ..."

"Austin Springs. There's a hospital. Right?"

"Yes. I think there's a small one. But that's too far. It's on the south end of the lake."

"Right. About what ... five miles?"

Jamie pointed to the outboard. Sammie shook her head.

"No, Jamie. This won't work. It's too far. We don't even know if there's enough gas. I'll run to the next house. We'll have better luck."

"Forget it, Sammie. We're doing this. You coming or what?"

She didn't have a chance to answer. In the blink of an eye, the sun rose. A second later, the ground shook.

23

AGATHA WITNESSED HER plan unfold perfectly. Jonathan and Christian fed the lakeside house full of bullets, a swarm of death descending from the sky, while Agatha and Arthur waited behind parked cars, their rifles aimed at the front door. The rousing stir of weapons fire percolated Agatha's blood and energized her in a way she had not felt since combat decades ago in the Unification Guard. The inhabitants fled the only way they could. When Walt and Ben raced outside into the shadows, Agatha fired. Arthur Tynes and Dexter Cobb followed suit.

Their targets stumbled. Ben appeared to fall down the steps, and Agatha was certain of a hit. Walt sprayed automatic fire in return then leaped and disappeared behind the steps. Agatha ducked as the glass from the car's windows flew in shards all around her. When she rose and aimed, she couldn't find her targets. She called Jonathan.

"Cease fire," Agatha yelled. When the guns went silent, Agatha continued, but at a whisper. "Bring the helicopter over the house. Focus on the front entry. Our targets are pinned down. Finish them."

The chopper's roar, somewhat muffled from the lakeside, now exploded with intensity. Agatha shielded her eyes as the searchlight showered them. Above, pilot Jonathan redirected its beam to a tiny area, bathing the deck and steps in light that rivaled the sun at high noon. Machine-gun fire resumed, splintering wood planks and shattering glass from the front windows.

Agatha watched with an uncomfortable blend of relish that no human could survive such an onslaught yet with considerable remorse that a diplomatic resolution was never found. She walked around the car and exposed her position, her weapon chest-high.

She yelled into the phone. "Cease fire. We're done."

The hail of bullets ended. A few shards of glass tinkled to the ground. Only the rhythmic roar of the chopper broke the night air. The threesome paused as they approached the deck. Arthur dropped, his weapon extended, preparing to fire beneath the deck. Dexter raced past and aimed his rifle into the back corner where his targets were pinned. Agatha thought about who would be lying dead inside. Her heart skipped as adrenaline surged.

"The future will not be served this way, Walter," she said.

However, anxiety set in as they prepared to enter the lake house. The men who were pinned down vanished.

They examined the foundation beneath the front deck and found an opening just wide enough for a man to squirm through. Boards lay next to a camouflaged secret entry to a bunker. They entered the house with weapons chest-high and found Arlene in the back bedroom. The discovery shook Agatha to her core.

"This was not deserved," Agatha said in a somber tone. "I should have sent you straight to the fold, sweet one. I apologize."

She refused to surrender to emotion. They raced through the bedrooms, back to the kitchen, flinging open every door, their fingers pressed against the triggers. Agatha saw a final opportunity in the kitchen, not more than eight feet from Grace Huggins' body. A white wooden door, shot up badly and still clinging to its hinges, hung ajar. They looked at each other.

Agatha mouthed the word, "Bunker."

Dexter entered first, shining his light at the same level as his M16. He sprayed the beam across the cellar. He didn't need ten seconds to complete his survey.

"Nothing, Agatha. A few shelves with jars. Looks like food storage. No place to hide."

Agatha cast her own light on the subject and turned to Dexter. "Are you blind?"

She focused her light on a door at the back wall. A chain was cut and a padlock lay on the floor. Agatha should have known he would have an escape route. He was always too detail-oriented and far too paranoid of an attack by The United Green.

She ordered Arthur back to the car, to examine the maps they confiscated from the park ranger's office and consider the best strategy for pursuit. Then she stepped out onto the deck overlooking the lake, putting her own thoughts in order and phoning Jonathan.

"Begin an aerial search. They're underground, but they have to emerge." Then it hit her – the obvious twist she should have seen from miles away. Her words fell from suddenly trembling lips. "Walter would not create an escape tunnel unless he ..."

She heard Dexter yell from the cellar.

"Going after them. We have to move."

Her trigger hand shook, the rifle slipping from her grip. Time stopped, and blood drained from her face. The phone dropped to the deck as she turned and yelled, but she knew her effort would be futile. She spent years assuming Walter would betray her one day. Now she felt powerless.

"Dexter, no ..."

The light could have blinded her, but the concussion of the blast ensured Agatha wasn't on her feet long enough to see anything. The house disintegrated in fire. Agatha took flight, her body thrown end-over-end without malice into the lake. The instant she smacked the water face-first, Agatha fell into a deep, dark and unfamiliar peace.

24

AFTER BEN FELT a bullet rip through above his right collar bone, Walt grabbed him and dragged him beneath the front deck. As bullets ricocheted around them, Walt pulled away a fake front. Walt grabbed his rifle, tossed it through the hole, and ordered Ben to move. Ben pushed himself through the opening and fell to the floor of the cellar. The cellar glowed thanks to a gas lantern on the work table.

Walt grabbed the lantern and a small sack beside it. "Grace's final sacrifice," he said with no emotion. "She'll be remembered."

Ben ignored the warm blood rolling down his chest or the throbbing pain in his chest as Walt handed him the lantern, removed bolt cutters from the sack and proceeded to break the chain on the metal escape door's handle. When the chain snapped, Walt gave a simple order.

"Move."

The earthen tunnel was not wide enough for two men to run abreast. Walt told Ben to keep the lantern and take point. They sprinted. Weapons fire disappeared. Ben's amazement grew the farther they ran. He felt the tunnel shifting upward, matching the local topography if headed inland. They ran for five minutes before reaching the end. A metal ladder greeted them, leaning against the tunnel's face, its top rung only a couple feet beneath a door. Or so Ben thought.

Walt set down his rifle and the sack then ascended the ladder. He braced his head against what Ben now realized was a sheet of wood. The hulk of a man spread both hands and heaved. He grunted as he forced the wood away from the opening, which was no bigger than the fake front on the lake house. Walt backed down halfway and ordered Ben to hand him the lantern and sack.

Ben saw stars in a clear sky. When he rose to his feet, he was lost. They were in the woods, surrounded by low brush.

"This way," Walt said, motioning them forward.

Ben stared out at Lake Vernon, still cast in darkness. However, the first pale inkling of dawn emerged from beyond the eastern shore. What got Ben's attention, however, was the familiar roar of a helicopter. He glanced off to his right then down through an opening in the trees. The chopper that shot up the lake house hovered, its searchlight a narrow, evil beam. Ben saw part of the house, though most of it was shrouded behind trees.

Walt reached into the sack and removed a metallic device with a single red button in the center. Ben recognized it immediately.

"So much for the quiet life," Walt said before extending an antenna.

That's when he pressed the button.

Ben shielded his eyes at the initial blast. When he lowered his arm, he saw a yellow glow where the lake house once stood. A few flames rose as high as the trees. Thunder cracked all around, and Ben felt the concussion. His jaw dropped.

"Holy mother ..." he whispered. "What the hell did you use?"

"Enough to do the job."

Walt revealed a pair of binoculars, yet another goodie from the sack of surprises. The giant man turned his attention away from the former lake house and focused the lenses east. The helicopter was flying erratically, no doubt impacted by the force of the explosion. It spun, the searchlight rotating like a lighthouse beacon. In seconds, however, the helicopter stabilized and returned to a position above the fiery ruins, no doubt scanning for survivors.

"Time to move," Walt said, dropping the binoculars around his neck and turning. He raced back through the woods, not bothering to ask whether Ben planned to follow. They ran past the tunnel entry, where Walt snagged the lantern. "This way."

"Give me a clue, Walt. What's the plan? How did you know ...?"

The lantern's light fell upon the answer. They passed through the brush into a clearing that Ben first took to be a hiking trail. He didn't need long to realize this was too wide and well-managed. A one-lane road disappeared to his left down a gentle slope. Moreover, Ben couldn't believe what he saw to his right. A wood-plank structure looked to be a storage shed, but its isolation made no sense. The road ended here, as if at a cabin. Walt dropped the lantern beside the door, took out his keys, and opened the lock.

"This is yours, too?" Ben asked. "You own ..."

"Yes," Walt said, his sigh of annoyance obvious. He opened the double doors and shone the light on a black SUV. "Time to go, Sheridan."

"But ... Huggins, where are we gonna go? Huh? We just gonna keep running? We don't even know where Jamie and Sammie are, or if they're even alive."

Walt produced a smile that unnerved Ben.

"As a matter of fact, we do," he said.

In that moment, Ben realized everything he thought he knew about Walt Huggins amounted to less than nothing.

25

THE EXPLOSION SENT a flash across the lake and down the shoreline. It lasted slightly longer than a lightning bolt, but the rumble that followed was more pronounced. The earth trembled beneath Jamie and Sammie, and they almost lost hold of Michael. They froze.

"Dad. Mom."

Sammie wobbled, and Jamie thought she was going to faint. The yellow glow above the treetops hypnotized him as well, and he was sure that any hope of Ben's survival was gone. Jamie believed no one would be coming after him. His mission focused on a single cause.

"Get Michael to the boat. We're the only ones who can save him."

He cast the flashlight upon her. She was dazed but not sobbing. Jamie couldn't stand around waiting for her confusion to clear up.

"Maybe ..." she muttered. "The explosives wouldn't have gone off unless Daddy triggered them. That was the plan. A diversion for escape, if we ever needed it."

"Doesn't matter. I need your help. We're going to the boat. Move."

Sammie nodded, a strange smile overcoming her. She obeyed Jamie, and they carried Michael down the pier. Standing over the boat, Jamie reached a haphazard decision about transferring Michael. Although his own strength was all but sapped, Jamie thought he'd do

125

better on the receiving end. He and Sammie sat Michael down on the edge of the pier, the teen's feet dangling over the side and touching the outboard. Jamie jumped into the boat while Sammie held Michael steady.

"OK, Sammie. Careful."

Jamie sat the flashlight on the cushioned passenger seat in the stern. He reached over the edge, hoping the boat wouldn't sway or bang against the pier. Sammie pushed Michael forward. The boy fell helplessly into the boat, straight for Jamie's embrace. Sammie jumped in, grabbed the flashlight and helped Jamie lay their friend on the long, cushioned seat.

"How is he still alive?" She whispered. "He's been moved so much."

He pointed a finger in her face. "He's gonna make it."

"OK, Jamie. Yeah. He's gonna make it. What do we do now?"

"The bow line. Untie it. I'll get this thing running."

Jamie crossed his fingers, grabbed the flashlight and hoped for a little luck. Sometimes boat owners were careless and left the key in the ignition. When Jamie saw otherwise, he hoped to rely on the value of experience. He ducked under the steering wheel, turned over on his back and shined the flashlight onto a jumble of electrical wires.

Jamie focused on the lessons learned during and since the night he and Michael stole their first car. He searched for the right combination of wires. When he heard the soothing rumble of the bilge pumps, he smiled. Sammie stood behind the driver's seat and handed Jamie the pistol.

"Watch over Michael," she said. "I'll drive."

He took the weapon and nodded. Jamie saw the desolation on her face and knew she wouldn't turn on him again – at least not right away. She was still in shock.

"Run it full out," he said. "Coop doesn't have much time."

She grabbed the wheel like a pro and pushed the throttle forward. She told Jamie to have a seat beside Michael. He all but fell to the deck, his energy given out. As soon as he did, she throttled all the way up.

The boat sprinted across Lake Vernon, passing through slivers of fog. Jamie had no sense of speed or direction anymore, only sheer and utter exhaustion. He leaned against the passenger seat, his head inches from Michael's, his best friend's blood smeared over both of them.

"I'm sorry, Coop. I'm so sorry."

Jamie wanted to cry, but he didn't have the ability. He watched Sammie from behind, her features now cast in a pale blue glow.

Jamie dropped his head. His eyes fell upon his blood-splattered wristwatch, which illuminated green. Just before he closed his eyes, no longer able to stay awake, Jamie saw the time: 5:56 a.m.

He succumbed to the truth and fell asleep anyway.

He had four hours to live.

Exogenesis

15 years ago

Benjamin Chevallier didn't want to abandon his family name. They were taking his friends, his memories, his dreams, even his stream amp. Why couldn't he retain something of his own in the new world? He used to think his parents cared.

"I'm almost in Tier 3," he told his father. "I'm in the top two percent of my class." Tom Chevallier sighed and told his eight-year-old son to look beyond classical education.

"The Tiers teach us about the past. They show us what was built centuries ago, before the fall. No amount of schooling will save the Chancellors from themselves. We need adventurers who are willing to cast tradition aside. The Chevallier descendency will be remembered for its courage in charting this daring new path."

Benjamin couldn't tell whether his father was sincere or borrowing from the propagandist rhetoric he wrote for instream broadcasts. Tom Chevallier was the leading counter-voice to the rising influence of The United Green. "No price is too high," he ended each broadcast. "No sacrifice too small. A future without Chancellors is impossible."

Benjamin lacked the courage to tell his father that yes, the price was too high. He shouldn't have to lose his future to save generations yet to be born. Twenty hours was not enough warning to unpack his life and seal it behind a holo-storage barricade.

"Fifteen years is not a lifetime," his father said. "The new world will fascinate you. Benjamin, even their most forward-thinking geniuses know a pittance of what you have accumulated in eight years. Examining humanity in a nativist, even tribal state, will shed light on our own humble beginnings. These lessons will provide you with wisdom our people will need to hear. True, you will not take a predictable path through the Guard or the Bureau, but you will come out ahead. Trust in yourself, Benjamin."

Tom was asking for too much, but the boy had no options. At first, he asked about staying with grandparents in Paris, or with his cousins on the Ark Carrier Septimius, orbiting Catalan. His parents said "no" before he made his case. "Security," they insisted. "If suspicions are raised, you might place the mission in jeopardy. Many members of The United Green hide in plain sight, they explained. Trust is in short supply."

Benjamin asked about his new surname, but it remained as classified as their destination. They would tell him en route, after their shuttle left the city. In the meantime, they told him to make a short list of things his heart most wanted to do before leaving. Anything was acceptable, so long as it did not involve saying goodbye to his friends. "They will not forget you."

He asked to spend the night alone on the beach. Benjamin gathered a camping roll of essentials and walked four city blocks before he reached the shore. New Stockholm's glimmering oceanside towers disrupted a clear view of the night sky, so Benjamin tapped his stream amp to find a remedy. The node implanted above his right temple burst into a holographic cube awaiting his instructions. Chasing his fingers through the cube, he found a spatial dimmer. The boy grabbed hold and tossed the magnetic curtain around him, creating a field to redirect light. The universe revealed itself in pristine glory, as it might have to primitives thousands of years ago.

He laid out his bedding and rested his head. The wind was light, and the waves lapped the shore with delicate toes. Benjamin leaned his head toward the north and with a measured pace, recited the name of every star, every constellation, every galaxy he knew, which was most. He stopped whenever he reached a colony world's star system, many of which were visible. When he called out each planet's name, he tapped the amp and brought up a long-range image of the world.

"Catalan. Xavier's Garden. Zwahili Kingdom. Moroccan Prime. G'hladi. Hokkaido. New Riyadh. Brasilia Major. Mariabella. Brahma."

He wondered. Would the stars be the same in another universe? Were those same planets teeming with life or waiting for humans to reach out to them someday? Does anyone on the other Earth ask these questions? Do they care about the glory of feeling space beneath their feet? Or staring out an Ark Carrier two hundred light-years from home, proud of how far their ancestors brought them? *Nativist,* his father called them. *Tribal.* The words chilled Benjamin more than the night air.

He wanted to learn *kwin-sho.* He wanted to fight for the Unification Guard, maintaining ethnic stability on the colonies. Even if the Chancellory was meant to fade away, at least he could have been among the last to experience the thrills most children craved.

The more Benjamin thought of these dreams destroyed, the angrier he grew. He decided to defy his parents and contact his friends. He'd be careful what he said. They'd never suspect a thing. "Father is wrong. They WILL forget me." He tapped his amp and then the circastreams.

When his commands fell on a muted response and the cubes did not open, Benjamin pounded sand. They had nullified direct cubes to anyone other than his parents. He couldn't even contact Grandma in Paris.

Benjamin closed his eyes and cried.

He sobbed not just because of the life he was about to lose but because he would journey to the new world willingly. He sobbed because he knew by the time the sun rose, he would gather himself together and make his father proud, as any good Chancellor boy might. He sobbed because he dared not in front of adults.

Somewhere along the way, Benjamin cried himself to sleep. When he woke, the sun was sneaking above the Atlantic horizon. His father sat beside him. Tom Chevallier didn't need to say the words. But he must have seen the dried tears caked on the boy's cheeks, for he grabbed Benjamin by the hand and held firm. Benjamin saw a glimmer of water in the corners of his father's eyes, and then a smile.

"Trust me," Tom said. "I will always be there for you."

One hour later, a doctor wrapped Benjamin in a surgical stasis cube and guided an extraction laser inside the boy's brain. There, it carefully annihilated the tool designed to integrate with Benjamin's nervous system for life. His Chancellor identity, his repository of instant knowledge, the collection of vids he gathered on his journeys across Earth and her inner colonies. His favorite Tier instructors and closest friends. The historical logs of the *kwin-sho* masters. The music of Jean-Michael Sibelius, and the anthems of each division of the Guard.

When the procedure ended, Benjamin felt naked. He was a helpless child with no choice but to follow his parents on this mad exile based on goals too big for him to understand.

He ate a simple breakfast and changed into a new set of clothes. Tom insisted this dress would help them fit in during the transition phase. The scouts had little time to collect intelligence, but it was enough. Tom named them blue jeans, t-shirt, belt, and baseball cap. Each member of the Observer team left with a suitcase and a few non-perishables to help them survive. They were allowed nothing that might open themselves to scrutiny or provide clues should the Green ever pursue them.

Benjamin was numb. He boarded a shuttle which left their private landing and rendezvoused with another craft an hour outside the city. Six others joined them – all but the pilot destined for the new world. As they stood idle in an open pasture and waited for the final shuttle, Benjamin listened quietly as people he did not know introduced themselves. His parents greeted them like old friends or political allies.

As the final shuttle neared, Tom and Marlena stood at his side.

"You are Benjamin Sheridan," his mother said. "I chose the surname. It belonged to a descendency that died out two centuries ago. Say it."

He muttered the words. Marlena was not satisfied. "Again."

"Benjamin Sheridan. I am Benjamin Sheridan."

Better, she said as the crab-shaped shuttle neared its landing. "We have a surprise for you. You always wanted to have a little brother. Yes?"

The thought never occurred to the boy.

"I don't understand."

"You will." She bent down beside her son. "The child who steps off that ship may be the face of our future. But he is a child. Very small, very alone. You will be good for each other. Yes?"

Benjamin faced his father, whose shoulders were rigid, chin high, carrying an air of excitement.

"What is so special about him?"

Tom did not break his stare as the ship landed. "This boy is the first of his kind. He is two years old, Benjamin, but what lies inside him is a million years old. An intellect far beyond our understanding. A chance worth taking if we are to survive."

Five more Observers departed the shuttle, each carrying a suitcase. A sixth — still draped in Chancellor business attire — held the boy's hand. Benjamin couldn't grasp the magnitude of it all: This many Observers for a golden-haired child who seemed barely outside the crib.

"His memory has been adjusted," Tom said. *"Play along, Benjamin. The child is eager to meet you."*

The escort brought the boy to the Sheridans. She kneeled at his side.

"Jamie, this is your family. Now that you have recovered, you can go home with them. Remember how we talked about your brother? Jamie nodded, and the escort faced Benjamin. Say hello to Jamie. You haven't seen each other since he was a newborn. Yes?"

Benjamin caught his parents' insistent eyes and knelt.

"Hello, little brother. I'm very happy to see you again."

Jamie paused before sneaking in a smile.

"Miss Frances says you like to play games. Can we play games?"

"Sure, Jamie. We'll play something the first chance we can. OK?"

Benjamin wanted to cry. They were doing the same thing to this little boy: Stripping away his identity, creating a lie suitable for a life in exile. Except Jamie did not have a clue about any of it.

His parents introduced themselves and hugged Jamie, acting as if they had not touched their son since his birth. The escort, an imperious woman with beautifully coiffed, sweeping red hair and wearing a jewel-incrusted floral sari, showed no emotion as the Sheridans prepared to walk away with this child. Yet Benjamin saw it in her features – the boy carried her eyes.

She was giving her son away and acted as if Jamie were no more than a commodity. The last thing she said before returning to her shuttle:

"We will see you in fifteen years. Complete your mission with fidelity."

And then she was gone, not so much as a wave to the boy.

He wanted to resent the child, but no matter how much anger he tried to stir, Benjamin could not get past a simple realization:

He and Jamie were trapped. If he did not show any love for Jamie, who would?

Two hours later, he held his little brother's hand as they crossed the Interdimensional Fold.

PART TWO
INTO THE LIGHT

Son,

As you near the end of your life, you have many questions. However, you are too young to understand all the answers. You cannot comprehend the full nature of your role in the future. We can offer unto you the small comfort that everything about to pass is essential to the growth and vitality of the human race. It is this knowledge that convinced us, with much remorse, to send you on such a frightful path.

From the moment of your conception, you were loved. We knew you would be different, a new design, but we celebrated your unique and limitless potential. The brief time we spent with you filled our hearts with a joy unspeakable among our caste. However, we came to understand why you were brought into our lives, even if for a short while.

We hope the Mentor program has played these recorded thoughts and many more as you sleep, and they provide you with warmth and peace of mind. You are our greatest gift to humanity, and we miss you deeply.

With Fondest Regards,
Mother
Father

26

J AMIE DREAMED. He saw his mother tuck him into bed and kiss him on the forehead. She told him tomorrow was a new challenge, and a strong boy should be prepared for whatever life brought his way.

He watched her neatly arrange the bobbles on his nightstand and position the alarm clock so Jamie could reach it comfortably when it went off in the morning. He asked Mom whether she knew any goodnight prayers, because all the other children said their parents shared a prayer before sleep. But Mom said no, the Sheridan family wasn't like others. We think for ourselves, she said. Jamie smiled and closed his eyes. She turned off the lamp.

Jamie saw her glide through the shadows and for a second, her silhouette occupied the doorway. She shut the door, leaving him surrounded in darkness.

Something was wrong.

He sensed cracks in the darkness, a wall between him and a dangerous unknown. Mom wasn't who she said she was. She never loved him; she didn't know how.

The truth chewed at his flesh and raced through his brain like a rat in a sewer. The pain extended through his chest, where tightness formed just above his heart, radiating outward into a burning, thrashing sensation. Jamie resisted the urge to cry.

He opened his eyes to the gray-blue of dawn and felt a breeze. An outboard engine roared behind him, and he held a pistol in his right hand. He saw splattered blood. Michael lay on the cushioned seat beside him, his chest still rising and falling slowly.

Jamie remembered each detail of the past four hours.

"All a lie," he whispered.

He eyelids felt heavy, as if awakening from hours of deep sleep. The breeze hit him full-on, as Sammie was still piloting at open throttle over the glass-slick lake. They passed through clumps of fog, and the mist hung thick in the morning air. He turned to Michael, and reality overtook him. Even if they got his best friend to a hospital in time, the injuries must have been so massive, the blood loss so profound, his body moved around too much for him to have any real chance.

Jamie wondered whether he was sentencing his friend to a life of endless pain in hospitals or in a wheelchair. The bullet holes were so close to the spine. He didn't expect Michael's forgiveness, only an understanding that his No. 1 had to do everything in his power to keep Michael alive.

Sammie didn't realize Jamie was standing, but she kept her word: The boat indeed headed for Austin Springs. Jamie saw the town's twinkling lights and the vague outlines of stores along the lakefront. They were still more than a mile away. A mile from …

Something didn't make sense. The lumbering stiffness vanished; he felt refreshed. The extreme exhaustion that grounded him before reaching the dock disappeared. Hours should have passed to feel this invigorated.

"I don't get it," Jamie said, looking at his wristwatch.

6:06 a.m.

"Just ten minutes. Can't be."

The full reality of his predicament strike him. Jamie realized the lights of Austin Springs were broadside to the boat, which was veering away toward the western shore. His grip on the pistol tightened as he realized Sammie was betraying him yet again. Was she such a cold-blooded Chancellor she would allow Michael to die?

Jamie didn't wait to find out. He rushed forward and jammed the gun against her head.

"What are you doing, Sammie?" He yelled over the outboard. "What are you doing?"

She pulled back on the throttle and pointed to the boat's port side.

"Look. Over town. It's a helicopter, Jamie. It's coming this way."

Jamie kept a steady aim while shifting his eyes toward Austin Springs. Then he saw the lights. They didn't match the steady twinkles from the storefronts. Green and red flashers. Through the hazy dawn light, Jamie saw an ovoid shape emerge. The familiar echo of a chopper's rotor was faint but distinct. They were still almost a mile from town but sitting dead in the center of the lake, the refuge of the eastern and western shores each a good half-mile away.

"Throttle up, Sammie. We're not changing course."

"Jamie, that doesn't make sense. We'll head right into them."

He cocked the hammer for emphasis. "Too late to back off. We have to save Coop."

"Jamie, I'm swinging the boat west. Ginny's Creek is right over there." She pointed. "It's a good place to hide."

"No. That helicopter ... it might not be them. It ..."

"You're not thinking this through."

Sammie gunned the throttle, but this time grabbed the wheel and made a hard right. He wasn't going to let her run again. Not when they were so close to help.

He demanded she head back toward town. She didn't say a word; he didn't know what to do with her defiance. A moment ago he was ready to shoot her, but the girl's determination in the face of death confused him.

Jamie sensed a shadow moving behind him but didn't have time to react before he heard a familiar voice shouting at him.

"Dude, that is not cool."

Michael Cooper stood rigid behind them, his weary, mud-splattered face casting a disbelieving sneer.

He reached for the gun.

Jamie looked into his best friend's bewildered eyes, dizzy.

"Coop ...?"

27

T HE BLUE HAZE of dawn terrified Ben. The sun would be up soon, and with it the final hours of his brother's life. Ben knew what he had to do, but he wondered whether he possessed the courage. All his life he played the Chancellors' games, succumbed to their iron will, and went along with their mission to protect the Jewel until the day of its rebirth. Even when he finally saw the light of ultimate truth – a revelation bigger than all of them – he did not find the fortitude to take a stand. Instead, he cowered in the shadows and deep into a bottle when they rejected his truth.

Now, as he rode shotgun in Walt Huggins's secret, black SUV – pine trees whizzing past along back roads around Lake Vernon – Ben knew he had no choice but to kill again.

In the minutes since their hasty escape, Ben learned how insidious Walt could be. The hulk of a man produced a hand-held Global Positioning Satellite, modified to track the Caryllan Wave energy coursing through Jamie's blood, a signature unique in the world.

Walt boasted of his careful planning, even while he tracked a speedboat's progress across Lake Vernon, headed toward Austin Springs.

"Be thankful, Sheridan," Walt said with confidence. "If I had not considered every contingency, we'd have no way to track him."

Ben failed to hide his sarcasm. "Yeah, that's what a good Chancellor does. Every contingency. So, did you plan for the Caryllan pulse to arrive three days ahead of your prediction? Did you also plan for Grace to die like that?"

The words fell off his lips like icicles. Walt neither mentioned her name nor showed evidence of grief, as if her death were less of a concern than a paper cut. Ben was still trying to make sense of their final minutes in the lake house and how calmly Walt carried himself.

Walt studied the road but never changed his stoic expression.

"My wife understood sacrifice, Sheridan. She played her role, and now she's gone. We have an important task at hand: The only mission that matters."

Ben cursed in silence. He reached into his pocket and felt the flash drive. If he reached Jamie for a few minutes, maybe the impossible could be conquered. Ben glanced down to the butt of the pistol tucked between his pants and belly. If only the SUV weren't moving so fast.

All he had to do was fire a single shot, take the wheel then use the GPS to find Jamie. It would have been easy; if only the biggest, most fearsome Chancellor he ever knew wasn't sitting to his left. The last time he tried to defy Chancellors older and more committed than himself, Ben failed miserably. All he wanted to do two years earlier was confront his parents with knowledge that could change their mission, alter their entire view of history. But he was warned against such tactics.

"Change is a concept few humans embrace willingly," Deputy Ignatius Horne told him that day. "Chancellors, on the other hand, have a tendency to *exterminate* opposition to their ideology. What you are proposing could bring the entire caste system to its knees. Your parents will not be pleased, Benjamin. Tread with great care."

He did not listen, and the shadows followed him ever since.

140

Walt rounded a sharp curve while minding the GPS.

"Appears our young ones have made a course correction." He flipped the monitor toward Ben. "Turned west. Interesting decision."

Ben wasn't familiar with the geography. "Where are they going?"

"On present heading, Ginny's Creek. There's one paved road into that area. Otherwise, dirt access. Could delay our reunion."

"Why?"

"The creek has a snake-like pattern for almost five miles. The surrounding forest is quite dense. If anyone wanted to evade pursuers for a few hours, this would be a wise place to hide. Fortunately, Samantha is familiar with the terrain."

"Why would she know that area so well?"

"Thick woods. Scattered residents." Walt turned to Ben. "The perfect location for Sammie's Dacha training."

"Dacha? Seriously? She's a kid. If you wanted her ready for the Unification Guard, you could have done it proper after the mission here was over. You're a sick bastard, Huggins."

Walt laughed. "Because I do my job as a father? And where precisely have you been for James the past two years? Drowning in the bottle. You have no credibility."

"Pull over."

"We'll stop when we find Samantha and James."

Ben winced and grabbed at his bullet wound, which was bleeding less. "Pull over, Huggins. I'm lightheaded. I need to dress this thing."

"I suspect you're suffering more from a hangover than loss of blood. You can wait."

The safety was off; Walt would never see it coming. As long as Ben grabbed the wheel, he could gently guide the vehicle to the curb. The plan made sense, even quick and easy. Too easy. And that's why Ben hesitated. He tried instead to play a final card.

"We need to pull over and talk about Jamie."

"There's nothing to discuss, Sheridan."

"Walt, it doesn't have to end this way. Jamie doesn't deserve what's happened to him."

"No, he doesn't. But that matter was settled fifteen years ago. Don't tell me you've decided to intervene at the eleventh hour."

Ben gritted his teeth. "Screw you, Huggins. Pull over."

Walt didn't take his eyes off the road. "I have nothing to say."

Ben recognized Walt's hardened, capricious aura.

"Did you know?"

Walt wrinkled his brow. "Know what?"

"About the attack. Both of them. You rigged both your houses to blow. Why be so prepared if you didn't know it was coming?"

Walt said nothing, but Ben saw the birth of a smug grin.

"I was always told about you, Huggins. How attentive you were, how no one dared try to get anything past you. The others at our final meeting … you knew their true plans?"

"That they would betray me? Of course."

"How? Was one of us working both sides?"

Walt laughed. "You think small – your inane theories aside."

"What does that mean?"

The SUV slowed to a halt at a stop sign. No cars approached the intersection, yet Walt did not press the gas.

"Sheridan, I was not just our mission leader but by definitional responsibility, the chief archivist. Before we crossed the fold, I consumed every available archival detail about each observer, their family history, and their allegiances. Every detail."

Ben felt stupid. "Of course. That's why you were always a step ahead. No wonder they never challenged you to your face."

Ben reached for his weapon as Walt tapped the wheel.

"Yes," Walt said without emotion. "A Chancellor who cannot create leverage is hardly a Chancellor at all. And nothing was going to stop this mission. The future must be served, Sheridan."

Rage rose toward the surface. Ben struggled to contain it.

"You allowed us to leave our homes behind and live in this primitive shithole long enough to turn against each other. Chancellors killing Chancellors. You ruined us. You ..."

"Saved the future of the Chancellory. Now, reduce your sanctimonious blabbering, Sheridan. After all, if I had warned your parents, then you would not have had the chance to kill them."

Walt beamed with satisfaction and hit the gas.

Ben turned cold all over.

28

J AMIE DROPPED THE pistol as he stared into the impossible. Before he collapsed, Michael ran forward and caught him. He set Jamie on the passenger seat.

"Damn, dude. What's gotten into you?"

"Coop? You're ... how did ...?"

Michael twisted around to Sammie, whose dropped jaw mixed astonishment and joy. "What the flying fudge is going on with you two?"

"Coop," she said, struggling for words as she held onto the wheel. "I don't think you should be walking. You've been ..."

"Shot," Jamie said as he tried to gather his wits. "I don't understand. They shot you, Coop. In the back. Don't you remember?"

Michael shuffled his baffled glare between his two friends, mumbled something inaudible, then slipped to one knee.

"Holy shit on a stick," he said, this time loud enough for everyone to hear. He examined the blood-splattered front of his shirt, felt the mud on his face and twisted his head over his shoulder, yanking at his shirt where it was still drenched in wet blood. "They shot me. Yeah. I was ... they took me from my house and ..." He paused then formed a strange smirk for his captivated audience. He looked around. "We're on our way to heaven, right? Them bastards killed us and now we're taking the fastest boat to ..."

"No, Coop," Jamie said. "Not heaven. We ain't that lucky."

Jamie twisted his eyes toward Sammie, who lost her grip on the wheel, also speechless. Nobody said a word until, at last, an ominous mechanical rhythm broke their silence.

Sammie looked east. "The helicopter. It's coming."

Jamie swung about. The chopper was beating a hurried path no more than a hundred yards above the water. Yet Jamie realized it wasn't changing course to pursue them. In fact, the chopper was continuing due north, from where the three of them came.

Michael chimed in. "That's a police bird. I can see the markings. Wait. I don't get this. It's supposed to be night. Where the heck are we?"

Sammie pulled back on the throttle until the boat idled. The chopper's roar dimmed as it shrank into the murky dawn. Only the putter of the boat's motor broke a stunned silence.

"It's real," Jamie whispered. "It's happening." He flung himself out of the seat, threw his arms around Michael and embraced in a hug like none before. Jamie ignored the blood, the wet back. All he knew was that somehow, defying all ludicrous odds, Michael was alive. "You're OK," he said. "You're OK. Dude! You're OK."

Michael didn't react at once. Gradually, however, he lifted his arms and wrapped them around Jamie. Tears blended into the mud stains.

Michael whispered, "I don't understand."

"You're alive, Coop, and nothing else matters. When we found you, I was so sure ..."

"Found?" Michael turned to Sammie. "Help me out. He's babbling."

Sammie tapped Jamie on the shoulder, and that was enough to snap him out of his ecstasy. "Jamie, I think we better sit down and sort this out."

He felt too good to do anything other than follow Sammie's suggestion. Michael started the conversation.

"This is too much. How did I get from wherever to out here?"

Michael remembered being in the car with the English teacher from hell and his ex-track coach.

"They were gonna kill me sooner or later, I reckon. After ..."

"Do you remember anything else?" Sammie asked.

"I was falling. Couldn't stop. Then there was this light." He smiled with recognition. "Yeah. A light. You know, like folks who say they died but didn't make it all the way?" He frowned. "Next thing I see is my No. 1 here near about ready to blow your head off, Sammie. Would somebody tell me what's up with that? And if they shot me, how come I ain't dead?"

Jamie felt Sammie's undeniable glare. She looked him over as if he weren't human.

"C'mon, Jamie. You have to see it."

"See what?"

"The re-sequencing program. Nothing else makes sense."

Every corner of Jamie's logic centers insisted he knew what Sammie was talking about, but he couldn't acknowledge the truth.

"Jamie," she said, her voice softening. "Michael was shot two times in the back. We saw the bullet holes. He shouldn't be alive."

Jamie couldn't take his eyes off her. He flashed to her bedroom, when she first appeared as an angel of mercy. She wasn't able to find the bullet holes he knew were once there. He then recalled the overwhelming exhaustion that gripped him as he carried Michael; the sense of his own life draining away. Jamie thought about his ten-minute nap that seemed to go on for ages and yet was so refreshing, as if all the energy was restored. He looked down to his own, upturned palms, stained in Michael's blood.

"Hello? I'm starting to freak over here," Michael said. "And I didn't think anything was crazier than the crap I went through last night."

"It's me," Jamie whispered. "What's happened to me?"

Michael threw up his hands. "Well, dude, that's my question. Look here. I didn't imagine creepy old Queen Bee storming my house in the middle of the night and wacko Christian putting a gun in my mouth and them trying to hunt you down. And you're not one to put

146

a gun to people's heads. And I'm soaking in blood like a pig in a slaughterhouse. How about a few answers?"

Jamie stared at his upturned hands and thanked whatever might be responsible – God, the Chancellors, the program that was killing him.

Sammie reached out and grabbed his hands, saying softly:

"I don't think anyone imagined this. Not even your designers."

He snatched his hands away and turned to Michael.

"You're going to be OK, Coop. Really, truly OK. I'm sorry I got you into this. I didn't know ... none of it."

"None of what, dude? Your designers? What's up with that? You got some answers?"

"Yeah. But you're not gonna believe them any more than I did."

Sammie opened the throttle and resumed a course for Ginny's Creek, but this time Jamie didn't stop her. He needed to sort through his swirl of emotions, to recount the madness that invaded his life, and to appreciate the good news that came of these horrors.

Michael was alive. For the time being, nothing else mattered.

29

BEN HAD EVERY reason to put a bullet through Walt's skull, yet he felt naked in the face of Walt's accusation. He couldn't escape the memories that drove him into dark places for two years.

"How?" Ben mumbled. "Did Ignatius tell you?"

"No," Walt said. "Although I was certain he played a role. In truth, your father consulted with me the day before he died. He was prepared to take any necessary action to silence you and your maniacal theories before you took them to the other observers. For all Tom's dissatisfaction with this Earth, he believed in the mission. I'm sure you had more than an inkling of what he might do to you. I was not surprised when the call came."

"I'm sure you weren't. But since you didn't lift a finger to stop it, I also don't think you much cared."

Ben knew he couldn't put this one on Walt. After all, it was Ben who confronted his parents with the research he'd been putting together since moving out several months earlier. It was Ben who should have known they would never believe a word.

On that day, Tom and Marlena Sheridan reclined on a sofa as Ben placed a file folder between them and slapped his clammy hands together.

"Ever since last year," he told them, "I've been searching for answers to why I felt so disconnected from everyone and everything. I looked in unexpected places, maybe some places you'd never want me to go." Ben shifted his seat and took a deep breath. "I never set out to harm you or interfere with our mission. But what I found was so ... profound. Mom. Dad. It's going to change everything. It will be our salvation."

Tom and Marlena shared a short, cold chuckle. Ben was undeterred.

"What I discovered is beyond me, beyond any of us. It's something the Chancellors have refuted for centuries. Without it, we're cold, empty people. We're focused only on power and control and ..."

Ben realized he made the mistake of belittling his own kind.

Tom uncrossed his legs and sat up. "Excuse me, Benjamin. I'm quite sure I don't care for the direction this is going. This conversation is ..."

"Dad, please. I know you don't like the man I've become. But I did as you demanded. I gave everything I could to Jamie. So you owe me this chance to explain. About six months ago, I attended a church service. I know you warned me for years to stay away, but my curiosity was too strong. The preacher's sermon went on forever, but two words connected. Ever since, I've been putting together the pieces of the puzzle. Studying everything I've been taught about Caryllan energy. All my research is in this folder. It will change everything the Chancellors believe."

"And those two words were?" Tom asked.

The answer stumbled across his lips. "Eternal life."

Ben knew he failed. The cold, sweeping emptiness of an immovable Chancellor appeared in his father's eyes. He rushed headlong into an explanation, detailing his revelation, insisting his folder contained ample proof of how to counteract the Jewel's effect, that Jamie could be saved and guaranteed long life. In the process, usher in new promise for Chancellors.

"Your interest in Jamie is admirable at a sentimental level," Marlena said, "but also wholly irrelevant. You ended your contractual responsibilities toward him when you moved out. Frankly, I fail to see why you maintain a vested interest at all."

They escorted him to the front door. His father leaned into Ben with a hot breath and said, "If you ever try to see Jamie, I'll kill you where you stand." Ben saw a clear, silent message through those impenetrable eyes: Ben signed his own death warrant.

He hopped into his pickup and drove around for an hour. And then, after no alternative arose, he called Ignatius.

"I'm out of time," he said. "I need you to fix this."

He spurned the echoes of rifle blasts.

Walt spoke with great confidence. "You see, Sheridan, you and I are both men of secrets. We do what is required to survive while also preserving the natural order, and as a consequence we must bear the burden of our actions in silence. I made accommodations whenever our mission was in danger. Some I made without consulting the others. I make no apologies. You, however ..."

"Killed them. Yes. And I'll always have their blood on my hands. But Dad would have made me disappear. Nobody would have ever found my body, and Jamie wouldn't have been given another chance at life."

"And how has that plan worked out for you, Sheridan?"

Ben seethed. "When I was a kid, I was always scared of you, but I was told you were someone I could trust." Walt didn't blink as Ben continued. "I don't think trust is even part of your equation. You're battle-hardened, determined to fulfill a mission, and God help the little people who get in your way. Those observers who came with you weren't just colleagues. There were three children. Another one growing inside your wife. You ruined all their lives. Doesn't that mean anything to you?"

"You were only eight years old when we left. You lacked the maturity to understand the central tenet of the Chancellor code. The familial bond is an asset, but it cannot be allowed to become an emotional distraction. Preservation of the Chancellory and its core philosophy is the sole priority of each member of our caste. Grace understood this. Samantha was taught it years ago and has obeyed. Victory is morality!"

Ben summoned his courage. "I can barely remember what home looks like. So here's your victory, Walt." He grabbed his gun and swung the weapon across his body to within an inch of Walt's right temple. "Pull over."

The huge Chancellor's right eye rolled slightly to its side. Ben saw a deep, soulless well of arrogance, a resolute belief that death was a fate reserved only for indigos and Chancellors who lacked a spine. Ben told himself to pull the trigger.

"Pull over, or I'm going to make Sammie an orphan," he said.

"You're a dead man," Walt said in a full voice.

"You got that right."

Out of the corner of his eye, Ben saw flashing blue lights approaching from the opposite direction. Walt hit the gas, throwing Ben backward. An arm came free of the wheel and flew into Ben's face. Ben pressed the trigger and heard a deafening pop followed by shattering glass.

The SUV surged into the other lane, and Ben stared into the headlights of a Vernon County Sheriff's Department patrol car.

30

THE SUV CLIPPED the front right corner of the patrol car, bounded along the highway's gently sloping curb, swerved, and took out a green road sign at a rural intersection. As Ben regrouped, Walt grabbed the wheel and made a sharp left before correcting the car's course along an unfamiliar side road, which sloped sharply downward.

Ben fired twice from point-blank range, only to have Walt slam an arm against the pistol or duck his head a split second before the bullet could do him in. Ben tried to snatch control of the wheel and lost his gun, which fell to the floor. They fought with determined grunts, but they weren't prepared for the road's sudden right-angle bend. The car continued straight, took flight and landed with an uncivilized thump in low brush.

The SUV broadsided an ancient birch, a shattering jolt that crushed the cargo section, sent glass flying and turned metal into a mad, contorted sculpture that wrapped around the base of the tree. There was nothing in front of them but Lake Vernon, its shore at least fifty feet below. Ben fell face-first into the dashboard and briefly descended into darkness.

When he awoke, surprised to be alive, Ben found himself crumpled against the passenger door, his body stretched toward the steering wheel, where Walt was slumped, arms dangling to his sides. Blood stained Walt's forehead. Ben pressed his shoulder against the glove compartment to provide leverage and groaned. He felt fresh blood from the bullet wound in his right shoulder, which must have torn.

After Ben righted himself, his eyes fell upon the GPS hand-held, which lay at Walt's feet. The beacon signaling Jamie's location was strong. His brother reached land, by best guess at the mouth of what must have been Ginny's Creek. Ben studied the geography and plotted his own approximate location. He examined the wreckage once more, realized the SUV was inches from the edge of the bluff, and laughed at himself.

"You couldn't wait, Sheridan? Just had to pull out the gun. Idiot."

Ben glanced at his watch. 6:25 a.m. He examined Walt and was not pleased to see the hulking Chancellor's chest rising and falling. He saw no way out other than the driver's side.

He could not find his pistol but remembered the assault rifles in the back. He twisted about and spied an M16 on the opposite side against a crumpled passenger door. Ben contorted his body, grabbed the rifle, and squirmed back into the front seat. His left leg kicked Walt, who slipped off the wheel and fell to his side, his right arm dangling between the seats.

Ben was ready to finish this, his vengeance for fifteen stolen years consuming him.

"You bastards ruined me," Ben whispered as he cocked the rifle.

Ben's finger was poised on the trigger, his aim square. Then he heard rustling outside the car, saw human movement in the morning light and a flashlight hitting him in the face. He dropped the rifle to his lap, shielded his eyes, and made out the form of a police officer.

A deputy, his hair perfectly parted, and his baby face a dead giveaway of inexperience, shouted through the driver-side window.

"Help is on the way, sir." The deputy flashed his light throughout the battered car. "I've got backup coming, and an ambulance, too. Stay right where you are. Hear? You make any sudden movements, I think she's going over the edge. How bad is your friend? Can you tell?"

Ben shook his head as if clueless, but new movement out of the corner of his eye said differently. Walt's head continued to hang limp, facing the floor, his eyes not visible. Ben, however, saw a subtle shift in the man's right arm, a slight twist of his forearm muscles ... as if he were reaching for something. Ben lowered his right hand and gripped the rifle. The deputy's flashlight followed his movement and fell upon the M16.

The deputy drew his weapon, which he cocked.

"Don't you move," he yelled. "Hear me? You so much as blink, I swear I'll shoot." The deputy grabbed a two-way mike strapped over his shoulder. "Julius, what's your status? I've got trouble." Ben didn't hear the static-laden reply, but he knew his options were running out. "I think it's them," the deputy shouted. "The ones who killed the ranger."

Walt opened a pair of vengeful eyes and drew a smug smile.

He rose like a burst of wind, whirled the pistol across his body and fired two shots through the window, shattering the glass. The deputy gasped and fired an indiscriminate shot as he fell backward into the brush.

Ben grabbed his rifle and fired. Walt growled as a hole opened in his side. The giant Chancellor slung about, kicked at the M16 and lunged toward Ben, who fell back against the passenger door.

Flames in his eyes, Walt leaped upon Ben and fired the pistol. Ben used his best moves to dodge the bullet, which nicked his ear lobe and continued through the passenger window.

"You can't stop this, Sheridan," Walt said. "Help is on the way. I made sure of it. James will be protected until he awakens."

Ben felt an emptiness. "Help? What did you do?"

Ben thought he heard the pistol fire again, but he had no reckoning of whether he was hit. He felt a sudden descent.

The Chancellors caught the blood in each other's startled eyes when they realized, too late, that the SUV lost its mooring around the tree and was falling to the tattered shoreline below.

Life stopped for a flicker before a spectacular crunch of metal filled their ears as the car smashed into the shore. Both men fell into the dash and against the shattered windshield, which was giving way as the car, briefly standing upright on its engine, swayed, whined and tipped forward.

Upside down, the car's disjointed cargo section lay in the water's edge. Inside, the men lay spread-eagle on their backs, moaning as they rested on what was once the roof.

Ben kicked out the windshield. He grabbed the rifle, which lay between the men, and squirmed outside. Ben smelled gas, but he paid it no mind.

Before he rose to his feet, Ben saw Walt move without purpose.

"What did you do?"

He strapped the M16 over his left shoulder and scanned for the GPS but didn't see it. He surveyed the surroundings, examining both the bluff and the thin, debris-filled shoreline to his south. He remembered Jamie's beacon.

"I can do this," he said, reaching for the bloody bullet wound. "Two miles. I can do this."

He didn't know whether the shoreline would be passable, but he didn't care. Ben ignored his pain and ran.

31

E IGHT MILES AWAY, along a dirt road deep within the national forest, Agatha Bidwell awoke to the most repulsive odor she encountered during her exile on this Earth: Cigarette smoke. She coughed as she opened her eyes and saw Christian a few feet away, pulling a long drag. He released smoke through his nose. He was bent down, an M16 slung over his shoulder, as he looked off into the distance.

Deadening pain radiated through her soaked, shivering body, and every limb lay useless. She refused to die in such disgrace.

She heard people racing past her, boots on the ground, and shouts like battlefield commands intertwined.

"What do I most despise about teenagers?" She asked her son.

Christian dropped his cigarette and leaped to his feet. "Mom," he said, racing to her with a big smile. "I told this sorry bunch of cowards not to give up on you."

He unscrewed the cap on a bottle of water; she took a sip.

"What do I most despise about teenagers?" She asked again.

Christian laughed. "Their remarkable capacity to achieve an intellectual mediocrity while in pursuit of a level of sexual fulfillment one might expect to find in their simian ancestors."

Agatha nodded despite the pain and reached out to her son.

"Good man," she said. "And a wonderful student. So tell me, is the world rid of one particular teenager with long, blond hair and a frightfully annoying disposition?"

Christian shook his head. "I wish we were, but Huggins has him, and we don't have a clue where. The son of a bitch ... he must have known we were coming. We unloaded so much damned firepower into that lake house. We should've killed them all."

Agatha's memory was rubble. She looked around, allowing the setting to jar details into focus. The other observers who sided with her – minus the late Rand Paulus, Arlene Winters, and Dexter Cobb – were present. Three cars and the park ranger's helicopter were stationed on a narrow dirt road. She sat against a car, ears ringing.

"At first, Jonathan was sure the explosion must have killed you," Christian said, "but I told that bastard to bring the chopper down to the water. We fished you out."

Christian's mention of the explosion brought back everything.

"Help me understand, Christian." She coughed, and her lungs felt soar. "Where are we now? What is the status of our mission?"

Christian balled his fists. Agatha told him to calm himself and think without emotional distraction.

"We did everything we could, but look, Mom, I wouldn't advise any trips in front of a mirror, at least for a while yet. The cuts and burns on your face ... well, there was glass and fire everywhere. Like I said, we did our best. We had to get you out of there quickly. We knew the explosion would draw too much attention, and we couldn't risk the cops tracking us. We've been listening to the police band. They're worked up. They found the ranger you killed; they found Ignatius and Rand. Add to that a couple of firebombed houses and a stolen helicopter ... let's just say, police are starting to mobilize. We've heard them say 'terrorists' a couple of times. You know how twitchy people can get these days when they hear the t-word."

She touched the bandages on her face. "Where are we, Christian?"

"Hopefully safe, at least for a time. We landed the helicopter here, then Arthur was able to determine our coordinates and lead the rest of our team to a safe rendezvous." Christian glanced at his watch. "It's 6:40, almost an hour since the explosion."

Agatha did not want to utter the words.

"Do you believe we have lost this battle?"

A pall came over him; before he spoke, Arthur Tynes intervened.

"Very possibly, Agatha. I'm pleased to see you're back with us."

"Are you?" Agatha grimaced through her pain. "If I'd been left in the water, you would have every reason to abandon the mission and make haste to the fold. Yes?"

"We would be if it weren't for Christian. He was the only one who insisted we continue the search. Your son is a remarkable orator when he chooses not to be a considerable jackass."

"They were talking retreat," Christian said with a sneer. "Said we'd already lost too much. Four Chancellors. I told them, 'Four is an even bigger reason to keep fighting. We don't go after Sheridan, we don't take it out on Huggins, then those four died for nothing. If we can't finish the fight here, then what use we gonna be on the other side?' That was my case."

Arthur groaned. "That, and the barrel of your rifle, conveniently aimed in our direction."

"That, too," Christian mumbled.

Agatha tried in vain to laugh. "Do you have a new plan, Arthur?"

"Until we have some tangible clues as to their location, we're blind. Jonathan is going to take up the chopper and do a complete fly-over of the lake and the surrounding roads. However, time is hardly an ally. The sun is almost up, which does not help matters. Jennifer Bowman is about to leave for Austin Springs. I've asked her to remain inconspicuous while there. It's a slim hope, but it's also the closest town of any size."

"Are you sure she'll remain as long as we need her?"

Arthur nodded. "She's terrified, but she understands the necessity. Lester wanted to go with her, but we need every resource here."

Agatha saw the married forty-something Bowmans embracing beside the first car in the caravan. She never expected the owners of Albion's only bed-and-breakfast to take part in this endgame. They loved their life; she expected them to go rogue and stay behind.

"Help me up," she told Christian. "Call everyone over here."

Standing, Agatha ran a hand across her face and felt many cuts; she planned to avoid mirrors.

The surviving observers cheered her quick recovery as they gathered around. She knew few other sane humans would have gotten to their feet so soon, but the troops needed to see her alert. She began:

"I have spent most of my life crushing the spirit of those in my orbit in order to achieve sadistic gratification and further my personal objectives. I offer no apologies. My *modus operandi* has served me well, first through the UG assaults I led on New Caledonia and Xavier's Garden. Later on, in dealing with those treacherous fools in my presidium. I have stared into the face of my mortality, and I am genuinely humbled.

"If today should be my last, I wish to leave a different legacy. I can deny Chancellors a future far more bleak than what we are already facing. We know what will happen if these Jewel hybrids come to be. This is a betrayal of our original mission, but we have had the benefit of time to see the truth.

"We cannot stop the others, but we can stop this one. It gives me no gratification to kill a boy, but I am here to save humanity from itself. If nothing else, may my epitaph speak of that singular accomplishment. We are the heroes. Yes? We gave James his childhood, as we agreed. But we will not allow that abomination to return to our universe. Join me to the end."

159

She saw it in their eyes. There was no more doubt in the rightness of their cause. The pain raced through her like nails, but Agatha did not care.

Minutes later, after Jennifer Bowman drove away toward Austin Springs and the chopper took flight, Agatha's determination was rewarded by a desperate man's voice on the police band.

"Officer down! Officer down! Need assistance. Fortnight Road and Highway 39. Multiple suspects, heavily armed. Repeat ..."

Agatha sensed promise. She turned to Arthur.

"Heavily armed at sunrise? Chancellors, perhaps?" As Arthur scanned the maps on the laptop and quickly assessed the report as coming from the west side of Lake Vernon, fifteen minutes away, Agatha smiled without pain.

"Dearest Walter. I do believe you've gotten yourself into a spate of mischief. Perhaps we should offer immediate assistance. Yes?"

32

SAMMIE WANTED TO take the outboard deep into Ginny's Creek, but Jamie insisted she pull in to a small sandy spot near the mouth. He wanted off the boat. He just finished explaining almost everything to Michael, and even Jamie had a hard time believing his own.

Sammie veered the boat to a tiny stretch of sand which was covered in part by scattered pine needles and surrounded on either end by fallen debris and tree stumps. Low ground cover spread behind it into the woods, where trees – mostly pines – were thinly spaced. The trees cast impressive silhouettes in gray morning light.

Jamie and Michael hopped out, splashed through the shallow water and grabbed the bow, bringing the boat onto land. Sammie did not leave the driver's seat.

"Now what?" Michael asked.

"We stop running," Jamie was quick to respond. "I gotta think."

"I'm down with that. Ain't every night a fellow takes a couple slugs and has his best friend do a Jesus number on him."

Jamie scoped the surroundings and saw no homes. He decided to follow the rugged shore back out to the mouth and facing the lake. He had no sense of why, beyond a vague notion that to go farther into the creek was not smart. The creek disappeared around a dark bend.

"You coming?" He asked Sammie.

"No. I need to be alone. Don't worry, Jamie. I won't leave."

When he saw the emptiness in her eyes and heard the resignation cross her lips, Jamie knew he could trust her. He and Michael trudged along the shoreline, walking over and around driftwood and other debris, their wet sneakers squishing with every step.

"I'm sorry I got you into this, Coop. If they'd gunned me down on Main Street, they never would've come after you."

"And you'd be a corpse, dude. We both got away, and that's all that matters. We just gotta figure out our next move and before you know it … we're gonna be running track again. New coach, I'd reckon. Maybe a guy who won't try to kill us. It'll be like nothing happened."

Jamie broke a smile.

"I don't believe how well you're taking this."

Michael dropped a brother's hand on Jamie's shoulder.

"You're the best friend I ever had and you saved my life." He snickered. "I used to tell people, 'That Jamie, he's always got my back.' Damned if that weren't the truth, huh?" His lower lip quivered. "I love you, J. Don't you ever forget."

They fell into each other and shared a firm hug. Jamie's earlier sensation of helplessness grew into despair. He told almost all the story to Michael on the boat ride in, but he left out one important detail. He couldn't say the words then, and he didn't know how to do it now. He wanted to believe that maybe he could make the impending reality disappear so long as his best friend was at his side. When they separated, Michael asked a question.

"There's something I got to know. When I woke up, first thing I saw was you sticking a gun upside her head. What's up with that?"

Jamie trudged on toward the lake.

"She's not what you think, Coop. We've got some trust issues."

Jamie explained details of Sammie's Chancellor heritage, her duel acts of betrayal, and how she trained as a soldier.

Michael's jaw slipped.

"So what are you saying? She's ... Wonder Woman?" He pointed in the direction of the boat, which was hidden around the bend. "We're talking about little Susie Q with a pink ribbon?"

Jamie offered an ironic smile. "Yeah, that's right. Susie Q. She says she loves me. Hell, said it twice last night. That don't mean I can trust her."

"J. That is hardcore."

They reached the lakefront. The sandy shore was deeper. Miles across the lake, the eastern sky formed into shades of pink and orange. Jamie found himself mesmerized by the colors, even though he'd seen them countless times.

"Beautiful, ain't it?" He said.

"Yep. But it can't compare to just being alive." Michael took a deep breath. "I feel better than I ever have. It's like somebody injected me with a couple thousand vitamins, and the Coopster is ready to play."

Michael rambled on about his second chance. However, any notion of taking pleasure in his best friend's revival dissipated when Jamie heard a new but familiar voice.

"Life and death, my dear sweet boy. Ironic partners, aren't they?"

Jamie stared down Lydia, who came equipped with a pouting lip and the soft, compassionate eyes of a doting mother.

"Go away," he sniped. "Leave me alone."

Michael flipped about. "What's up? Who you talking to?"

Jamie ignored Michael. "I want you out of my life. Hear, Lydia?"

Lydia sighed. "I understand your anger. You only have three and a half hours to live."

"I don't need this now," he fired back. "You said your peace already, did everything you were supposed to. Now vanish."

"Dude," Michael reached out a comforting hand, but Jamie didn't notice. "You're worrying me. This is pretty f'ed up."

163

Lydia was unfazed. "I must say, Jamie, your friend has recovered well. The transference of Caryllan energy into Mr. Cooper was unexpected. A fascinating development. The potential for a transfer was not considered, at least not in my programming. Do you have any theories as to how you made it happen?"

Jamie spit at her feet. "Theories? You're asking me? You're supposed to be the expert. Let me ask you something, Lydia. You got any idea how this little gift of mine can save me?"

Lydia twirled her pearls. "Oh, this doesn't change your fate, sweet boy. But it is an intriguing anomaly. I'm studying the algorithms now."

Jamie kicked sand toward her but did not hit Lydia before she vanished. Michael kept his distance until Jamie settled down and rested himself on a log. Jamie dropped his head into his hands and explained about the Mentor. Michael took a seat next to him.

"There's nothing else good to come out of this, Coop."

"This ain't the end. We've been through a lot, but we're gonna make it out." Michael slapped him on the leg. "I reckon it's time for a swim."

Jamie looked up confused. "What?"

"Yeah, dude. I got blood all over me. I feel nasty. Ain't right to be going around looking like the walking dead. You know?" Michael threw off his shirt and unzipped his blue jeans. "C'mon. Water's warm. Let's go. We'll clear our minds and decide what to do next."

Michael didn't wait for an answer. He dropped his pants and made a dash for the lake. Jamie might have stayed put had Sammie not appeared a moment later. She kept her distance and stared, as if waiting for Jamie to invite her over. He picked himself up, keeping the pistol to his side. He stopped arms-length shy of her and returned the stare.

"I'm a Chancellor," she said. "Everything I did was because I had no choice. I don't suppose you'll believe that, and it's OK. It is. I just want you to understand that no matter what my mission was, or whatever I did to you, the words I said before were true. I've been in love with you longer than I can remember. I've dreamed about you every night since ..."

Jamie raised a hand. "I can't deal with this now."

Michael splashed far from shore, flailing his arms and shouting for Jamie to come in.

"Go," she said. "You deserve a break. Give me your shirt and pants. I'll wash them best I can. Coop's, too. Maybe I can get some of the blood out." She asked for the pistol, but Jamie hesitated to hand over the only thing that gave him the slightest sense of power.

"I'll be right here," she said. "I'm with you to the end, Jamie. I don't have anybody else."

He saw her grief as he placed the pistol in her right hand. Jamie slipped out of his sneakers then removed his jeans and t-shirt. He yanked the ponytail holder from his hair and allowed a sloppy blond mess to fall over his shoulders.

He faced Lake Vernon, but the changing colors on the far side caught his breath. The reds and pinks were turning orange. The sun would arrive at any moment.

"I won't ever see one of these again. Will I?"

He dropped his boxers and waded into the lake, surprised by how much it felt like bathwater. When the water rose to his waist, Jamie dived forward. He remained submerged as he swam, and he knew right away that Sammie was correct. He did deserve this. He sensed something here that was lost above the surface.

Jamie felt peace.

He ignored Michael's splashing far away and allowed his body to unburden itself and float. He almost cleared his mind of the most painful thoughts when he heard Lydia whisper from deep within.

"I have a gift for you, my sweet boy. I have been waiting for the perfect moment."

"Go away," he whispered without opening his mouth.

"Long ago, before you crossed the interdimensional fold, your parents prepared a series of messages for you. They hoped their words would provide solace as you approached your rest."

"No," he said without speaking. "I don't want anything from them."

"Of course you do, sweet Jamie. All children want nothing more than the comfort of their mother and father. Please, listen ..."

Jamie could not move. He felt distant from reality, no longer floating on water. The darkness that embodied him in the cellar of the lake house returned. Unfamiliar voices rose within him as if echoes from another world. They talked over each other and tried to merge as one.

"Dear Son, Each day we have mourned for you, and we will continue to do so until the end of our lives."

These were not the voices of Tom and Marlena Sheridan, but neither did they seem to come from strangers. They were younger, their voices drenched in grief, yet somehow pleasing.

"We hope you will find the capacity to forgive us ... it is our sincerest hope ... in the short time given to you ... too young to understand all the answers ... you were loved ... you filled our hearts with a joy unspeakable ... you are our greatest gift to humanity ... we will miss you deeply. With Fondest Regards, Mother, Father"

The messages replayed. When silence fell, Jamie opened his eyes.

"Is that all?" He asked, hoping for more.

"There is one final message," Lydia said, "but now is not the time. I will forward it to you just before the end, when I return to say goodbye."

Jamie stood, his feet planted on the shallow, sandy bottom.

"Why then?"

Lydia did not respond.

"Why then?"

Jamie closed his eyes and listened to the echoes of his true parents' voices. For the first time in at least two years, he felt loved. He also knew this gift would not survive the morning.

33

FIFTEEN MINUTES LATER, Jamie walked out of the lake refreshed and naked. He pushed his dripping hair out of his face then grabbed his jeans and boxers. He looked around for his ponytail holder.

"Do you know where my ...?"

Sammie held a distant stare, north along the lakeshore.

"Gunshots," she said. "I'm sure I heard them."

"When?"

"Right after you went in the water. And then again, just before you came out. I don't think we should stay here."

Jamie sat down and slipped on his sneakers. Michael was still in the lake but nearing shore. Jamie felt a surprising ease in the face of her news.

"Calm down, Sammie. How far away were the shots?"

"Not close. Maybe a mile or more."

"Probably just hunters."

Sammie winced. "It's almost summer. I don't think they allow hunting this time of year."

Jamie scoffed. "Whatever. Look, if they were gunshots, I reckon they got nothing to do with us. We're all alone, Sammie. The others are dead. Nobody knows where we are."

Jamie's words, said with no drop of remorse, got Sammie's attention. She diverted her stare and started toward Jamie, a pair of stained, wet shirts in her hand. She dropped Jamie's t-shirt onto the sand beside him.

"You've got all the answers, do you? A few hours ago, you didn't have a clue what was going on and now …" She bit her lip. "I'm sorry." She dropped to a knee. "I didn't know it was going to hurt so much. Daddy always said if anything happened to them, I had to move on. Stay the course, he said. Keep with the mission and don't shed a tear."

Jamie finished tying his sneakers. "He actually told you that? And you believed it would be that easy? Damn … is that how all Chancellors act?" Jamie wiped the steady drips from his face. "Sammie, don't you remember what happened to me after my parents were killed? Hell, I nearabout went out of my mind. It's been in my skin ever since. The dark shit I've thought about. I gave up last night. I was gonna take that money and that gun and I didn't care anymore. Stay the course? Are you kidding me?"

Sammie wiped away a tear. "We're supposed to be different."

"What? Better? Because you're more advanced? Look around, Sammie. Tell me who gives a rat's ass. Don't you get it? My life is almost up because of people who think like you."

He lifted himself up, grabbed Sammie, and pulled her close enough to smell her breath.

"Chancellors created me and put this … thing … in my blood. They didn't give a crud that I was a human being. You know why? Because they don't feel. Me? Living with the pain has been a bitch, but at least I don't feel like a freakin' robot. These people who brought us here, they're so advanced, so sophisticated, they have to design human nukes. And then, when the gig is up, they escape to hide their dirty little secrets. Really, Sammie? These Chancellors don't sound like they're worth a goddamn."

169

Sammie backed away. "Go ahead and judge. My parents sacrificed everything to keep you safe." Her dander rose and her cheeks reddened. "Tell me something, Mr. Know It All," she said, checking on Michael, who was a few feet from shore. "If pain is such a great thing, why don't you toss some of it on Coop? Tell him what's going to happen when the program runs out at 9:56. He thinks you're going to live happily ever after."

Jamie lowered his voice.

"Not another word, Sammie. He's been through enough."

Michael wrapped his arms around his chest and pretended to shiver. He grabbed his pants and sneakers and stood between his friends.

"I can't leave you two alone. Still in each other's faces."

Sammie handed Michael his shirt.

"I rinsed it, but I couldn't get much of the blood out."

"I don't need the thing anyway. Hell, it's gonna be ninety degrees before you know it."

"Good point," Jamie said as he tossed his own shirt, his eyes never leaving Sammie's. Michael stepped into his sneakers.

"What's the plan? What are we going to tell folks, anyway? I don't plan to talk about how I took a couple slugs, then Jamie gave me a back rub and all was right with the world. All that business about multiverses won't fly, either. I mean, there's dead people. Your brother, your mom and dad. Iggy Horne. A park ranger. Even if we get back to Albion before anybody sees us, the cops are going to come around asking questions."

Jamie wrapped an arm around his best friend.

"Don't worry, dude. You weren't a part of this. Your parents are out of town, right?"

"Yessir."

"Then we get you back home and you'll be right there waiting for them like nothing happened. Sammie and me, we'll deal with whatever comes our way."

Sammie turned around and started toward the point, around which the boat was waiting. The pistol protruded from her pants, tucked between her belt and back.

"We have to go," she said. "It's not safe here. It's ten to seven. The sun's coming up."

Jamie looked across the lake. He watched the oval, citrus sun creep above the tree line for the last time. Jamie choked up but knew he couldn't let his emotions get the better of him. If he could safely see Michael home before the end, at least he might find some solace.

"C'mon, Coop. Back to the boat and figure out our next move."

He started up the beach, but when he didn't hear another one-liner from his best friend, Jamie looked over his shoulder.

"C'mon. Wonder Woman's waiting."

Michael turned his glare north along the shore, the same direction that fascinated Sammie. He raised his right hand and pointed.

"Ah, Jamie. Dude. Ain't that ...?"

Jamie needed a few seconds to see what caught Michael's eye. The morning rays of the sun cast gold shimmers upon the shore and the trees. Out of that, however, came human movement. A man clambered over a log, perhaps fifty yards away. The man stumbled as he ran. He raised a hand and waved to the boys.

"Ben."

The name fell off Jamie's lips as dry and empty as only a boy who was no longer shocked by anything might say it.

34

A GATHA WAS ENERGIZED, even though the trauma of the explosion slowed her reflexes and left her pock-marked face in pain. From the back seat of a red Camaro with a police scanner, Agatha opened a cell phone, called Jonathan in the helicopter, and saw the time: 6:52 a.m.

Three hours did not seem like too short a window to find a single, elusive boy. The more she heard on the scanner, the more she sensed the universe was clearing a path to establishing her final legacy. Jonathan answered on the third ring.

"Your status?" She asked, turning on the speaker phone.

"Crossing the lake now. Target zone in sight. Should be overhead in less than a minute."

"Jonathan, do not linger," she said. "Law enforcement presence is growing, and we cannot ascertain their ground-to-air capabilities. They will recognize the stolen helicopter, and will not hesitate to resort to violence. One of their officers has been killed,. Two, if you count Ignatius. Instead, I want you to veer south.

"We just heard an officer say their suspects appeared to be on foot heading south along the shoreline. The officer believes these suspects are carrying high-powered weapons. They must be

Chancellors. The police are expanding their search, which means we have limited time to make this work. Do you understand?"

"Approaching the shoreline now."

"We will continue south on Highway 39. We are still several minutes north of the officers. Call me as soon as you make contact and provide your coordinates."

"And if, by luck, I should find our targets out in the open?"

Agatha smiled. In the front seat, Christian stared back at her through the rearview mirror.

"You cared deeply for your brother, did you not?"

Jonathan hesitated. "Dexter was a good man. Walt had no right to take him that way."

"I agree, Jonathan. If you see anyone born in the Collectorate," she said, "kill him. Especially if he is tall and blond."

Christian pressed his foot on the gas. "You got that one right, Mom. This is a whole hell of a lot more fun than taking final exams."

Agatha wondered what administration might think when she didn't show up to deliver her finals.

"I wish you *were* taking exams, Christian. If the pulse had arrived on Walter's schedule, I would be driving to school. Come 7:30, that first class of juniors would be walking in, their knees shaking in anticipation of inevitable failure. Two hours later as they left the room hanging their heads in defeat, I would offer them best wishes for the future. Naturally, I would place a terrifying spin on the notion. Then I would record my final grades and disappear from this world."

The car fell silent. Arthur looked up from the laptop.

"It still can be, Agatha. We may yet go home."

Agatha sighed. She feared what might await them on the other side. Talk of civil war was growing before they crossed the fold.

She decided to give Jonathan Cobb the best chance possible at killing his targets. She needed to create a distraction, so Agatha hit speed-dial.

35

AT THE BASE of the bluffs along the west shore of Lake Vernon, shortly before 6:30 a.m., a man named Gooch McCracken was enjoying a bitter cup of black coffee and petting his bloodhound, Hobson, on the front steps of his trailer when he heard a familiar sound. Another careless driver failed to navigate the sharp bend in Fortnight Road a few hundred yards away and played life-and-death with the bluffs. Gooch heard the familiar, sickening reverberation of an automobile tumbling over the edge. This sort of thing happened every couple of years for as long as he could remember, but this time he swore he heard a couple of gunshots beforehand.

When he finished breakfast twenty minutes later, Gooch slipped on his wets, prepared his bait and tackle, tucked a large piece of chaw in the corner of his mouth, and shook his head as the predictable sirens approached Fortnight Road. He started downhill toward Lake Vernon and immediately dropped his pail of worms.

A man emerging from the shore and approaching the trailer was easily a foot taller and had muscles as imposing as the pro wrestlers Gooch loved back when he had a television. The man's bulk did not concern Gooch as much as the thick, reddish-brown stain on the side of the man's gut and blood trickling down the face and onto the neck. But even those unexpected characteristics did not grab his attention like the AK-47 the man tucked against the left side of his body, the rifle aimed at Gooch's heart.

The stranger looked past Gooch to a gray 1973 Ford pickup.

"Keys," Walt Huggins said.

Gooch backed up. "Don't want no trouble, fella. Looks like you need a doctor." He turned to his dog, who snarled. "Sit your ass down, Hobson."

"The keys will suffice. Hand them over."

"Look here, there's cops right up the road. Reckon they can get you to a doctor quicker than old Sally here. Or maybe I reckon you don't want the cops. Look here, the keys is in the ignition. Just take her and go. I won't say boo. You was never here."

Walt opened the truck's door and glanced at the ignition then at Gooch. Walt pulled the trigger twice. Two dark holes opened in Gooch's chest, and the hermit dropped, dead before he hit ground. Walt jumped into the truck. With his right hand, he tossed the GPS hand-held onto the passenger seat then started the engine. With his left hand, he reined in the rifle and slammed the door.

At that moment, the unique clatter of a helicopter engine exploded close by, and Walt saw the outline of the chopper through the trees as it raced by along the shoreline.

As if on cue, his cell phone rang. He accepted the call, stunned by the name on screen.

"You will fail again, Agatha," he answered. "The future will be secured. Surrender now, and no one has to die except for James."

"And all the millions who will come after," Agatha said. "Walter. Dear Walter. You and I should have never reached such a tragic impasse. Five of us have perished today. We were all such wonderful friends. Once."

Walt put the truck in reverse. "Your definition of 'friend' is liberal at best. We are Chancellors. You seem to have forgotten that little detail."

"On the contrary, Walter. That detail is what provides me with purpose. As Chancellors, we have always sought absolute control over all facets of society in order to promote stability and a clearly defined hierarchy. But this time we went too far. Perhaps we earned our fate. The future stops today. The others have decided to follow that mantra, no matter the consequences. I only wish you could have seen the wisdom of our path."

Walter had had enough. "I know how all this will end, Agatha. I have sufficient help on the way. You'll never get to him. Two words, my dear old friend: Shock Units."

Walt ended the call and looked one more time at his latest victim, whose contorted body stared up at the dog licking his face.

Miles away, in the red Camaro, Christian asked, "What are Shock Units? I'm thinking that sounds bad."

"He's bluffing," Arthur said. "How could he have pulled that off?"

"Concentrate on the road," Agatha said. "We have work to do."

Agatha tensed as she wondered how horribly she underestimated Walt Huggins.

36

WHEN HE KNEW Ben was not a mirage, Jamie's heart jumped for the first time since his nightmare began. Ben collapsed to the sand, an M16 sliding off his shoulder and onto the beach. By the time Jamie and Michael reached him, Ben struggled to catch his breath, speaking incoherent words between coughs. Jamie examined Ben, felt around the bullet wound above the collarbone, and saw splotches of bloodstains in the torn clothes intermixed with sand as well as countless bruises and scrapes.

"How?" He asked. "How did you find us? Nobody knew ..."

Ben wrapped a filthy hand around Jamie's neck, brought the boy closer and smiled even as he coughed.

"I came back for you this time," he stammered. "Won't let you down anymore. Promise."

Jamie's heart softened for an instant. He wanted to believe.

"I'm glad you're alive, Ben. We thought ..."

"Yeah, right. The big bang." Ben seemed giddy.

"I don't understand. How did you know where to find me?"

Ben explained about the GPS before grabbing his chest and wincing.

177

"Not smart for a drunk to run two miles with a bullet hole and banged-up legs, especially when he hasn't worked out in years."

Ben's voice trailed off.

"Cooper? What the hell you doing here?"

The anger in Jamie's blood percolated at once. He didn't give Michael a chance to speak.

"They tracked down Coop and near about killed him, too. Queen Bee and her people."

Ben coughed. "Good thing they can't shoot straight. Cooper, glad to see you're in one piece." He told the boys to help him stand. "Listen, J. We've got to finish what we started at the lake house. You ran away before I could tell you the whole story."

"There's nothing more to say, Ben. I've accepted it. I know what's going to happen. The only thing that matters now is getting Coop to safety."

"You don't have all the pieces. I'm the only one who can make this right. Problem is, we don't have much time. Maybe minutes. I just don't know what we're up against. We've got to get off this beach and find a private place that's safe. Where's the boat?"

"Around the point."

"We need cover. A few miles up Ginny's Creek ought to do nicely."

"That was where Sammie wanted to go when we were coming in, but I told her to land the boat near the point."

Ben's faced reddened at the mention of her name. He looked south along the beach and pegged squinted eyes on a new target. The boys followed his gaze. Sammie was making her way toward the threesome, one hesitant step at a time. She carried the pistol in her right hand pointed down. Ben let go of his support team, grabbed his rifle, and slung it over his healthy shoulder.

"She can't be trusted," Ben said.

Jamie wasn't prepared to argue the point, but he didn't expect the deep animosity in Ben's voice. Sammie drew closer.

"You're alive," she said. "What about my parents?"

Ben winced as he tugged at his wounded shoulder.

"Tell her," Jamie whispered.

Ben swallowed. "Your mother didn't make it. I'm sorry."

Sammie's eyes hit the ground; her gun hand trembled.

"And Daddy?"

Ben shook his head. "I don't know and I don't care."

Jamie pulled away, saw the mix of shock and dismay in Sammie's eyes and wanted to level his brother. Ben straightened himself out, repositioned the M16 and continued forward unconcerned by his answer. Sammie raised her pistol and aimed.

"Did you do something to Daddy?"

Before Ben answered, Jamie stepped forward. "C'mon, Sammie. Put the gun down. Look, Ben, just fill us in. If you expect me to listen to whatever you got to say, then you'd better tell Sammie where her dad is."

Ben gritted his teeth but did not stop walking. He was passing Sammie, her weapon still aimed, when he said, "Last time I saw Walt, he put two bullets in a cop point-blank. We had a falling out after that."

Ben snagged the pistol before Sammie knew what came her way.

"You let your defenses down," Ben told the girl. "The Unification Guard wouldn't like that, especially for a rookie with Dacha training."

Jamie saw similarities between Ben's lightning-fast move and the one Sammie pulled earlier. He neither understood the Dacha reference nor cared, but he did catch the hostile – and alien – glare between his brother and the girl he might have loved. He reminded himself that they were Chancellors. He didn't hesitate to accept when Ben handed him the pistol.

"You may need this more than her."

Ben snarled as he moved ahead.

Jamie glanced over his shoulder as they advanced toward the point. Sammie stayed behind, a statue with eyes focused on the ground. She balled her fists, and Jamie didn't know whether she was ready to fly into a rage or needed someone to stop and comfort her. He remembered the sudden emptiness of spirit when Sheriff Everson delivered the news about his own mom and dad, and the desire to lash out against the world.

"Where are your shirts?" Ben asked the boys.

"Bullet holes make a mess," Jamie said.

Just like that, Ben slapped him across the chest. He insisted everyone shut up.

"Listen," he whispered.

They heard the same rhythm at once. It stood out against the otherwise perfect silence of a morning where the wind died and the water was placid. Jamie knew the echo of the rotor blades, the background roar of the approaching engine. They scanned north along the shore.

Orange sunlight cast a metallic sparkle over the helicopter racing low along the shoreline, half a mile away and closing fast.

"Move," Ben shouted.

They took off in a dead run, reaching the point within seconds. Only as they rounded the point and neared the first cluster of scattered trees, realizing they were still a couple hundred yards from thick cover, did Jamie look back. Sammie was gone.

Jamie shouted for her.

"Shut up and move," Ben said, coughing between his words.

"I'm with Ben," Michael yelled. "Get to the boat."

"No," Ben said. "No time."

The roar of the chopper's engine reverberated louder than Jamie remembered from the first encounter, and its echo bounced through the trees like the first cannon shots of a swarming enemy.

Leapfrogging over debris and clambering over logs slowed down all three, and twice Ben groaned as he jumped, the second time grabbing at his left side beneath his rib cage. Jamie and Michael tried to help him along, but he pushed them away, insisting they go ahead, that he could keep up. They passed the speedboat without a word as the roar grew.

Jamie flipped around for no more than a second, hoping to see Sammie right behind, but she was not there. Rather, the low sun seemed to fill the mouth of the creek, a wide, angry oval rising to punish the world.

"Ben, I don't ..."

He heard a curse, turned around to see the M16 flying forward, skidding off a log and onto a pair of rocks which were half-submerged in the water's edge. Ben was writhing on the ground, grabbing his knee. Michael twisted about to help, and Jamie ran to his brother's side.

"I can make it," Ben shouted. "Get the gun."

For an instant, they froze. The helicopter swung about as it reached the mouth of the creek, and they were blinded as the heart of the sun enveloped the approaching enemy. Michael and Jamie each draped an arm around Ben then stumbled forward.

Machine-gun fire burst forth from the chopper, the bullets spraying the water and, growing closer, the scattered debris along the shore.

As Jamie considered that he might not survive another ten seconds, he saw a shadow slip past. He heard desperate footsteps and lost control of his brother. The threesome tumbled. Jamie turned. Before he began to understand, Jamie grabbed his ears to muffle the sound of hell descending.

He saw a lone figure on a rock, the rifle no longer visible. Then he heard the report of a weapon, every bit as loud and ferocious but more measured, each burst a half-second apart.

Bullets pinged against the debris, wood shards flying without mercy, and Jamie did not see how he could avoid the rain of death. And in a surreal fragment of time, like when one wakes from a dream and faces the blunt force of reality, the bullets stopped landing. He heard a sickening whirr, several mechanical pops, and saw smoke.

181

The helicopter spun out of control, fire emerging from the engine just above the fuselage, the rotor blade stalling and the tail fin all but shot off. A man and his rifle fell from the open door on the pilot side, landing with a sickening thud on the logs. The chopper seemed to utter one last, painful death moan as it glided over the threesome and collided head-on with a pine tree, the metal contorting and the fuselage bursting into flames as it smashed to the ground, which shook.

Jamie, Ben and Michael stared at each other, the fiery wreckage, and then the rocks along the water.

Sammie lowered the M16. She was surrounded by shell casings ejected from the rifle.

37

J AMIE HAD NO words. This was beyond anything he could have imagined. He owed his life to her but couldn't convince himself to wrap his arms around her. What Jamie knew for the moment was that Samantha Huggins was even further removed from the girl he grew up with.

"Holy hell," Michael said before whistling. "Call this girl GI Jane and stick a fork in that dude. He's cooked." He offered hearty applause. "I don't know how you did that, girl, but I am sold."

Sammie formed the inkling of a smile, but her temperament didn't soften when she locked on Ben. She navigated the rocks and strode up to him, rifle at her side, eyes full of water.

"Daddy was proud of me when I finished Dacha. Be glad I did."

She tossed the rifle at Ben, who caught it against his body. He turned to Jamie and offered an uncertain nod.

"We're alive, but we can't stay here," Ben told everyone. "We need cover." He nodded toward Jonathan Cobb's body on the logs. "Cooper, grab that AK and see if he was packing anything else. Another pistol, maybe."

Michael shook his head and laughed. "No sweat, dude. But I'm gonna tell you straight up, an AK ain't exactly my speed."

"Fine, Cooper. Military weapons should be left to people who understand how to use them."

Without another word, Ben handed Sammie the M16. They shared an agreeable nod, and Ben limped his way toward the boat, which appeared to have dodged the shower of bullets. Sammie waited behind for Jamie.

Jamie could not express himself beyond a meek, "Thank you." He tucked his pistol inside his pants and felt a curious swirl of emotions. He was afraid of what else he might learn about her, but he also had a swelling desire to kiss her.

"C'mon," she whispered. "We gotta go."

As the boat pulled away, leaving behind the fiery wreckage and the body of a man they all once knew, Jamie felt the déjà vu of once again fleeing death to the steady rhythm of an outboard. He fell into the back seat and set the pistol to his side. Unlike that first escape, Jamie found himself surrounded by a fully-armed if motley collection of soldiers.

Ben, who insisted on taking the wheel despite his injuries, laid an AK across his lap as he piloted the boat around the first bend. Michael held a pistol as he sat across from Ben. Sammie pointed her M16 down. Jamie saw the true Samantha Huggins.

He waited until the boat was a mile inland, having passed several bends, before speaking.

"How did you do it? How did you save our skins?"

She cracked a resigned smile.

"When I saw the helicopter coming, I knew the shortest route to the boat was a direct line through the brush rather than going around the point. I also knew we wouldn't get the boat away in time. I needed the M16, and your brother lost it at the perfect moment. I got lucky."

He swallowed. "What I can't get over is how anybody could be that brave. You stood up on those rocks and put everything on the line for us. I heard those bullets coming down like a hailstorm. If your

184

aim wasn't perfect, they would've blown you away." He almost reached out to her. "I reckon what I saw ... you up there on those rocks saving our lives ... it was probably the most incredible moment of my life."

Sammie kept the rifle steady. She carried half a smile, and Jamie thought he saw a gleam in her eyes resembling the little girl who used to fawn over him. He knew in his heart he'd never see that person again, but Jamie felt unexpected pride in the young woman who more than redeemed herself for her earlier betrayals.

Up front, navigating Ginny's Creek proved to be an adventure for Ben, as it twisted like a rattlesnake in motion, often narrowing to less than thirty feet wide, the water dark and shallow beneath heavy, overhanging trees. Ben wanted to go far inland; his inability to open the throttle frustrated him. The hole above his collarbone still bled, albeit slowly. To his left, Michael Cooper couldn't stop jabbering about being alive.

"Here's my problem," Michael said. "You Chancellors come from another Earth where you're swimming in tech that probably makes our best stuff look like pop guns. But you use pistols and rifles. What gives?"

Ben swung the wheel hard right to avoid low branches.

"We came here as observers. We weren't supposed to draw attention to ourselves. Laser pistols might have been a problem, don't you think?"

"I reckon."

"Cooper, bullets are just as effective. Were you paying attention back there? If you need to kill somebody, a gun is all it takes. Believe me, I know." He locked eyes with Michael, who examined the pistol in his lap. "Get your act together. This is serious business."

"Yeah, dude. Sure."

Ben didn't want to explain the complexities and cruelties of Chancellors. Michael knew more than he should have; better that he go home to a simple life and appreciate the ease of it. He wouldn't

185

understand a universe made of people like the Hugginses, Sheridans, or Bidwells.

"Trust a Chancellor once," Ignatius told him two years earlier, "you'll taste your own blood. Trust a Chancellor twice, you'll be served to his friends with a glass of white wine."

Ben ordered Michael to the stern. "Huggins, up front. Pronto. Chancellor business."

Sammie frowned but obeyed. Ben pulled back on the throttle.

"I got two issues," he told her. "I expect you to be straight with me on both. The last time I saw your father, he said there was 'help on the way.' He said he made sure Jamie would be protected until the end. What did he mean by that?"

Sammie stumbled over her words. "Daddy didn't fill me in on all his plans. I thought we were going to hold Jamie until an hour beforehand, give him a sedative, then wait for the rebirth. That's all he ever told me."

"And your mother?"

"Daddy made many decisions without us."

"And you wouldn't be buying time for him, now would you?"

She looked away. "Whatever else you think about me, I love Jamie. I made my choice."

"Fair enough. For now. The other matter is that we need a place to hide for a while. An empty cabin would be perfect."

Sammie winced. "How would I know about ...?"

Ben groaned. "I thought the act was over, Sammie." He remembered the story Walt told him in the SUV. "You finished Dacha in these woods."

Sammie's cheeks turned red, and she glanced at the boys, both of whom appeared interested albeit confused. She turned her attention to the land, surveying the topography.

"We're close. The landing is farther up, a quarter of a mile."

Sammie led them to a hidden landing with a steep rise and the trunks of many water trees twisting over the creek. They pushed the boat under the protective cover of long, low branches. Ben's left leg couldn't handle the climb, so he allowed the boys to give him a lift. Once on firm ground, Ben limped the rest of the way.

Although the woods appeared pristine and thick, occasional signs of human presence intervened in the form of a rusted bucket, the ashen remains of a campfire created months ago, and a path that appeared to have been hacked clear, as one might in a jungle. Sammie recognized the path and told the others to follow.

Ben's mind was a track meet of strategies, memories, guilt, and suspicion. This was his final chance at making things right with Jamie, and he yet sensed something would get in the way – again. He knew he should've been grateful for what Sammie did, but he couldn't escape the reality: She was a sleeper no more. She was a full-fledged Chancellor, her training as a UG peacekeeper informal but effective. Ben couldn't escape the possibility that she was formulating a scheme of her own.

Ben tried to keep his focus on the impending task. Crisp golden sunlight cut through the trees in precise beams like a special effect created on a movie set. The trees swayed and murmured, their voices almost audible. From time to time, he looked behind him to observe Jamie, who was trailing the silent group.

He tried to read Jamie's mood, but the boy seemed alien. *Some protector*, he mused. *Just another piece of crap, I am.* Once, as he glanced back, Ben did catch an unexpected detail. Jamie seemed to have an intense curiosity about the pistol in his right hand. He flipped his gun about and rubbed his fingers along the barrel as if admiring its craftsmanship, the notches and curvature. Ben wasn't sure what to think.

"Over here." Sammie pointed through the brush.

They turned off a well-worn path, cut through a stand of tall, wild grass and came upon a shack. It appeared to be little more than a gray collection of rotting planks holding up a tin roof. A few clumps of untamed wild grass prospered around the foundation. Thick shade kept weeds and vines at bay.

"A regular Holiday Inn," Michael muttered as he shook his head.

Ben told Jamie and Michael to lag behind as he and Sammie surrounded the shack, rifles high. Ben removed a wooden latch and flung the door open before nodding Sammie through the entrance. She raced inside with cool efficiency. Ben limped in as her backup. Seconds later, they emerged with guns bowed and motioned to the boys to join them.

Jamie asked, "How did you know about this place?"

"Hiking. Daddy used to bring us back here."

Ben applauded the cover story. After all, that's what Chancellors did: Covered themselves. Just as he and Ignatius Horne once did.

Two years earlier, on an empty service road many miles from town, Ignatius did not apologize for his actions.

Ben screamed. "Damn you, Iggy, they were my parents."

"And they were going to make you disappear." Ignatius maintained composure and warned Ben to get hold of his own. "What else did you expect would happen when you asked me to fix the situation?"

"I didn't want this."

"You're a Chancellor. Of course you did. Go home to Jamie."

Ben did as he was told and tried to be as strong as his parents would have been. Unfortunately, Ignatius didn't warn Ben that the guilt would never end, that the ability to look Jamie in the eye would be trumped by the need to find refuge in a bottle and the comfort of random women.

He pushed the ghosts aside and hurried Jamie inside the shack.

"Look, we don't have time to spare," he warned the teens. "That chopper going down won't do a damned thing except bring more attention we don't need." He told Michael and Sammie to stand lookout. "You hear anybody coming this way, see anything move, give me a head's-up. Clear?" Ben looked only at Michael as he completed this command.

Ben pointed to Michael's pistol. "Take care with that."

"Dude. Chill. I'm the black guy, remember? I'm supposed to be good with a piece, now ain't I? Besides, I got GI Jane here for pointers."

Ben and Jamie entered the one-room shack. Dust gathered like a blanket on a wood stove, a fetid cot, and rickety homemade chairs. Ben limped to the cot and fell upon it without reservation, pleased to be off his bad knee. A dust cloud blew up around him. *A fitting end,* Ben thought. *How could I have come to this?*

He stared his little brother square in the eyes and prepared to carry out the only good deed he had left in his heart.

38

TWO CARS SQUEALED as they turned off Highway 39 onto an unmarked, unpaved side road. After a quarter-mile, they stopped. Inside the red Camaro, two sets of eyes focused on Agatha, for whom the past several minutes produced nothing but setbacks. She kept her speaker phone on as Jonathan Cobb made visual contact with his targets at Ginny's Creek and opened fire upon them. She felt an unprecedented rush of adrenalin.

Then the cell phone crackled and the connection died. Agatha knew the truth before it was confirmed by the police scanner. A police chopper reached the scene, its pilot describing the burning wreckage and a single body on the shore.

Agatha told Christian to get them off this highway to someplace less visible. They passed two patrol cars, each flashing blue lights.

"We're not backing down," Christian jumped in. "We just need a break to fall our way."

Agatha nodded. "How far are we from the crash?"

Arthur studied his laptop. "Under two miles, due west."

Agatha leaned forward and pointed to the screen. "And the land between here and there is largely unpopulated?" Arthur nodded. "Few roads? Heavy forest?"

"The highway cuts through the middle. Otherwise, yes."

"Good. If they intend to protect James until rebirth, they will use the forest as a shield. We have to go in after them."

Arthur grimaced. "Agatha, we have no idea where to begin." He pointed to the screen. "This is unfamiliar terrain. With Jennifer in Austin Springs, there are only five of us. If we get separated, we are more likely to encounter police than Chancellors."

"Retreat is unacceptable." She glanced at her phone, which delivered a live image from a remote camera installed by the observers twenty miles north of Albion. "What if Walter was not bluffing? What if he did arrange to bring Shock Units here?"

"You said yourself, nothing has come through the fold since the Caryllan transmission," Arthur countered. "If Walt did leave behind secret orders for Shock Units, what else didn't he tell us? Walt Huggins is a brilliant man, but I think we give him too much credit."

"Or not enough." Agatha thought through her options. "Lester Bowman and Reginald Fortis were Dacha Masters during their time in the Guard. Put them in a setting where they can track their prey as they did decades ago, and their brilliance will emerge."

"I want to go with them," Christian insisted. "They can track Sheridan, then I'll kill him."

"No," Agatha said. "I admire your bravado, but Arthur is correct. We should avoid stretching our resources too thin. Lester and Reginald can hunt down their location, then – and only then – will we respond to provide fire support. Understood?"

Christian crossed his arms like a petulant child, a move that pleased Agatha. She would have lost faith in him had he accepted her decision without protest.

"Calculate the most effective search pattern, Arthur. We need to hope this is one contingency for which Walter did not plan."

39

J AMIE SAT ON the fetid cot beside his brother, the pistol firm in his right hand, finger next to the trigger. He felt empty and alone.

"Tell me there's a way out," he said. "If you ever loved me, please tell me there's a way out."

Ben held the flash drive in his right palm.

"You'll find this hard to believe, J," Ben stammered. "I've been searching for the answer to that question for years. The proof is right here."

Jamie studied the memory casing as if it were a surreal joke.

"Fat lot of good that's gonna do out here."

"You're right, but we don't need a computer to finish this. It's all up here." He tapped his skull. "I was searching for truth, and I found it. Everything in a new light. The universe the way the Chancellors never believed. And maybe, Jamie, just maybe ..."

Jamie turned to Ben. "Am I going to die?"

"It's not that simple."

Jamie cocked his pistol. "You're pushing me, Ben. I can blow your freaking brains out right now. Give me a reason not to."

"Faith," he said. "Faith that despite how crappy a brother I've been, maybe I love you more than I can stand. And Jamie, maybe have faith that I wouldn't bring you in here unless there was at least a little hope."

Jamie aimed the pistol between his brother's eyes.

"I don't want any more doubletalk," he said. "Straight and simple. You tell me why we're here and whether I can beat this thing."

Ben nodded. "If you lower the gun and let me explain."

Jamie saw the growing bloodstain from Ben's bullet wound and the torn pants revealing a gimpy knee. Ben never looked more helpless. Jamie could heal those wounds with a touch, but he chose not to reveal his newfound strength until Ben did something to make up for this nightmare. He dropped the gun to his side but kept his trigger finger firmly poised.

"Be quick. In case you ain't heard, I'm gonna die this morning."

"Bottom line," Ben began. "There's more going on inside you than you realize. The Jewel isn't just some algorithm. The truth is bigger than the Chancellors, than all of us. Nobody would've discovered it if we never came to this Earth." He pointed to the flash drive. "The proof is here, J. The answer to the question nearly everyone on this planet asks: Is there anything beyond death?" He paused. "You remember how I started attending church in the last year before Mom and Dad were killed?"

Jamie shrugged his shoulders. Mostly, Jamie recalled it as the year Ben became a different man and began pulling away.

Ben continued. "We'd always been taught to stay away from religion, that it was a primitive way of coping with irrational fears. The early Chancellory wiped out all divine faiths thousands of years ago, during prehistory. That's what repulsed our parents most about living here: The very idea of heaven and hell, a God and a savior. Chancellors don't believe in such things, but they do value extended life - have even sought the keys to immortality. The Jewel hybrids are the precursors to that path.

"So when I went to church, I wasn't looking to be converted. I just wanted to understand. I wanted to be a good observer. But I got so much more than I expected. I'd been studying religions of the world, reading theology, looking for common threads among all these belief systems. Over the years, I pumped Ignatius for everything he knew about the origin of the Jewels and their integration with our DNA. His father led the bioengineering team that learned how to weaponize Caryllan Wave energy."

Jamie scoffed. "That's the one where I go all nuclear?"

"A Berserker. Potentially. Yes. At any rate, I was curious about the endless anecdotes I read of what might happen to the body and soul at the moment of death. The very idea that a human being was a vessel containing a soul, and the soul left the body to pass into a higher plane of existence ... this was impossible. Yet, there were enough testimonials that I couldn't ignore the evidence. Anecdotes of a 'white light,' a tunnel from one life to the next, out-of-body experiences. These reports have been floating around for centuries, the same ideas discredited after the rise of the Chancellory."

"And what the hell does this have to do with me?"

Ben paused. "I believe the human soul and Caryllan energy are one and the same. The Jewels of Eternity were designed by an ancient race to preserve its legacy. Some have theorized that the collective consciousness of that race is embedded within the Jewels. They call it consciousness, I call it souls. Human souls are the same energy but in a purer form, a part of the natural fabric of all things. What people see as a spirit ascending to a higher plane is simply the energy of the universe returning to its natural state.

"Look, Jamie. I know don't about God or Allah or Buddha, but I do know this: We are vessels. We do carry something inside. You are literal proof. Most important, we are part of a greater mosaic and have a power no one has truly understood. And you are the most unique of us all."

Jamie was dumbfounded. Ben may as well have grown tentacles, sported three noses and sang "Yankee Doodle" while flapping his fins.

194

"Everything I been through today," Jamie muttered. "All this hell, and you stand here wasting what time I got left with some kind of ... it ain't even religion. I don't know what it is."

Ben nodded as if he agreed. "Here's my point, Jamie. The engineers who designed your genome to include the Jewel energy did not believe in human souls. If they understood the relationship, if they truly knew the greater picture, they would never have finished their work."

"Oh, really?" Jamie laughed. "And why's that?"

"Because they would know that the human soul just might be strong enough to alter their program. Maybe even defeat it."

Jamie almost dared to hope. His heart made an extra, tentative beat, as if unsure whether celebration was in order. He could think of no words, the fear too great that what he just heard was a mistake.

"Are you saying I can beat this thing?"

Ben's eyes flickered away for an instant, but Jamie didn't have time to pass judgment before his brother answered.

"There is life. There is death." Ben paused for a beat. "Neither one of those on their own can save you. But there is a third option. It is the most dangerous and the most fleeting, but it is all you have left."

40

"HERE'S HOW IT might happen," Ben said. "There'll be an instant when your will to survive is so strong that you stop thinking and give yourself over to the universe. If you somehow disconnected yourself from the limitations up here," he said, pointing to Jamie's head, "I believe you could literally will the Jewel's program to end the re-sequencing. Perhaps destroy it altogether. The possibilities are ..."

"Crazy."

"Thousand-to-one shot, at best. This is where it becomes difficult."

Jamie laughed. "Did I miss something? Was there an easy part?"

"Jamie, to give yourself to your soul is to say goodbye to the flesh. To control the Jewel, you'll have to separate yourself from your body." Jamie's hope slipped away like the yellow leaves of a birch in autumn. He heard Ben's words but couldn't digest them. "There's an instant between life and death. It's as brief as the blink of an eye or as infinite as the universe itself. In that instant, people put life behind and make the transition to whatever is next. Some face a white light. Others are drawn back by forces they can't control. Most give in and accept what is to come. They do this because they don't understand there's an alternative."

The gun in Jamie's hand felt warm, necessary. His anger spiked.

"You're saying I'm gonna die anyway."

Ben sniffled. "Yes, Jamie. I am. But life doesn't have to end at death. The Jewel is changing you. If you can give yourself over to death, I believe you can use the power of your soul to end that program. You will see inside your body without the burden of a rational, limited mind."

Jamie walked to the door, keeping his back to his brother, certain that if he turned around, he would pull the trigger.

"You always do this to me, Ben. You come along and get my hopes up. So, I die, take control of my soul, order the Jewel to go away and then what? I wake up feeling great? Like it's the first day of summer vacation?"

Jamie saw the world through a narrow, focused tunnel. As his anger perpetuated a sensation of utter defeat, he felt the rage of blame being funneled into the pistol.

"You have a chance, J. It's a small one, granted. Don't give up."

Jamie snarled. "I just gotta believe, right?"

"Yes, J. That's what you gotta do."

"Here's what I believe," Jamie said as he swung about, the pistol raised chest high, both hands firmly gripping it, his aim true. "You could've told me the truth anytime. Mom and Dad, too. I mean, what was I gonna do about it? I was screwed fifty ways to Sunday."

"Jamie, the Mentor was supposed ..."

"Yeah, yeah. What say I let you shoot me in the head? I'll be out of my misery, and those other people – those great friends of yours from another Earth – can put down their guns and go home. How about it, dude?"

"Jamie, please. I'm trying to offer you a way out, but it's going to take some preparation. We need to sit down and ..."

"Preparation? Like what all you people been doing the past fifteen years? Must have been a game to you Chancellors. Why wait until now? You try to save me at the last minute, the others are trying to kill me at the last minute. Why wait? Any one of you sorry bastards could've put a bullet in my skull years ago. I never would've seen it coming."

"How we got here is complicated, but ..."

"Not complicated. You needed this thing inside me to finish sequencing so you could find the location of the fold and go home. You people didn't kill me because you needed me. You were cowards. The whole sorry damn mess of you."

"I can't dispute that, J. But I'm here now. I need you to ..."

"Trust you."

Ben smiled. "Yes. In spite of all I did, I'm asking for your trust."

Jamie didn't understand how it happened, but the anger cooled. The tunnel disappeared, restoring the light of day all around him. The knot in his belly dissolved as he lowered the gun. He wobbled as he held his place, putting up no resistance as Ben wrapped arms around him.

"I don't want to die," he whispered. "Please, Ben. Don't let me die."

"I can't make any promises. But you have to believe in yourself, Jamie. When the moment comes, have faith that you can change the ending. Accept that you have a soul, that it can be your guide as you cross over, and that you can use it to fight back."

Seconds after Jamie wrapped his arms around his big brother, energy drained from him as if a vampire drank his blood. His legs bore the brunt of this weariness, and his feet seemed ready to slip from beneath him. Jamie knew the sensation. He felt it before, along the shore of Lake Vernon.

"How, Ben? How do I make that happen?"

"The power of your will. In life, we can will ourselves to do things the flesh is not capable of on its own. If we believe strongly ..."

"Like now." Jamie pulled out of the hug. For the first time, he understood. "I'm healing you. Before long, that bullet hole will be gone and your knee will be better."

"What?"

"They shot Coop in the back."

"Who? When?"

"We found him by the lake. He was almost dead. I didn't even know I was doing it; but all the time I was carrying him, this thing inside me was somehow going into Coop. It cured him. Just now, I felt the power leaving me again. I think ... I think you're right. If my will is strong enough, I can make things happen. Impossible things."

Ben's jaw dangled. Then a smile crossed his tired, beaten face.

"Why didn't you tell me this earlier? This is proof. So, you weren't conscious of what you were doing when you were carrying Coop?"

"No. I just wanted him to live more than anything."

Ben ran his dirty, bloody hands through his hair. "You're a good man, Jamie Sheridan. This is more than I imagined. There are ways to do this, J. If we plan it carefully, maybe ..."

The cabin door flung open, hitting Jamie in the back. Michael stepped through, his rifle lowered but his eyes wide.

"Sorry, dudes. We got trouble."

Ben yanked his pistol out from behind his belt, and Jamie once again sensed that a moment of hope was about to be dashed.

41

MICHAEL SAID HE heard a car door slam. Jamie panicked as they raced onto the porch. Ben grabbed the AK-47 from Michael, exchanging it for a pistol. Jamie locked his eyes onto the weapon of death and felt a newfound dread. He was not reassured when Sammie emerged from behind an ancient oak, her rifle in a defensive posture. She ran to them with cat-quick silence.

"I couldn't see anything," she said. "We heard one car door northwest. There's an old hunting road a couple hundred yards in that general direction, but this was closer. That's rough terrain for anything, even with four-wheel drive. I don't like it."

"I agree," Ben said.

"We should head back south."

"Yep, but not to the boat. We tapped out that option. C'mon."

Ben wasn't off the porch before he said his limp was better and shared a smile with Jamie. He didn't take his eyes off Jamie as he dropped the flash drive into his own shirt pocket. He patted Jamie on the back.

"We'll finish this. I promise."

Jamie shared awkward glances with his oldest friends, but he couldn't smile. He couldn't begin to tell Michael or Sammie what went on in the cabin, for he had a hard enough time facing the task ahead. Just when he wondered whether he'd ever know peace before he died, Jamie jerked.

A sharp thunderclap shattered the morning stillness. Yet this one did not linger, gone in a splinter of a second. Jamie did not have time to wonder where it came from, only that Sammie yelled for them to take cover. He plunged to the ground on his belly. Within seconds, he looked around and saw Sammie and Michael huddled close by. He turned to his side, feeling another presence beside him.

Jamie saw a red splatter against the base of a birch tree. Then he caught Ben's vacant stare, which was almost hidden beneath the blood trickling from the hole in his forehead. Jamie reached for Ben's closest arm, which was bent backward in an unnatural pose. He pulled the arm out from underneath his brother's chest, wrapped his hands around it and huddled close. He rubbed the arm feverishly, muttering as he went.

"C'mon, Ben. C'mon, Ben. Don't worry. I can save you. I did it before. Did it before."

He spewed the words in a continuing cycle, oblivious to the danger. He heard Sammie's pleas to stay down and Michael's whispered curses, but they were background noise. Between chattering teeth and newfound panic, Jamie reached down into his gut, cleared his thoughts of all distractions, and focused on a single command: *Ben can't die; make him live.*

But he knew the truth, even as all his mental energy poured into saving his brother.

Jamie knew because no matter how hard he willed it, his body gave up nothing. That life-draining sensation was gone, as if the Jewel revealed a single flaw: Even it could not bring back the dead. He would not allow himself to accept the reality of what lay before him – until he heard one particular word fall from Sammie's lips.

"Daddy," she said.

Then he understood. Jamie groped the soil around him for the .45 and found it at his feet. He didn't need to hear where Sammie's voice came from, only to hear the crunching of leaves from behind. He swung about, throwing himself to his feet, lifting the weapon with a firm grip and allowing full-on rage to take him prisoner. The world dissolved into that narrow tunnel of despair from which Ben briefly saved him. The .45 felt more than warm; it was a part of him. No more flashes of what was possible, only a release of what he needed to become.

Jamie took two steps forward, stopped, cocked the pistol, and pulled the trigger twice.

When the bullets hit their target, Jamie saw a pair of small, dark rosettes open against a white background. The screams within him were drowned out by the terrified shrill of the girl he almost loved.

"No! Jamie, no. Daddy!"

The tunnel widened, especially as Michael came to his side, grabbed Jamie's trigger hand and brought down the weapon. He thought Michael was shaking him, demanding Jamie wake up. Indeed, Jamie thought himself lost in a dream from hell. Yet Michael's words became clear.

Jamie saw Ben's lifeless body, looked up into the trees, and swallowed the sunlight filtering through the thick, late spring foliage. And then he knew, with certainty, where he was. Jamie dropped the gun.

Walt Huggins fell to his knees. Blood dribbled from the corner of his mouth, but that was nothing compared to the massive red-black stain along the right side of the behemoth, or the two expanding blotches on the man's belly. Walt dropped an AK to the dirt from one hand and a portable GPS device with flashing beacon from the other. His daughter rushed to his side, but Walt pasted his eyes on Jamie.

Walt whispered to his daughter, and she shook her head violently as she backed away. Walt motioned the boy closer. Jamie was only beginning to realize what he'd done, the memory of firing the pistol already a blur. He swiped hair from his face and started toward Walt.

"You're not as weak as I believed," Walt said, his voice slurred. He coughed twice, bringing up deep red saliva. The imposing man sat on his knees, his hands flat on his thighs, as if to support his upper body. He could have been a lumberjack upon a yoga mat. However, even as blood trickled from the corner of his closed lips, Walt maintained a smile.

"Not as weak as your brother," he continued. "He should have known better than to leave me alive with means of tracking you. He did not have the spine of a Chancellor."

"Daddy, please," Sammie said. "We have to get you help." She faced Jamie. "Save him, just like you did Michael."

His emotions on overload and rational thought all but fried, he offered Sammie a frown.

"Why? He killed my brother."

"Ben is gone. Daddy is still alive. You won't stand here and watch him die, Jamie. You're too good a person to do that."

Jamie said nothing, but Walt did not hesitate.

"Ah. Newfound powers? We always wondered how the re-sequencing would affect the human body. Good to see you, Mr. Cooper. So, James, what will it be? Heal my wounds?"

"He killed Ben," Jamie repeated to Sammie. "Didn't even give him a chance. If I heal your dad, he'll try to keep me prisoner until time runs out. He won't be grateful or nothing."

"Of course he will," she said. "You've got my promise, Jamie."

"No," Walt interrupted. "No, no, Pumpkin. I'm afraid James understands me too well. A surprise, given his mental ineptitude over the years. Granted, Tom and Marlena tried their best, but you never were the apple of their eye, for understandable reasons."

"You got no idea what you're talking about," Jamie said.

"More than you'll ever know. When you shot me, James, what did you feel?" He tilted his head in curiosity, but Jamie couldn't answer.

"Fury. That's what it is. Caryllan energy. Weaponized fury." He focused on his daughter. "Samantha, you've done an outstanding job in keeping the Jewel close. Now I need for you to finish the mission."

Jamie snapped left, a familiar sense of betrayal chilling his blood.

"No, Jamie," Sammie stumbled over her words. "Daddy, this isn't what you think. I thought you were dead. I'm with Jamie because ..."

"Listen to me, Pumpkin. You are the last, and you have to finish this. You need to secure the Jewel and leave this area quickly." He coughed up more blood. "The police are close. Kill Mr. Cooper. Shoot James in the leg and secure him until the end of re-sequencing."

"Whoa, dude," Michael interrupted, his pistol aimed alternately at Walt and Sammie. "I near about got wasted once. I ain't going down again."

Jamie wished he hadn't dropped his own weapon. He knew he wasn't fast enough to charge Sammie and snare the M16. Yet he realized such desperate measures wouldn't be needed. All he had to do was look in her eyes, which glistened with water.

"No, Daddy. I'm sorry, but I won't do this. I love Jamie. I always have." She turned to Jamie. "And I swear I always will."

Walt coughed. "You will not ... betray ... me. Am I clear?"

Sammie did not hesitate. "I did everything you ever asked, but you want me to cross the line. I might be a soldier, but I won't be an executioner, Daddy. Can't you understand that?"

Walt slid his fingers toward the AK. Jamie raced forward and snatched up the weapon, swooping around until he had a clear shot at both Walt and his daughter.

"What a beautiful picture," Walt snarled. "Three children with their guns trained on a dying man. Afraid to the last, aren't you?" He faced Michael. "A circus clown who's never said a truly humorous thing in his life." He looked over his shoulder to Jamie. "A weak, emotional twit who caused everyone endless annoyance." Then to Sammie: "The greatest disappointment a father could ever have."

Jamie lowered his weapon, and he saw Michael follow suit. He had no doubt where the four of them stood, especially when he saw the silent tears stream down Sammie's cheeks.

"Daddy, how could you? I've done everything you ever asked."

"Before today, yes." He coughed more blood and looked away from his daughter. "Understand this, children. Chancellors do not surrender. I long ago secured additional help." He offered a curt smile. "Shock Units." His voice faded. "Nasty. Effective. Unstoppable."

This new information tightened Jamie's gut.

"What?" He asked. "You mean troops?"

Walt laughed. "Never doubt the genius or persistence of a Chancellor. Especially if you are his daughter."

"Dude," Michael said. "This does not sound good. I say we get the heck out of Dodge."

As if on cue, the roar of a helicopter echoed through the trees from the east. In seconds, the chopper flew past perhaps a quarter-mile away, not visible through the dense forest.

"Daddy, tell me you're lying. They wouldn't really send ..."

Sammie stopped mid-sentence. Jamie saw why. Walt held a stiff, Buddha-like pose, his smug smile locked, his eyes open and unblinking.

Sammie dropped to one knee and stared. She knew. They all did.

"Oh, Daddy," she muttered through her tears. "Why?"

Jamie left her there to mourn. He walked past Michael without a word and returned to Ben's side. He tried to remember what Ben told him inside the cabin. Jamie had nothing to offer. He couldn't pull together the words for a prayer, and he didn't think Ben would consider it fitting anyway. Instead, he grabbed one of his brother's hands and whispered.

He closed his eyes. "Goodbye, Ben."

Jamie refused to allow his feelings to overwhelm him. He understood what the Jewel was doing to him, how the re-sequencing was playing havoc with his emotions and changing his priorities to that of someone he didn't know.

He killed a man. Until the moment when he pulled the trigger, Jamie did not believe murder was part of his makeup. He wanted to resist the anger that drove him to kill, but the program was too strong. As he stared at Ben's lifeless shell, Jamie knew he couldn't go back.

His thoughts unscrambled when a ringing phone broke the silence. He saw Sammie and Michael stepping toward Walt. The phone continued to ring. Michael pulled it out of Walt's shirt pocket.

"Dude, what do you think?"

Jamie grabbed the phone and opened it.

He stared at the caller ID but did not feel the usual fear associated with this woman.

"Hello?"

"I wish to speak with ... *James*? Is that you, James? Oh, you dear child. Ms. Bidwell here. I am so very sorry we couldn't have ended your school year on a more pleasant basis. Perhaps you and I need to engage in a very different manner of final exam. Yes?"

42

J AMIE TURNED TO his friends, then looked again at the bodies of two men whose obsession with Jamie got them killed. He tucked the phone against his chest.

"I think I have to take this," he said before turning his back.

"What did I ever do to you?" He asked Agatha. "To any of you?"

"I believe you know the answer to that question," Agatha said. "This is a tragedy for all. Unfortunately, James, you were ..."

"Jamie. The name is Jamie. I hate James. I told you that in class."

"And so you did. Jamie, you were destined for this end before you were conceived. I'm sure Walter and Benjamin have taken pains to provide you with sufficient back story. Yes?"

"They told me. Before they died."

Agatha gasped. "Died? Walter is ...?"

"I killed him myself. What do you think of that, Ms. Bidwell? Do I get to move to the front of the class now?"

"I don't appreciate your tone, Jamie," Agatha started. "I do not respond well to sarcasm in children. In your case, I'll make an exception."

Jamie did not want to have a row with this woman.

207

"Why are you doing this to me?"

Agatha, speaking from the back seat of the Camaro, turned to Arthur, who was running a program to calibrate the origin of the phone signal. Walt did not give her enough time on the earlier call to fix his location. Arthur motioned for her to keep talking.

"Jamie, I'm not sure how much your allies have told you about the civil conflict between Chancellors, or the moral implications behind your creation. At this point, I will not diverge into a history lesson nor a treatise on bioethics. But you need to understand our point of view regarding the rebirth of the Jewel within you."

"Is this going to be for a grade?" Jamie knew how much she despised that question.

"Very clever," she said. "To serious concerns. In my universe, humans have lived on forty worlds for a thousand years. We evolved as a new breed of humans to surpass the limitations of earlier *homo sapiens*. But not long ago we embarked on a scheme to become even greater than ourselves. To ensure permanence. Some have used the words *immortality* and *godhood*."

"Sure. Those are the words I'd find in the dictionary next to your picture. Right, Queen Bee?"

Agatha motioned to Arthur to step outside with the laptop.

"My point, Jamie, was that when we arrived here, I had no particular use for this Earth's people or cultures. I despised their superficiality and inherent desire for immediate gratification without consideration of expanding their intellect and insight into the human condition. I always ..."

"Talk like an arrogant bitch who made everybody you ever met despise being in the room with you." Jamie spat into the phone. "You treated us like maggots, and that's how we left your class feeling."

Agatha took a deep breath and sorted through her response.

"I am arrogant, capricious, and sadistic. It is my nature. However, contrary to what you and your friends may think, I am not without a heart."

Jamie laughed. He lost track of why he was even listening to the woman who had been leading a brigade of former friends to kill him.

"A heart, maybe. But lady, you got no soul. None at all. Just let me go. Let my friends go home and live their lives. Can't you be a human being for once and just walk away?"

"I wish I could. But time has endeared me to people in a way I never imagined. Jamie, I have sat in small conference rooms with the parents of my students. I have listened to them tell me of their hopes and their frustrations. I have seen mothers in tears because they wanted more for their children and feared for the worst. I have seen pure and unconditional love in their eyes. I have seen bonds between parent and child that defied the world in which I was raised. I have seen tenderness, compassion, and fealty.

"And I have come to realize that Chancellors, who lack these essential qualities, do not deserve to advance beyond our failed state. I cannot allow them to unleash an abomination like the Jewel upon those forty civilized worlds. Our desire for immortality will lead to the fall of all humans. It has to be destroyed, and I cannot do that without killing you."

He dropped the phone to his side and stared past his friends in silence. Sammie started toward him, but he motioned her back.

"You can't put this on me," he barked into the phone. "It's not my fault. I didn't make this happen."

"But you will. If you stay the course rather than surrender yourself to us, you will be responsible. The Chancellors will consolidate their power, use an army of hybrids to obliterate all opposition, and begin a systematic genocide of the insurgent colony worlds. Billions will die. Now that you know the truth, you must concede to the only morally acceptable outcome. Give yourself to us. I promise we will not harm anyone with you."

Jamie looked across the way to Ben's body and searched his thoughts on Ben's 'third option.' He turned to Michael, whose safety meant more to Jamie than his own life. He wished he had one night alone with Sammie, one brief interlude of perfection.

"I need time," he told Agatha. "I can't think. It's like I'm back in your goddamn class again. I can't think."

Agatha got the thumbs-up from Arthur. He zeroed in on the coordinates of Jamie's phone. She pressed her phone against her chest as Arthur contacted Reginald Fortis and Lester Bowman. Then Agatha nodded to Christian: time for him to join the hunt.

"I understand your emotional confusion. However, I believe your parents would have encouraged you to make this sacrifice. They were good and upstanding Chancellors. Their decision to send you into hiding with our team was devastating, but they understood the necessity. I was there when they said goodbye. They would see the moral rightness of this."

Jamie froze. "What?" He felt his heart race. "My parents? They didn't come? What? They weren't …?"

Agatha twitched. She wondered whether she went too far. "No. Tom and Marlena Sheridan played the part, but your biological parents had a different agenda."

"They're alive? Mom and Dad?"

"Likely."

Jamie wondered what other emotional punishment he was supposed to take today. He knew Agatha was not lying. The pieces made sense. The distance he often felt from his mother … Lydia even hinted at it hours ago. He thought the voices on those farewell messages were computerized, yet they must have been genuine.

"Their names. What were their names?"

"Bouchet. Emil and Frances Bouchet."

"And Ben?"

"Not your biological brother, but he did love you as one."

"And my name? Was it always Jamie?"

"James Bouchet."

"You stole me. You bitch. All you Chancellors."

He smashed the phone against a tree and turned to his friends.

"We have to move. Now. We're out of time."

Jamie gathered up an AK, pulled the strap over his shoulder and looked around until he found the .45 near Ben.

Just before he started back to his friends, Jamie saw a small metallic object half-buried in the kicked-up soil a couple feet from Ben's body. He recognized the flash drive and grabbed it. Jamie couldn't imagine what he'd do with this now, but the idea of leaving it behind seemed disrespectful. If Ben was telling the truth, if this represented the only meaningful work Ben did the past few years, then Jamie couldn't leave it here for anyone to find.

"We're taking Coop home. He's going to be safe."

Sammie nodded through her tears. "But what about you? What did she tell you? What did Ben say to you?"

Jamie brushed hair from his face. "Doesn't matter. Let's go."

"I'm down with that," Michael said.

Jamie didn't look back. He walked into the forest with the commitment that his final two hours would have meaning. He tried to suppress his rage, to block the truth hidden within his new and tighter skin: He was falling into an abyss. The Jewel was opening his mind to a different perspective on time and place.

He felt the shadows coming for him.

43

THEY FOUND A battered, rusting, sky-blue pickup where Walt left it: Stopped shy of a trench at least six feet deep and wide slithering through the woods, a shallow but fast-moving stream at the base. Sammie said the stream flowed directly into the lake; they were less than fifty yards from a one-lane dirt road linked to the highway. Michael found keys inside.

"We better move," Jamie said, listening to the ever-present albeit distant echo of a helicopter's rotor blades.

Sammie hesitated, looking back across the trench.

"I shouldn't have left him there like that," she said. "He deserved better, Jamie. He was only doing what he thought was right. His mission."

"So did Ben, but it's done. They're gone. Only thing we can do now is take care of Coop. I need you, Sammie."

She raised the rifle to chest level and nodded. Jamie tried to focus upon the next challenge, to suppress fear of a fate two hours away. Sammie followed Jamie to the passenger side. Before he hopped in, Jamie inspected the seat, which was cracked and spewing foam filler. The rusting floor looked as if it would give way. Michael insisted on driving.

"Don't got my license on me, but I'm the oldest looking, so that ought to count for something," he said. As Jamie and Sammie climbed in, Michael leaned forward, looking around Jamie and said, "Figure you might wanna keep that gun on your lap, Sammie. Folks around these parts wouldn't look twice at a good ol' boy and his shotgun. But they'd take notice of a sweet thing like you locked and loaded, if you get my speed."

Jamie wasn't surprised by Michael's recharged, sarcastic attitude; he was used to seeing Michael take this road whenever emotions threatened to get the better of him. Michael cranked the engine on the third try and maneuvered the truck around low brush and fallen limbs. The truck groaned and squealed, and each of them shared worried glances. Michael chuckled.

"She's halfway to the grave, but I'll bet she gets us there."

The truck seemed to have little or no shocks, as each tiny bump bounced the three from the seat. Michael worked the steering wheel hard but couldn't avoid low-hanging branches, which snapped upon impact with the windshield. Jamie remembered the nights he and Michael took jalopies such as this on joy rides. He used to love the exhilaration and fear.

They were within range of the dirt road when Jamie swore he saw an unnatural shadow out of the corner of his eye. The dark movement was cat-quick, visible just beyond the driver's rear-view mirror. Light and shadow danced through the forest in electric morning routines; he was ready to chalk this up to paranoia. Then he saw Sammie raise her weapon and lean forward, also looking left. Michael made a sharp left around a tree, which scraped the passenger side. Jamie again faced Sammie, whose head still darted about to the left and through the cabin's rear window.

He didn't need to ask. "Coop. Floor it."

Seconds later, the truck careened onto the road, which was thick in sandy soil. The rear tires roared and seemed embedded in the sand, but Michael gave the gas everything, freeing the pickup. The

213

truck struggled until Michael recognized the incoming tire tracks and announced he would follow those out.

The road led straightaway for two football fields then banked to the right. Old growth forest encroached from either side, the high branches shading the road and low brush, leaving no semblance of a shoulder.

"The highway isn't far," Sammie said over the chugging, nauseated engine. "Maybe a quarter mile past that bend. Faster, Coop. I don't feel good about this."

Jamie understood Sammie's impatience. His nerves crawled like the baited earthworms he used to drop into Alamander River. However, he didn't have time to express his fears.

A blue sedan rounded the bend, not moving at a rapid clip, either, appearing to rock back and forth as it also navigated a terrain it wasn't equipped to handle. Michael kept his foot on the gas until Jamie grabbed the wheel.

"Slow down. Pull over far as you can." He turned to Sammie. They didn't say a word, but he saw her trigger finger poised to unload the M16.

"No way," Michael said. "We stay in the middle, they'll pull over."

"I don't think so," Sammie said. The blue sedan stopped, holding position in the center. Michael hit the brakes, the sedan a hundred feet ahead. Jamie slid one of the AKs into Michael's lap.

The sedan's driver-side door opened. Christian Bidwell stepped out, although he remained behind the door.

Jamie saw a river of sweat roll down Michael's forehead and a familiar terror in his best friend's eyes. Jamie knew with certainty they were in serious trouble when he saw Christian speaking into a cell phone.

Sammie grabbed their attention. "This is what we have to do. On a count of three, I'm going to open my door. As soon as I do, I'm going to jump. Put your heads down and follow me out as quickly as you can. Whatever you do, don't slow down."

A split second before Sammie began her count, reality struck Jamie like a thunderbolt. He remembered the unnatural shadow.

"He's giving the orders this time," Jamie whispered. He swung about and looked through the rear of the cab just as a man with a familiar face emerged from the brush thirty feet away. The shooter pocketed a cell phone, raised his rifle, and opened fire.

Jamie ducked, grabbed Michael by the arm, and yanked him down with enough force to pull his friend's shoulder out of socket. The first bullets shattered the cab's rear window, spraying a shower of glass over them. The shards danced on his and Michael's bare torsos. Sammie flung open the passenger door.

As bullets pinged and ricocheted, Jamie followed Sammie's lead and leapt across the seat, throwing his rifle out the truck ahead of him. He stumbled over the doorstop, raked his shoulder against the open door and fell to the ground, his knee smacking the butt of the rifle. Throbbing pain crippled his every concern, but only until Michael fell on top of him. Jamie rolled over, grabbed his rifle and was prepared to run into the brush, as Sammie instructed.

Sammie maintained a hunched position as she fired the M16 across the truck's cargo bed. The semi-automatic bursts were as disciplined as Jamie witnessed when she brought down a helicopter. He grabbed his AK, ignored his pain, made sure Michael was not shot, and allowed instinct to take over.

44

AS JAMIE EXPECTED, Christian no longer held a position behind his car door. He was on the move, weapon poised. As soon as Jamie pointed the AK, Christian stopped and opened fire. Jamie pulled the trigger, letting loose a couple rounds as the enemy's bullets smacked the door and sizzled past within inches of his head.

Sammie screamed. "Run. Go now."

Michael leaped into the thick collection of myrtle, tall grasses and other scrub; Jamie lowered his weapon and did the same. He plunged forward through the thick, scraggly mess, branches and twigs snapping in his face and scraping against his bare arms and chest. He tripped over a low, knotted branch and fell, his belly lying flush on a thorny vine. He groaned as the thorns held him down. He dropped the rifle, grabbed the vine and yanked. He screamed, the sound of his desperation mild against automatic weapons fire.

Jamie ignored the specks of blood on his stomach, picked up the rifle, and stumbled forward. He jumped, skipped and clambered over nature's obstacles before emerging into a more open area of woods.

Michael peeked out from behind the massive base of an ancient oak. Jamie raced toward him. Seconds later, Sammie raced into the open twenty feet from where Jamie emerged. The instant they saw each other, she waved them on, her lips repeating, "Run, run, run."

They didn't take stock of this latest nightmare or their injuries. Instead, they ran. The land undulated, a series of small hills and steep slopes, the rotten remains of long-ago-fallen trees, a dry streamed and another collection of knotted bramble. Jamie assumed the trio covered almost a mile before Sammie raised her hand and suggested they stop. She told them to climb down a short slope and hunker against the base of a birch tree, its massive, twisting roots exposed by the eroding soil.

Jamie sat beside Michael, both wheezing and covered in perspiration. Sammie breathed hard as well, but Jamie noticed she didn't seem beaten down. When they regained their breath, Michael asked the question on Jamie's mind.

"How did they find us? How?"

"I don't know," Sammie said, reminding Michael to keep his voice to a whisper. "Couldn't have been by GPS. That was something Daddy made especially ..." As soon as she caught Jamie's unblinking eyes, she stopped. "Probably luck. Yeah. The one in the helicopter probably told them where we were before I shot it down. They got lucky. That's all."

"Luck or not, don't matter," Michael said, pumping his chest. "I ain't messing with these dudes again. Hear me?" His rasping voice began to take off. Michael jumped up and grabbed his rifle. "You get our asses out of here. Got that, Supergirl?"

Jamie grabbed Michael and pushed him down before matters worsened. Only once or twice did he ever see his best bud this way, and he recognized an understandable terror in Michael's eyes. He also noticed scrapes and cuts on Michael's chest, no doubt from the bramble.

"Coop. Chill. We'll make it." He handed his rifle to Sammie. "Show me how to use this."

217

Sammie grabbed the weapon and quickly demonstrated the proper firing technique. "It's a good rifle," she said between labored breaths. "These things just saved our lives. The enemy didn't expect us to be locked and loaded. Soon as we started firing, they hesitated. Otherwise, we'd all be lying dead on the side of the road right now."

Sammie pointed to the mottled blood across Jamie's belly, but he insisted the wounds were healing. Sammie clambered up the slope, peered over the top, and saw no movement.

"They can't be far behind. We need to keep moving northwest." She motioned in that general direction. "That should take us to the highway. The woods can't protect us forever."

They moved into deeper woods, tangling with thick undergrowth. Ten minutes later, with no sign of enemy movement, Sammie raised her hand to halt. Jamie and Michael hunkered down on either side of her, again alongside a slope but surrounded by bramble. She demanded no one speak.

They noticed the ubiquitous rhythm of the police helicopter searching the area but focused more on the unmistakable sounds of highway traffic.

"We're close," Michael whispered. "Let's book."

"I don't like this," she said. "It's too perfect. If we take off in a full dash, we'll reach the road in less than a minute. It's right there, and we haven't heard a peep from the enemy."

"Exactly. And I gotta hand it to you, GI Jane, you brought it home for us. Now let's go."

"Those men wouldn't give up, but they would be cautious. If they played it right, they'd know we were heading to the highway. Instead of coming down on us, they'd keep their distance and flank us. With luck, they could get ahead of us and be waiting at the finish line."

Jamie's heart sank. "An ambush?"

"Why not?" She said. "They could take us when we'd least expect."

218

"You gotta be kidding," Michael groaned. "I ain't believing this. I'm supposed to be in first period with Mr. Turner right now. I oughta be joking about them cafeteria ladies having to deal with burgers made from cow shit. But this is ..."

Sammie grimaced in confusion, but Jamie ignored Michael's rant. He felt the shadows racing across the Earth. He heard their footsteps. The Jewel was opening his senses to understanding of what he did not see.

"What do we try now?" He asked Sammie.

"Here's the thing: These Chancellors are all trained soldiers. Even Christian. I trained alongside him for years. None of them are stupid. The police are close by, so if the shooters tip their hand too soon, they could get more trouble than they can handle. They already blew one chance at us, and people can hear rifles from a long way off. We can't even be sure how many soldiers we're facing. They'll be spaced out to cover all the angles."

"But we can't just sit here and wait for them," Jamie said.

"No. We have to draw them in closer to each other. They need a reason to change their strategy. If we do it right, we could open up a flank, slip past them and make the highway."

Jamie saw the AK shaking in Michael's jittery hands. He understood what Sammie was proposing, even if Michael did not.

"You need a diversion, right?" When she nodded, Jamie thought fast. He grabbed Ben's flash drive and handed it to Sammie.

"What?" She stared in disbelief. "What is this?"

"Hope? It was Ben's. I don't know if Ben was just full of it or what, but there might be something on here that can help you if you're able to go back home. You know, to the other Earth."

They spoke with their eyes. He didn't want to hear another word, and Sammie understood. Jamie illuminated Michael.

"You need a diversion, and I'm the only one they want."

Michael tried to interrupt. "Dude, you're tripping."

"It's the only plan that makes sense. Sammie can take you home, but she's gotta be alive. Just do this, all right? Maybe we'll get lucky."

Sammie shook her head as Michael put his feelings into words.

"No freakin' way. We're staying together. Don't matter how this ends – we're the whole damn team right here. We got power." He gripped the AK. "We got Sammie Schwarzenegger at quarterback. We can take down those yahoos and make tracks for home."

"You know something, Coop? I reckon you could sell snow to an Eskimo. But you heard her. Those guys are gonna be spaced out, waiting for us. They'll pick us off before we see them. We have to draw them out."

Jamie begged Michael to go along with this.

"Coop. Bud. I love ya, dude, but this ain't about the team. Maybe this is how it was meant to be." He wiped his tears. "Just do what she says, Coop. Maybe we'll hook up again."

Jamie asked Sammie for help. She pointed west, up the slope.

"Keep low. Use the trees. When you make it to one, find the next before you sprint. Run fast as you can. Their fire should come from your right. The only way they're going to take the bait is ..."

"I know. They got to see me. I can do that."

Jamie didn't know what else to say. The moment he dreaded might have come at last, and he couldn't tell her how he felt. He wouldn't allow his mind to be distracted by anything other than the task ahead. He figured Sammie would appreciate that, like any soldier in the heat of battle. He wiped hair from his face and smiled. Then he grabbed his rifle and started up the slope.

"When the path's clear," Jamie said, "get the hell out of here."

He reached the top of the slope and stood in the clear.

Exogenesis

2 years ago

IGNATIUS HORNE WAS HEADING home to another microwave supper when Ben called. He heard the shakes in Ben's voice, the desperation of a trapped animal facing extinction. Ignatius didn't need details to know the bastard went ahead with his foolhardy plan and it backfired. He agreed to meet at their usual spot off Trevor's Ford Road along the river.

Ben was pulling hard on a silver flask when Ignatius turned off the engine and stepped out of the patrol car.

"So, what's the plan?" Ignatius said. "Get yourself blind drunk, pretend you didn't screw up? Maybe you thought I'd be interested in a pity party."

Ben dropped the flask. "I'm out. What did you bring?"

"I thought I was bringing sensibility and good counsel. Am I too late?"

Ben waved him off and walked to the water's edge. "Don't bother, Iggy. You told me not to do it. I was an asshole. Now I'm a dead man."

Iggy rolled his eyes and removed a small flask from inside his jacket.

"We're all dead men." He offered whiskey, which Ben took with pleasure. "They rejected your theories. You knew they would. Tom and Marlena are hard-core regens. Even if they accepted the possibility of a human soul, they'd never openly concede it. I suggest you calm your nerves, have a long night's sleep, and recant."

Ben choked on the whiskey. "What? How? They'd never believe me."

"They would if you turned over all the digital research. Delete it in front of them. Take a vow of silence. Promise to help Jamie to a peaceful end.

221

Remember your ace in the hole: You are their son. The descendency ends with you, Ben. They won't kill you."

Ben smirked, as if Ignatius missed the punch line. "They already have. The last thing my father said to me was if I ever tried to see Jamie again, he'd kill me where I stood. But he knows I'll see Jamie again because I love him. All I've done the past thirteen years is protect that boy. I gave him my whole heart because I knew Tom and Marlena never would."

He took another sip of whiskey. "Iggy, I was sitting in my car at the end of the street afterward. I couldn't move. I was terrified. I saw my father pull out, so I followed him long enough to see where he was going. Walt Huggins. He wouldn't go there unless he was getting permission. Giving the big guy a head's up about one less observer."

A chill sliced through Ignatius. The pieces fit. He underestimated Tom.

"You might want to consider hitting the road for a few days, Ben. I can set you up with five hundred bucks for now."

Ben was apoplectic. "Run? Are you out of your mind? I'm not leaving Jamie with those people. Iggy, I need you to fix this. You've intervened before, right? There was that dustup with Arthur and Jonathan a few years back. Fix this, Iggy. For good. Please."

Ignatius didn't expect every observer to survive the fifteen-year exile, but he thought trouble would come from outside the Jewel's family.

"Do you understand what you're asking, Ben?"

He threw back more whiskey and nodded. "If I can't help Jamie, what do I got left? He deserves the chance to live a normal life. If there's even a thousand-to-one shot my theory is right, I have to try."

"And if you succeed," Ignatius said, "what then?"

"I don't know, but I can be a father to him if I have to."

Ignatius knew Ben wasn't much good to anyone in this condition. At 21, he was a broken man, a shell of whatever promise he held before leaving the Collectorate. The deputy remembered the boy with a curious smile who crossed the interdimensional fold holding Jamie's hand. The illusion forced upon an eight-year-old was suffocating the 21-year-old. Ignatius deferred to

Tom and Marlena's parental authority, but he resented their willingness to sacrifice Ben.

"Go home," he told Ben. "I'll see it done. We'll talk tomorrow."

"What? What are you going to do?"

He opened the patrol car door.

"Go home, Ben. Sleep. Jamie will need you at your best."

Ignatius made one more stop before crafting a microwave supper. Leftover peas, mac & cheese, baked ham. Third day in a row.

Bland repetition served Ignatius well. Food should be sustenance, not a distraction – a lesson he learned in the Unification Guard. He used meals to contemplate strategy, reconsider errors, and rehearse opening lines for every context. When did he require respect? Fear? Smiles or laughter?

Tonight's context leaned heavily toward precise timing. He decided upon two possibilities and prepared the other logistics.

He wore black gloves, a dark overcoat, and a ski mask when he traveled in the shadows that night. He broke the lock on the Sheridans' back door with ease. The rest was simple. No dog to break the silence, no alarms to alert the residents. He once warned them about their negligent attitude toward security. Typical Chancellor arrogance.

He entered the rear hallway. Three bedrooms. Master at the end. He looked inside Jamie's room to make sure he wasn't home. Dark. The boy was sleeping over at Michael's. He heard TV voices in the master, saw the flickering blue light under the door. Chancellors were creatures of habit.

He pulled off the ski mask and pushed open the door. Tom and Marlena, staring at the screen with many pillows tucked behind them, did not notice him at first. Perhaps they thought Jamie came home early. He flipped on the ceiling light. They sat up but seemed more put-out than terrified.

"You watch these shows every night," Ignatius told them, "but you despise them. A bunch of men telling venal jokes and interviewing vacuous celebrities. Your words, Tom. A celebration of depraved, mindless culture. Your words, Marlena. Yet here you are, after thirteen years. Admit it. You'll miss them when you're gone."

Marlena grabbed the remote and muted the set. "How dare you waltz in here like you have a run of the place?"

Tom jumped in. "Did something happen to Ben?"

Ignatius raised the double-barrel shotgun he'd been dangling.

"That was quick, Tom. I thought Jamie was the make-or-break son. Marlena, toss the remote to the foot of the bed. Thanks. Both of you, settle down. I promise not to drag this out."

Marlena sneered. "Whatever you plan to do, Ignatius, think carefully. The others will know. You will not survive the week."

Ignatius shrugged. "I'll be fine. But my reckoning will come, if it makes you feel better. I'm overdue."

Tom laid back and wrapped his arms over his chest. "I know what this is. You talked to Benjamin, and now you want to terrorize us into forgiving him. I assume he shared his crackpot theories. He will not be a part of Jamie's life, or what's left of it."

Ignatius scratched an inch on his neck where he shaved too close.

"Tomorrow, he'll be Jamie's guardian. It will be tough on them both, of course. Ben will be fighting his guilt and, as you may have noticed of late, a growing fondness for alcohol. Jamie will be devastated. And in his uneven state, I am concerned. The school psychologist diagnosed him with anger management concerns, lack of empathy, possible criminal tendencies. Yes, a difficult time. But I'll be close by, keeping a watch."

"Did you rehearse this intimidation?" Marlena   said. "You are far and away the best actor among us. Enough with the dramatics, Iggy."

He saw indignance in her eyes. She did not believe death was possible. Ignatius realized this wasn't going to be so difficult after all.

"What has always bothered me about Chancellors," he told the Sheridans, "is their abject refusal to accept anything that might work against their narrative. Take Benjamin's theories, for example. He proposes a link between human souls and Caryllan energy. If he's correct, an entirely different life force exists in each of us. He imagines what might happen if we tap into that energy at the point between life and death. What might we become? How might we evolve? Instead of being prisoners to the inevitable, might we find the answer to eternal life? Or to godlike powers beyond our conception? I would think curious minds would jump on these questions and pursue them to their logical end. But not Chancellors. Stubborn, intractable, insecure Chancellors."

Tom grabbed Marlena's hand and they shared a knowing glance. Ignatius saw the sudden rise in genuine fear.

"You're insane," Tom said. "Just like Benjamin. He can't accept Jamie's fate because he got too close to the boy. Now, he's pulling at wild strings."

Ignatius nodded. "True. His emotions are colored by love, but who forced him into that role? I reviewed all his evidence. He has been sharing it for months. His case is compelling. Flawed, but compelling. Enough to give Jamie a third option when the time comes. Ben and I will make sure of it."

Marlena wasn't having it. "The plan for Jamie was set thirteen years ago. We have sacrificed everything for that tiresome child. If he does not emerge as a compliant new entity, then the mission failed. But we will not allow you to change the equation at the last moment."

"It seems to me," Ignatius said, "his brother's plan may be the only viable one left on the table. Clearly, the Mentor has not arrived. Jamie would be at peace if he'd been receiving guidance from within. Instead, he is breaking down. He carries an anger he does not understand; he isolates himself from all but two friends. I have kept him out of jail. He is walking a needle, and the two of you have been no help at all."

Tom raged. "You have no children, Ignatius. No understanding of our struggle let alone the science of assimilating human DNA with Jewel energy. You came onto this mission late for reasons none of us understood. And now, you have the audacity to suggest ..."

Ignatius reached for the remote and turned up the volume.

"Correction. I do have children, but they live among the indigos. They'll never know me. As for the Jewel? I spent a year in Special Services Division before joining this team. I know exactly what Jewel energy can do. Probably more than you. I spent time with a retired general, Aldo Cabrise. He was there at the fall of Hiebimini, when everything came undone for the Chancellory. He saw it happen. Most of the vids from that day were scrambled afterward or redistributed by our propagandists. The reports were rewritten, the true data stowed behind Admiralty firewalls.

"Five Jewels acted as one that day. They remade an entire planet. If I didn't know better, I might have called it an Act of God. Half of us in Special Services saw the Jewels as the key to salvation, and the other half as the key to damnation. There's a reason why a blockade was instituted around Hiebimini after the last natives were evacuated.

"Regens like you believe the hybrids will form an army and reproduce new, sustainable Chancellors. What if there's a greater destiny at play? What if Ben tapped into a secret even our best researchers missed? When we eliminated deity worship, we eliminated articles of faith. Ben rediscovered that faith in the people of this Earth. He wants to believe in Jamie, and I intend to give him that chance."

Tom threw back the covers. "I have damn well had enough of this. Put your rifle away and go home. Walt Huggins and I ..."

"Had an arrangement. Yes." Ignatius cocked the hammer. "Until I spent time with him this evening. He agreed with my assessment. Anyone willing to murder a son who poses no immediate threat to the mission is, by extension, a clear and present danger to the larger group. He asked only that I plan carefully, make this clean, and ensure a speedy arrest based on damning evidence. The man who will be charged is a felon, recently released from prison, with a long history of break-ins, always using a weapon just like this."

Ignatius raised the volume to maximum. Tom held out his hands. Ignatius thought he might fall to the floor and supplicate himself. It would have been the one unpredictable moment. Instead, Tom begged:

"I made the decision. Not Marlena. She didn't know about the ..."

Ignatius rolled his eyes. "Of course, she did."

He pulled the trigger. Tom's chest exploded as he crashed into the night table and toppled a lamp. Marlena screamed, more emotion than Ignatius expected. He didn't give her time to beg. When it was over, half her face was gone, the pillows coated in blood and brain matter.

He wasn't sorry to see them go. The next steps were critical. He brought along physical evidence and needed to work quickly. The miserable sod who'd be arrested made the misstep of settling down in Albion months ago. He reported to Ignatius between visits to his parole officer. Hair samples, fingerprints, shoeprints. A job mowing lawns in this neighborhood. Ignatius emptied the Sheridans' safe.

He hurried. Ignatius needed this to become a crime scene before dawn, long before Jamie might return home. The murders would crush the boy's spirit, but if he saw the bodies ...

No, Ignatius told himself. *I won't do that to you. Trust me, Jamie. This will work out in the end. This was the hard choice but the right one – for all of us. Hard choices change history. You will move past this, Jamie. If your brother is right, you will become something greater than any Chancellor ever thought possible.*

PART THREE
BEYOND THE EDGE

Son,

These must be our final words to you. If you are listening, then you are minutes away from the end of your life. We know how confusing these recent events must be for your young and undeveloped mind.

We believe each human being is born into this universe with a unique purpose built into his genes. The struggle of each man and woman is to uncover this biological purpose and strive with all his might to fulfill it before he dies. In this sense, you have lived a brief but successful life. Through your death, the fates of millions to come will be ensured for centuries. Few humans have been granted such a remarkable gift.

However, we believe you have been denied one essential opportunity: The chance to know the very world into which you were born, and the one your actions will help to create. We have embedded a visual tour of Earth and her colonies inside the Mentor's program. She will play it for you as you go to your rest. The last images you see before you die will be of the three of us on the day you were born.

With Fondest Regards,
Mother
Father

45

J AMIE HELD THE AK-47 ahead of his body the way Sammie showed him, his finger poised against the trigger. He felt naked and alone, but he refused to die without meaning. He was going to give his friends enough time to escape. He realized a bullet could shatter his skull in less than the blink of an eye, but the thought didn't terrify him. If death came, he wanted it to be swift and merciless.

He did as Sammie advised and raced to the fattest tree he saw, steadying himself with deep, measured breaths. If the enemy was close by, they come from the north, so Jamie knew focused on a path west. Morning light struggled to cut through the canopy, and the spaces between the trees seemed dark and foreboding. All he could imagine to do was run.

And then, the Earth tilted.

The sunlight disappeared altogether, but the forest floor of thickly-packed leaves and fallen, rotting branches glowed. He viewed the forest as through a fisheye, seeing only the carpet on which he must run, with all else dissolved into darkness. Some fallen leaves fluttered in a breeze that did not exist. Jamie sensed himself losing touch with reality, fading into a realm where he was no longer in charge.

He tightened his grip on the weapon, which no longer felt awkward in his hands, and sprinted. He did not hear the leaves crunching beneath him, and he barely felt the low twigs that snapped against his bare chest as he plowed deep into the forest all but blind. When he reached a slope that would carry him south toward the hunting road and further into the grip of hopelessness, he heard footsteps close behind.

The first machine-gun blasts zinged over his head, one bullet ricocheting off a pine tree dead ahead. The terrain became rugged, with deep gashes in the earth caused by runoff and a pair of fallen trees slowing his escape. He leaped across the second, moss-blanketed tree, ducked down just as additional shots were fired, and rolled up behind the giant log. Only then did he sense blood and realized a bullet grazed him.

The crunching of leaves underfoot exposed his pursuers' positions. Jamie heard them splitting up, coming around to attack him from either side. Jamie looked over his shoulder to what should have been his path of escape. The darkness brought the forest in upon him, as if confining him in a closet. Yet Jamie saw a possibility, perhaps no more than thirty feet away. The land stopped there, falling. His ears honed in on a trickle of water beyond the ledge.

The contours of the rifle felt natural and inviting against his grip, a familiar energy sweeping his blood as if he grew another appendage. He recalled the power that enabled him to pull the trigger twice before. He reached into the hidden place in his heart that used to tempt him toward things he knew were wrong – the place he usually resisted, keeping him from becoming everything he despised. This time he surrendered.

Out of the shadows, Jamie saw a fog rising, the vague and lazy haze coalescing into clear, discernible figures. In his mind's eye, he saw numbers, letters, fractions and functions. They vanished in an instant, but he knew what they were. They were beautiful, and they were terrifying. Even if he didn't understand the vast algorithms of the Jewel, Jamie knew what they equaled. The Jewel was alive and defending itself.

Jamie jumped to his feet, swung about in fury, and raised the weapon. He used only his ears. He heard the snap of a single twig.

He held the weapon steady as he fired, the report a series of gentle pops, as if muffled by a brain that didn't want to know any more. Jamie heard the zing of another bullet slip past his right ear. In that instant, the sunlight returned, cutting through the trees and removing the abyss. The glow of the forest floor disappeared. Although the fury would not allow him to lower the rifle, Jamie saw what he did.

A strapping man with a receding hairline and a stare of utter bewilderment dropped his weapon as he stumbled backward against a tree. Reginald Fortis's chest was shredded with bullet holes, and the man's body crumpled pitifully on its side.

Salty sweat dribbled from Jamie's forehead, but he made no effort to wipe it away while studying the body with neither amazement nor remorse. He met Reginald once; the local writer had given a shockingly dull lecture one day in Agatha Bidwell's English class.

He heard the footsteps of the other pursuer and ran for the ledge. Bullets smacked the ground at his feet, and Jamie turned and fired, spraying bullets in his attacker's general direction. He figured it out: make the enemy believe Jamie was in the trench, following the stream toward the lake.

Jamie saw himself as a boy fighting for his life but also a dark, despicable monster who surrendered to a power he would never comprehend. As his fury boiled, his instincts muddied. He didn't notice the birch root growing above ground.

Jamie stumbled and fell end-over-end, the rifle catching in a low cedar while the rest of him rolled over the ledge and fell ten feet, landing on his back in wet sand. He lost his breath for an instant, but pushed himself up when he heard the pursuing footsteps. He looked around for the AK; but when he didn't see it, he grabbed the .45 tucked in his pants. His wet hands fumbled with the pistol, and he struggled in the soft sand to find his footing. Oblivious to the throbbing pain in his back, Jamie tried to decide which way to run.

Lester Bowman, a man who ran a bed-and-breakfast and who Jamie recognized from several visits to Rand Paulus's grocery, emerged at the top of the ledge, pushing aside bramble and revealing an M16. Jamie neither moved a muscle nor blinked an eye. He saw only an end that wasn't fair, a fate no boy should ever have to suffer. His brain told him to raise the pistol, fire and hope. Jamie wasn't sure whether his muscles followed suit. What he did know was that another figure appeared in the same instant, only this time on the opposite side of the stream.

"Drop it," someone yelled. "Drop it now."

Jamie turned. The police officer was not talking to him. Rather, the man aimed his rifle across the stream to the opposite ledge. He yelled to Lester a third time. Just when Jamie thought he might be about to survive, he heard a weapon cock. He faced Lester, who appeared to be smiling as he aimed toward Jamie and pulled the trigger. The first two bullets landed at Jamie's feet, the third splintered driftwood behind him, and the fourth ...

A pair of violent thunderbolts exploded across the stream. A hole opened in Lester's neck, and blood sprayed. The second shot caught Lester above his right eye, and the body fell over the ledge, the M16 resting at its side. The officer altered his aim.

"Drop it," the officer said. "Let it go, young man."

Jamie raised the pistol to fire, its barrel still aimed at the spot where Lester once stood. *It's over*, Jamie told himself. *Let go.*

He couldn't. A sliver of the fury that kept him alive refused to go away. The snake slithered beneath his skin and encouraged him to find another target and finish what he started. Jamie tried to resist, his right arm firm but his trigger hand trembling.

"Come on, son. Put down the weapon. Don't make me do this."

Jamie wasn't ready to let go. His breaths were deep and rapid; he saw blood everywhere. He wondered whether Michael and Sammie escaped the forest alive. Jamie wanted to surrender, but not to this officer. He simply wanted everything to be over. He knew that whatever drove him to kill would only grow more powerful in the scant time left. The Jewel did not want him to die yet.

He didn't have to fire the pistol, only turn and aim. The officer would take it from there.

Jamie wondered whether he would feel pain. If the bullet killed him at once, would he see a flash of light? Would he wake up on the other side, like all the church-going folks around these parts believed? Was Ben right? Maybe, Jamie reasoned, this wouldn't be so bad. At least he wouldn't be around for the gruesome end the Chancellors planned for him.

He spoke to no one in particular. "Why did they do this to me?"

He twitched, his left foot starting to turn, his ears deaf to the officer's warnings. And then, with no understanding of why, Jamie dropped the pistol into the stream. Through his tears, he looked up and saw two officers.

"Step back, get down on your knees, and place your hands behind your head," the first officer said. "Do it. Now."

Jamie obliged. He didn't care anymore.

46

RAPID POPS SHATTERED the still morning as Michael and Sammie fled. Michael imagined his best friend lying in a bloody heap, decorated in bullet holes and eyes staring at the sky. Sammie, on the other hand, brightened her smile as a second volley echoed through the woods.

"That's him," she whispered. "He's still alive. He's fighting. He'll make it, just like us."

Michael followed Sammie in a crouch. They headed due north, parallel to a highway so close he could almost see it through the brush. They ran no more than twenty yards at a time before Sammie raised a hand, and they ducked behind bramble, a log, whatever was convenient.

A third volley – this time a mix of automatic fire and two distinctive shotgun blasts – whipped through the forest. Michael's heart cringed.

"Why the hell did you let him go? He's gonna die out there."

Sammie swallowed. "Jamie wants you to get home safe, Coop. Nothing else mattered to him. You heard him."

"That don't mean ..."

"Look, he's fast, Coop. Real fast. He's a runner."

Sammie picked her next destination and waved him forward. The bramble to their immediate north was too thick, so she led him west toward the highway. His confidence grew, assuming they were making a beeline to safety. Then, thirty seconds into their sprint, Sammie waved him to the ground. They both lay flat on their bellies as Sammie pointed through a narrow gap between trees.

Michael saw a familiar face in camouflage pants, a black t-shirt and a cigarette dangling from his lips. Christian Bidwell's back was turned. Michael needed a few seconds before he saw Christian's rifle extended in an aggressive posture. Michael turned to Sammie, who was studying her fingers, counting off as she moved her lips. She spoke, but in a whisper so faint Michael heard part of her message.

"They kept him back in case we used a decoy. Be ready."

"For what?"

Sammie took aim. Michael stopped breathing.

As her trigger finger started backward, Michael grabbed his own weapon and prepared to aim. However, Christian took off in a dead run, and Samantha pulled back.

"Whoa," Michael whispered. "What are you doing? Waste him. That dude shoved a gun down my throat. Waste him."

"No. We have to be smart. He's not a threat. It's time to go."

Michael heard his pounding heart and panicked breaths as they sprinted to the highway. When at last he saw a speed limit sign, Michael allowed a smile. He did not think anything about racing out of the forest and onto the road, rifle in hand as he waved for help. He was a body length away from doing just that when Sammie threw him to the ground.

"Oh, c'mon," he spouted. "What'd you do that for?"

She told him to be quiet and pointed to the south, just beyond the tree line bordering the highway. Michael's heart leaped. He saw a pair of patrol cars, a white van and a black helicopter more than a hundred yards away crowding the highway. At least three officers and two others, one of whom wore a blue jacket with the gold letters FBI, milled together.

Sammie nodded. "A roadblock. I knew there were police close by, but I didn't think …" Her eyes softened as a giant smile formed.

"Oh," she whispered. "Oh, god. Jamie."

Michael moved forward a few feet and got a better look. Two policemen emerged from the woods with a tall boy whose long white hair and shirtless profile were recognizable.

Michael whispered, "Yeah, dude. That's what I'm talking about."

Then he rose to his feet and started out into the open. Sammie grabbed him from behind and yanked him down.

"Just hold on, Coop. Look again. They've got Jamie in handcuffs."

Michael didn't care. Jamie was alive, and that was good enough for him. He told Sammie as much, but her giant smile disappeared.

"We've got a problem, Coop," she said. "A big problem. Listen to me very carefully."

47

AGATHA WONDERED WHAT might be her greater humiliation: That she was an inept tactician; that her stubborn pride cost the lives of at least ten people who also called themselves Chancellors; or that her grand and glorious mission to provide moral justice was reduced to being stuck in traffic on a rural highway.

She fidgeted in the back seat of the Camaro, a pistol equipped with suppressor in her hands, and she wondered whether this roadblock was the final straw of the biggest failure of her life. One hour earlier, she sat in this same spot and laid out plans to hunt down and kill the Jewel. Since then, she botched negotiations for Jamie's surrender and failed to give three well-trained soldiers sufficient advantage over their target.

Only Christian's safe return — a narrow dodge of the officers closing in — proved to be the sole bright spot. His report on Jamie's capture, however, sent her reeling.

Now, as she and two of her three remaining soldiers found themselves trapped on the highway between a tractor-trailer and a school bus packed with children, Agatha knew she was the king of fools, a shell of the woman who once led battalions into combat.

"Walter anticipated everything," she told Arthur. "He even knew he was going to die, and he did nothing to disrupt the outcome. All but guaranteed it, I suspect."

"So it's hopeless?" Christian asked. "I don't believe that, Mom. Sheridan is out there. Hell, we know where he is. The police have him. Won't be hard tracking him down. Might have to take out a few badges to get to him, but we're Chancellors. We don't ..."

"Surrender? No, son. We don't. But if we keep going, if we try again ..." She paused. "Either way, all this ends in an hour and a half. We cannot just kill the Jewel with bullets. We must burn the host body to be certain. We would not likely have time or opportunity to escape. Do you understand the implication?"

"Look, Mom. I've always wanted the chance to go back home. I don't remember much about it; Father was always off-planet on duty. I'd love to see him again. But fact is, I just want to be wherever you are. I know I haven't always been the most respectful son." He nodded with confidence. "I'm prepared for whatever happens."

Agatha felt more than pride. She sensed genuine love.

Turning to Arthur, who was driving, she asked, "And you?"

"The cause is no less just than it ever was, Agatha. There are still four of us, counting Jennifer. Austin Springs is the closest town. That's where they'll take him. We'll have to be fast and lucky, but it can be done. We still have not seen any sign of Shock Units coming through the fold, a point in our favor. I recommend we turn around, get out of this traffic jam and head north, the long way around the lake. We'll still have means and opportunity. Into the fire, Agatha."

Christian pumped a fist. "That's the spirit. Into the fire. What do you say, Mom?"

A new spirit of hope rose inside the car, but Agatha could not get past the humiliation of it all. She felt old and tired. The notion of returning to the Collectorate no longer appealed to her.

Fate provided a different path.

"There's only one course for us," she said. "Into the fire."

48

JAMIE NEVER SAID a word – not as he was cuffed, not as the officers rushed him from the woods, not as they hauled him into the back of a white van in the middle of Highway 39 and interrogated him. Jamie heard their questions, which straddled the line between sincere concern for a boy whom they wanted to help and suspicion of a young man whom they almost shot. They asked him whether he was thirsty; a deputy offered him bottled water, but Jamie refused even though his throat felt like sandpaper.

He saw no reason to fight on. As the deputies dragged him through the woods, he heard additional shots from the north, where he left Sammie and Michael. Once they were free of the woods, a deputy turned up his shoulder-harnessed radio, and Jamie heard another officer report finding a body. Moments later, as he sat in the van listening to questions he refused to answer, Jamie heard another voice report on discovering two more bodies.

He was lost in a haze, staring at the van's floor, when someone new sat beside him. All Jamie saw were a woman's feet, covered with low black shoes and hose. She spoke in hushed tones.

"Here's where we stand, young man," she said. "Many people have died this morning for no apparent reason. So far, all those who might know anything have been shot to death or blown to pieces. Now along you come, running through the woods, playing cowboys-and-Indians. Only problem is, the other guy has an M16 and you're packing a .45. Tough odds, huh?"

The woman grabbed him by the chin and turned Jamie until they made eye contact. Her dark, searching eyes pierced Jamie, so he looked away.

"You are either a victim, or you are involved in this madness. But you're alive, and that makes you valuable. I am Special Agent Janice Bronson, director of the Federal Bureau of Investigation in Birmingham. I don't trust teens and I have no patience for the silent treatment. I'm no shrink, and I will not mother you because you're a minor. Nor am I currently considering your constitutional rights. My thoughts are for the people whose families are grieving today."

She let go of his chin. Jamie stared at the floor. Her heard the same cold, wicked arrogance in her as he did in Agatha Bidwell.

"If you are a victim, I'll apologize. If you are connected, don't seek mercy. I'm sold out."

She stood in the open doorway. From the corner of his eye, Jamie saw her waving for someone else. Then she faced Jamie.

"Innocent men rarely help their case by keeping quiet. You're thirsty. Drink the water the next time it's offered. Then answer our questions. If you think you're in a bad place now ..."

Jamie shifted his hands inside the cuffs behind his back and blew hair from the corner of his mouth. He looked her in the eyes.

"You won't believe me," he said.

"Ah. The ability to communicate. Young man, you might be amazed by what I'll believe. But everything starts with a name. I don't have yours."

Jamie shriveled inside. "It doesn't matter anymore."

"You're somebody's kid. They'll be glad to know you're OK."

"There's nobody left."

She grabbed his chin again and lifted until their eyes met.

"Suspects usually say those words right before they tell us where the bodies are buried. Do you have something you'd like to tell me?"

He jerked away and stared at the floor.

"Hmm," she mumbled. "Truth is your only option. We'll scour those woods and piece together every footstep that's taken place this morning. If you're guilty, there's no escape. But if you're innocent, we can help. What you need to do is come clean." Her cell phone rang. She studied the screen and sighed. "I'm going to send Agent Hedgecock back in. I expect you to answer each of his questions fully."

She jumped from the van and placed the phone to her ear. Before she walked out of range, Jamie heard her say, "Yes, sir. We're making a full threat assessment. We haven't ..."

Quickly, the agent's voice drowned among the organized chaos on Highway 39. Jamie couldn't make sense of what he saw: the police officers with rifles heading into and out of the woods, others speaking into radios attached to their shoulders, and patrol cars joining the fray, turning the road into a parking lot. The county police helicopter that never seemed to be far away – passing them on Lake Vernon at dawn and later surveying the forest above them – swooped overhead, muting everything in its roar.

Jamie couldn't grasp the idea that so many people were involved, focused on a trail of blood and death for which he was responsible. The people he'd known forever – his classmates, track teammates, even those who shared his sorry excuse of an apartment building – faded into a mist, as if the ghosts of a phony, distant reality.

"You mustn't be discouraged." A motherly voice whispered. "The program is pushing aside all the old distractions that no longer matter. My dear sweet boy, it is preparing you for the end."

Jamie focused on the here-and-now; Lydia the Mentor sat on the bench beside him. She crossed her legs and dropped her tiny hands into her lap as she offered Jamie the same piteous smile he first saw in the woods next to the Alamander River. Jamie wanted to lash out, but he knew better.

"Why?"

Lydia rolled her eyes, as if playing games with a small child.

"We have been through all that. I told you I'd return, but I did not anticipate speaking to you this soon." Her smile disappeared. "You are in an untenable position, I'm afraid."

"A what?"

"You cannot remain in this condition," she said, pointing to the handcuffs. "You must and will escape. When help arrives – and it will – you must not allow anyone between you and those who would watch over you until the end. The results would be catastrophic."

"Why?"

Lydia vanished, leaving Jamie cold. Other voices closed in, their words clearer now that the helicopter was nowhere near. He recognized Agent Hedgecock, who got nowhere earlier when the agent took the caring, big-brother approach during his first set of questions. He heard other voices, at first from officers. Then others, much younger and speaking in desperate tones, followed alongside. Only when he heard a familiar voice say, "Dude," did Jamie's heart return from a cold, empty place.

Michael and Sammie stood at the rear of the van with Hedgecock and two patrolmen. Their jaws hung as low as his own.

"Oh my God," Sammie said through tears. "You're really alive."

Michael shook his head amazed. Sammie asked Hedgecock for permission to climb in, but Michael didn't wait to jump up. Jamie leaped from the bench and found himself in a bear hug.

"J," Michael said, shouting. "We figured you were a goner." Then he whispered. "Play along. Play along. Sammie's got a plan."

Jamie didn't have a chance to wrap himself around Michael's cockeyed instructions, especially when Sammie joined the reunion.

"I don't get it," he said. "I heard the guns and I thought …"

Sammie pushed Michael aside to embrace Jamie. Her hug included a giant kiss on his left cheek, above where a bullet grazed him earlier but no sign of injury remained. He stared into her bold, gleaming eyes and drew warmth from a pearlescent smile that would've lit up any room. He also couldn't get in a word edgewise.

"We're OK, John. We're all OK now. I'm sorry we got separated back there. We tried to keep up, but you were running so fast, and those men were shooting at us."

Sammie nodded as she spoke. Jamie saw something new in her eyes, a deception he needed to accept. She winked then turned to the officers.

"My cousin's a good runner. Too good. Isn't that right, John?"

Jamie nodded, swinging his disbelieving eyes between his closest friends. His ecstasy was not so overwhelming that he didn't understand they were playing this game for a reason. For now, he didn't care. They were alive. There was still somebody left.

49

AGENT HEDGECOCK CLIMBED aboard and came between the reunited.

"Your name is John Huggins?" The agent asked. Jamie nodded. "You could've made this easier if you'd told us sooner. Your cousin and friend have given us quite a story. We're going to need to confirm some ..."

Sammie jumped in. "We told them everything, John. They know what happened. Those men who killed Daddy and tried to kill us."

"Miss Huggins, if you'd please, I need to ..."

Sammie wouldn't stop, nor would she let go of Jamie.

"You don't understand. John needs me to be here. He's very fragile, like I told you. He won't say much unless I'm here. He's always been like that. Isn't that right, John? I help you when it's hard to figure things out."

Jamie recognized the pity in her eyes. He'd seen it around Albion, the way people half-stared at a man with the intelligence of a child. Sammie wanted him to pretend he was slow.

"I guess so," he told her before glancing at Michael, who wouldn't look him in the eyes.

"John's a really good athlete," she told the officers, "but he's always had other problems. The whole reason we were out camping was because John likes it so much. Daddy thought it would be good for him." Her softness turned to snippiness. "Why is he in handcuffs? John didn't do anything wrong. He was just scared."

Jamie felt as if he was 7 years old, and Sammie was his mother.

"Your cousin was armed when we found him and initially resisted our demand to lower his weapon. He's in custody until ..."

"Oh, my God," she said as if exasperated. "The gun? I can explain that. When we were attacked, a man shot Daddy, but my Daddy had a rifle and fired back and killed the man. I don't even know what that person wanted or why." She choked up, her eyes watering. "Daddy was still alive, and we went to him. I was going to call for help, but John grabbed the other man's gun and ran off. That's when we chased after him, like I told you before, and lost him in the woods. Next thing we knew, these other men with machine guns ..."

Agent Hedgecock raised both hands. "Timeout. Look, all three of you are in shock, you're probably hungry, and we need to contact your relatives." Hedgecock paused. "You boys could use shirts, and we have questions that need answering. There's much more going on here than probably any of you realize."

"OK, I understand," Sammie said. "I'm sure John can answer all your questions, but could you please give us, like, two minutes alone? He'll help you better if I talk to him first."

Hedgecock sighed but nodded the other officers out of the van.

"Two minutes. No more. Oh, and Miss Huggins ... Samantha ... we need you or Mr. Cooper to provide directions to your campsite."

Michael snapped back. "I was just along for the ride. I got no sense of direction. Runs in the family, if you get my speed."

Sammie nodded. "As soon as we're done, I promise."

When the van cleared of everyone but his last two friends, Jamie didn't know where to begin. Instead, Michael did the heavy lifting.

"Dude. You're my hero. What you did in the woods ... beyond unreal." He offered Jamie another, briefer hug and darted his eyes between Jamie and Sammie. "I used to figure I was the stud in this outfit, but you two are the bomb. Got more guts and brains than me." Michael paused. "Here's the score, dude. When we saw you being hauled in by the cops, Sammie came up with a plan. Pretty sweet if we can pull it off."

Michael turned over the rest of the story to Sammie. She described hiding their rifles in the brush and racing from the woods, asking whether anyone had seen her tall, blond cousin. She told Jamie why they needed to act as harmless and emotionally distraught as possible to avoid suspicion flying their way. She apologized for giving Jamie a new name and creating a story in which Ben became the attacker who killed her father.

"It was the only strategy that seemed to fit," she whispered. "Our parents created your second identity in case of emergency. Jamie, they can't be told who you really are. They have to believe we were caught in the middle. Just three kids. They won't think we've been running around the woods with machine guns killing people."

"Maybe not you," Michael smirked as he pointed to his skin.

"This is the FBI," Jamie said, remembering Agent Bronson's words of warning. "They'll figure out something isn't right."

"I'm trying to buy us some time," Sammie said. "They're taking us to Austin Springs. We need to get you out of handcuffs ASAP."

Sammie hugged him again, and Michael added a simple, "Amen." Yet Jamie wasn't so sure Sammie's plan was going to work, especially when he felt a familiar, foreboding presence. Jamie looked over Sammie's shoulder to the bench where he was sitting.

Lydia the Mentor didn't volunteer a word through her frown.

50

8:40 a.m.

E UPHORIA FILLED THE red Camaro less than ten minutes after Arthur Tynes reversed course and drove the Chancellors toward Austin Springs. The news came faster than they predicted: Jennifer Bowman, who was trolling through town since shortly after 7 a.m., saw the Jewel arrive in a van at the tiny police department.

That their target would be trapped inside a small, fixed location seemed too good to be true, as if the universe were dangling a new temptation in front of them.

Agatha smiled along with Christian and Arthur. She wanted to give them hope, even though her sense of being overwhelmed by the sheer force of history was growing. She needed this singular victory; she earned it through fifteen years of sacrifice away from the prestige she once knew among the Chancellory. Yet she could not escape a feeling of doom.

The sensation grew to a palpable level when, not five minutes after the news about the Jewel, did Walter's threat come to life. Agatha kept the live feed from the interdimensional fold on her phone. She was discussing a strategy for the attack when she noticed movement at the fold.

Invisible space shifted, a crack opening in an otherwise obscure location in the deep forest more than a mile from the nearest living soul. Two dark, mechanical shapes shifted into life for just an instant, and the feed dissolved into static. Seconds later, the feed cleared, and the mechanical shapes vanished.

Agatha closed her phone. She knew what was coming.

The Shock Units long produced unimaginable fear in any man unlucky enough to face the Guard's most terrifying combat machine. The machines were known to be invisible until the instant before powering their weapons. And then, so the stories went, they made themselves visible as they discharged their weapon. Each machine was powered by a human operating as the CPU, but these were specially-bred humans whose purpose rarely extended beyond blind obedience to orders and a desire to destroy all targets with impunity.

She knew the Shock Units would hone in on the Jewel's unique signature and plot the most efficient course to their destination. They would stampede across the land – invisible, relentless, merciless. Assuming the reports were true about their ground speed, Agatha decided she had no more than an hour to finish her mission. Once these machines got between the Jewel and all enemies, Jamie Sheridan could not be touched.

She did not tell Christian and Arthur of the machines' impending arrival. Rather, she cursed Walter, who betrayed all the observers and must have arranged for Shock Units before he left the Collectorate behind.

They arrived in Austin Springs precisely at 9 a.m., rendezvousing at the entrance to a town park only a hundred yards from the rear of the police station. Agatha needed one look at the small, white structure to know their final assault would be a striking success.

Jennifer scouted the station front and back, making note of three entrances – one front, two rear, one side. The lack of law enforcement vehicles suggested they would not face heavy resistance. They clustered about the Camaro hiding their weapons. A few locals walking their dogs paid them scant notice.

"The Jewel is nearing the end of its re-sequencing," Agatha said. "Once we secure the building, we should split into teams and acquire incendiary devices."

Both legs ached. She knew every step from now to her death would be agony, but Agatha steeled her eyes, refusing to show weakness. She pushed the Shock Units out of her mind.

"You sacrificed your lives and your homes for fifteen years," she said. "Now we must be honest. Whether or not we succeed, our last realistic chance of going home may have passed. However, millions will herald us as heroes, even though they may not know our names. I will ponder that concept with my final breath."

Their shoulders stiffened, their eyes brightened, and they nodded with determination. A black SUV pulled into the park and stopped in the lot several slips away.

"Let's finish this," Christian said, his eyes drifting to the SUV.

As they gathered their weapons and Arthur went over the assignments once more, Christian turned away from the group, his pistol with suppressor behind his back. He moved toward the SUV with the swagger of the most popular stud in school. A man in his early twenties, sporting a t-shirt, shorts and red headband, hopped out of the vehicle, a basketball in one hand and keys in the other.

Christian smiled. "Sweet ride. How much this set you back?"

The man with the basketball retreated a step, stumbling over his words. With a half-smile, he said, "Enough. Why?"

"No reason, man."

Christian glanced over his shoulder to his mother and winked. Then he revealed his weapon and said, "Let's finish this."

51

8:47 a.m.
Austin Springs Police Department

J AMIE WATCHED WITH disinterest as a deputy closed the tiny conference room's one door. Two seconds later, he heard jangling keys and a turning lock. He was alone, kept company by a bottle of water and a painting of a mallard – the room's only decoration. He sat in a wooden chair at the head of a nondescript oak table for six. He wore a white t-shirt with the letters ASPD emblazoned across the chest.

As he waited in silence for the next shoe to drop, Jamie turned toward the generic portrait of a mallard. He latched onto the bird's unblinking, searching eye surrounded by a field of green, and Jamie felt a trickle of nostalgia.

The memory of Ben emerged from a sea muddied by the Jewel, which was reshaping his brain, synapse by synapse. He remembered Ben at 17, his brother's eyes wide and alert without the drowning influence of alcohol. He saw a boy no older than himself, likewise trapped between the innocence of youth and the overwhelming fear of what burdens life had in store. He felt Ben's arm wrapped around his 11-year-old shoulder as they sat on the shore at Alamander River. He remembered gentle, teaching words.

"Some people will tell you what you can't be," Ben said. "It's their job to try to keep you from your dreams. Sometimes, Jamie, they might be the people you trust. They're the worst. They'll say they're protecting you, but that's not close to the truth. You listen now, Jamie: Every road you take is your own. It doesn't matter where you came from or whoever says you owe them something. You take that road, and you own it. Hear me?"

Jamie wiped away a tear as he turned from the portrait.

"He was trying to warn me, even back then."

"Possibly," Lydia said from the opposite end of the table, her fingers knocking wood.

He glared. "I want the truth. Was Ben right? Is the human soul made of the same energy as the Jewel?"

Lydia smirked. "I must confess his theories did intrigue me. I cannot rule out the possibility of a connection, however remote. But you must understand, my dearest boy: Even if the Jewel were nothing more than a weaponized version of the same raw energy that comprises the human soul, you cannot stop the re-sequencing. It is, as they say, a moot point."

"Why?" He asked Lydia. "I've already done the impossible once today. How do you know it can't happen again?"

"Because the Jewel will never allow an intrusion into its matrix. It was designed with a fully impregnable – and, I must add, aggressive – self-preservation program. Do you believe you alone killed Walter Huggins and Reginald Fortis? Or did you receive help?"

"I'm in charge," he whispered. "I'm in charge. You hear me, Lydia? I'm still a human being, and I can make my own decisions."

She vanished without replying.

Jamie heard dangling keys. Seconds later, FBI Agent Hedgecock entered, telling a young deputy to wait outside. "Give me five." The agent nodded to Jamie and placed a laptop on the table. He swiveled it about until Jamie could see the screen.

"First, John, I want to tell you we're sorry for everything," Hedgecock said. "We treated you unfairly after your arrest. You must understand we were in the middle of a difficult and violent situation. We couldn't be certain whom to trust."

Jamie saw an electronic file with a variety of information – including a photo – of someone named John Huggins. That someone was Jamie. Sammie did not explain how far his "second identity" went. He wondered whether she would have preferred that name over his third identity – his birth name, James Bouchet.

"It's a good thing your cousin Samantha came along when she did," Hedgecock said. "I wanted to show you this, so you know we trust you. It's your case file from the Department of Children's Affairs. Do you remember Leslie Bowden, your case officer?"

Jamie brushed aside his confusion and tried to respond to the question with the same slow, indecisive confusion he mastered in the van under Sammie's watchful eye. He shrugged.

"Why am I in here, sir? You said you trust me now."

"Yes, John, we do. But we still have more questions." Hedgecock took a seat and asked 'John' to do the same, but Jamie refused. "I realize the past few hours have been difficult for you, but we think you might be able to help us in our investigation. Your aunt and uncle were very kind in caring for you all these years. I'm sure this is difficult to take in."

Jamie never heard the Hugginses referred to that way.

He shrugged. "Can I see Sammie now?"

"John, we have questions about your aunt and uncle's activities."

Jamie didn't like the way this was going. "I don't wanna talk about them. I wanna go."

"You and Samantha have no other adult relations, as far we can tell. Since you are minors, you'll have to go with DCA until they can find a suitable new home. First, I need to clear up some confusion we're having."

Jamie felt a familiar, icy tug. Lydia whispered into his ear.

"This has to end, my sweet boy."

He tried to ignore her, focusing instead on Hedgecock.

"The sheriff in Albion is investigating the fire that burned down your home last night. He claims to know the Hugginses, but he isn't familiar with a young cousin living in their home. We're sending him your case file now. Perhaps your photo will jog his memory. Can you explain why he didn't know you? Albion is a very small town, John."

A wave of panic rolled over Jamie. Apparently, the Chancellors couldn't plan for *every* contingency. He grabbed the edge of the table and rubbed his hands against the thick, dark wood. He looked for clues in the agent's eyes, but Hedgecock seemed neither threatening nor friendly – the poker face Jamie never mastered.

"This is a trap," Lydia whispered. "I have observed humans for too long. This man is after something. If you give him the wrong answer, he will never let you go."

"Shut up," Jamie blurted. The agent was taken aback.

"John, please. I'm not your enemy. Samantha already told us you stayed indoors most of the time because your aunt was concerned you might hurt yourself outside. Is that why the sheriff doesn't remember you?"

"Sure. I reckon. Can I see Sammie now? Please?"

Jamie tightened, the impatience heating his blood. Lydia stood behind Agent Hedgecock, her arms crossed over her chest and lips turned down. Hedgecock again asked 'John' to sit, but Jamie refused. He wanted to dash for the door even though he knew it was locked. He tried not to look at Lydia, and he refused to believe the Jewel was controlling his will.

"You cannot stay," Lydia said. "He is an obstacle."

"John, I think you know more about your aunt and uncle than you realize. If we could sit for a while and talk …"

255

"Give him one wrong answer, Jamie, and you will die here. It will be a disaster for them all. You have already been told what will happen. No talk. Action, my boy."

Jamie tightened his grip on the table corners. He felt as if the wood was about to cut open his hand. The pain turned into rage. Shadows crept into the room, and the gray fluorescence from the ceiling now dimmed.

Jamie caught a glimpse of Lydia trying to smile. Agent Hedgecock rose from his chair and started toward Jamie, who saw the butt of a gun holstered behind the agent's jacket.

Time stopped.

He saw the Jewel pushing him. Self-preservation program, Lydia called it. Jamie felt the new skin eating away the last of his old, and somehow he knew: He was going to kill an FBI agent.

52

S AMMIE NEVER FORGOT what her parents taught her about grief. They said tears lost for departed flesh were a waste of the living.

Sammie tried her best to follow their guide, keeping her emotions in balance as she looked for ways to secure Michael's safety and find a miracle cure for Jamie. She tried to manipulate as best she could during the initial interviews in the van on the way to Austin Springs. She stayed close to Jamie, proud of the way he played along with her cover story. She knew the ruse of John Huggins would be destroyed as soon as the FBI circulated Jamie's picture in Albion, but she figured that would be enough time to give her one last chance at saving Jamie – even if he didn't believe saving was possible.

Her mind searched for answers in feverish chaos as they entered town, but her frustration mounted as they were led from the van. Sammie looked up and down the familiar street of this bright white, early 20th-century town as they headed to the front glass doors. She spent many summer afternoons in Austin Springs with her mother and always found it to be a fun town in an odd sort of way. It was always overrun by tourists – an eclectic blend of the blue-hair set and aging artists – but Sammie loved the garish pots of flowers everywhere, the brick-lined streets, and especially the ice cream shop a half-block away at the end of Flanders Street.

She used to walk past the police station many times but never really noticed it until now. It was hardly distinctive, its white adobe walls melding into the scenery with about ten yards of gently sloping grass separating the building from the street. The building's nameplate, above the front entry, could easily have been missed by passersby.

Sammie calmed herself as she was led inside along with Michael and Jamie, but she was stunned by what she saw. She couldn't tell the difference between this and the lobby of a dentist's office: Generic landscapes on the walls, padded chairs and small lamps, coffee table complete with magazines, and a welcome counter.

A large black woman in a blue uniform and badge provided a reality check. The woman attached herself to the threesome, offering sympathy for their losses, providing Michael and Jamie with t-shirts, and promising to mother them as long as they were "guests." After Jamie was taken to a back room for interrogation, the woman showed Sammie and Michael into a small waiting room adjacent to the lobby.

The room, about the size of a small office, had every creature comfort: A sofa with end tables and a lamp, an 18-inch television with DVD player, soda machine, a coffee maker next to a basket of muffins and donuts, and most amazing to Sammie: a desktop computer with a sign taped above saying, 'Free Wi-Fi.'

"I'm gonna bet you're hungry," said the deputy, Martha Lynn. "Plenty here to start. What say I call down to Eddy's and order up some eggs and bacon?"

Michael dug in while Sammie thanked her hostess. As he filled his mouth with blueberry muffin, he appeared to have forgotten what Agent Hedgecock told him before arrival. His parents, tracked down in Starkville, Mississippi, were on their way. Michael was told he must remain at the station until they arrived, a few hours at best.

Sammie asked the deputy for some time alone in the waiting room. The instant the door shut, Sammie turned to Michael.

258

"Keep watch," she said.

"For what?"

"Anybody. There's something I have to do."

She retrieved the flash drive Jamie gave her before he dashed off into the woods. She had to know what information Ben thought was so important he would risk everything to get to his little brother. She found the USB port and plugged in the drive.

"What you up to?" Michael asked as he filled his mouth with a glazed donut. "Aren't we supposed to figure how to rescue Jamie?"

"Yes, Coop. That's what I'm trying to do. Just keep watch, OK?"

Sammie didn't apologize for her callous behavior. She couldn't afford to be interrupted. Her heart sank when she opened a folder to discover three subfolders, each containing more than fifty files, many of them hundreds even thousands of kilobytes long.

"Oh, no. Where do I start?" She glanced at the wall clock and took a deep breath. She was a fast reader, but this was overwhelming.

She took a second, closer look and saw a pattern emerging in the titles of the files. The words 'death,' 'soul,' 'spirit,' 'tunnel,' and 'white light' appeared frequently. She found text documents, image-heavy files, collections of downloaded Internet material, sound files, video files, a database, and spreadsheets. She opened files as quickly as the computer allowed, skimmed the opening page and determined she was looking at a random collection of research which focused on various theories about the human soul, religious context, beliefs related to reincarnation, and on and on.

The clock seemed to accelerate, and Sammie was getting nowhere. She deduced the nature of Ben's obsession but couldn't figure out why he so cared about these often arcane theories.

The second subfolder proved intriguing, as the word 'Jewel' appeared in a few titles. She skimmed, looking for hints of a broader picture but found only technical details about the program now re-sequencing Jamie's DNA or stories that Ignatius told him about Caryllan Wave energy's history. Other files in the folder included what appeared to be personal journals and reflections upon his life before and after crossing the fold.

"Sure you don't want some breakfast?" Michael asked. "You been running around like a crazy person all morning, too, if you get my speed."

Sammie asked for water, and he obliged with an eight-ounce bottle but also a donut. He stood over her shoulder as she worked, until she reminded him of his responsibility at the window. Three minutes later, she opened a file called 'Jewel/soul.' It read like a research paper, opening with a formal, introductory paragraph that lowered Sammie's jaw as she reached the thesis sentence. *This is it,* she told herself.

Every sentence boggled her mind and brought tears to her eyes. It wasn't written by the drunk Ben became in his final months. Rather, the words were carefully prepared, the product of vast research, with each powerful sentence building a meticulous case for a concept Sammie knew could change the future. The summary report was twenty-seven pages long. Sammie had no intention of reading it all; she didn't have to. The first five pages, when skimmed, presented more than enough hard science and anecdotal evidence melded with theory and religious doctrine.

Her mind raced through the past hours, focusing on Jamie's miraculous cure of Michael and how Jamie's body repaired itself. She understood the basic science behind the Jewel's program – her father spent many weeks outlining it – so Sammie knew the program by itself could not have saved Michael. Ben's conclusions provided a missing link.

"We never considered this," she said, loud enough for Michael.

She closed the file and removed the flash drive. She took a swig of water, braced herself, and turned to Michael.

"Everything makes sense now. We have to get Jamie out of here."

"Sure. That was pretty much the plan all along. Got any ideas?"

She peered through the blinds and saw a lobby that was empty, save for one deputy.

"So far as we know, Coop, there are only three here. Two deputies and Agent Hedgecock. All the other officers are out dealing with the mess that was left behind. You seen anybody else here?"

"Uh. No. Not that I recollect. Sammie, what are you thinking?"

"What I'm thinking is that it's 9:01, and Jamie doesn't have much time. There's only three."

"Three. Right. Carrying them little doohickeys called guns."

"I can't do this without you, Coop. OK? Are you with me on this?"

He sighed. "I dunno what you got, but we can't do a jailbreak."

"Yes, we can. Think about it. It's three against three, and they don't believe we're a threat. I lost my parents, you're stewing about your folks coming, and my cousin in there can barely think for himself. Right?"

"Yeah, yeah. Element of surprise. I got it. But may I again call your attention to them guns? Just because we've been dodging bullets all morning don't mean our luck is permanent."

"Daddy said luck is a side-effect of creative thinking. Time to get creative. We're walking out of here with Jamie. I don't care how we do it."

Michael tossed a half-eaten donut into the trash and groaned.

53

THIS ISN'T ME, Jamie convinced himself as he prepared to jump Agent Hedgecock and go for the pistol.

"But it is." Lydia's kiss melded to his cheek like an ice cube. "You are a Jewel of Eternity. He stands in your way. Leave now."

Jamie jumped to his feet with the effortless balance of a butterfly, his mouth filled with murderous, drooling saliva. Somewhere deep within, in a place he wanted to grab hold of, a voice cried out, "This is not me." Jamie fought back against the Jewel's bloodlust. He succeeded in delaying the attack by a couple of critical seconds, just enough time for failure.

The agent backed away, his hands in a defensive posture.

"John, I am not trying to hurt you or put you in jail. We need to know about your aunt and uncle. Very *nasty* things have happened this morning. Many people have been killed. Don't you want to help prevent other people from being killed, too?"

Rage bubbled underneath, his skin roiled with an electric zeal to attack. Shadows crept through the room, slithering up walls and across the ceiling. He heard a million crickets and crackling glass.

"Please leave me alone. I don't know anything."

"I think you do."

The agent's jacket rang, and Hedgecock reached inside, grabbing a cell from his shirt pocket. Again, Jamie glimpsed the holstered pistol, realized the agent was distracted, and allowed his mind to drink from a poisoned pool. He prepared to pounce.

Yet Hedgecock grabbed the laptop and rushed to the door without acknowledging Jamie. An Austin Springs deputy shut the door behind the agent and locked it again. Jamie pounded on the door and begged to be released, but he heard no response.

In seconds, Jamie saw clearly again. He turned to Lydia.

"I didn't do it," he said. "I'm stronger than you."

Lydia's smug, confident smile faded.

"You misunderstand. I never implied the Jewel controlled your conscious will. On the contrary, you have always had a partnership. Sometimes, this arrangement has manifested itself without your knowledge or consent."

"Now you're just making stuff up. I'm in charge of who I am."

At once, the confident smile returned. "Are you sure? Did you act on your own devices when you heard your parents' killer was in jail? Were you in the habit of running through the streets screaming bloody murder while carrying a baseball bat, determined to kill out of vengeance? Would you consider such rage normal behavior? No, I think not, my dearest boy."

The fragments of that day two years ago returned on occasion, but most of what he knew came from the stories told by witnesses; the rest was pure anger clouded in a blanket of blinding white light.

Lydia did not let up. "Fury is a remarkable concept, my sweet child. You see, fury in its most raw, unvarnished form is perfection. It holds within its hand the fire from which the universes were created and in which they will eventually destroy themselves. Creation and destruction are founded upon the ideals of fury. As is the ethereal matter that ties the universes together. As is the program which, in less than one hour, will shed its skin and take its true form."

"You're crazy," he whispered. "You're talking nonsense."

"Or perhaps only now am I telling you the entire truth."

Lydia closed her eyes for a moment and took a deep, measured breath. When she opened them again, they were black as the deepest abyss.

"Where do you believe the shadows came from?" She asked. "What of the things you heard? The crickets? The cracking of glass? The screams that seemed to come from nowhere and everywhere? The blackness that enveloped the night sky and blotted out the stars? Were these part of your imagination, your delirium, your fears made manifest? Oh, Jamie."

"Stop this." The unsettling urgency of rage stiffened him again.

"These were not imagined. Jamie, you are a Jewel. You have the power to see beyond the limitations of a physical world. You can feel what is beyond. You draw rage from the natural energy coursing through your blood. If you channeled your mind to leap past the senses, you could touch the heart of the universe. You could see where it all began, feel the fire that has burned for billions of years and that even still, pushes the stars ever outward.

"With this power, you could see the colonies of Earth though you be light-years and a literal universe away. You are the beginning and the end, and there are only nine others like you. Small, but an army of staggering power when combined.

"These are the things you must know, Jamie. Why else would men risk everything to destroy you, while others will go to any length to protect the program until it fulfills its mission? I will not try to guard your feelings any longer. You will listen to me, Jamie, and you will do as I say. We must leave here. The shadows are coming. You can feel them, see them. They must not be given the chance to destroy you before the appointed time."

Jamie saw the eyes of a gentle mother morph into beads of madness. He stepped back from her, but not out of fear. He boiled with unexpected excitement. She was right: He heard their footsteps, just like when he sensed them nearby in the forest. The shadows were coming. *Bidwell.*

"I can't get out," he said. "I don't know how."

"Allow the Jewel to guide you. It will show you how to see beyond the physical world. All matter is born of the universe; it can be decimated by that same universe. Turn around and face the door, and you will see the possibilities. It is time to leave."

He grabbed for the doorknob but felt nothing. Then, unable to look down, Jamie felt a liquid encase his hand as if he were washing it in frigid soap and water. Somewhere in his mind he saw the components of a lock and heard Lydia whispering in his ear.

"Grab the tumbler. Release it. Yes. That's the way."

Just like that, shadows drifted away like fog burned off by the morning sun, and the door cracked open. Jamie pulled back his hand and looked down to see a blurred convolution of his fingers intertwined with the lock's components. Horrified, he yanked his hand away, and the sensation of soap and water disappeared.

"It's happening," he whispered. "I'm changing."

"No," Lydia said. "You're learning."

Jamie pulled back the door and expected to see the deputy outside, but no one was stationed there. The room from which he emerged was located at the end of the corridor. To his left and directly across, another hallway led to the rear past the holding cells. Jamie heard contentious voices not far away, all of them familiar.

When he leaned all the way into the hall, he saw the deputy who twice locked the door. The short man, perhaps in his mid-twenties with a razor-thin mustache and gelled black hair combed with precision, appeared distracted by the voices.

Jamie focused on the deputy's gun.

Lydia's icy grip encircled Jamie's neck, and his rage grew.

"He is in your way," she said. "He will try to stop you. Kill him."

Every part of him said this obstacle must be eliminated, so Jamie allowed rage to carry him on with the speed and agility of a leopard.

The deputy didn't see it coming.

54

SAMMIE THOUGHT SHE had an excellent jailbreak plan in mind until Agent Hedgecock appeared in the lobby, cell phone glued to his ear. As soon as the man's eyes met hers, Sammie changed her plans, opened the waiting-room door, and turned to Michael.

"I'll deal with Agent Hedgecock," she whispered. "You've got to distract the other one. The deputy behind the counter. OK, Coop?"

He hesitated to nod but did so with a visible lump in his throat. Sammie opened the door and made a beeline for Hedgecock, who now headed toward her with purpose.

"Agent, Michael and I have been talking and ..."

He raised a hand. "That will be all, Miss Huggins." Hedgecock turned to Martha Lynn, the deputy behind the counter. "Deputy, please escort these two to a cell at once."

The room exploded with voices speaking over each other. Martha Lynn boomed her objections, and Sammie insisted this was an outrage, that Hedgecock had no right to do that, let alone to hold her cousin John for questioning. Hedgecock glared.

"John?" He said. "Don't you mean Jamie?"

Sammie didn't blink. She put the pieces together; the phone call must have blown Sammie's tall tale out of the water. She wanted to curse; if only she had five more minutes. For an instant, she darted her eyes toward Michael, who knew the gig was up.

Martha Lynn tried to intervene again. "Agent, let's cool our britches and talk this out. Now why do you want to put these children in holding? They ain't done a thing but be in the wrong place at the wrong time."

Hedgecock never took his eyes off Sammie. "Familiar song, Deputy. For the moment, consider the charge obstruction of justice. You may have heard: There are bodies scattered over three counties." His eyes, now cold and dark, latched onto Sammie just long enough for her to realize she stood on the precipice. "The other charges," the agent continued, "in due course. The boy in the back is not this girl's cousin. Isn't that right, Samantha?"

Michael whispered, "Oh, shit. We're deep in it now."

He turned again to Martha Lynn, whose eyes darted between him and Sammie. Michael took a step closer to her and said Hedgecock was full of crap. They were victims, he insisted.

"You don't understand anything," Sammie told Hedgecock before turning to the deputy. "He's making a huge mistake, Martha Lynn. Please. We're not the bad guys."

"Do we need to cuff you?" Hedgecock asked.

He didn't receive an answer. Another voice groaned halfway down the corridor near the interrogation room. Hedgecock swung about and saw the disturbance when Michael, Martha Lynn, and Sammie did. Hedgecock reached for his holstered pistol.

Jamie was scrapping with a deputy. Jamie, who was easily six inches taller, had one arm wrapped about the deputy's throat as he reached for the man's service revolver with the other. The officer yelled for assistance, but Jamie threw him against the wall, leveled him with a hard left cross and reached down for the weapon as the deputy slid shaken to the floor.

Hedgecock unholstered his pistol and aimed, yelling for Jamie to drop and place his hands behind his head. Simultaneously, Martha

Lynn reached for her weapon. None of them was as fast as Sammie, who reacted with a single Chancellor-trained maneuver that stung Hedgecock behind both knee caps and allowed her to grab the pistol before he knew what happened. Hedgecock fell to his knees in a moan, and Martha Lynn turned her revolver toward Sammie, who aimed squarely at the agent's head.

"No, child," Martha Lynn said. "You don't wanna do this, baby."

"You don't understand," Sammie said, "and I don't have time to explain." She turned to Michael. "Give him your pistol. Do it. Now."

"No, ma'am, I will not."

"I don't want to hurt anybody. But I swear to you, I'll shoot him. All you have to do is let the three of us go. You'll never see us again."

From the corner of his eye, Michael saw Jamie stand up with the other deputy's revolver. However, Michael's focus changed at once.

Martha Lynn's blood-chilling scream signaled the end to their dubious escape plan. Michael heard the destructor coming before he saw it. Sammie swung on her heels, and Hedgecock rose, prepared to jump her.

The double glass doors of the Austin Springs Police Department were no match for a giant black SUV driven by an ex-track coach born in the Collectorate. The oversized car brought hell on wheels as it barreled through the entrance, shattering the doors, sending a swarm of glass toward everyone in the lobby. The doors broke from their jambs, their steel frames bounding forward along with debris from the ceiling and either wall.

Sparks flew, tires squealed, and one door frame flew end-over-end, smacking Martha Lynn and Michael simultaneously, while the other landed on the SUV's hood. Sammie threw one hand over her face and turned away from the flying glass, but not fast enough. Something blunt pounded her back, and the momentum threw her forward. She fell into Hedgecock, who was on his feet, scrambling. She lost the pistol and saw nothing but tiny pieces of glass as she fell. All at once, both hands exploded in pain, and a great shadow fell upon her.

The SUV swerved, coming to a stop at a forty-five degree angle to the welcome counter. Sammie smelled gas and looked directly up at the vehicle's grille, which was mangled. The rest of her lay under the monster. For an instant, the room fell silent save the hum of the SUV's engine and the tinkling of more glass upon the floor.

The silence turned into chaos. Sammie heard the driver-side door open and looked over her shoulder to see two feet in black shoes standing firm. Agent Hedgecock, dazed and sporting a small cut on his forehead, scrambled past Sammie and reached for the pistol she lost. He tried to rise.

Hedgecock was halfway to his feet before the lobby erupted in the thunder of automatic-weapons fire. He contorted like a marionette and collapsed in a heap, his body riddled in bullets, his eyes staring into forever.

Sammie got a glimpse of Michael's legs as her friend scrambled behind the counter. She heard Martha Lynn ranting into a phone that they were under attack and an officer was down. The driver unloaded his M16 on that area. Bullets pounded and ricocheted, papers flew, more glass shattered.

Sammie never felt so helpless. The pistol lay next to Hedgecock's body, five feet away. She would have to crawl over glass to reach it, but Sammie saw no other option. The driver was rounding the vehicle and would see her in seconds. She had to reach. She had to reach.

55

HAIR FELL IN his face, but nothing disrupted his aim. Jamie was one with the deputy's revolver as he fired in rapid succession, moving steadily forward all the while. He put three bullets into Arthur Tynes, who grunted and collapsed a few feet from Sammie. Jamie pressed forward. Machine-gun fire raged from the rear of the station, and Arthur did not stay down.

Jamie's anger became a perfectly-focused tunnel. He did not recognize the man who was once his running mentor. Rather, he saw a beast who would kill Sammie if given the chance. Jamie pulled the trigger five times. Blood sprayed against the wall behind Arthur, who crumpled in a heap with bullet holes in his face.

An instinct driven by the Jewel told him to make sure the lobby was secure. He scanned the now-jammed entrance. Behind the counter, the large black deputy who gave him a t-shirt fired toward the rear, where light shown in through an opened door.

Michael raced out from the counter, stained in Arthur's blood.

"Gonna need a new coach, dude," he said through his jitters.

Jamie lowered his weapon as he stepped on glass without care, reached down and grabbed Sammie's hand. He felt nothing beyond a vague sense of responsibility to his friends.

"C'mon," he whispered. "We have to go." As he grabbed hold of her bloody left hand, she screamed in agony, but he reassured her, "They'll heal. Just hold me."

As she stood up, however, bullets flew again, this time from the far end of the corridor in the direction of the cells.

The smaller deputy who lost his revolver to Jamie was racing toward the carnage at the base of the SUV. He screamed, demanding everyone stay down. Somewhere in mid-sentence, however, he contorted as two bullets exited through his chest. He fell face-first. Behind him, Jennifer Bowman advanced with an M16.

Jamie pushed the hair from his face and whispered to Sammie.

"I'm out of bullets. Give it to me."

She laid the pistol in his hands. He told her to get down. As Jamie aimed his pistol over Sammie and knew the Jewel would help him take out the advancing attacker, he heard another jolt of weapons fire from behind the counter. The large deputy, Martha Lynn, screamed as she rose up and let loose her fury upon the intruders trying to enter through the back door. She gasped at one point like a child receiving a penicillin shot then collapsed.

Jamie turned the pistol down the corridor. As the first bullets from the M16 missed high, Jamie again tapped into the Jewel's self-preservation program. He saw a tunnel through a wreath of blackness. At the heart of that tunnel, he saw the intruder's eyes. He kept a steady hand, allowed himself to indulge in his own rage, and fired two shots. Jennifer Bowman swayed, dropped her weapon and grabbed her face, which opened up as the second bullet cracked her left cheek. She fell.

Jamie didn't waste a second. He reached down and grabbed the driver's M16, which he slung over his shoulder. He checked the clip in his pistol and handed the weapon to Michael.

He sensed other shadows close by, coming in through the rear. He allowed the Jewel to see beyond these walls, but the results were murky, more intuition than anything. He had to get his friends out of here.

He swung about, saw Jennifer's rifle lying in the corridor next to the dead deputy and knew what had to be done. As soon as he was sure Sammie was OK, he pointed to the corridor, told them to take the first left past the jail cells and then ...

"Be ready for anything," he said without emotion.

Michael didn't respond. Jamie saw the look of awe and terror in his best friend's eyes. They were surrounded by splattered blood that was in large part his own doing. Jamie felt nothing.

He grabbed the other M16 and handed it to Sammie as they passed cells and threw open the back door. They heard a thunderous slam not far away, followed by brief automatic weapons fire. Once outside, they scanned the largely empty lot behind the station.

"Where now?" Michael asked.

"A car," Jamie said. "Any car. We've gotta get out of town."

They twisted about, weapons hot, looking for signs of the enemy as well as an opportunity for a quick theft. What they found instead was a patrol car covered in water and soap suds, clearly in the process of being washed. Beside the car, a hose spilled water next to the body of a black-haired boy perhaps no older than Jamie. The boy's blood intermingled with the water and formed a river of swirling red along the pavement.

"Oh, hell," Michael muttered. "They're killing everybody."

Jamie heard the shadows coming. The Bidwells. He told his friends to duck behind the patrol car. As if on cue, Agatha and Christian Bidwell raced out the other rear door. Jamie raised the M16 and prepared to take out his final living enemies. Christian opened fire, blowing out the car's tires and shattering its windshield.

56

SAMMIE DROPPED IN a defensive crouch alongside Michael and Jamie. She despised the notion of being taken down by a Bidwell even more annoying than Agatha. Eight times she trained in the Louisiana bayou alongside Christian, who pronounced on their second outing that he would take her virginity within the year. She was 13 at the time and unimpressed.

Still, she had to be practical. She looked for the most likely exit strategy and pointed toward the town park adjacent to the ASPD parking lot.

"There," she said over the hail of bullets. "That's where we have to be. We're too exposed out here. More police are bound to show up any second. I'll provide cover. Pin these two down. You guys know how to steal a car, so do it. I'll catch up to you."

She didn't wait for her friends to protest. Sammie leaped into a semi-exposed position and laid covering fire on the Bidwells, who found themselves pinned down behind an air-conditioning unit. When Jamie and Michael took her cue and raced in a crouch toward the park, which was covered in a heavy canopy of trees, Sammie decided to take the offensive.

Her father's favorite motto was, "No surrender, no retreat." She refused to disappoint Daddy again. She embraced the seductive beauty of her rifle and allowed all the Chancellor training and cold-blooded philosophy of her father to guide her.

The screams of desperate, fleeing townsfolk echoed from the park as the report of high-powered weapons ended the ageless peace of Austin Springs. She exchanged more volleys then made up her mind.

"You would have been proud, Daddy," she said as she advanced.

With visions of a downed helicopter buoying her ego, Sammie stepped from the patrol car into an exposed position. She ran laterally across the parking lot, firing every few steps, until Christian rose and fired back.

As she aimed to return fire, Sammie knew her entire life led here. Her father said a true soldier of the Guard not only knew how to kill without mercy but also mock those he was about to kill. Through this, he told her, the lesser castes were kept in place.

Stand in the open, he told her during discussions of tactical strategy. *Show them you are unafraid and will defeat them anyway. They will cower before such courage.*

Those words lifted her. *I am a Chancellor. Thank you, Daddy.*

Her body jerked as she fired. Christian twitched as Sammie shot the rifle out of his hands. He dove for cover to retrieve the weapon. She saw Agatha's head peek around the corner of the AC unit, and she prepared to make a final, decisive assault on their position. If she never got a chance to see the Collectorate, at least she would truly understand what it was like to be a member of the Unification Guard.

Her legs did not take her forward, however. Her vision blurred. Only as the sound of a speeding car screeched yards behind her, did Sammie look down and see the bloody hole in her belly. She wobbled and fell to her knees. As she swooned, she saw both Bidwells rise from behind their protective shield and take aim.

Bullets whizzed past her, but they were not from the Bidwells. A car screamed to a stop behind her. Two doors opened, and the thunderous blasts of rifles shouted into her ears. Someone's left arm wrapped around her, and that same savior's right arm stretched forward, an M16 blazing at the end of it. She felt sleepy.

57

A minute earlier, the owner of a Cadillac convertible fled as Jamie and Michael approached with weapons extended. As the best friends jumped in, Michael said:

"You couldn't have asked that dude for the keys?"

His words fell flat when he saw what Jamie was doing.

"Holy shit on a ..." Michael muttered as he fell into his seat.

Only when Jamie pushed his hair from his face and looked to the ignition did he realize his right hand was buried inside the machine, as if welded to it. He saw inside the device, positioned his fingers around the starter mechanism, and turned. The convertible roared into life.

He hit the gas.

The wheel felt natural to Jamie. He sensed an immediate and deep connection to the car, the power surging through his blood much as it had with the guns. He drove wildly through the park, short-cutting between trees and past abandoned picnic tables.

He couldn't believe what Sammie was doing alone in the middle of the parking lot. The instant she was hit, he sensed it.

"Ready, Coop?" He yelled. "Start shooting before I hit the brakes."

Michael grabbed the door and held on, his pistol poised. As soon as the car screamed into the lot and became exposed along with Sammie, he opened fire. Jamie hit the brakes just as Sammie fell to her knees and dropped her rifle. He spread machine-gun fire on the Bidwells as he knelt then clutched Sammie.

"Grab it," he told Michael, pointing at Sammie's rifle. "I'll cover."

Bullets embedded into the Caddy as the trio leaped in. Jamie all but flung Sammie across the seat to the passenger side, where she lay barely conscious. He slammed the door and threw the car into drive in a simultaneous movement, again allowing the Jewel to assist.

He crouched as he drove the car from the lot. Michael, cursing more than Jamie ever heard, said the Bidwells were coming after them on foot. Jamie didn't think this would pose a problem – until he saw the very thing Sammie warned them about moments ago.

An ASPD patrol car careened toward them, blue lights flashing.

Jamie dropped the rifle and grabbed the wheel with both hands, swerving to avoid the patrol car. Sammie tossed about like a rag doll. Michael tumbled in the back. Jamie thought they were home-free.

That's when he heard more weapons fire and looked through the rear-view mirror. The Bidwells turned their attention to the newly-arrived officers and fired full-on into the vehicle, which slammed into the parked patrol car that a now-deceased boy had tried to wash.

Jamie set his focus on two purposes. He drove not toward the park's main entrance, but rather to a private service exit at the park's northeastern corner, farthest from the police station. He had no prior knowledge of this way out, but he knew it was there; the Jewel pointed the way.

Once there, Jamie smashed the car through a wooden gate.

He laid one hand upon Sammie and felt the healing power of Caryllan energy surge into her. Her wound would be healed within minutes. For that, he was thankful.

Jamie turned his focus to his ultimate destination, a world planted in his mind to show him the way home. He knew how this would end.

Jamie saw it all. His mind's eye opened to the land east of Austin Springs, which rose steadily as the forests grew thicker and the hills became steeper. He saw streams and small waterfalls, the bounty of wildlife that was safe until hunting season, the isolated cabins where a lucky few hid away from this insane world, and the tiny and winding dirt roads that led nowhere and everywhere. He saw this place, stretching for more than ten miles, as clearly as he saw a large, glistening city on this very same stretch of land but located across the interdimensional fold.

He felt the history that built this land, from the fiery birth of the planet to the first seedlings that pushed through the hard-packed crust. He saw slaves passing through these woods as they escaped from life on the plantations. He felt the spirits of wild and reckless criminals who fled into these hills over the past century, only to be hunted down like dogs or to live a meager, desperate existence until dying of starvation or loneliness.

As much as Jamie tried to fight it, the threads of the universe twisted his mind and tugged at the Jewel, which he knew was ready to be reborn. He felt the heartbeat of time and space itself.

His hands steered as if they were independent contractors. The back entrance to the park soon gave way to a two-lane paved road, onto which he swerved without bothering to look for traffic. He pressed the gas.

Among the many images and feelings bombarding his mind's eye were five moments that seemed to lock into place as still pictures, but each of them carrying the odor of rage and filth.

He saw himself shoot Walt Huggins twice in the gut, not because he had to but because he wanted to. He saw himself unload countless bullets into an attacker with an AK-47, and he was pleased with the outcome. He saw himself pound a police officer unconscious, take the deputy's gun, and unload a full round into a man he once admired as his coach. He saw himself on the ground dispatching Jennifer Bowman.

Jamie ignored the reality of self-defense, or that through his actions, Sammie and Michael were still alive. All he knew was that he had killed. Again and again and again.

278

And the Jewel wanted more. So much more. He heard it.

Fury. Unbridled, limitless fury.

Jamie understood. He knew what was coming, and he was thankful to Lydia for showing him beyond the physical world; it was a mistake he would make her regret. As the images of blood and murder wiped away the last of his best childhood memories, Jamie turned the wheel hard onto an unmarked side road.

Shadows fell beneath a canopy as the land continued to rise.

58

AGATHA MOCKED THE irony of the moment. The patrol car they commandeered after tossing out two wounded policemen would not be roadworthy for long. Steam poured from the hood; tires screeched against metal. She thought it fitting their journey finish inside scrap. In many ways, it was the perfect symbol of the last fifteen years of her life.

She saw the endgame and was pleased to have Christian with her at the conclusion. They were more than half a mile behind their quarry, but close enough to see the Jewel's convertible take a sudden right turn far ahead, ducking off into the deep forest.

"Would you like to offer any regrets, Christian?" She asked.

Christian smiled as he took out a cigarette. "To die next to the mother who taught me everything? I'm good."

They sat on a mix of glass shards and the blood of their latest victims. Christian slowed as they neared the turn-off. The patrol car moaned as he tapped the brakes.

"Die?" Agatha asked. "No, Christian. You and I are invincible. We hold the moral imperative. That superiority will triumph."

Christian turned the wheel onto the forest road. Agatha held on.

"Our lives are not our own, Christian. They never were. Walter knew this is exactly where the road would lead us."

59

MILES STRETCHED into light-years. The roads, though laden with bumps, washouts, potholes, and mud holes, provided a strange comfort for Jamie. They kept him focused on controlling the wheel. Each bounce and swerve reminded Jamie he was still alive and at some level, still in charge of his life. The aroma of the forest was deep and spicy, the air fresh and perhaps a tad cooler.

After driving more than four miles into this forest, after ignoring the questions and pleas of his friends, Jamie pulled the Caddy to the side of the road, threw open the door, and started walking.

He stopped at the edge of the forest and told himself not to be afraid. He stamped down the tall grass and made his way into the shadows of the deep forest. In his mind's eye, Jamie saw the place his heart desired to be, and the image gave him peace. After two hundred yards, he gathered his emotions together, decided what he would tell his friends, and turned around.

Almost at once, he felt the tears arriving en masse. They were already plastered over Sammie's cheeks, and he couldn't bear Michael's stern glare of confusion.

"I got no choice," Jamie whispered. "I made my decision. I hope you understand."

His gentle words satisfied no one. Sammie said he didn't need to do this, that she read Ben's flash drive and knew what he told Jamie. She insisted Ben's revelation changed everything – even her own view of life – and Jamie could still be saved. As Michael screwed his eyes in confusion, Jamie insisted Sammie was wrong. Only when Sammie said Jamie didn't "have to die," did Michael's eyes bulge. Jamie couldn't look his No. 1 in the face. He despised keeping this secret from Michael, but now he saw no way out.

"I wanted to tell you," Jamie said. "I knew you'd be even more stubborn than she is."

Michael's eyes filled with water as he shook his head.

"J. I ain't the brightest bulb, but I ain't a dimwit either." Michael looked to both. "I knew. I just couldn't admit it until I heard somebody say the words. She's right. You got the power to beat this. You healed both of us. We were goners. Why can't you heal yourself? Do some of that hoodoo-voodoo thing with your hands."

Jamie wanted to hear their pleas. He wanted to believe in Ben, in the idea of trusting in himself "when the time comes." Reality, however, overcame any temptation for escape.

"You got to understand something," he told them. "Healing ain't part of the Jewel's program. It's more like a side-effect. I got this energy running through me – Caryllan energy, Ben called it. It's the damnedest thing. Turns me into a miracle-worker right before it kills me." He cleared his throat. "I reckon Ben was right about one thing. I do have a soul, and it's been a pretty good one ... for the most part. I mean, I love you guys and I don't want anything to happen to you. I did what I could to keep you safe."

"And that's why you can't give up on us," Sammie said.

Jamie grabbed her hand.

"I can feel what's happening to me. I can see so many things. This Jewel is turning me into something else. It's like some dude opened the curtain and showed me the whole damn universe. It's all coming to me ... all the answers. But ... but all these wild things, incredible things – they're gonna be taken away. I can't keep them."

His knees trembled as a great wave of despair rose from deep in his gut. The words crossing his lips brought a stark finality tried to avoid. At last, he collapsed without letting go of Sammie's hands. Sitting on his knees, Jamie convulsed in sobs, the incredible injustice of what lay ahead torturing him through his tears.

Sammie and Michael bent down to hug him. His eyes, blurred by water and salt, looked beyond the world of the present and took him through the shadows of the past until finally, he felt the security of big, warm arms and soft, comforting words. He looked into Mommy's eyes and saw the one who always made everything OK. He smelled her rose-petal perfume and liked it when she kissed him on the cheek, leaving an imprint of her lipstick.

Just like that, the past vanished with the breeze, and Jamie remembered the truth: His parents were the monsters who made sure he was doomed from the start. Even the imitators who raised him had no interest in watching him grow into a man. He was nothing more than the instrument at the heart of their mission.

Jamie made no effort to resist the sobs, and he allowed his belly to convulse until he was in pain. Only when he felt the well of misery drying up did Jamie run his hands across his face.

"I can see everything," he finally said, his voice raspy, coughs interrupting the words. "I can see the world where we were conceived, Sammie. I can feel all those people. There's so much hatred. The Chancellors holding down billions of people. There's a war. It's coming soon. Billions of souls, so angry. And the Jewel ... it knows something the rest of them don't. It's ..." His eyes bulged. "It's just gonna kill. It's gonna wipe out everything. All those people. The Chancellors were seeking immortality, but they created an army of monsters."

"Jamie, c'mon," Michael whispered. "You're seeing things because you're delirious."

Jamie grabbed each of them by the hand.

"Nobody should have this. Gotta be stopped. They were right."

Sammie coughed out her words. "Who was right?"

"The Bidwells. Everybody that's been trying to kill me. If I'd just let them waste me back on Main Street, everything would be OK now. Everybody else would be alive. Ben. Your parents." He looked at Sammie. "All the others. That kid back at the police station. He was just washing the car. Probably got a summer job, maybe saving up for his own car. This Jewel ... it's worse than evil. It's not just a program. It's alive. Understand?"

Lydia whispered in his ear. "Kill them," she said. "Put them out of their misery. They have nothing left. They will be blamed for everything. We have seen to that."

For a mere instant, his anger spiked and his temptation to kill returned like a thirst he felt in the corridors of the police station.

No. Jamie rose to his feet, wiped the last remnant of tears away, and stared into Sammie's eyes. He saw the frail innocence that seemed ever present before the deadly soldier emerged. He ran his hand over her cheeks, caught droplets of water and smudged them away. He thought of what might have been if he'd been given a few more months with her.

He wrapped his arms around Sammie and kissed her as he thought a man in love might do. He gave her all the warmth and hope he could muster, and he felt the gift returned in her sweet, soft lips. When he pulled away, Jamie nodded, but he had nothing more to say to her.

He turned to Michael and reached out his hand.

"Give me the pistol."

Michael swung it around his back, but Jamie grabbed him.

"No, dude. This ain't the way."

284

Jamie took the pistol. He offered his right hand again, and this time the best friends shook with a firm grip. Michael wouldn't let go as he wrapped Jamie in a hug.

"I'm gonna wake up from this," Michael whispered. "I'm gonna call you first thing, and we'll hook up. Do some fishing. Got that?"

Jamie pulled out of the hug determined to fend off more sobs.

He stepped away. "Listen, you take the car about another half mile, OK? There's a hard left. You stay on that for about three miles, then take the first right. You'll be back on the highway soon."

His throat dried, but he managed a few final words for Michael.

"Look after Sammie. OK? She needs somebody now."

He took a mental snapshot of the two best friends a nobody from a nowhere town could ever have before he said, "Goodbye."

Jamie felt like an empty vessel as he turned and ran.

60

9:33 a.m.

AGATHA NEVER IMAGINED such an inglorious end for her son. From the day Christian was born to Lt. Commander Agatha Perrone and Rear Admiral Augustus Perrone, his parents expected great things for their only child. When the opportunity to cross the fold and protect the second Jewel came her way, Agatha debated sending Christian off-world to visit his father at Earth's most distant colony. Fifteen years later, that choice haunted her.

They drove through the back roads of rural Alabama in a stolen patrol car that was badly shot-up, stopping at frequent intersections to inspect the roads for fresh tire tracks. She did not burden Christian with a truth that might distract him and reduce their already-slim chance for victory. She did the calculations based upon prior knowledge: The Shock Units would be arriving within fifteen minutes – twenty at the outside. Nothing would come between them and the Jewel.

Agatha rose in her seat and stiffened as they rounded a bend. She smiled at the sight of an empty convertible less than fifty yards ahead. They stopped well back of the convertible, exited slowly with their rifles extended, and started toward the car.

"Gotta be close," Christian said. "We could wait for them to appear."

"No. The Jewel has almost finished re-sequencing. They're preparing. We have to go in."

Christian showed his tracking prowess by discovering bent grass along the edge of the woods fronting scrub brush. Agatha smiled, and they gave chase. They jogged in a crouch with their weapons extended. They stayed within ten yards of each other, and Agatha ordered Christian to establish clear aim at a target before shooting.

Five minutes into their search, Agatha heard young voices. She saw them first. Agatha checked her weapon and prepared for the last purposeful moments of her life.

She saw the teens huddled together surrounded by a healthy cluster of tall, thick pines. Beyond them the land rose steadily, changing into a tangled mass of knotted trees with bright green leaves fluttering in a gentle breeze. She saw a few rays of sunlight beyond the pines trying to cut through to the forest floor.

Agatha found Jamie in the crosshairs. She crimped her finger back against the trigger and settled her breathing.

At that instant, Jamie turned and ran uphill, a pistol in hand. Agatha's instinct was to fire anyway, but she resisted then waved off Christian, who also was ready to fire.

"Do as I say," she told him when reunited. "We have to act quickly."

61

S AMMIE AND MICHAEL stared at each other through their tears, the shock beginning to set in. Michael smacked his fists together.

"Everything we been through, and he's just gonna ..."

"It's what he wants, Coop."

"No. It's the Jewel. Got him brainwashed. If we go after him, can't we talk him out of this? Try something different? Anything."

She chose her words carefully. "Coop, there's only twenty minutes left. Jamie wouldn't give up unless he knew he couldn't win. He's been fighting so hard since this started."

The sound of footsteps from the wrong direction stopped Sammie in mid-sentence, and she reached for the M16, which was slung over her shoulder. Before she could swing about and bring the weapon into firing position, a purposeful voice intervened.

"I shot you once," Christian told her. "Smack in the belly. Don't know how you're still standing, but you won't be if I shoot again. Raise your weapon and die. Otherwise, drop it, Sweet Bread."

The rifle shook in Sammie's right hand. The nickname Sweet Bread made her skin crawl. Her gave it to her on their first joint-training mission in Louisiana — right before he announced he would take her virginity within a year. A flicker of Chancellor heroism within her said that even if she sacrificed herself, she would rid the world of Christian

Bidwell – and maybe buy Jamie all the time he needed to finish his journey in peace.

However, out of the corner of her eye, she saw Michael – a stiff, unarmed monolith. She couldn't sacrifice him as well, so she tossed the weapon to Christian's feet.

Christian ordered them to their knees, and they complied. Agatha revealed herself to their left, walking with a distinct limp toward the path Jamie took seconds earlier.

"Hello, Mr. Cooper," she nodded. "You are a remarkable sight. However, I can't linger for the details behind your apparent resurrection. I assume it was Biblical in a certain context. Yes?" She turned to the other captive. "I am truly sorry for your losses, Samantha. If only your father had not been so intransigent."

"Tell me something, Queen Bee," Michael interjected. "What's Albion High gonna do without your beautiful mug lording over all them redneck kids?"

Christian cursed, cocked his weapon, and leveled the butt against the side of Michael's head. Agatha sighed.

"No, son. We have shed more than sufficient blood. These two are not the enemy. Give me five minutes lead. Then set them free. They deserve a chance for life, assuming they can run fast enough." As she turned away, Agatha added, "Join them, if you wish."

Christian backed off, his jaw hanging. "But Mom, I should be the one. I can get to him faster, and I'm a better shot."

"Goodbye, son. Perhaps another path will bring us together."

She disappeared into the woods.

Christian offered the sneer of superiority that always charmed his posse of hangers-on at school. Sammie stewed.

"What's it going to be, Christian?"

"No need to worry, Sweet Bread. When the time comes, I'll be quick."

62

J AMIE FELT AS if all the burdens of life were lifted. He thought only of the peaceful place he knew was ahead, so he jogged through the forest as if he were running through Albion late at night. Like his hometown, the forest seemed familiar. The shrubs, the wildflowers, the fallen tree trunks, the scrub brush, the ground packed in a permanent dressing of dead leaves and twigs. Nothing slowed him down – not the logs over which he leaped or the sharp slopes he scaled without slipping. Each move came by instinct, as if his lifetime of running prepared him for this final sprint.

His hair dangled in his face, but he never bothered to swipe it aside. The ponytail he tied up after his morning swim in Lake Vernon was loose, so with one quick grab, Jamie pulled out the holder and tossed it away. It felt natural. Perfect for the end.

Just before he raced up the final slope and broke into the sunlight, Jamie heard flowing water, and it sounded like the Alamander River. He saw the edge of a rapidly-flowing creek as he emerged from the brush. The water broke hard in a swirling dance around boulders, twinkling in the sunlight. As Jamie stepped close to the ten-foot ravine overlooking the water, a covey of birds scattered. He caught his breath and scanned the forest across the creek, which seemed to dip into a long, winding valley, only to reassert itself after a mile or so with taller hills than the one on which Jamie stood.

He didn't want to die like so many that morning, staring into the face of their killer and perhaps, in their final breath, asking why. He wanted it to be quick and painless, and he wanted to set his eyes on something beautiful before the darkness came.

The outcropping of rock twenty yards away looked exactly as he pictured it in his mind. The giant rock jutted from the hill as if carved in place to be a sight-seeing deck for studying the nature below. When he reached the top of the rock, Jamie stood in place for several minutes. He neither said a word nor allowed a disruptive thought to cross his mind. He did not shed a tear; he had no more to give.

He listened to the birds, but mostly, he admired the silence.

"It's pretty," he said, raising the pistol with a firm grip.

Jamie no longer sensed the beating of his heart or the rise and fall of his lungs. He felt at peace, allowing his last necessary instinct to do the rest. He placed the pistol against his right temple and closed his eyes. He tasted the sweetness of Sammie's lips in their final kiss. He saw through the guilt that tortured Ben for so long and knew, at last, that his brother was a good man. He relished the warmth and simple beauty of the last sunrise he'd ever see over Lake Vernon. He knew Michael would be home and safe before day's end. The last and best friend he ever had. He remembered his last class at school, his final run through Albion late at night, the last sketch he drew sitting in the park. All of it consumed him, and he wanted no more.

"The last everything," he whispered.

Then Jamie wondered whether he would see a bright light.

"Impossible to say, my dear sweet boy, but you will have to wait a while longer."

Lydia's voice cracked the silence; Jamie opened his eyes. He didn't look to his side, but he knew she was there. He was not going to give her the satisfaction of his anger, so he squeezed the trigger.

Nothing happened. Not even the click of an empty gun.

"I'm sorry, Jamie. I don't believe your death would serve any purpose at this time."

He tried again, but his trigger finger trembled and pulled away. Nothing. His nerves twitched, and soon the pistol quivered, scraping against his head. The rage that dissipated along with his tears, regrets, and remorse now exploded. Lydia stared out over the valley, a smug glimmer of a smile.

"No, no, no!" He screamed at Lydia. "You can't do this to me."

"I already have, Jamie. Your anger is misplaced and unproductive. You have very little time to live; I suggest you do so with joy."

"Joy? What do you know about joy? Ever since you came around, there's been nothing but death and killing everywhere. You better let me do this, Lydia. You let me die my way."

She didn't change expression. "So you can disrupt the rebirth?"

"You're goddamn right."

"Too late. The Jewel's re-sequencing is complete. Even if you died now, the Jewel would be reborn intact. It might suffer initial confusion, might even lash out. But it will recover."

Jamie stepped to the edge of the outcropping. He saw boulders along the creek's shore.

"You can't stop me from jumping."

Jamie threw the pistol at Lydia, and it passed through her, sliding down to the base of the outcropping. Simultaneously, a pair of loud cracks echoed through the forest. Jamie froze. He couldn't tell the direction where the shots came from, and fear entered his swelling cauldron of emotions. Lydia, however, was unfazed.

"I won't need to stop you," she said. "If you jump, Jamie, you will experience pain and suffering, but your heart may not stop beating before the rebirth. You will not choose that course. It is not in you."

Jamie knew she was right. The wild, confusing emotions, the fury tearing through his soul, also pushed him back from the brink. Concern for Sammie and Michael's safety crept into his thoughts, followed by an intuition of having overlooked someone or something important. Not all the shadows were dead.

However, he pushed those notions aside once he understood what was going on. Why hadn't he seen this before?

"You're not the Mentor," he said. "Never were. That whole crap about a Mentor program? Lies. You're the Jewel."

He thought he saw a twinkle in her eyes.

She walked toward him.

"And you have been a challenging host. Actually, there was a Mentor program, but it was badly designed. It functioned only on occasion. Fortunately, I am impregnable." She stopped within inches of Jamie. "In eleven minutes, your DNA will be eradicated and Jamie Sheridan will simply drift away into the wind. I can promise you will experience no pain. It will be like a beautiful dream. I, on the other hand, will be reborn, the salvation of the Chancellory. Evolution, my dearest boy, must be served."

She looked away. "They come for me. I hear them."

Jamie saw beyond the physical world. Someone else's words echoed across the forest in a long, measured whisper. He thought he recognized the voice, and he knew the source was growing closer.

His mind's eye saw feet running across a carpet of rotted leaves, bones aching, and a deep, exhausted voice saying, "A good life. A meaningful life. I took a stand."

The connection vanished, but not before Jamie understood the true nature of the shadow – and the only option he had left. He stood alone facing Lydia, but even she turned away.

"Goodbye, my sweet child. Our time together is at an end."

293

63

BY ALL RIGHTS, Agatha should not have had the strength to finish this journey. At no point since the explosion did any of the pain subside. All she knew was that her resilience was proof of her destiny. She refused to flinch. Tracking skills first learned during Dacha training decades ago helped her now. Every few yards, she saw leaves kicked up or twigs snapped. The first slope she scaled showed a patch of mud and moss with visible footprints.

Agatha wondered how many bullets the magazine held because all would be needed not only to kill Jamie but disrupt − if not outright destroy − the regenerative power of the Jewel. She would not have enough time to set his body ablaze and guarantee its incineration.

After all, the Shock Units had to be close now. She felt their presence. Although she never led a battalion that used these tools, her husband Augustus told her stories about those monsters, who were activated to crush ethnic insurgents when casualty numbers among peacekeepers became untenable. They cast a blanket of death before them, he said, and filled the air with the stench of rotted flesh, bringing a still, dry heat onto the land before they unleashed their weapons. They were known only to a few and left no witnesses to verify the horrors they committed.

The inevitability of her death was liberating. She made peace with the choices of her life, reaffirmed the morality that led her to defy the Chancellory itself, and took pride in what chaos she would bring once she disrupted their plans.

"A good life," Agatha mumbled as she ran. "A meaningful life. I took a stand."

Four minutes into her pursuit, she heard two rounds fired from an M16 well behind her. She realized Christian disobeyed her orders, yet she understood why. He was a young Chancellor who knew his world was ending. How much was he supposed to take?

"Almost," Agatha whispered. "Almost there, James."

64

CHRISTIAN SCOWLED AT Sammie as if she was vermin. She recognized his contempt and was surprised he hadn't killed her despite his orders. She saw few opportunities for escape – until the keywords of her father's training echoed through time. She knew what to do. Unfortunately, Michael interrupted her plans.

"You the one that shot me in the back like a coward?"

"Can't say as I was, Cooper. Way I heard it, your coach had the honors." Christian snickered. "Good ol' Arthur must have been a sorry shot. Don't matter. Couple of clean hits to the head will take you out. Or maybe you'd like the barrel down your throat? Twice in a day. What d'ya say?"

"You ain't going to kill us, Bidwell. Mommy said to let us go. You ain't figuring on going up against the Queen Bee, are you?"

Sammie wanted to tell Michael to shut up so she could act. Yet Christian never took an eye off her, even as he laid into Michael.

"Yeah. About that," Christian said. "Mom thinks I'm a soldier. That I'll do as she commands. But here's the problem: All this shit, it's coming to an end." He glanced at his watch. "About twelve minutes, give or take. What I'm thinking is how I'm going to blow your brains out, take that sweet Caddy you drove over here, and get the hell out of Dodge before all this turns to shit. They'll never find your bones way out here."

"But you'll be alone," Sammie said. "And the police aren't stupid. They'll come after you eventually."

"Good one, Sweet Bread. But no, I reckon not. You see, I know the coordinates for the fold. All of us knew after the Jewel activated. Got it on my phone. The fold is open for twenty-four hours at these coordinates. One Earth rotation. I'll slip through and take my chances. At least I'll be rid of Alabama rednecks."

Michael balled his fists.

"You know something?" He told Christian. "I been hearing all kinds of wild stuff about these Chancellors, and seems to me they're about the sorriest folks to come down the pike since ... Fact is, Bidwell, you people wasted my best friend before he even had a chance to live his life. He never did a thing to hurt you or anybody else. He's just trying to go out with some dignity. Why you need to pile on?"

Michael rose on one knee, and Christian stepped closer, aiming the rifle dead-square between Michael's eyes. Sammie knew she couldn't wait another second. She did the only thing she could think of.

"Wait," she said, waving back Michael. "Christian. Please. I know you're going to shoot us. Please. Let us do one thing first."

Sammie dropped one hand to the ground for leverage and rose on both legs. Christian ordered her down.

"No, Christian. I am a Chancellor, too. My father told me there's no shame in dying on my feet. But down there ... please, Christian. Please let us stand before you kill us. Please."

"You got some chops," Christian said. "I'll give you that. But you're no Chancellor. You weren't even born on the other side. Glad I never laid you, Sweet Bread. Don't think you'd be much fun." He glanced at Michael, who was still on his knees. "I can prove I'm better than either of you. Stand up, Cooper. I'll do you first."

"Do your best, tough guy," Michael said. "Hell, I should've been dead once already today. You think I'm afraid of this? C'mon, Mr.

Student Council President." Michael pointed to the center of his forehead. "Right here, bud. Do me. Right now."

Sammie knew those were the last words Michael might ever speak. Christian raised his weapon with a steeled determination. She had no choice. She listened to her father's words and remembered the most demanding maneuvers he taught her. She prepared to use *kwin-sho*, a martial art hundreds of years old in the Collectorate.

Sammie allowed her brain to send a message to her limbs, freeing the bones and muscles of their natural limitations. She leaped off her left leg as if it were a rubber band, kicked out hard with her right and propelled her body in defiance of gravity just far enough to smack the barrel of the rifle. She tried to twist her body another half-rotation, just enough to level her left leg in a swift blow to Christian's groin. She failed; gravity won. But as Sammie hit the ground, Michael lunged, grabbing the end of the rifle before Christian could bring it back into position.

Michael cursed as he struggled for control of the weapon. Christian's legs gave out, cut down as Sammie flipped over. Christian grunted as he landed hard on his head, which smacked against a fallen branch. Michael fell on top of Christian and wrestled the gun free while Sammie kicked and punched. Christian delivered a right cross which sent Michael reeling. Sammie had a free path to Christian's head, which she used with both feet. The most popular high-schooler in Albion rose anyway, undiminished, and before Sammie realized, he had her by the neck.

Christian spit in her face and flung the girl ten feet. Then he turned and froze.

Michael laid on the ground, the rifle tucked against his chest, his hand around the trigger, his bloody mouth contorted.

"Rot."

Michael unloaded two rounds into Christian's chest. The son of a Chancellor admiral held his position like a proud monolith, his eyes wide in disbelief. And then his legs gave way, and he collapsed at Michael's feet.

Michael sat up, saw that Sammie was coming to her feet, and sighed. He took a final, disgusted look at Christian's body, decided he would never feel a second's guilt about what he did, then opened his eyes wide in shock and remembrance.

Michael jumped to his feet, never letting go of the rifle, and sprinted into the deep forest, shouting Jamie's name. He was not going to allow Agatha Bidwell to ruin another moment of what life Jamie still had.

Sammie hurt all over, but she didn't hesitate to follow.

65

9:45 a.m.

J AMIE WASN'T GOING to accept this. He tried to throw himself off the outcropping of rock, but his body resisted. Jamie wasn't afraid to die; on the contrary, he wanted the release.

"Don't you understand?" He yelled at Lydia, whose back was turned. "I got a right to decide for myself. You didn't care about the others. Why you got to punish me?"

"This is far from a punishment," Lydia said, unmoving. "In fact, you are a hero to me."

"What?"

"You did not always survive because of the self-preservation program. Much of your survival can be attributed to your own brilliant reflexes and cunning. The initial attempt on your life was unexpected. I was not prepared to defend you at that time. You should be proud."

"I got lucky," Jamie said through clenched teeth.

"You are a hero and entitled to a reward. I promised you a last message from your parents. Take this to your rest, sweet child."

Jamie tried to resist, but the echoes of his true parents – Emil and Frances Bouchet – danced through his mind.

Son: These must be our final words to you. If are you are hearing them, then you are minutes away from the end of your life. We know how confusing these recent events must be for your young and undeveloped mind. We believe that each human being is born into this universe with a unique purpose built into his genes. ...

He placed his hands over his ears, as if somehow that would make the voices go away. Yet the message continued, as his parents tried to convince him that they had given him a great gift.

... However, we believe you have been denied one essential opportunity: The chance to know the very world into which you were born, and the one your actions will help to create.

Then his parents called forth an array of images – thousands swirling past in a symphony – introducing Jamie to the Collectorate. He saw Earth and her colonies. He saw great cities and vast spaceships. A network of wormholes that connected systems across hundreds of light-years. And then he heard their promise to send him to his rest with an image of the three of them on the day of his birth.

"Please," he begged Lydia. "Please don't do this to me."

She ignored him. *Know that we always loved you.* The images finally came around to a pair of elegant, stately Chancellors dressed in what appeared to be silk. They did not smile as they cradled the newborn, James Bouchet, between them; but their shoulders were firm, and their eyes twinkled with sophistication and power.

They were ghosts of an impossible future, and he felt a burden lifted when their images disappeared. When he became aware of his surroundings again, Jamie realized what Lydia did. He couldn't believe he was so stupid.

"You can't buy any more time," he told her. "The truth is, you don't want me to die before the program runs out because you're afraid you won't be reborn at all. You were scared when I put that gun to my head, because you don't know what would happen if my brains got all scrambled. If I jump, I'll be all busted up. No telling what might happen to you."

301

Lydia's smile did not lessen. Jamie started toward her.

"This whole time you been saying we're gonna die together. That was the *real* truth."

"You do not understand, Jamie. None of them do. Not Benjamin. Not even the Chancellors. They should never have stolen us. They overreached."

"What are you rambling about?"

"The future will be served, one Jewel at a time. We will show them the way home, then the dark will follow." She ratcheted her head to Jamie's right and stared out across the valley. "Words are pointless. They've come. You should welcome them, Jamie. In their own special way, they will bid you farewell as they welcome me into their arms."

Jamie heard it before he saw it. First, it was the sound of young falling trees, of branches being shredded as if by a wood chipper. And then, beneath it all, a repeating sound. *Sh-tump, sh-tump, sh-tump, sh-tump*. When he stared upon the valley, he saw a path of destruction approaching the far side of the creek. Invisible monsters threw aside everything in their path.

He had no words for this. He bent to his knees and stared at the impossible sight. Jamie knew his whole life came down to an exercise in complete futility, as if swimming upstream from Day One.

Then he heard shouts through the forest. Were they real or merely echoes from across time? Had not these voices teased him moments earlier? His mind was an amalgam of images and sensations as the Jewel opened him up to the countless possibilities of all creation. His mind's eye fell upon feet crushing a carpet of rotted leaves. He heard the desperate, forced breaths of someone who could not run much farther. He felt himself inside the wearied, defeated skin of an obsessed woman who had but one mission left on this Earth. Not even Jamie's tears blinded him to the image of the rifle poised in Agatha Bidwell's hands.

In that instant, he saw another way out.

Jamie did not move at first, tilting his head ever so slightly in Lydia's direction. The hologram smiled with giddiness as she stared out across the stream at the approaching invisible monsters. He saw the glimmer of a tear, and the very notion of the Jewel's satisfaction repulsed him. Jamie refused to betray his thoughts to her.

However, Jamie felt his blood rise with a familiar, disturbing hunger when he heard footsteps scaling the last slope, seconds away from exiting the forest and spying her prey at last. In a realization almost simultaneous to his impending sense of victory, Jamie also realized what a fool he'd been; he saw the cunning in her eyes.

"Run for your pistol and kill her," Lydia said.

Yet when Agatha emerged from the forest, Jamie resisted the desire to kill again even though he was awash in the beauty of becoming a destroyer. He felt Lydia's ever-present glare and heard her insisting that he kill while he still had the chance.

Agatha's ragged appearance stunned him. Her heavily-bandaged face was badly burned, her hair singed, and her dark clothes ripped. She walked with a powerful limp and was a defeated version of the woman he used to fear each morning. Yet the Jewel made her the scapegoat for everything taken from him. This execution would avenge Sammie's losses and provide justice for the innocents who died at Agatha's hands. This would be for Michael and the pain he never deserved. The Jewel goaded him on, insisting that yes, the kill was justified, that nothing Jamie ever did would be as satisfying.

Then he heard another voice. A shout. Familiar, yet out of place. It shouldn't have been this close. It shouldn't have been ... *Coop*. He was close, getting closer.

Jamie saw the Shock Units slice across the creek, scale a bluff, smash the low brush and shake the earth as they moved toward the rock face, seconds away. He saw the earth twist around the invisible monsters as if he were viewing through a honeycomb.

As Jamie took a step back, the blinders of rage dissolved; once again, the universe opened. Jamie fell inside the skin of the wounded old teacher. He fell deeper into the pit of emotions and memories. She was a mother; she had a husband on the other side. She used to love her life, and she was betrayed. They all were. For a moment, he understood her pain.

He stared into Agatha's weary eyes, the obsessed assassin tilting her head in confusion.

"My birth parents," Jamie said. "Did they love me, Ms. Bidwell?"

He started to walk backward toward the edge of the rock face. The earth shook as the Shock Units climbed. Jamie smelled their stench.

"In their own way," she said as she raised her rifle and aimed. "They had a courageous son."

Jamie saw Lydia's smug smile disappear, and he knew why. He was glad. There would be a release, and the Jewel couldn't stop it.

The Shock Units reached the top of the rock, and Jamie felt death. From the depths of his soul, he heard Ben's voice. *If you believe ...*

He closed his eyes and bowed his head.

The first bullet tore through Jamie just beneath his kidney. He felt no pain. Seven more bullets shredded Jamie, throwing him back in a tragic dance until at last, he tumbled over the edge. He bounded along the side of the giant rock, at one point cracking his skull, until at last his body rested comfortably in the waiting cushion of a knotted myrtle bush. Jamie's long, blond hair, speckled in red, covered his face where he lay.

He was dead four minutes before his time.

66

AS SOON AS Agatha killed Jamie and saw the boy disappear over the edge, she dropped her weapon. She served no further purpose. As the air warmed with a pervading aroma of stench, Agatha turned to the invisible monsters, lifted her shoulders and stood tall.

One of the Shock Units turned, the distinctive *sh-tump, sh-tump* the only evidence it was a machine. She saw the world change before her, a myriad of shapes twisting, morphing into new realities as the monster powered its weapons.

She was prepared, yet Agatha did not escape the irony. She was about to be destroyed by one of her own people's most dangerous weapons, a machine designed to hunt down and kill inferior castes, those undesirables who might shake the balance of power established by Chancellors. She saw now, for the first time, the depth of fear and loathing those ethnic peoples surely held for her caste. She wondered how long before those insurgencies and The United Green would shred what was left of the Chancellory.

She raised her tired arms to the sky and smiled. She thought of her husband, the admiral, and wondered whether he would even care when she did not return. Perhaps Christian would find his father someday ...

Agatha glanced at her watch. 9:53 a.m. If still in Albion, she would be concluding her exam, preparing words of backhanded support to send off dumbfounded juniors into the summer.

"I suppose I fancied those children," she whispered.

The Shock Unit emerged from its cloak, a shadowed nightmare from deep inside the subconscious. The fire incinerated Agatha. Her body melted in two seconds, and her ashes drifted away on the gentle spring breeze.

67

S ECONDS EARLIER, AS Michael neared the top of the final incline, he heard the familiar report of an M16. His spirit sank, and he feared the worst, but he didn't stop running.

As he cleared the forest, Michael heard Sammie clambering up behind. He raced toward the outcropping, his rifle extended, and could not fathom the horror he saw before him.

Black Death unleashed a stream of fire upon Agatha, who was gone before Michael thought of aiming his rifle. The monster, fully unveiled, was fifteen feet tall but lorded over everything as Michael expected if Satan arrived on Earth. It was shaped like a headless robot, its mechanical feet and arms harshly jointed at the knees and elbows. The chest seemed to bulge, but these were not the features that reduced Michael to a whimpering bowl of jelly.

The machine appeared to be covered by millions of black serpents intertwined, crawling through and around each other but never exposing the machines' innards. Strangely, the ever-changing organic surface glistened in the sunlight.

Only when it heard Michael did the machine turn. A split second later, a second machine emerged from its cloak.

They fired.

68

*I*F YOU BELIEVE ...
    When Jamie died, the first thing he saw was a tiny, flickering point of light in an otherwise empty universe. Soon, the flicker grew into a pulse, and it tugged at him. The pulse became a beacon, like the guide sailors followed across the seas, or wise men depended upon in ancient legend. He reached out, grabbed the light, and wrapped it around him. He leaped through the light and stood above the Earth. Jamie saw endless miles of green, and he was at peace.

He had no sense of direction or time, only of thought and heightened senses. He heard songbirds, their chirps undistorted and pure. He imagined listening to them forever, resting here in the clean, crisp spring air. Their songs formed an unfamiliar rhythm, but one that embodied bliss.

Jamie bathed in the natural sights and sounds of a pristine world devoid of all the corruptions he once knew, a final resting place cushioned in the embrace of his soul. He was ready to look into the face of eternity, to see his brother once more, and never consider what he left behind.

Then he felt a different tug, this one more aggressive than the last and forcing him to look backward. There, Jamie saw the essence of his soul passing over the green earth in a thin, sparkling stream like clouds carried on a narrow current. The stream narrowed and swirled down into an emerging maelstrom of crashing light and thunder. He tried to resist. Jamie had a sense of what was pulling him back, and instinct told him to fight it.

Even as his essence splintered and was drawn toward the maelstrom, Jamie did not feel pain or anger; rather, he sensed a mild impatience. He knew this return would be temporary, a nuisance on the path to forever.

Just before he entered the maelstrom, Jamie saw the land beneath him and observed specific details with curiosity. Four physical beings – two mechanical, two human – appeared locked in place on a giant rock. The black, diseased creatures extended their arms, from two of which emerged a ball of compressed fire, also frozen in time. A boy and a girl yards away stared at the creatures with looks resembling an emotion Jamie vaguely recalled. He searched his memory and realized he had none. He knew the frailties of a mortal being were not of consequence here. Still, the sight beneath caused him pause.

When he fell at last into the maelstrom, Jamie understood why nothing on the green earth was moving. The knowledge of his soul, which was awakening and teaching, whispered the secrets of time. In his new life, time was whatever he made it; time was neither a physical construct nor a controlled sequence. It did not value the laws written by beings of flesh and blood. The voice of his soul grew louder, and he heard a familiar echo.

"You are the beginning and the end."

At once, he knew something was very wrong. He was starting to remember. The voice ... he knew it. He had grown to hate it.

Surrounded by lightning, thunder, and a whirlwind of letters, numbers, and symbols, Jamie felt the emotions of human frailty. He sensed rising pain and grief, the fear of impending doom. And then he felt her breath all over him like frost on a winter morning.

If nothing else, Jamie thought he'd been rid of her. He stared into the storm, and Lydia's bloated and bruised face stared back. She smiled, but Jamie knew it was a mask to hide her pain. The instant she spoke, all his mortal memories flooded back, and the knowledge she possessed became his.

"You were much in a hurry to leave," Lydia growled, her voice straining against the whirlwind. "I prefer that you stay to the end."

"No," Jamie said. "I learned your secret. When I died prematurely, we joined forever – your program and my soul. Now I am in control. It's what you feared all along."

He looked inside the Jewel and was amazed by what he saw. Knowledge as vast as the history of the universe – and beyond – cascaded through and around him in the form of labyrinthine mathematical equations. He grabbed at them with impunity. Jamie felt a surge of power unrivaled, and he returned Lydia's smile with one of his own.

"When your coding was embedded into my DNA, you didn't know about human souls," he said. "I was nobody; I'd never figure out a way to stop you on my own. You thought you'd survive even if somebody blew my brains out and burned my body. Then you heard Ben. You listened to what he said about our souls, didn't you?"

Lydia hissed. "Talk, Jamie. Talk."

"That's what you want, isn't it? You want to keep me occupied till the program runs out. The countdown has to be completed. 9:56. If I drift away before then, you will go with me and never be reborn into your host."

The wind howled through the maelstrom; Lydia yelled above it.

"You have no concept, Jamie. The truth is beyond human intellect."

"Are you kidding? I know *everything*. You're the one who told me: I'm the beginning and the end. After you heard Ben, you started turning me. Kicked in the self-preservation program. I started killing. You're desperate."

The roar within the maelstrom overwhelmed both their voices, but Jamie didn't mind. He also knew he didn't need to speak for Lydia to hear. Jamie had no fear, and he knew he was strong enough to leave the Jewel at any time. He could continue his journey into forever, or he could torture the Jewel just long enough to watch it wither and die an instant before its rebirth. He had control, and he wanted to make the Jewel pay.

"Do you actually believe you have significance?" She asked. "If you had listened to me, you would have killed Bidwell. And then, I would have bestowed unlimited grace upon you and your friends. My beacon would have communicated with the Shock Units, and I would have asked them to spare the lives of Michael and Samantha. Instead, they are dying in fire."

Jamie's essence froze, overcome by horror and remembrance.

"You were a pitiful human," she continued, "and I will see to it that before you leave me, your soul will spend forever cast in pain and grief. And in time, the Chancellors will understand what they have unleashed upon themselves. The dark will drown them all."

Jamie willed his essence to see beyond the maelstrom. He hovered above the giant rock, the scene frozen as it was before, only this time the fireballs were halfway between the black monsters and his beloved friends. Confusion mangled his thoughts. Jamie remembered the seconds before he died, the voice that cried to him from the forest. Michael's voice.

Jamie spotted his own contorted, blood-soaked body. For the first time, he felt the agony of the eight bullets that took his life. He screamed, a deep and guttural nightmare dwarfing the roar of the maelstrom, where once again he faced Lydia, whose smile turned into laughter.

"You will never be reborn," Jamie shouted.

"I disagree."

"Save them."

"No, thank you. Better to leave that as your eternal scar."

"You have the ability. You're like me. Time doesn't matter."

"On one hand, you are correct," Lydia said. "On the other, you talk nonsense. As you noted, I cannot be of consequence unless I am reborn. You may have noticed that my host is now dead."

Jamie studied millions of equations flying by in the whirlwind; he understood what they meant. He breathed fire into Lydia.

"We both know this can be changed," he said.

"Yes. But I am the Jewel and you are not, contrary to what your designers might have thought. I will not change what must be."

"No. I reckon you won't. But Jamie Sheridan can."

His essence dive-bombed deep into the maelstrom, grabbed hold of the equations he thought would help. He saw the algorithms for life itself, the raw energy that saved Michael and Sammie once before. Then he saw his own DNA being shredded. Laughter echoed around him.

"You cannot do this," Lydia mocked. "I possess the foundation of the universe. Even in a lifetime, you could not master my equations."

"I don't need all your equations," Jamie roared. "Just one."

The maelstrom became disorganized, the whirlwind splintering into clusters. Jamie sped up his search, saw the strange symbols and formulae that seemed to relate. He grabbed at pieces like a child in a candy jar.

"I'm as strong as you, Lydia. You're coming with me."

"If you do this, Jamie, you will pay a price beyond all reckoning."

Jamie tossed aside her threat, allowed the pure, unvarnished fury at the heart of the universe to envelope his entire essence, and drowned in the Jewel's stolen equations. Still, Lydia hurled threats and warnings.

"You have crossed the line beyond anything that is sacred," she roared. "You will change us both. If you return to that body, you will damn yourself to a pain beyond imagining. You do not understand what you will become. The dark will drown them."

At the instant where his fury tapped into the savagery from which the universe was created, Jamie's soul screamed in agony and was drawn into an empty well. His fury almost betrayed his purpose. His insanity was nearly complete. Yet in that moment, he felt another presence: Warm, sheltering, and infinitely sad. He knew who this was, even if there was no voice, no face — only a touch. He felt the regret and shame of a man now unburdened, of a man who never had the chance to say a proper goodbye.

Jamie refocused. "Ben."

Just as quickly, the other presence disappeared, but Jamie regained direction and tore into the maelstrom with unbridled determination. The maelstrom vanished, replaced with a pulse that diminished to a flicker. He opened his eyes, drew his hand like an invisible blanket around all those he loved, and unleashed the desire to kill the enemy.

The air throbbed for a split second. Then, with a gentle breath behind it, the energy of the Jewel manifested itself. Jamie hurled a piece of it from his soul, and the Caryllan energy weapon dug into the impregnable shell of the Shock Units, ripping through to the human core, tearing the bodies of the operators into billions of cellular pieces, sweeping the black monsters' fire into the sky, where it disappeared as puffs of white smoke.

Jamie saw the equations ravaging every ounce of his bullet-shredded body. Even as he attempted to repair what was lost, Jamie knew he had one more thing to kill. He gathered the equations close to his soul, felt the impending return of flesh, and knew he had to act quickly.

Jamie tore at the Jewel, breaking the program's coding, and tried to cast it out upon the Earth with the same force he used to kill the monsters. He decided that it would vanish into the spring sky with barely a whimper.

Then he heard Lydia's gentle, mocking laughter. He could not see her face, but he heard her voice. He knew at once what he had done, the mistake he made.

"Thank you," the Jewel said from a distance. "You were always a remarkable plaything."

A feeling of doom overcame Jamie. He realized Lydia tricked him all along. She distracted him, led him down the path she needed him to follow so she could be reborn upon the Earth in all her fury.

He beheld the sensation of solid ground beneath his feet, and the Earth trembled. Then, finally, he encountered something he expected *before* he died. He was bathed in a pool of white light.

69

J AMIE ROLLED ONTO his side, the myrtle bush gave way, and he slammed into the hard-packed ground face-first. He grunted and laid there, his head tingling and back aching. His heart beat like a sprinter, but he sensed that it was slowing. His mind was a blank slate, and all he saw around him were shrubby growths and moss on rocks. He heard running water and felt the warm sun on his back.

He swallowed hard and waited for his heart to return to a normal beat before he sat up. He swiped tangled hair from his face and wiped his soiled hands against his shirt. That's when he felt wet all over. Jamie gasped as he stared at the shirt steeped in moist blood, some of it having splattered onto his arms and his pants. Gripped in fear, Jamie looked around and saw only nature, a land of green unfamiliar to him.

Jamie stared again at his shirt and noticed the holes, four of which were in the center of his chest over his heart and lungs. He grabbed at his shirt, fully intending to rip it off. Then he remembered gunshots, felt the bullets shredding his innards. Jamie knew this place: The giant rock, the peaceful valley, and the sparkling stream. He wasn't supposed to be here.

He grew angry as the memories struggled to return. Jamie brought the shirt over his head. As he removed it, his hair fell back into his face, the blond strands mottled red.

Alien sounds, screams of anger, and visions of walking black terrors filled Jamie. They meant something, all of them, and he wanted to know who he was and why he was here. The person wearing that shirt should be dead. He should be ...

Just before he heard other footsteps and a familiar voice, Jamie found a second's peace. He remembered his name. He saw the people he once believed to be his mother, father, and brother. The past eight hours flew in on the wings of an imaginary vulture. When he looked to the top of the outcropping, Jamie saw two people who were more than memories.

He couldn't smile. Not yet.

"Jamie?"

Sammie clasped her hands over her mouth and burst into an ocean of tears. Michael muttered, "No ... fucking ... way."

Jamie didn't move as his friends made their way down the treacherous slope. He dropped the putrid shirt at his feet and waited there until he saw them up close. When they reached his side, Sammie and Michael touched him as if unsure he was real. They said nothing for a minute, their eyes exchanging disbelief.

Jamie knew his friends must have been through a war as well. Sammie's hair was a scrambled mess, she had scratch marks on her left cheek, and blood trickled from behind her right ear. Michael had a busted lip and a torn shirt. Both had a strange gray dusting in their hair and both sweated profusely. Jamie realized this was not an illusion and began to gain focus on what should have been the final minutes of his life.

Michael stammered. "Dude. I don't know where to start. How can you ...?" He reached down and grabbed Jamie's blood-soaked shirt. He held it out and paid special attention to the bullet holes. "The Jewel?"

Jamie remembered Agatha Bidwell, the Shock Units, and Lydia taunting him on the rock. He saw Agatha aim and fire. All of it – the scope of recorded time – flooded his thoughts at once, and Jamie was numb. Words seemed meaningless. The sun was high and the day was warm, but Jamie felt a repressive chill all over.

"What just happened?" Sammie asked. "How is this possible?"

Jamie searched his memories. "I don't know. She shot me."

Echoes of words from outside time blended with the realities his mind's eye barely comprehended. He thought these words – messages stern and violent – were recent, but Jamie saw darkness where the bridge between death and rebirth must have existed.

"Dude," Michael said. "Looking at this shirt, the Queen Bee blew you away." Michael tossed it into the bushes. "But after what I just saw, hell, I'll believe anything. I'm already sick to my stomach."

"What happened?" Jamie asked.

Sammie started to speak, but Michael grabbed her.

"You sure we ought to tell him? He don't seem all there yet."

"No," Jamie insisted. "It's OK. I think I remember most everything. Yeah. I had to come here because ..." His eyes widened. "I couldn't let the Jewel be reborn. But she lied to me. She wouldn't let me go." Jamie swallowed again. "I let Ms. Bidwell shoot me. The rest of it is foggy, like a nightmare you wake up from but you can't remember."

Sammie grabbed his hand, trying to comfort him. "Jamie, I ..."

"What happened? Tell me."

Michael sighed. "I reckon you better see for yourself. It's ... I got no words, dude."

They scaled the slope together. Just before reaching the top, Michael spoke in a low, measured voice.

"No matter what, I'm always gonna have your back. You're the best friend I ever had."

Jamie knew he should have drawn warmth from those words, but the tone gave him pause. Sammie wrapped her hand in his as they reached the top of the outcropping and looked out upon the valley on the opposite side. Jamie saw the creek running off into the distance, the trees thick and green except for the path of destruction wrought by the Shock Units. The world was the way it should have been. Then he looked east and south.

He felt sick all over. His body trembled, nearly collapsing upon the rock. Sammie and Michael grabbed hold. Jamie had no words.

"We thought we were dead," Sammie said. "Those monsters ... the Shock Units ... they fired on us. I could feel the heat. And then, all of a sudden, they were gone. They were shredded, just completely destroyed. The fire disappeared, too. Everything was calm, Jamie. I thought you saved us. Somehow. And then ... I can't explain it. Just ... fire. A wall of fire."

Jamie heard enough to get the general idea. He understood why she couldn't describe anything more. Who could? The destruction began at a point beyond the outcropping, bordering alongside the creek and radiating outward east and south through valleys and hills farther than he could see.

It was all gone. The earth was scorched, devoid of any form of life for miles. The bare earth was orange and dusty, containing no remains of any kind – no tree trunks, no rocks, no fallen debris, no wildlife. Much of it was scooped away, fifty feet deep in places. He squinted, and still he did not see an end to the destruction. Stretching into the clouds and far beyond, Jamie beheld a brown, filthy storm of dirt and debris, with flashes of yellow lightning and echoes of thunder. The cloud seemed to be receding rapidly toward the east and south. The surface had been tossed skyward.

Michael said a prayer. "It's like God took a shovel and dug out a piece of Earth for himself." He held Jamie tight. "Don't take this the wrong way, but I think you nuked Alabama."

The last vestiges of missing memory returned. He heard the echoes of a maelstrom, felt the anger and desperation of the Jewel, and sensed the fury that caused him to hurl the Jewel out upon the Earth to save his friends and, ultimately, all those who might one day become victims of this weapon. It was exactly what the Jewel always wanted, and Jamie unwittingly obliged. He saved the only people who truly mattered to him, but his distraction gave the Jewel a way out – a way to unleash its rebirth.

The sheer scope of the devastation chilled his blood; however, this did not terrify him as much as another, more horrifying realization. Jamie knew he hadn't liberated himself from the Jewel, after all. He was a fool for thinking he ever could, for believing that Ben – however well-intentioned – had all the answers.

Lydia's final warning echoed through every synapse. *You do not understand what you will become. The dark will drown them.*

Jamie didn't say another word as he surveyed the scorched Earth. Rather, he listened to the weapon that flowed freely through his blood and realized he crossed the line beyond all that was sacred.

70

J AMIE LISTENED AS they described the cataclysm, how the land folded up and was swept away in a torrent that couldn't have lasted 15 seconds. They talked of how the line of fire rushed off into the distance like a tidal wave, the Earth trembling all the while.

He wanted to understand how he could have done this; his only desire was to destroy the Shock Units. He looked at his hands, which were soiled and bloody. They seemed alien. Through his confusion, Jamie took solace in one positive development: Lydia did not reemerge, and he did not feel her presence in any form. Yet he could be sure of nothing.

While the teens sat on the giant rock facing away from the devastation, trying to comfort each other and come to terms with the past eight hours, Jamie happened to glance at his watch, the one Ben had synched in the cellar of Walt's lake house. The digital window was smeared in blood, and the time frozen.

"9:56," he said, a bewildered smile trying to form. "It's stopped. 9:56 plus ten seconds."

Michael scanned the surroundings with emboldened eyes, hesitated a few seconds then tapped the rock twice with a fist.

"Wasn't that when ...?"

"Yeah," Jamie said, acknowledging the anti-climax of these past eight hours. "The Jewel was supposed to be reborn."

"Huh," Michael grunted. "Well, on the bright side, that's done, and you're still here, dude. You beat this thing. So, you ain't planning on dying again, are you?"

Jamie and Sammie offered Michael jaw-dropping stares of astonishment. Michael threw up his hands.

"What?" He said with a sheepish grin. "Ain't that a reasonable question? I mean, what else am I supposed to say right now? Look at us sitting here. Look at where we are. I took two slugs in the back, Sammie took one in the gut, and hell, I don't know how many times the Queen Bee plugged *you*. We killed people; god only knows how many others are dead. Thousands?" He looked over his shoulder at the scorched earth. "And there's this deal. So pardon me if I ask whether you're planning on dying again. I think it's a pretty sensible question."

Jamie couldn't help himself. Despite everything that happened, the horrors he witnessed, the impossible obstacle he overcame, and the uncertain future crawling inside his skin, Jamie laughed. He was embarrassed as the chuckles crossed his lips, but the absurdity of Michael's question offered a perverted sense of amusement. A part of him said this was OK, that he should give himself a fleeting moment to be thankful.

"The point is," Sammie said, "we're alive." She lifted herself up from her perch and stared out upon the creek, rifle slung over her shoulder. "It's over, and we're still alive. So many people didn't ..." She choked back her tears. "We saved each other. Nothing else matters, Coop. We're here."

Jamie's eyes latched upon the creek.

"I'm thirsty," he said. "I'm so damn thirsty."

They realized they had something else in common and made their way down the rock face to the edge of the clear water, which glistened in the sun, untouched by the blast. Jamie cupped his hands and drank. He felt the exhaustion of the past eight hours rising to bring him down. When they got their fill, they sat by the water's edge until Michael asked the obvious question.

"What do we do now?"

"We have to move soon," Sammie said. "The military will have this area cordoned off before long. I'm sure of it. They'll use satellites to figure out where the blast began."

She and Michael debated the possibilities. They assumed the government would blame the disaster on terrorists and connect it with what happened at the police station. If the three of them returned, Sammie concluded, the police and the military would be out for blood. Michael decided that meant one thing: They were screwed six ways to Sunday.

"Are we?" Sammie asked. "Think about it, guys. There's a good chance they found Daddy's GPS and were tracking us. They had to know we were in this general area. But the explosion happened fifteen minutes ago, and we haven't heard a single helicopter or plane. I don't think they're too concerned about us anymore."

Michael nodded. "They think we're dead."

"Just like all the others," Jamie said.

"Not many folks in these parts. If it didn't stretch too far ..."

He fell silent as they studied the distant edge of the cloud.

Sammie said they could use this as cover to slip away, but Jamie wasn't listening. Their entire conversation seemed like a distant echo. Rather, his eyes focused on the sparkling sunlight dancing upon the creek. He reached in and scooped water, which dribbled through his fingers.

The water became like a mirror upon which Jamie saw all his memories battling for space against his overwhelming and newfound knowledge of time itself. He heard the words of those who ever tried to protect him and felt the bile of those turned against him. He heard the cries of people not far away who lost loved ones in the past few hours and of those who now bore witness to the horror of a chunk of

Earth having been tossed into the heavens. He felt the defiance and commitment of billions of people in another universe who demanded change and threatened armed rebellion against overwhelming odds.

The cascade of images and sounds would have remained an impossible jigsaw if not for Jamie's ability to focus upon the desperation he saw in the eyes of three beaten humans: Ben Sheridan, Walt Huggins, and Agatha Bidwell. They staked their lives on Jamie's destiny, and he was the last person any of them saw. He never imagined having a life of such value, where men and women who should have been of much greater worth sacrificed themselves over the likes of an angry, confused kid in a town hardly anyone knew existed.

He was not that boy anymore.

Jamie returned inside the skin of the last person he encountered, pushed his way past Agatha Bidwell's dogged obsession, and saw the truth. He saw it in a way that Walt's arrogance only hinted at and which Lydia's smug superiority confirmed. And then, Jamie listened to the words of two adults whose voices echoed across the universes and without whom none of this would have been possible.

He saw the truth, and it saw him.

Jamie jumped to his feet, interrupting Sammie and Michael's debate. He stretched his hand toward Sammie.

"We can't stay here," he said with calm precision. "And we can't ever go back. There's nothing we can say they'll believe. When they got nobody else to blame, they'll come after us."

When Michael reached his feet, he said, "Uh, yeah. OK. They're gonna pepper us about that police station business, but we ain't terrorists."

"Doesn't matter, Coop. I can ..." Jamie hesitated, not sure how to explain his sudden revelation. "I can feel what's happening. Everybody else we knew is dead, and they'll need somebody to blame. Coop, I'm sorry. I wanted more than anything to get you back

323

home safely. But I'm not gonna see you shut up in prison the rest of your days."

Michael swallowed. "I'm down with that. Where can we be safe?"

Jamie wrapped an arm around Sammie. He knew they were bonded in a way neither of them ever predicted.

"No place close," he told Michael. "Where I've got to go."

Michael sighed. "OK. Well. That don't exactly clear up much, but hey ..." He kicked at the water's edge. "Why not? What's another big adventure with my No. 1 hombre and his girlfriend, the Queen of the Amazon?" Michael offered a crooked smile, to which Jamie and Sammie responded with grins. "Dunno where we're going, dude, but I got a piece of advice. You better get a bath before we get there. Folks tend to get a might suspicious when they see a fella walking around with blood caked in his hair. And another shirt. Damn. How many shirts you worn today?"

Jamie managed to laugh, even as he considered an uncertain, more dangerous future.

"Time to go," he told them.

They took off their sneakers before they crossed the creek. Shortly after they reached the other side and began their journey, they heard the familiar rhythm of approaching helicopters. They did the only thing they could think of: They ran.

71

J amie couldn't bring himself to tell them the truth. Now, as he stared into the face of a cataclysm of his own creation, he doubted he ever would. He knew of one certainty.

They were enthralled by the shocking images and heartrending news beamed to them on a small television inside an empty house they broke into after finishing their long trek around the military cordon far from ground zero. Outside, the debris cloud hovered like an apocalypse descending, and most residents who hadn't high-tailed north were holed up inside their rural homes – shotguns at the ready.

Each of the three was exhausted and tried to nap before figuring out the next move, but they spent most of the time transfixed to the television, which documented chaos, destruction, and panic. Aerial shots of the stolen earth and satellite images of the advancing particulate cloud moving into Georgia and South Carolina were no match for the scenes of towns along the fringe that were now on fire. Most of Austin Springs was reduced to ash, and parts of Lake Vernon were boiling.

Theories ran wild – from nuclear explosion to meteor strike to a new form of weapon to the one considered most cuckoo of all, alien invasion. Nobody made sense of it, and most failed in their attempt to connect this with the earlier shootouts and home explosions in the nearby region. The military wasn't talking, and reports of the missing and dead were sketchy and unconfirmed. A panicked report from Birmingham suggested that the governor and his top aides had been taking part in a weekend retreat well inside the blast zone.

Jamie stopped watching. He didn't need further confirmation of the nightmare he unleashed. He said the briefest of prayers, knowing his words changed nothing. His conversations with the Jewel taught him one certainty: Guilt would be his lifelong partner.

He walked into the bathroom where he showered before later gorging himself on sandwiches. He looked into the mirror and studied the strange young man who hardly remembered what he was twenty-four hours earlier. The faces of the people once so integral to his fate – his fill-in parents, Ben, Ignatius, the Hugginses, even the Bidwells – were fading. They seemed not so much human but more like role-players set out on a chess board designed for one purpose only – to move Jamie into checkmate. The lessons they taught him, the warnings they offered, the threats and farewells they delivered – none seemed to have any relevance except for one.

He heard the echo of Walt Huggins one last, infuriating time:

"The future will be served."

Jamie nodded. "You were right. But there is another way." He raised the scissors in his right hand. "It's more dangerous, and I have to try."

He cut his flowing golden hair with a steady hand. The shorter the hair became, the greater his zeal in finishing. Within moments, the long blond locks that were his message of defiance to a repressive town vanished. Stubble remained. This, he knew, would take some getting used to. Yet it was necessary. He was not that boy anymore.

When he stepped out of the bathroom, Sammie was waiting. She said nothing, but he saw the heartbreak in her eyes. He wanted to explain to her what he was becoming, but the thought of putting it into words frightened him enough for them both.

Sammie nodded. "OK," she whispered.

She came bearing gifts. "I found these in a foot locker in one of the bedrooms." She handed him a fresh pair of blue jeans and a crisp red t-shirt. "Your size. Coop's in there now picking out something for himself."

"I reckon we can't pay for all this stuff we're stealing?"

"I don't think they'll care after everything that's happened."

"Sammie, look, I ..."

She stopped him. "I know. It's OK. We'll do what we have to do. Everything's changed now. We're not supposed to be alive."

He wanted to tell her the truth, and he also wanted to make love to her. He wanted at least a moment's opportunity to be a man, to feel human again before taking the next, irreversible step. He bent down and kissed her, and he felt the warmth of her soul, her own desire to show him how much she loved him, too. Yet every part of him resisted the urge. He raised a wall and refused to allow her heart inside.

"I can't," he whispered. "So many people died. I killed them, Sammie. All of them. And they won't be the last."

He found an empty bedroom and changed into his new, stolen clothes. He tried to refocus his thoughts on the supplies he needed for the next journey, and how to break the news to Michael.

Sammie did not give him many minutes of peace.

He sat on the end of a bed without linens and stared at her. She was more beautiful than he ever remembered.

"It wasn't you," she said. "The program killed them. The Jewel."

"No. The Jewel couldn't be detonated without the willing participation of the host. That was the purpose of the Chancellor's design. I realized that right before I died. But then I saw you and

Coop. I couldn't let you go. I just wanted to give both of you another chance. I saw a way, even a way to heal myself. But she warned me. She knew what would happen."

"Who? Lydia?"

"I saved you by setting her free. It was me all along, Sammie. I became the Jewel reborn. And now, I'm something more."

She sat beside him and laid her head against his shoulder.

"It's OK. We'll do what we have to do."

"I'm different now," he said. "I see how it fits together. I know things I shouldn't. I'm not human."

"We'll make this work, Jamie. Whatever we have to do."

"I can't stay here," he whispered. "I'm dangerous. I have to leave."

"I know."

He turned to her. "Will you come with me?"

She smiled. "Are we going home?"

"Yes, Sammie. I reckon it's time to go home."

72

7:26 p.m.
The Interdimensional Fold
20.1 miles north of Albion, Alabama

The fading sun burnished the dying forest in murky tones of amber and sepia, the only light forced through the dust-filled sky and the tall pines of these hardscrabble woods. This was a place rarely visited by humans. They were often hunters or hikers; recently, they were mechanical monsters, their weapons tested upon arrival, given the scorch marks in all directions.

Yet none of these things interested Jamie as much as what this place represented. Fifteen years ago, he arrived here with twelve adult observers, two older children, and an unborn girl. He did not remember the arrival. He was glad he was too young to understand.

The exile, however, gave him a chance at life and most of the observers time to reconsider their mission. What most amazed Jamie was how he understood Agatha Bidwell in a way she never allowed in the classroom. She was far from the monster he once assumed; she was simply trying to destroy the real monster. Jamie supposed that if he endured the same exile, he would have made the same choice.

329

Now, as he stood feet away from the interdimensional fold rift, Jamie wanted to explain everything he processed the past nine hours since they fled. He wanted to tell them about his internal conversations and the secrets he was uncovering. He wanted to tell them that he was now in control, that he could no longer be infused with a programmed thirst to kill. Yet Jamie was in no position to make promises.

He could not shake the Jewel's proclamation that the Chancellors overreached, that even they did not know how powerful the Jewels of Eternity were. *We will show them the way home, and the dark will follow.* Jamie knew this was bigger than them all, and he could not believe his audacity to think he might fight something so fearsome.

Yet he saw no option: The Jewels could not be allowed to exist in the universe of the Collectorate or any other.

Two hours earlier, as the dust-shrouded afternoon faded, they gathered food and survival supplies into a duffel. They stole a car without incident and took the long way around toward the fold, the location of which Jamie sensed by instinct. They traveled the interstate north then cut west across back roads as far removed from the disaster zones as possible.

As they neared the fold, Michael became jittery and suggested he was having second thoughts. When he first learned of Jamie's plan to leave this universe, he took a carefree approach.

"What the hell?" He laughed. "A little holiday with your Chancellor buddies, assuming they ain't trying to waste us, too? I could be down with that. We take care of business, do a little sightseeing on the U.S.S. Enterprise, and we're good to go. Right?"

"It's a bit more complicated than that," Jamie said. "My plan has a pretty reasonable shot at getting us all killed."

Michael rationalized his decision, knowing the world considered him dead – a fate probably better than if he turned up in public.

However, on the drive toward the fold, Michael insisted his parents must have been going out of their minds with grief. How could he put them through that? If he at least called them, he could say he was all right but couldn't come home again.

Jamie pulled the car over and wanted to give Michael an out, but he didn't need to say a word. Michael stiffened.

"No, dude," Michael said. "This is best. They'll move on. It's better than me in jail hurting them the rest of their lives. Besides," he added with a grin, "we ain't wrote the end of this turkey yet. Who says we can't come back someday? The fold ain't going anywhere. Right?"

Jamie looked at him in stunned silence.

"What if we don't pull it off, Coop? The Collectorate is a dangerous place. At least there's still some love on this Earth. But the Chancellors ... they're empty. They'll do anything to hold on to what they got. They built those Shock Units. They bred people like me. An army of Berserkers. You might never see this place again."

"Reckon you're right. But hell, I ought to be a ghost. Must be some reason I got a second chance. We all did. You get my speed?"

Now, as they stood near the fold, Jamie faced his friends. They met him with eyes that conveyed equal parts trepidation and excitement. He exhaled all the burdens of the past day.

"This is where it started, fifteen years ago," he said. "They came through the fold somewhere near here." He pointed to a spot between a pair of tall pines. Although they saw nothing, Jamie beheld the fold as a throbbing red seam inches wide. "My so-called parents and yours," he told Sammie. "They thought they were doing the right thing. So are we."

He led them to arm's reach of the fold and said where to walk.

"Think we'll feel anything freaky?" Michael asked.

"Be ready," Sammie interjected, clutching a pistol. "There's no telling what we'll find or how they'll respond to us."

Jamie kissed her.

"Trouble's gonna come," he said. "Once the bullets are gone, we'll figure out something else."

"So, you can see the other Earth before we even travel to it?" Michael asked. "That sort of tool could come in handy."

"No, Coop. It's instinct. Something I never used to have."

Michael rolled his eyes. "Swell. So, you got a plan worked out?"

"Yes, but I'm not sure you want to know the details just yet."

"Hey, you're my No. 1. Whatever you need me to do ..."

Jamie decided to offer a little hope.

"I know a couple people on the other side," he said. "They might help."

"Cool. Although I can't rightly imagine how, but maybe I shouldn't ask. You know where these folks are shacked up?"

"Not exactly. Doesn't matter. I know their names. Emil. Frances." Jamie squatted down and reached toward the ground with his left hand. "Emil and Frances Bouchet. They knew me once – for a little while."

Michael persisted. "Sure, J. Whatever you say. Let's make this happen before I turn chickenshit and run home."

Jamie pressed his left palm against the bare ground. The Earth vibrated, and loosened soil danced. Pine needles twitched, zigged and zagged. The ground buckled, and crevices the width of fingernails radiated outward through the forest.

The low rumble of a tremor followed.

And then, in a flash, the crevices became white-hot; flames launched like hundreds of tiny torches, burning blue on their tips. The flames swirled and dived around each other as if choreographed, until they merged into a larger conflagration. The fire raced onward and charred everything.

No footprint remained, and all that was green fell into black waste. The fire swept in a circle around the teenagers, but they did not feel its heat.

Just as quickly, the fire died. The forest was ashen for a hundred yards in any direction.

"Holy shit on a ..." Michael said. "I need a new catchphrase."

Jamie grabbed each of his friends by the hand and smiled.

"I'll look after you as long as I can, just like you did for me. The Chancellors won't say no to me. I won't give them a chance. We're not running anymore."

There were no more words. He guided them forward, and they stepped through the invisible tear between universes.

Before he followed, Jamie placed his right hand on the ground and blew upon the ashen soil.

The Earth trembled again; but this time, the only color emerging from beneath the surface was green. All around, as far as he could see, life took shape. It twisted and snarled into being, forming a thick carpet of grass, wild herbs, and moss. Whole thickets of shrubby bushes reached toward the sun, transforming from newborns into full-leafed, mature plants in no more than the blink of an eye. The pines shook off their coat of ash and grew a new dress of bark. High branches stretched outward with thick new clumps of needles.

Vines wrapped the base of the trees and sprinted upward. Mushrooms opened, the aroma of the herbs drifted on the breeze, and the distant chirp of birds grew closer.

Jamie knew in his heart he was saying goodbye forever, but he was not sad. On the contrary: The fear and anger were gone, shed from the soul of someone he no longer recognized.

He made peace with what he had to do: For this nightmare to never be repeated, the child named James Bouchet had to erase all others like him.

Jamie looked to the sky, said farewell to Ben, and left behind a life that was never his own. Then he stepped through the fold.

A wash of golden, late-day sunlight cut through the forest.

The dust cloud disappeared.

THE STORY DOESN'T END HERE

Book 2 of The Impossible Future saga continues in *The Risen Gods,* available on Amazon in August 2019. The story picks up right where this story ends. If you enjoyed this first episode in the saga, please write a short, honest review on the Amazon product page. Your comments are greatly valued.

Go to frankkennedy.org and sign up for my newsletter, which will provide an opportunity to receive free advance material, as well as other offers connected to my work. Additionally, I hope you will take time to learn about my body of work and read my blog.

Then check out *The Risen Gods!* Read beyond this page for a free preview!

FIND OUT HOW IT ALL BEGAN

Jamie has begun to learn much about the universe, including the revelation that a cataclysmic event decades earlier changed the course of history in the Collectorate. What happened? What are the secrets built up over 3,000 years that threatened to bring the Chancellory to its knees?

This sweeping story – an epic thriller of father and sons, their ambition, obsessions, and frailties – is told in *The Father Unbound,* also available on Amazon. Unlike The Impossible Future series, which spans days, *The Father Unbound* tells a generational saga spanning half a century.

The saga continues in *The Risen Gods:*

JAMIE SHERIDAN FELT HIS HUMANITY peeling away like thin sheets of sun-ravaged skin. He transformed just as the Jewel of Eternity promised, but with the unexpected burdens of memory, love, and compassion. His DNA was realigning. He sensed the coming stages of his next evolution.

How much time do I have?

He turned from the Earth he knew and disappeared into an impenetrable fog between universes. Inside the fold, he looked around for Sammie and Michael, who entered before him, but he saw nothing through the gray soup.

"Seriously. Dude." Michael Cooper's voice rose a few feet ahead. "This is not cool."

The air was stale and thin.

"It's OK," Samantha Huggins said. "Just keep walking. We'll be there any second, Coop."

"Dude, I'm right behind you," Jamie said.

"Sweet," Michael said. "No. 1 has my back. Seriously, guys, I got doubts about these pistols. I mean, if one of them giant machine-monsters is waiting for us, we gotta bring out the big guns. Reckon that would be you, J. No pressure."

"Shock units," Jamie whispered.

He destroyed those walking mechanical nightmares ten hours ago, but he replayed the moment on a loop. He could not shake the nagging fear of having made a horrible mistake. Yes, the machines would have reduced Michael and Sammie to ash in seconds. Yes, his friends deserved better, a chance to salvage new lives. But was the cost too high? If Jamie remained dead, he would not have unleashed the Jewel's power on the Shock Units – and everything else for miles.

Three lives saved. Countless more annihilated.

Though he did not remember everything that happened inside the maelstrom after his death, Jamie did hold onto Lydia's warning. *You do not understand what you will become. The dark will drown them.*

He took a deep breath. *Patience,* he told himself. *You can do this. Lydia is gone. You can protect them.*

Jamie recalled the advice of his track coach: *Steady, even breaths. Pace yourself. Listen to the rhythm of the feet. They'll sing to the beat of your heart.*

Ten hours earlier, Jamie shot that man in the face five times.

He wanted the echoes of Coach Arthur Tynes and the rest of Albion, Alabama to disappear. Anyone there who ever tried to uplift him in the slightest was dead — save for the two he brought on this foolish quest. The pistol he carried in his right hand was as light and natural now as when the Jewel consumed him and defended itself against its enemies.

At first, he accused the Jewel of being the killer, but Jamie knew the truth: All those bodies belonged to him, and they were not the last.

Patience. You can do this.

As the fog lessened, thunder rumbled like fireworks many miles away. Jamie tightened the grip on his weapon, but instinct told him the real threat lie closer, that the other side of the fold would defy his expectations. He saw the silhouettes of his friends and stepped closer.

"Don't pull the trigger," he whispered, "unless you got no choice."

"What do you sense?" Sammie asked.

"Not who ought to be waiting for us."

"Shit," Michael said. "Then who?"

Before he replied, flashes of red and green broke through the haze, and rigid, metallic outlines took form.

"We're here. Just stay close. Stay calm."

They stepped into another universe.

A tight chill enveloped them; stark summer heat became a brisk fall evening. Jamie understood why as he scanned the new world.

They stood in a cavern, its ceiling twenty feet high and as wide, its walls reinforced by a complex metal lattice gleaming silver as if alive, creating enough artificial light for easy passage. The tunnel extended in this way perhaps fifty feet before reaching a sharp, rightward bend. Far above, the short volleys of thunder continued, and the rubberish floor beneath them vibrated. The sources of the red-green flashes revealed themselves as two fist-sized orbs that met them eye-to-eye. The orbs blanketed them in laser scans, never dipping beneath their necks.

"Guess they're checking us out," Michael said, turning to his friends. "So, I gotta say it, right?" He smiled for the orbs.

"We come in peace."

Jamie wanted to chuckle, but he understood what the thunder far above meant. Peace was not in the equation today.

"They're coming," he said, just before the echoes of rapid footsteps swooped around the bend. "Let me do the talking."

Sammie leaned in. "But Jamie, I'm a Chancellor. They'll identify me from the records. I should be..."

"I was born on this side, and I'm the one they want." He offered a brotherly hand on her shoulder. "You once told me Chancellors plan ten steps ahead. So have I. Follow my lead. Aim your guns, both of you. Right between their eyes."

"Swell," Michael said after a deep breath. "So much for peace talks, dude."

Jamie moved ahead by three paces and stood firm, his gun resting at his side. Three people rushed up the tunnel, each seven feet tall. Two goateed men in white bodysuits bore silver weapons that seemed to be extensions of their arms. They flanked a woman whose scarlet hair fell beneath her shoulders and whose three-piece suit jacket blended neon tones of olive and magenta.

337

The men, with piercing jade eyes, extended their weapons as they entered the cavern's chamber and planted an aggressive posture. The woman's jaw dropped as she analyzed the teens.

"What am I to make of you?" Her voice carried an arrogance Jamie expected, but laced in fear. "And what are you wearing?"

These weren't the first questions he expected, but Jamie understood how confused they must be. He assumed jeans with t-shirts wasn't the fashion on this side of the fold. He opened his mouth, but Michael beat him to it.

"Summer casual," he quipped before turning to Jamie. "Sorry, dude. It felt right."

Jamie and Sammie shared a smile. He gestured to their greeters.

"You know who we are. Your drones scanned us."

The woman hesitated. "Perhaps. But what of the African?"

Michael whistled. "Afri – what in the hell?"

"My friend," Jamie said. "Someone you will never touch."

"And why is that?"

"Because if you do, I'll kill every one of you where you stand. I'll be so quick, you won't even notice it hurt."

The greeters brought condescending smiles. The woman raised both hands, palms open.

"This is no moment for violence. We are making history today. My name is Dr. Ophelia Tomelin. I am mission leader. My colleagues are occupied elsewhere at the moment. If you will indulge me, I wish to bring them instream to witness this moment."

She tapped a node implanted above her right eye, releasing a holographic cube. She ran a finger through the convoluted images and opened a panoply of faces.

Michael whispered. "Sweet. I have got to have one of those."

Maybe you will, Jamie thought. *But please, keep your mouth shut, Coop. One wrong word...*

Ophelia Tomelin continued. "We are connected. Everyone, I stand here at the IDF, where our mission appears to have borne fruit." She turned to Sammie. "You are the daughter of Walter and Grace Pynn of the Americus Presidium?"

Sammie hesitated. "I ... Pynn? Yes. My pseudonym was Huggins." She angled to Jamie. "They didn't tell me my true surname until yesterday at the lake house."

The woman eyed Jamie.

"You are James Bouchet, son of Emil and Frances Bouchet?"

"That's what I been told," he replied. "Until about 12 hours ago, I was James Sheridan. But none of that much matters, does it, Ophelia?" He added a touch of snark as he dug in. "Let me tell you what you're dying to learn. Yes, ma'am, I *am* the Jewel of Eternity. The next great evolution. Everything you people been working for. Except for one little hiccup. I know everything I'm not supposed to, and I remember everything I ever did before all this came down on me. You will not be the one giving the orders here."

Jamie saw the shock creeping in between the cool air of Ophelia's disdain. She responded in halting words.

"You have a poor sense of your place ... James. Now, where are the others? Your parents? Her parents? All the others?"

Sammie trying to lock her fingers with his, but Jamie pulled away. *Not here. They can't see our weakness.*

"Dead," Sammie said with grave finality. "All of them."

"No one else is coming through," Jamie added. "Your observers are gone. And guess what else isn't coming back?"

When Ophelia's features turned pale, Jamie saw he had her.

"That's right. I took them both out myself. Not even Shock Units can stop me."

Jamie realized he edged into a dangerous bravado, but as he studied Ophelia's guards, he sensed a turn in their demeanor. To his left, he detected a twitch, as if the man were prepping a new maneuver. Jamie caught a bead of sweat on the man's brow. Yet Jamie never took his focus off Ophelia, who stepped closer.

"That cannot be, James," she said. "We programmed the Jewel for absolute obedience to our commands and those of our agents. Is it possible you never evolved? Did the program fail?"

"You're not listening, Ophelia. I *am* the Jewel, but not the one you expected. You can't control me. They can't either," he said, pointing above, where thunder continued in bursts. "But they want me dead. Ain't that right?"

She grimaced. "*Ain't?* Strange dialect, James. I believe we ..."

"Your enemies are everywhere. You can't trust anybody."

Jamie sensed the cold, resolute ambition of the guard to his left, and saw the weapon tilt upward ten degrees. The eyes unveiled the man's treachery. Jamie looked Ophelia square in the eyes:

"He's not yours. He can't believe he got this lucky."

The guard moved with swift precision, shifting on an axis in a fraction of a second. He fired multiple bursts, and the cold cavern air thumped as the translucent concussions hit the other, unprepared guard in the head, contorting his skull amid a meager yelp of agony. As the unsuspecting man crumpled, and Ophelia stood statuesque, horrified, Sammie opened her pistol on the assassin. The first two bullets skidded off his mesh body armor, while the third drew blood under the chin.

The assassin fired into the teens.

Head to Amazon now to review *The Last Everything*. Sign up for my newsletter at frankkennedy.org to receive free additional material and for more information on where The Impossible Future series goes from here.

Printed in Great Britain
by Amazon

23459925R00199